BOOK OF DEAD THINGS

Greetings from the dark.....

Alan Smale

BOOK OF DEAD THINGS
— Expanded Edition —

Edited by
Tina L. Jens and
Eric M. Cherry

Twilight Tales
Chicago, Illinois

Twilight Tales Presents...
BOOK OF DEAD THINGS

Copyrighted as a whole by Tina L. Jens and Eric M. Cherry © 2007, all rights reserved.

All stories used by permission of the authors. Further *Acknowledgments* on page 6.

Cover art and interior illustrations pp. 255 & 276 Copyright © Alan M. Clark, reproduced here by permission of the artist

Skull and graveyard illustrations Copyright © 2007 Robert T. Garcia, all rights reserved.
Cover and interior design by Robert T. Garcia
Garcia Publishing Services, 919 Tappan St., Woodstock, IL, 60098 / www.gpsdesign.net

Twilight Tales
5529½ N. Kenmore #2C
Chicago, IL, 60640

Visit www.TwilightTales.com for more
information on this and other Twilight Tales titles.

Library of Congress Control Number: 2007902465
ISBN: 978-0-9779856-3-0

First Edition, June 2007

Printed in the United States of America.

TABLE OF CONTENTS

7	Introduction, *by Tina L. Jens*
11	Perfect Rings of Calamari, *by Dan Waters*
14	Wearing the Dead, *by Alan Smale*
30	Love in the House of Nowhere, *by John Weagly*
36	Lorelei's Little Deaths, *by C.S.E. Cooney*
51	For Five Minutes, the Deep, *by Jude Walter Mire*
57	Upon the Midnight Clear, *by Stephen Dedman*
67	Demons in His Art, *by Chris Kozlowski*
69	Soul Collector, *by Craig D.B. Patton*
73	Dad Brings A Deader Home, *by Yvonne Navarro*
85	A Patchwork of Poems, Reanimated into Something Barely Alive, *by Katherine Norem*
87	The Tatesville Curse, *by Andrea Dubnick*
99	Children of Stone, *by Tina L. Jens*
109	The Cemetery Plant, *by John Peel*
117	It Ain't Much to Brag About, But It's All Mine, *by Bill Breedlove*
136	Death, Dying & 3 Credits, *by Ken Goldman*
147	The Mud, The Blood, and The Bones, *by Christopher Fulbright and Angeline Hawkes*
163	Frankenstein, *by Jo Fletcher*
165	Jimmy and Me and the Nigger Man, *by Scott A. Cupp*
176	The Horror of No Beer, *by Richard Gilliam*
179	But Somebody's Got to Do It, *by Edo van Belkom*
186	I Fuck the Dead, *by Sukie de la Croix*
189	Blood of the Rose, *by Karen E. Taylor*
194	White of the Moon (A Lullaby), *by Jo Fletcher*
196	The Alberscine's Vigil, *by Thomas J. Strauch*
216	Sent Down From God, *by Randy Miller*
230	The Midnight El, *by Robert Weinberg*
240	Heart Beat, *by Sèphera Girón*
253	The Dead Boy at Your Window, *by Bruce Holland Rogers*
257	Five Places You Must Visit After You Die, *by Tom Barlow*
270	Mobly's Big Idear, *by Stephen C. Merritt & Alan M. Clark*
278	Mummies, *by J.D. Smith*
279	The Mummy Lost Her Sarcophagus Where a Mother Found Her Soul, *by Martel Sardina*
289	Hell's Deadline, *by Suzanne Church*
293	Naked Lunchmeat, *by Brian Hodge*
304	Charlie Harmer's Last Request, *by Brendan Detzner*
312	Exodus, *by Lawrence Schimel*
314	Cold Comfort, *by Michael Penkas*
320	Interlude: Blood, Snow, and Sparrows, *by Joshua Alan Doetsch*
328	About Our Authors

ACKNOWLEDGMENTS

The editors would like to thank Edward DeGeorge, Mike Penkas, Jude Walter Mire, Martel Sardina, Craig Patton, Charlie Brown, Wally Cwik, John Weagly, Barry Jens, and Nancy Garcia for their many hours of copyediting and proofing. This book could not have happened without you.

"The Cemetery Plant" by John Peel © 2007.
"Charlie Harmer's Last Request" by Brendan Detzner © 2007.
"Cold Comfort" by Michael Penkas © 2007.
"Death, Dying & 3 Credits" by Ken Goldman © 2007.
"Five Places You Must Visit After You Die" by Tom Barlow © 2007.
"For Five Minutes, the Deep" by Jude Walter Mire © 2007.
"Hell's Deadline" by Suzanne Church © 2007.
"Interlude: Blood, Snow, and Sparrows" by Joshua Alan Doetsch © 2007.
"Lorelei's Little Deaths" by C.S.E. Cooney © 2007.
"Love in the House of Nowhere" by John Weagly © 2007.
"The Mud, The Blood, and The Bones" by Christopher Fulbright and Angeline Hawkes © 2007.
"The Mummy Lost Her Sarcophagus Where a Mother Found Her Soul" by Martel Sardina © 2007.
"A Patchwork of Poems, Reanimated into Something Barely Alive" by Katherine Norem © 2007.
"Perfect Rings of Calamari" by Dan Waters © 2007.
"Soul Collector" by Craig D.B. Patton © 2007.
"Wearing the Dead" by Alan Smale © 2007.

The following stories appeared in the original edition of *Book of Dead Things*:
"The Alberscine's Vigil" by Thomas J. Strauch, © 1997, 2007.
"Blood of the Rose" by Karen E. Taylor, © 1995.
"But Somebody's Got to Do It…" by Edo van Belkom, © 1998.
"Children of Stone" by Tina L. Jens, © 1999, 2007.
"Dad Brings A Deader Home" by Yvonne Navarro, © 1998.
"The Dead Boy at Your Window" by Bruce Holland Rogers, © 1998.
"Demons in His Art" by Chris Kozlowski, (originally writing as Chris K. McComas), © 1999.
"Exodus" by Lawrence Schimel, © 1995.
"Frankenstein" by Jo Fletcher, © 1994.
"Heart Beat" by Sèphera Girón, © 1999, 2007.
"The Horror of No Beer" by Richard Gilliam, © 1999.
"I Fuck the Dead" by Sukie de la Croix, © 1999.
"It Ain't Much to Brag About, But It's All Mine" by Bill Breedlove, © 1999, 2007.
"Jimmy and Me and the Nigger Man" by Scott A. Cupp, © 1989.
"The Midnight El" by Robert Weinberg, © 1994.
"Mobly's Big Idear" by Stephen C. Merrit & Alan M. Clark, © 1999.
"Mummies" by J. D. Smith, © 1999.
"Naked Lunchmeat" by Brian Hodge, © 1996.
"Sent Down From God" by Randy Miller, © 1996.
"The Tatesville Curse" by Andrea Dubnick, © 1999.
"Upon the Midnight Clear" by Stephen Dedman, © 1998.
"White of the Moon" by Jo Fletcher, © 1999.

Introduction
Tina L. Jens

As you might guess by the fact that I volunteered to edit a *Book of Dead Things* not once, but twice, I like monsters. I've only ever written two or three stories that didn't feature a supernatural entity. But the dirty little truth is: *I don't like zombies.*

I think they're boring, and I think anyone who can't manage to run faster than a shambling corpse, or who thinks it's wise to barricade oneself in the basement or an upstairs bedroom rather than running down the street or across the field (where one could easily out-distance them), deserves to be eaten. So let the idiots die in a cadaverous, cannibalistic orgy, but don't bother to tell me about it, and don't ask me to watch a George Romero movie with you.

The anthology guidelines said:

Full disclosure: we're hard to impress with...zombies. The mere fact that...a zombie is chasing (albeit slowly) his supper is NOT a plot for a story–that's simply what they do.

The anthology market update issued half-way through the submission period said:

A zombie story–especially of the flesh-eating variety–is a hard sell. If you must send a zombie story, send me one about zombies who aren't in the George Romero tradition.

Voodoo zombies don't eat flesh– if they eat meat or salt, they immediately walk themselves back to their grave and die again, according to the lore.

If you must send a flesh-eating zombie story, make it character-driven, and do not make the ending, "Then the zombies broke through the door and ate them." Or any variation thereof.

You might assume that authors would read that and think, "I shouldn't send this editor a flesh-eating zombie story."

I could have filled a city cemetery with all the flesh-eating zombies I received. Medieval flesh-eating zombies. Civil War flesh-eating zombies. Wild West flesh-eating zombies. Futuristic, post-apocalyptic flesh-eating zombies. Wholesome Midwesterner flesh-eating zombies. Inner-city drug lord flesh-eating zombies. Even the New Orleans voodoo zombie story had a flesh-eating aspect to it.

I ranted and raved so much that the Chicago gang that hangs out at the Twilight Tales weekly show will tip-toe up behind me, say *"Zombies!"* and run away to laugh hysterically from the safety of the next room. (I have got to get me a better class of friends…I'm certain the mystery writers would never do such a thing.)

The trouble was, in the end, some of the best, most-moving, most heart-felt, most-lyrical stories featured hungry, shambling corpses. Well, actually…featured is the wrong word. They featured wonderful, three-dimensional, believable characters who had to face an awful, icky situation and make tough choices, and they did so with dignity and grace.

So I can't say I don't like zombies anymore…but I can still say that I don't care who they eat for lunch.

—Tina L. Jens
Chicago, May 6, 2007

BOOK OF DEAD THINGS

Perfect Rings of Calamari
Dan Waters

I CAN WONDER WHY CERTAIN songs that sound good when I'm sober sound like hell when I'm drunk, and why certain songs that sound great when I'm drunk don't even register when my mind is clear. Aesthetics versus intellect, the varying states of mind—these are the colors but timing is the brush. The fried calamari tasted so good that night with Renee at the Sea View and the rings tasted even better after she squeezed a wedge of lemon over the platter, her fist passing in slow circles and sending a citrus mist onto our food. The first bite was buttery and soft, and the breading fell away when I used the wide serving fork to put some more on her plate. There were hot fried banana peppers mixed with the calamari. Renee was drinking a Corona from the bottle and there was beach sand in her hair.

She smiled, and timing really is everything.

I like calamari, sure. I still like calamari at the Sea View and I still like to play *Diver Down* on their CD jukebox, and when "Little Guitars" comes on I might even look at the doorway to see if she might be coming back. But I know she isn't, because it is all about timing and even if Renee came back from the dead wearing the same dress and we ordered the same food listening to the same music on a similar breezy June evening, it would never be the same. That's the sad tragedy of experience. I'll love calamari all my life, but I'll never replicate that taste again. Freeze those moments and lock them away because nothing in life is repeated.

I doubt myself. I'm wrong; she wore a white dress, a white dress and blue sandals and she had sand in her hair but her hair smelled like jasmine…but what does that all mean today? She's gone. Fried calamari with marinara on a picnic table at the beach makes for a very nice evening but it will never be that evening again, and that moment will never be this moment, even though the moon is full and there were as many clouds then as there are today. We saw the lighthouse that night but today there is a haze. I can see three seagulls whereas then I saw only two, and "Little Guitars" playing on my radio is more tinny than it was on the jukebox that night. The calamari tastes of freezer burn, but I want Renee so, so bad. I want her with me so we can watch the waves part like we did then.

I watch a wave crest, and the wave is seven feet tall, and I think I can see her at the deep green heart of that wave. I can't see the lighthouse because there is a haze and there was no haze that night and there is the nagging question of the extra seagull as I lift a stiff and cold bundle of tentacles to my lips and there she is.

There she is.

Renee is walking out of the surf. She stepped out of the seven-foot wave as it broke and there are no more seven-foot waves and only one blue sandal remains because try as I might I can never replicate that taste again. The white dress is transparent, slick with salt water. The transparent fabric clings to her like a film but it does not cling to skin because her skin is a ruin, a pocked and pitted seascape etched by tide and time. Her eyes so blue stare lidless at me from a short walk away.

I hurry to squeeze the rind of lemon over the plate, another detail out of sequence. Words do not express, I cannot speak, but on that night I told her everything. Renee does not say anything either, but the lips that I kissed and tasted the brine of hot peppers are gone, and the smooth cheeks I stroked in the glow of our second coupling hang in tatters. And her hair. Her hair has a great amount of beach sand but I am certain it no longer smells of jasmine.

What remains of her skin has turned translucent and it parts at the knuckles. I sit transfixed, watching the flexure of tendons on her skinless hand as she plucks a ring of squid from the plate.

"You've changed," she says. She chews and I can see teeth through the rents in her flesh, and when she swallows bits of matter come out the holes in her throat.

Timing. Everything is timing. The ring—the one of gold, not of cuttlefish—burns a hole in my pocket as it burned in my pocket last summer. Freeze those moments because they cannot be replicated.

But then she takes my hand and she leads me back behind the dunes as she did last summer, and the moon throws our shadows out onto the white sand the way it had that night. I kneel beside her and feel her skinless hands tug at the waistband of my trunks. Moments, those pristine moments that are the perfect intersection of timing and beauty, that pass are gone and we can never relive them except in our minds, no matter how much we might want to.

But that doesn't mean we have to stop trying.

She pulls me down to her and it is a different brine than that of hot peppers that I taste.

Wearing the Dead
Alan Smale

I GOT HOME FROM SCHOOL an hour late and roasting in my own juices; sticky with sweat and with angry tears still streaking my cheeks and itching my neck, because I'd been pummeled again at the bus stop and had to walk all the way home, and it was a real hot September day. All I wanted was to go inside and cool off and crawl onto my bed and cry some more, but—

A man I didn't know was sitting on our front step, bold as you please. He had his head in his hands, and he was a great big black guy, so wide I almost couldn't see the house around him. He was feeling the heat, too; his face shone, and the neck and armpits of his orange T-shirt were soaked.

I stopped at the curb, uncertain. My mom's crappy old Pontiac wasn't here yet, so she was still at the furniture warehouse. And the guy was blocking my route to my front door.

Just when I thought my day couldn't suck any worse.

Looking up the sloping lawn at him, I realized how dilapidated the house front was, the door frame warped from the damp and the frequent slamming. I fingered the key in my pocket and wondered if I was safe, even with the whole front yard separating us.

He turned to eyeball a Honda as it cruised past the end of our cul-de-sac and spotted me. "What's up, kid?"

"Hey."

"You live here?"

Don't talk to strangers. But what if they're between you and where you're going? I fumbled for an answer my Mom wouldn't belt me for if she found out about it. "Do *you*?"

"Nope," he said. "No sir."

"Then whatcha doing there?"

"Sittin'."

"You one of my mother's drivers?"

"Yep, I guess so." He peered at me again, maybe noticing the dirty tear-streaks. "You okay?"

I didn't trust him. I'd just fed him a good answer, after all, like a dumbass. "What's her name, then? If you know her, who is she, and what's the company called, huh?"

"Kim Straker's your momma. We work for Garton Furniture. And you'd be Trevor. You look like her."

Thanks a lot, big guy. "Thing is, that's my house. You've got to let me walk into my house."

"So? Come on up."

"Uh-uh." The phrase from the metro trains floated into my brain: *Please stand clear of the doors.*

He finally got it. "Oh! Right." And he stood up, dusted off his jeans, and shambled down the lawn to the road, while I backed up to preserve the distance between us.

"Your momma's got to help me, Trevor," he said. "Don't know where else to turn. Things are real bad."

I sprinted for the door. He didn't run at me, just stood there with his hands jammed deep in his pockets. I felt dumb for rushing, but I sure breathed easier once that door was slammed and locked behind me.

I flipped on the air conditioning unit in the window and craned my neck to look outside. He wasn't in front of the house anymore. I ran upstairs to Mom's room and didn't see him from there, either.

Damn. Where was he at? Out back? Under the windows, so close to the house I couldn't see him? *In* the house, somehow?

"You don't scare me, dipshit!" I yelled. Nobody called back.

I looked around some more, but I still couldn't see him.

I heard Trixie, though. Dead, but far from gone. The pitiful sack-of-potatoes dragging of her hindquarters, the scraping clatter of her front paws on the cellar steps. She mewled softly like a kitten, panting with that stupid dead-poodle grin. Chilling my spine.

Today sucked *hard*. I should have stayed in bed from the get-go. As if Mom would have let me.

I jammed my fingers into my ears against the dog's misery and kept on running from window to window, but I never did catch sight of the black guy again.

Mom came home with a headache, and the first mail she opened was bills, so it was cuss words and one cigarette after another, and I stayed real quiet. There was no mileage in telling her about the big guy. I could get into trouble for talking to a stranger, or for being so rude to him that he went away—and either would get me whacked upside the head. Maybe he would never come back, and if he didn't, then nobody needed to know he was ever here in the first place.

Mom worked in the office of a furniture warehouse, dispatching drivers to make deliveries and keeping track of what had gone out on the trucks and what was still in-store, waiting. She shared the office with a woman called Jildiz Bennett, who was all braids and sass and hands-on-hips. While school was out for summer and I had to be in the office, Jildiz was always nice to me, but Mom didn't like it when I talked to her. She said Jildiz was a point-scorer and a tramp and nothing but trouble, but I never understood why that meant I couldn't say hi.

I'd seen plenty of the drivers this summer; the warehouse was stifling and they often begged to come stand in the office for just a couple of minutes under the air conditioning. Big brawny guys, but always polite to my mom, even while they were scoping her out, and Jildiz too. Jildiz even more, I think, because she was the same color as they were, and she had very smooth shiny skin and lots of it showing. I didn't recognize the man on our doorstep as one of those drivers, but one big sweaty guy in a skullcap looks pretty much the same as another.

I sure recognized him when he came back at six, though.

When the doorbell rang I was up and out of my chair in a moment. Not many people came to call at our house. I glanced at him through the small, glass side-panel beside the door, and he gazed back, and I ran to Mom, who was in the kitchen leaning against the fridge with a small glass of something in her hand.

"What now, Trev? I'm busy."

"Big black guy at the front door. One of your drivers, maybe."

"Which one?"

"Hell if I know," I said.

Mom muttered a word I didn't like and followed me into the living room. "So, what, you just left him there on the step?"

"He's a big guy," I said.

"For God's sake, Trevor. You open the door, ask their names, 'who's calling, please? One moment.' It's polite."

"I was being careful."

"You're scared of every goddamn thing," she said, opened the door, and recognized him straight off. "What the hell you doing here, Robbie Dacks?"

He glanced back over his shoulder at the street. "Sorry, Miss Skim. Got a problem. Don't know where else I can go." That's how he said it: Skim, like the milk.

She fixed him with an unblinking stare. "This for real?"

"Yes, ma'am. I can't go home."

She closed her eyes. "You'd better not be shitting me, Dacks. All right then." And she opened the door wide enough for all of him to come inside.

Even though I was halfway across the room, it felt like he was looming over me. "Hi, Trevor," he said.

My mind went blank. "Who's calling, please?"

Mom sighed. "I swear the kid's retarded. Come into the kitchen, Robbie."

The heck with that. As soon as they closed the kitchen door, I scooted on over. Robbie Dacks was six inches taller than Mom and twice her weight. Eavesdropping is wrong, but I had to be sure Mom was okay.

Robbie Dacks was saying, "…and, Skim, I told him I wouldn't sell that shit no more, and that was that, and he could get off my porch right now."

"That wasn't too bright, Robbie. You should have kept your fucking mouth shut. Christ, don't look at me like that. I worry about you. You know I do."

God, my mom had a mouth like a toilet.

Robbie said, "Man's got to make a stand, Skim. Carryin' too many tombstones on my back already."

I went to my room. I tiptoed past the open cellar door, neck prickling with fear, but I didn't see any sign of Trixie.

Not yet. But it wasn't even dark yet.

I knelt on the bed and rested my forehead on the pillow. My heart was still pumping kind of fast.

It wasn't just the guy's size that freaked me out, or even his foul language. It was this: aside from the plumber, Robbie Dacks was the first man to set foot in our house since my dad died.

I cried when Dad passed away, and it seemed like I'd been crying ever since. The last thing he said to me was: *Be strong for your momma.* He surely meant that ironically. My guess is that I'd been strong for maybe ten seconds. But I was only eight years old, so it was a tall order to begin with.

He died in a hospital bed, with no hair left and the scrawny throat and patchy skin of a ninety-year-old, though he must have been under thirty. No one would tell me which cancer was killing him, and since Mom never mentioned him now, I didn't dare ask.

What I mainly remember from that night is crying endlessly. I was sure my heart was going to split in two, and the pieces come squeezing down my arms and out my fingertips. *That* feeling I'll never forget.

Also, I remember Mom trying to gather the strength to drive home, leaning her head back so the tears wouldn't make her mascara run, lighting each cigarette from the smoldering butt of the last. Saying, "All right, then. All right, then," but never standing up to take me away from the hospital room with its dingy, peeling walls.

In one year: my dad, and then Trixie. The dead dog. The dead, damned dog.

Mom appeared in my doorway half an hour later. "Come get to know Robbie. I got to dig out some stuff for him. And try not to say anything dumb-shit. He's our guest."

"Right." I said. *Nothing about Dad*, is what she meant.

She reached out and grabbed my chin, pulling my face upwards. "You been crying again?"

"No."

"For Christ's sake, Trev," she said and left.

She'd closed the cellar door in passing, and everything was quiet, so I didn't have to worry about Trixie. Just about Robbie Dacks.

"Hey, Trevor."

"Hey again, uh, Mr. Robbie. I'm here to be polite."

"Well," he said. "Me too."

"Please, won't you sit down?"

He sat down.

"May I get you something to drink?"

No, he was just fine.

Man, he was immense. How much did he eat?

"I didn't let on, about me being here earlier. Figured that'd be best for you."

"Uh-huh. I mean, yes. Thank you. That was most considerate."

"Your mom says you read a lot."

I stared back down the corridor towards Mom's bedroom with some desperation.

"You smoke? Drink?"

I looked at him. "No!"

"That's good. Don't you start up doing those things, whatever anyone tries to tell you."

"No sir."

Trixie's dead claws scrabbled faintly against the wooden stairs. The hairs on my arm came alive. It was clear Robbie hadn't heard a thing.

What the heck could I say next? "I see you have tattoos."

"Yep," he said, and pushed up the sleeve on his right arm. "Check this out."

They were hard to figure; dark shadows against his black skin. Against my better judgment, I was intrigued. I stepped forward.

It was a Celtic knot in a thick swirly pattern that went all around his bicep. He pushed up his left sleeve to show the silhouette of a heart with a long dagger thrust through it, ornamented with scrollwork.

"Neat. Got any more?"

Robbie hesitated, and I realized what a potentially stupid question that had been.

Then he grinned in a strange, sad way and hitched up his shirt to show me his back.

I was so shocked and startled that for a moment the whole world went hazy.

Earlier, he hadn't been using a figure of speech. The man had gravestones etched in dark ink all over his back.

"Put your shirt on, Robbie Dacks."

He looked at Mom as she walked into the room carrying two bottles of Bud. "Didn't mean anything by it."

"I know. Put it on. Trev, you hungry?"

I got made SpaghettiOs and packed off to bed so Mom and Robbie could drink the beers and eat proper food and talk some more. In my room, I gazed at the wall, too frightened to even blink.

I awoke just after two a.m. with Trixie scratching at the cellar door, needing to go out.

Dad had made it very clear: Trixie was my pet and my responsibility.

Besides, Mom couldn't hear the scratching and barking since Trixie died, so it was all down to me.

It's a little nervy getting up in the middle of the night to let a ghost-dog out to do her business. I dallied a little, pulling on my shorts and T-shirt.

I stuck my nose out around my door. If Trixie really has to, she can pass right through the cellar door—old dog, new trick—but tonight she was nowhere to be seen.

She was out there, somewhere.

I marched to the cellar door and yanked it open. Trixie wasn't there, so I padded to the end of the hallway, peeked round the corner into the living room.

And jumped about ten feet in the air when the voice came—

"Don't you be spyin' on me, Trev. I seen you there. Come on in, or go away."

Robbie Dacks, lying on the couch with a blanket over him.

My throat constricted. "Wasn't spying. Didn't know you'd stayed. I was looking for my…" Dog? "Homework."

His voice went gentle. "You afraid of me, Trev?"

"I ain't afraid."

He was grinning, I could tell from his tone. "Are too."

I took a deep breath, walked across the room to him. "Am not."

"Well, you should be," said Robbie Dacks. "'Cause you don't know me, and I could be anybody at all."

"My mom trusts you. Obviously."

"That's no guarantee."

I frowned at him. "You've had plenty of time to do something bad, if you were going to. But, you know? I'm the man of the house now my dad is gone, and I do want to know what you're doing here, Robbie Dacks, and why you call my mom Skim, and why you have a graveyard on your back."

My mom says I'm afraid of everything, but I'm not.

The gravestones represented deaths among his family and friends. Street deaths, drug deaths, stupid deaths. He told me about some of them, there in the creeping darkness.

Some of them had been his fault, Robbie Dacks's fault. Because of the stuff he'd been selling.

It was awful. I had to keep remembering to breathe. And he was talking like he'd forgotten I was just a kid. I swallowed, and my throat made a funny little noise, and he came back to himself.

"Sorry," he muttered, his head back in his hands. "Sorry, Trevor. I shouldn't have said all that stuff."

I reached out then and almost touched his shoulder with my shaking fingertips, but he recoiled as if I was holding a snake. "What the hell you doin'?"

"Nothing."

"Don't feel sorry for me. At all. These gravestones on my back? That's the point. They're so nobody feels sorry for me ever again."

"Right."

"And anyway, you don't touch nobody. You're a man now. You don't go sitting on strangers' knees, or letting them touch you, not at all, not unless your momma says it's okay, and if it don't feel right to you, not even then."

"I know all about that. I got good instincts."

He sighed. "Trev, I ain't gonna do nothing bad to you. But you don't *know* that, your own self."

"Yes, I do."

"And don't be looking for me to be your daddy. I don't know nothing about that."

He had no call to mention my dad. I drew back. "Anything else I can't do?"

"Your momma comes in, sees you sitting on my bed, now what's she gonna think?"

Now he was using words I understood. She'd pitch a fit.

"Don't be trusting what you think you know. Not till you're a heck of a lot older than what you are now. You hear?"

"Yes, sir."

But what I heard was the dragging sound start up, in the hallway. The hair on my shoulders prickled, and all down my legs.

Robbie saw my face change. "What? What's the matter?"

"It's my dog."

Trixie. I could hear the clatter of her front paws on the hardwood floor, the sliding of her paralyzed back end. I could hear her breathing, the shallow panting over a lolling tongue. I could smell her dead stink. She was through the cellar door, and she was coming for me. Closer to the corner, and closer still, and that chill that preceded her, that icy aura that all the walking dead must radiate, stealing the heat from the air around them and sucking it into the pale abyss of the ghost-world. My mouth was instantly dry.

"Ain't no dog here," said Robbie Dacks.

I went to Robbie then, knelt up on the couch right by him to get my feet off the floor. I was shaking. Some nights I can do what I have to, but the slithering, inevitable approach of Trixie on top of all those tales of senseless, callous street death…

"Hey, now. What was I just tellin' you?"

"I know," I said. "Shut up. This is an emergency."

And she came around the corner. Her paws first, then her white poodle face, her topknot. And the rest of her, dragging behind, her doubly-lifeless butt with her back legs splayed to either side of it, flat on the hardwood floor and dragging pitifully.

Tongue hanging out, breathless, she did the littlest of panting happy-barks when she saw us.

I swear Trixie doesn't even know she's dead.

I glanced at Robbie. "You don't see her? She's right where you're looking." If anyone else could see Trixie, it would be Robbie, who walked within a finger's-touch of death every day.

"Sure don't, Trev."

She leaned forward, gamely putting her front-weight into dragging her hind-weight along, panting happily in recognition.

"Well, that's 'cause she's dead. She's haunting me. I got to let her out. Wait here."

Robbie shrugged, bemused.

"And don't you ever laugh at me about this," I said. "Or I'll kick your ass."

I stepped off the couch. Close-up, I could see the blood matting the fur on her nose and right ear and clear across her right side. White bone-shards jutted out from her poor fuzzy head. Above the panting mouth, her gaze was blank.

Every night I see the wreckage of Trixie, I cry like it's the first time.

But I have a responsibility.

As I stood watching her pee in the front yard, I dried my eyes. It's lucky Trixie's a she, since girl-dogs pee sitting down anyway. A male dog would have about driven himself crazy trying to cock his back leg.

Waiting for her to drag herself back in, my fear faded. As she brushed past me, I breathed, "I'm sorry, Trixie."

She curled up on the mat. I stepped over her.

Robbie blinked at me, baffled, as I sat back down. "Don't tell Mom, okay? Swear solemnly you won't tell."

"Uh, I swear."

"I'm not crazy, Robbie. I'm the only one who sees her. She's haunting me because of what I did."

He scratched his back. "Sure thing."

And it poured out of me: how Trixie had been hit by a truck and dragged herself home, how Dad took her to the vet but couldn't bear to have her put down. Dad was already diagnosed by then and felt a strong bond with this stricken dog. Mom shouted at first about the messes the poor disabled poodle made, but then backed down because Dad was sick. And even once Dad was gone, Mom couldn't bear to take my dog away too. A rare instance of maternal compassion.

I took a long, jagged breath. Robbie knew almost all of it now. I figured I may as well tell him the rest.

Trixie had survived a pickup truck, only to be polished off by steps.

I'd been in the living room with Carl from my class. We weren't big pals, but we hung together some. He liked to come round. He said his parents didn't like him and his sisters wouldn't speak to him, but that's all I knew; our deal was that he didn't ask about Dad, and I didn't ask about his family.

Actually, I think Carl came to watch my mom. This was pretty soon after Dad died, when Mom would walk around the house in a daze wearing just a strappy top and a pair of Dad's old boxer shorts. I'd be embarrassed because she was drunk and she had freckles all over her shoulders and saggy arms, but Carl would gape at her like she was a supermodel. Sometimes you'd see quite a bit of Mom that she either didn't know she was showing, or just didn't care. She'd offer him a glass of milk, and he'd almost drop it because he wasn't looking at what she was handing him.

So Carl came for the show, but I didn't care as long as he'd be my friend.

He thought Trixie was kind of funny, and when he was around I saw the humor of it too.

Since I had company, Mom had put all Trixie's dog toys in the cellar to get her out of the way. So off to the cellar she went to find them.

Carl and I heard her go down the first step. Bomp.

The second step. Bomp.

Another: Bomp.

I looked at Carl, and we both started to smile in anticipation. We were just kids. But I should have known.

If I'd run, I *might* have made it there in time to scoop her up and save her.

I see it in my mind's eye: Trixie panting earnestly, best feet forward, taking the steps down with one forepaw and then the other, and her crippled hindquarters sliding to the side, coming down a step—bomp—then another—bomp; the scrabbling of her front paws as she tried to level herself off—clatter-clat—and then the dead weight of her rear overtaking her, dragging Trixie into a tumble, rolling over and over, out of control, bomp-bomp, ba-domp-ba-domp, DOMP, DOMP, and then a silence as she flew through the air, and a wet and final THUD-clang!—as she hit the concrete floor at the foot of the steps and rolled into the mess from Dad's various home improvement projects: spare tiles, Sheetrock, half-empty paint cans.

I waited for a bark or even a whine, but heard only silence.

In my heart I think we knew, even then, that she must be dead. But the sound of it was so comical, the pathos of her doom, the sheer banana-peel slapstick farce of it…and we were boys, and cruel, and we stared at each other for a single moment of horror, and then *I laughed*. And, freed up, Carl laughed too.

And we laughed til we howled.

I couldn't help myself. I really couldn't.

When I stood and tiptoed downstairs to pick up the pitiful corpse, when I felt how *cold* Trixie was, how broken, how sad, I stopped smiling.

I looked up the steps, and Carl was crying, standing in the doorway as I cradled Trixie's head, her blood slick on my bare arm, her bones poking out.

Embarrassed, chilled, trying to make it all stop, I said, "Hey, Carl. Come on, man. She was only a dog."

He turned, flicking teardrops onto the walls of the stairwell, and he ran and ran, and he never came to my house again.

"That's low," said Robbie quietly. "Laughing when your dog dies, Trev? That's low and mean. *Damn*, Trevor."

"I didn't know any better."

"Sure you fuckin' did."

I came out of the story and back to the nighttime living room and found my face hot and my stomach gripped with a huge ache.

Robbie thought I was a monster. This man who had dealt drugs and had gravestones tattooed into his flesh, I horrified him. "I've cried since," I said. "Often. Always."

Robbie looked carefully at the corridor, listening, perhaps. And then he said, "C'mere." And I did, and Robbie gave me a hug for about eight seconds, and I sobbed, and ghostly Trixie watched me mournfully from the floor with her pathetic head resting between her forepaws.

Then Robbie let go, and we sprang apart.

He said, "It's okay, Trev. Go on back to bed now."

"When I'm old enough, I want tattoos. Two of 'em. Will you take me?"

"Maybe," said Robbie Dacks.

As I walked past Trixie I heard her get up onto her front paws and pad-drag herself after me. I didn't turn. I just got myself back down the hallway to my bed and heard Trixie stretch herself across the doorway to protect me. And I fell asleep.

"Give me your key."

"What?" I raised my head an inch off the pillow and squinted.

"Robbie'll be staying here a while." I knew Mom was waiting for me to object, so I just leaned over to my bedside table and handed over my door key, calm as you like.

If she was surprised, she didn't show it. "And don't you tell anyone that Robbie is staying here. It's nobody's business."

Fine with me. I waited for her to go away, but she leaned in further and said, "This is important, Trevor."

"He'd just better be here when I get home," I said and let her try to guess what I meant.

My penance was a two-sided coin. Trixie was tails. Carl was heads.

He liked to trip me on the stairs at school. Many times I'd gone tumbling and crashing to the bottom. It was his joke, his cruel commemoration of our secret; Carl's way of getting back at me for having seen him cry over a dog that wasn't even his.

Today I should have seen it coming, but I had a lot on my mind. And I was tired, from the long midnight talks with Robbie.

Carl and Zeke strolled down the stairs towards me. Zeke was Carl's new friend. Zeke's older brothers were gang members with guns and all, and Zeke would be one too when he was old enough. I guess Zeke helped Carl to feel mean.

As I lay there at the bottom of the steps, Zeke wound up and pretended to kick me in the head, but didn't touch me more than a tap with his steel-toed boot. I cried anyway, and they laughed and hawked up some spit onto me and walked away.

"Don't show fear, man," said Robbie. It was two a.m., and I'd just let the dog out. "They know when you scared."

"So? If I talk back to them or act tough, they get me even worse."

"Uh-uh. They don't hate you like you think. If they did, they'd have messed you up bad already. You're just easy meat. If it gets to be work, they'll go pick on someone else."

"I don't think so."

"Trev. Who you think you're talking to? I ain't guessing. I *know*. For ten years I ate little snots like you for lunch."

I was heading for the school bus when Carl and Zeke jumped me, tossing me into the wall hard enough to bounce my head off it. As I sagged against the brick, Zeke faked a lunge to my eyes with the index and middle fingers of his left hand, then laughed like a maniac when I screamed and jerked my head aside.

I waited for a second to see if they were done, but they obviously weren't.

Okay then. *Robbie Dacks, I'm trusting you.*

"What the fuck you doing?" I said. "Shit-for-brains."

"Yeah?" said Carl in disbelief. Zeke smiled.

I put myself in his face. "You'd better not dick with me, or my mom's new boyfriend is going to chew you a new asshole."

"Oh yeah?"

"He's a big guy. You do *not* want to piss him off."

"So where'd this bad-ass motherfucker come from?"

They got a big laugh out of the MF word, under the circumstances. I laughed too, then said, "He come from nowhere, man. But he'll mess you up bad if you don't stay the fuck away from me."

Zeke said, "Your momma be Kim Straker, down at Garton?"

"Yeah."

"Skinny white bitch. Black bad-ass'd split your momma's skinny ass in two."

"My mom," I said with total conviction, "is tough."

"He not wrong," said Carl. "She one tough bitch. Nice tits. If she didn't stink of whiskey she'd be hot."

"What's his name, then, this big ol' bad-ass?"

"None of your fuckin' business."

"Yeah?" said Zeke. Then he inexplicably laughed and pounded me on the shoulder. "You okay, Trev. You the man."

And that was it; they just walked away, Zeke already getting out his cell phone to call his homies. I figured they'd forgotten me in a second.

How wrong I was.

I got home from school on time. The school bus dropped me at the end of our cul-de-sac, and I jived up to my house, beaming like a fool.

Robbie stood on our front step in his orange T-shirt, fixing up the front door. Even with his big bulk in the way, I could see how he'd replaced the warped wood, primed and painted the frame. It looked like a million bucks. Mom stood in the driveway, arms folded, wearing a look of startled pleasure.

"Well, shit," I said. "Here's Robbie Dacks, gettin' between me and my front door again."

They swiveled to look at me. "Trev?" said Mom, who'd never heard the S-word out of my mouth before today.

She didn't know me at *all*.

"Hey," said Robbie. "What's up?"

"Everything's up. I've got it all goin' on. I'm the man."

Robbie glanced at Mom. "That right?"

"I stood up to 'em, just like you told me. Damned if it didn't work out just fine." I was proud of myself and proud of Robbie. In five days he'd taught me more about looking out for myself than my mom had in the three years since Dad died. And it looked like he was sticking around. You don't fix up a front door you're not planning to use. "Oh, Mom? Newsflash. I was being bullied at school, but now I'm not."

Robbie looked surprised, but gratified. "Well, that's cool."

"Look what Robbie did," said Mom. Changing the subject, of course, but you know what? It didn't matter. I didn't need her approval.

"Looks great," I said, walking up the lawn.

Robbie looked back at the door. "Yeah," he said, and then allowed himself a little more rightful pride in his work. "Yeah! O-*kay*."

I pounded him on the back. "O-*kay!*"

And that's how come we were all facing away from the street.

The gangstas must have coasted around the corner with the engine off, because the roar of the semiautomatic was the first thing we heard. But Robbie, he must have had an instinct about it, because even as I felt the first bullets thud into him, he was already throwing me down to the ground.

The bullets lifted him up, big guy that he was, and smashed him against the house. He shook like he was shivering. Like he was cold.

His mouth was wide, but he never made a sound. Not one that I heard, anyway, over the clatter of bullets spraying the front of my house and my Mom's shrieking.

The car's engine roared into life and it did a sliding one-eighty on the street; an old, black, bashed-up Mercedes with guys in hoods leaning out the back windows. Like a movie or something. Then they were gone, tire-squealing towards town.

It seemed to happen so slowly, but it was over so fast.

I got to my feet. Mom still stood in the driveway, screaming, hands clutching her hair. So I knew she was all right.

Robbie was not all right. He was blown apart across the middle and bleeding like a fire hose.

Blood across the door and the siding, blood trickling down the driveway to the street, blood all over everywhere. His head cracked open from the force of being flung against our house. He was dead already.

Robbie couldn't be gone. He *couldn't*. Not like this.

I knelt by his side, the gunshots still ringing in my head.

His orange T-shirt was rucked up, tombstones glowing black against his coffee skin. I pushed the shirt up further and put my hand over a tombstone, and my heart welled up. In an instant it had filled my whole chest. I felt it pushing down on my bowels, squeezing through my arms like scarlet pulsing toothpaste, ready to blow my hands off. About ready to explode.

Mom walked slowly up the driveway.

Perhaps I expected her to throw herself across him and cradle his head in her hands. Or scoop me up and say, "Thank God you're alive, Trev, for a moment I thought I'd lost you forever."

She didn't do any of that. She just stood like a rail, looking down at the blasted body of Robbie Dacks, and then she tilted her head to stare at me with giant, horrified eyes.

"What have you done?" she whispered.

"Me?"

"You stupid shit," she said. And again, screaming, louder than the guns, slamming her fist into the air in front of my face with every word: *"You stupid shit! What have you done?"*

I got it, then. Of course it was me. I'd given him away. It was Zeke's brother's gang that Robbie had been hiding out from, all along.

Even without a tattoo, I'd wear Robbie Dacks's death burned into my back for the rest of my life.

I heard Trixie tumbling down the stairs to her doom: bomp-bomp, bomp-bomp, loud in my ears, ba-domp, ba-DOMP-DOMP. But I didn't need clues. I knew what I had to do.

Robbie's body cooled at my feet. Mom looked at me in fury and desperation, for me to explain, apologize, cry, anything.

But that wouldn't help. When I cried, I failed. Like I'd failed when Dad died.

Now, above all, I had to be brave.

Robbie couldn't be allowed to leave us. Without him, Mom and I would kill each other. She was almost set to kill me right now.

There was only one way to raise Robbie from the dead and keep him close by my side.

I looked into my mother's blazing eyes, inches from my own.

And I *laughed.*

Love in the House of Nowhere
John Weagly

T HEY'D KISSED BEFORE. A LOT. Veronica was a girl, and Jason was a boy, and they were both young adults. High school was behind them, and college was ahead, and she loved him. She was ready to try things with Jason that she'd only seen in movies.

They were sitting on the floor in the almost empty living room of a house where no one lived that stood beside a deserted road that no one used. The walls were made of cobwebs, and what light there was was lined with shadows.

When they'd kissed in the past, Veronica had been more focused.

Tonight was special. Jason had said he wanted to take her somewhere that meant a lot to him. When they pulled up in front of the old dark house, she'd almost asked if they could go someplace else. But then Jason turned to her and said, "Isn't it great?" The look on his face was so hopeful that she knew she couldn't say no.

Now she was starting to regret that decision. She pulled her lips away from his. "How did you hear about this place?" she asked.

"Rumors and urban legends," Jason said. "Don't worry. There's no one around. It's nice and secluded."

"When did they move out?"

"What? Who?"

"They. They who lived here."

"I don't know," Jason shrugged his shoulders. "This place has been like this for a couple of years."

Veronica pointed at an old mattress lying in the corner of the room. "How did that get here?"

"Maybe they left it. Maybe it came here on its own. Nobody knows."

Veronica stood and walked to the other side of the room. A broken mirror hung on the wall. She looked at her reflection in the glass and teased her hair. The air held a dense smell that made her sinuses itch. "This place gives me the willies," she said. "I feel like we're in one of those monster movies you make me watch."

"You look beautiful," Jason said.

Jason liked to say that with her blond hair and big eyes, Veronica looked like the actress Nancy Allen. Nancy had been Peter Weller's partner in *Robocop* and John Travolta's girlfriend in *Carrie*. Veronica knew that Jason really liked both of those movies, so she took the comparison as a compliment. Some of her friends at school told her that she was too pretty to date someone like Jason, who was kind of short and kind of dumpy, but Veronica thought comments like that were insulting to both Jason and herself.

"Beautiful or not," Veronica said, finishing her hair revision, "I still think this place is creepy."

"It's romantic," Jason said, walking over to her. "In a Boris Karloff sort of way." He placed his hands on Veronica's hips, turned her around, and touched his nose to hers.

Veronica smiled. "Did you bring other girls here, before you met me?"

Jason drew her closer. "If I did, none of them were as special as you."

"How many?"

"How many what?"

"How many other girls have you brought here?" Veronica asked, pulling away.

"Not that many," Jason said. "A couple. Three."

"Three?"

"Three. Four counting you."

Veronica leaned into him, placing her head on his shoulder. She liked the way his chest felt against hers. She could feel his heart beating. "I guess that's not that bad," she said.

They swayed in the night. There was no music, but the night was far from silent. The wind blew through the eaves of the house and created a song just for the two of them. Jason's hands moved up Veronica's back to her shoulders. She smiled.

They'd dated for most of the school year. Veronica had noticed Jason around school before, but she never really knew him. They didn't run in the same circles; Veronica was a pom-pom girl, and Jason was the president of the afterschool film club. When he asked her to the Homecoming Dance, she was surprised, but she said yes on impulse. The impulse had been right; they'd been together ever since.

Jason moved his face forward and let his lips brush hers. Out of the corner of her eye, Veronica saw something small flutter in the corner. She pulled away.

"I can't," she said. "It's too spooky."

"You want to go for a walk, then come back?"

"No, let's do something else tonight."

"But this is our last night together."

He was right. She was leaving for college the next day. Jason was leaving the following week. She wasn't going to see him for at least a month. Still, she wanted to wait.

"Let's give it a little time," she said.

Jason walked over to the mattress and nudged it with his foot. "I thought you were ready," he said.

"I thought I was, too, but I wasn't ready for…this."

"It's not that awful."

Veronica watched him. She didn't enjoy seeing Jason frustrated like this. "The first time I kissed a boy, it was in the McDonald's parking lot. I was thirteen. I was both overwhelmed and let down. The kiss was wonderful, but it was the McDonald's parking lot. After that, I swore that any other firsts would be perfect."

Jason nudged the mattress again.

"Don't you have any memories like that? Something important that you look back at and wish was a little bit different? Something significant in your life that you wish could have been just right?"

Jason thought for a moment. "Not really," he said. "I remember the first time I saw *The Bride of Frankenstein*. It was fine."

Veronica encouraged him with a nod. "Okay."

"And the first time I saw *Halloween*. That was good."

"Anything else?"

"And *An American Werewolf in London*. That went well."

Veronica didn't think he was getting it. Then she remembered something. "You haven't seen *The Exorcist*, have you," she said.

"No."

"Why not?"

"You know! It's considered one of the best of the best. When I see it, I have to be all alone, and it has to be in the middle of the night with all the lights turned off."

Veronica smiled. "See? That's what I'm talking about. The situation has to be perfect."

Jason nodded. "Okay. I see. We can still make tonight perfect; we can go somewhere else. I might have enough money for a hotel room, if we go to one of those places out by the factory."

"That's not quite what I mean, either," she said.

"Then what do you mean?"

He still wasn't getting it. It reminded Veronica of their first date. After the Homecoming Dance, they'd gone back to Jason's to watch a video. Veronica wanted to make out, but Jason was more interested in watching *Creepshow*, which he'd already seen ten times. They didn't end up kissing until the final credit had rolled. This was another one of those times that they weren't on the same page. She looked at the floor. Something with multiple legs scuttled across her field of view. "I just…I'm not sure I'm ready," she said.

"I thought you loved me," Jason said, sitting on the mattress. A puff of dust floated into the air.

"I do! But, how do I know you love me?"

"Of course I love you!"

"I know. But how do I know that? How do I know I'm not just one more girl? How do I know that I mean something to you?"

"Of course you mean something to me! I love you. What else can I say?"

Veronica walked over to a broken window that looked out on the overgrown front lawn. She understood that a lot of guys would say "I love you" to get what they wanted. They'd say anything! Jason wasn't like that. She knew in her heart that, despite his borderline creepy fascination with monster movies and his awkward ideas about romantic settings, he was a good guy. He meant what he said. He loved her, and she loved him. She also wasn't a foolish girl. She didn't expect to be with Jason forever. They were young; couples that met in high school and stayed together were a rarity. Still, she wanted Jason to be her first. But she had to know that it meant as much to him as it did to her.

As Veronica stared out at the empty night, an idea hit her. She turned to look at her boyfriend. He was still on the mattress, tracing his finger in the dust on the floor.

"You know that movie we watched, the one with the zombies?"

Jason thought for a moment. "Was it *Zombie*?"

"No, the other one."

"*Night of the Living Dead?*"

"No, but close."

"*Return of the Living Dead?*"

"*Return of the Return of the Living Dead!*"

"It was called *Return of the Living Dead, Part 2*," Jason said. "What about it?"

"Do you love me like that?"

Jason looked confused.

"Remember when that guy turned into a zombie, and he was trying to catch his girlfriend," Veronica said. "Then that other zombie came in and tried to catch her, too?"

"Yeah. They both wanted to eat her brain."

"And the first zombie said to his girlfriend, 'Honey, let me eat your brain! I'm the one who loves you!'"

"Yeah?"

Veronica crossed the room and sat next to him on the mattress. It was time to find out how he really felt. "Is our relationship like that? Would you let me eat your brain?"

Jason still looked confused. "You want to eat my brain?"

"It's a hypothetical question."

"I don't know," Jason said, turning his head and looking at the far wall. The lines on his brow deepened as he squinted his eyes. "It would depend on the circumstances."

"Think about it, Jason," Veronica turned his face back to hers. "You're done for, anyway. It's me and another zombie. No...wait...It's me and the other three girls you brought here. We all want to eat your brain. Would you choose me?"

"I'm not sure. This isn't an easy decision to make."

"Why? Are the other zombies prettier than I am?"

"Of course not. I just like my brain."

"Would you? Would you let me eat your brain?"

Something deep within the old house settled. Jason looked at her. To Veronica, it felt like he was seeing her for the very first time. The intensity of his gaze made her skin feel warm and her eyes tear up.

"Yeah," Jason said, brushing a strand of hair from her cheek. "Of course I would. You can eat my brain, if you really want to."

Veronica smiled and kissed him. It was a kiss she would remember forever. It was the type of kiss that, once it's broken, can never be found again. "By the way," she added after their lips broke, "you can eat my brain, too."

Jason lifted his mouth to her forehead and gently scraped his teeth against her flesh. "Yum! Brains! Love brains!"

Veronica giggled.

"So do you want to stay," Jason asked.

"I'm still not going to let my first time be in a spooky, dusty, crumbling old house."

"Oh."

"And I still think we should wait. A little while."

"Okay. So. What would you like to do instead?"

"I don't know."

They both thought for a moment. Something thumped in the floorboards beneath their feet.

"You know," Jason said, "I still haven't seen *The Exorcist*."

"I know. You're waiting."

"I think I've waited long enough."

Veronica's heart skipped a beat. "You mean tonight? With me? Not alone?"

"There's a first time for everything," Jason said.

Veronica stood, took Jason's hand, and led him outside. As the front door closed, the house sighed behind them.

Lorelei's Little Deaths
C.S.E.Cooney

LORELEI RAN TO HER DEATH on the moor.

The site was ideal for a tryst: bare rock, a lowering sky, and a high, lonely stretch of land where wolves howled on the horizon. Lorelei loved the moor. She loved the bleak earth, the treacherous heather, the hidden bogs. Sometimes, on special nights, like tonight, the boiling clouds above shredded to reveal a full moon.

Death awaited her by the skeleton tree. He lit the night. As soon as she saw him, Lorelei called out, "Hello! Hello!" and began to run faster, waving her arms like torches. The interrupted moonlight glittered on his answering smile.

"Hello, you," he said.

"Death, it is our anniversary!"

It was a bit tricky for Lorelei to enunciate while clambering over moss-grown boulders. To do this with any celerity was impossible. Death stepped out from the clawed shadow of the tree and offered her his hand.

"Up you go," he said and heaved.

The skeleton tree was dead, had always been dead, had been planted on the moor to mark something—a grave, maybe, or a battlefield where witches were buried. Once Lorelei gained her footing, Death leaned back against the trunk, crossing his arms over his chest. He had a slender, well-muscled chest, glimmery and milk-colored. He did not have any chest hair. Lorelei wriggled at the sight of him.

"Tonight will be the one thousand and ninety-fifth night you've killed me!"

"So many?" His smile flashed again. Lots of sharp teeth. Rows of them. "How shall we celebrate?"

"Do you love me?" Lorelei's bare feet danced on the moss. He wanted her, she knew it; his large nostrils flared to catch her scent. He wiped the palms of his hands on his trousers.

"Yes," he said. "I love you running to me, moist from the race. I love the colors you change when I place my rope around your neck: rose—indigo—mottled black. I love afterwards, when you are gone, and I sliver your flesh and eat my fill."

Lorelei had to clench her thighs against the throbbing. "Your words are poetry!"

Death made a low noise. Though, as usual, Lorelei never saw him move, in the split of a second she found herself displaced, pressed spine to tree, with the grave-glow of his body freezing hers.

"One thousand ninety-five." His murmur frosted the hollow behind her ear. "How shall it be tonight?"

"Like the first night." Lorelei kissed his forehead, his feral nose, the transparent eyelids that blinked closed sideways over lantern-yellow eyes. "Remember? I found you by this tree. And you said you were a monster and no one would ever love you, because you could only bring death. And I said…"

"You said that you would love me. The more I murdered you, the more you would love me, for you had been searching for me always. You were fourteen years old, and had never loved, never died. And now it's been one thousand nights. One thousand dreams…"

"One thousand deaths. And…ninety-five."

As on the first night, Death slipped his noose around her neck.

Lorelei's last unconscious thought was, "Yes, yes, *yes*!" And then, it burst from her. Life. Throbbing life. A lapful of life. She turned her head, biting her pillow to keep from screaming. Lorelei lay writhing, drooling, cursing her life—this staid, ho-hum, doldrums existence, wherein heart galloped and throat clanged and Death was banished. She missed him, she missed him, she missed the bones of him…

"Damn it!" Lorelei opened her eyes.

Like every morning, perfectly on cue, Marilee, her lady's maid, drew the drapes with a vicious whoosh and chirped, "Good morning, Lady Lorelei!"

Lorelei hurled a pillow at Marilee's mobcap. "Devil eat your *good mornings*, you pernicious crocodile in crinoline!" she spat. "I loathe your *good mornings*!"

Marilee caught the pillow, gave it a pert fluff, and tossed it back. She did this to irritate Lorelei, and Lorelei knew it, but she could not fire the girl for high spirits. She had tried.

"Did you sleep well, my lady?"

"No, curse your slimy eyeballs! I don't *want* to sleep well. How dare you ask me?"

Marilee did not turn her back all the way before rolling her eyes. "It's a fine, bright mornin'! As soon as yer up, yer da wants to see ye."

"I," Lorelei announced, "am not seeing anybody. Least of all the man whose ill-considered discharge inaugurated my abhorrent existence."

Marilee snorted.

Lorelei glared. "Marilee, I am going for a walk. Where is my shroud?"

"Just there, Lady Lorelei. If ye don't mind me sayin'…"

"I do, in fact."

"It's not really yer color, white." Marilee's pink little ladybug mouth quirked up in triumph as Lorelei's scowl deepened. "Washes ye out. Makes ye look a right ghoul, it does."

Lorelei darted out of bed, jamming her arms akimbo. "You've been sleeping with my father again, haven't you? Well, you're not his countess, nor never shall you be! The whole world agrees my mother was a night hag and deserved to be burned; but her blood was blue as sapphires, and you're just another roly-poly, red-blooded daughter of the moors. I defy you to say another word about my wardrobe!"

Marilee tossed her glossy black mane like an indignant mare, but she wisely buttoned her mouth. She was Lorelei's senior by only four years, but was the eldest of half a dozen siblings; Lorelei was an only child. Marliee had watched several brothers and sisters move through early adolescence with fixations on the melancholy and macabre. Apparently, they found it romantic. (Marilee herself had never undergone such a phase.) After a while, they had broken free of it—mostly undamaged—and had gone on with their lives.

Lorelei had been in such a phase for three years now and showed no sign of maturing.

Thinking her maid quelled, Lorelei sniffed. "Help me out of this nightgown. I'm soaked through. What a wreck! Bad enough to be alive, but to be alive in a *clammy* body! It's more than a reasonable girl can bear!"

Quarter of an hour later, no more or less reasonable than she ever was, Lorelei sat before her vanity, contemplating her cosmetics. She was dressed in her shroud, a flimsy, white dressing gown that was rather the worse for being Lorelei's favorite garment. It was threadbare, had lots of trailing bits and shabby lace and flounces on the hem. It had belonged to her mother. The Count had rid his house of every other trace of the late Countess, but that one item Lorelei would not relinquish.

"Lady Lorelei," she told herself, "you are looking spectacularly unwell!" Her reflection peered piteously back at her from the round, greenish mirror. "But unwell is still alive!"

Marilee plopped down on her mistress's bed. She watched as Lorelei leaned forward and concentrated with disturbing intensity on the transformation of her face. She wanted to ask: *Child, why do ye go on so? It's springtime! Yer young and rich and yer father's only heir. It's a shameful waste!*

But the maid had long since learned that comments of that sort would be met with—at best—contempt. At worst Lorelei might start weeping hysterically, pulling out her yellow hair by the roots and insisting she was not meant for this world; that the madmen who had seized and burned her mother over on the Continent should have stormed Ash Hollow and burned her too; that she was lost, lost, adrift in the bright cold light of day.... Marilee was in no hurry to incite such histrionics this morning.

Lorelei's cosmetics were laid out in as meticulous an order as instruments on a mortician's table. There was charcoal to enhance the circles under her green eyes. There was white paint to smear over her mouth and cheeks until her pallor was uniform. For her eyelids, there was a dark red pencil, which gave her the aspect of the living dead. When the applications were complete, Lorelei smiled into the mirror. She had cultivated a pathetic smile.

"That's better. Now he will recognize you."

Lorelei regularly walked a five-mile circuit through the moors, hoping for some sign of Death in her waking world. The path never failed to disappoint. Unlike the resentful wilderness of her dreams, the path through the real moor was laid out in tidy gravel and lined with flat, white stones. There were carts on the path, little girls on ponies, cheeky tourists on bicycles, and everyone staring at Lorelei like she came from a different planet, when really, Lorelei had been born and bred in that place, and it was no fault of hers she had turned out as she did.

"My lady!" Marilee followed Lorelei out of her chambers, through the trophy hall, and the gallery, down the stairs, into the receiving hall, and even out the front door, "Yer da—what'll I tell him? He wanted to see ye first thing!"

Lorelei turned sharply, planted herself in front of her maid, and grasped her by the elbows, shaking hard. "Marilee, Marilee, Marilee! Why must you badger me so? I can't stay in that house. It oppresses me! It weighs on my chest like an albatross! My father will look at me with basset hound eyes and tell me I must marry some marquis or duke, but how can he bear to part with me, and don't I look more like my mother every day, and what are we to do, et cetera…. How should I retort? 'I apologize, my lord, but being as I am, I am doomed?' It is too provoking!"

Marilee was seized by a sudden terror of this odd girl with her abrupt ways and relentless fingers and the red-rimmed green eyes that blazed so hungrily at her. There was a whine in her voice when she asked: "But what'll I tell him?"

"Tell him"—Lorelei ground the words between her molars—"that I am prostrate with galloping consumption!"

With that, she spun and bolted. What Marilee saw last were Lorelei's straggling locks, which she had not washed or combed, whipping past the gate like a butter-colored banner.

In waking life, the skeleton tree was not an imposing feature of the landscape. It was shriveled-looking and blottish, as if one strong gust would send it tumbling into some sinkhole. Nevertheless, Lorelei pressed her forehead against its black bark, hard enough to leave streaks of white face paint.

How often had she been tied to this tree and gutted with his hooks and scalpels? How many times had Death decorticated her, decapitated her, saw to every last minute-detail: scraped the nails off her toes, popped the caps off her knees, pierced his needles through her nipples, bit off her ears and nose and swallowed them while she watched? In waking life, no one paid her such close attention. They looked at her as though she were a circus geek, liable to chew the heads off chickens and paint strange runes with their blood. Death looked at her like he was the last man starving on a desolate world and she was a feast laid before him. Besides—if anyone was stranger than Lorelei, it was Death, with his crystal-bright yellow eyes and the way he glowed in the dark.

"Oh, tree!" she cried. "Skeleton tree! Witch tree, hanging tree, tree where he loved and murdered me! Help me! You who stand alone on this vast moor, surely you know my loneliness!" And Lorelei began to kiss the dead black bark with all the pent up fervor inside her, her arms wrapped like anacondas around the trunk. She thought she felt something snatch at her back, like branches or bone, but when she started away, nothing restrained her. She discovered, however, one witness to her ardent declarations. A ragged white crow sat perched on one of the tree branches, watching her with yellow eyes.

"Hello," she said.

The crow defecated politely, still staring at her.

"Are you a messenger?" In her eagerness, Lorelei's words tumbled over each other like blind kittens. "Did Death send you to me? Is he trapped in my dreams? How may I free him? Tell me! Tell me!" She reached to grab the bird, but at the last possible second it winged away, setting up a great scold and disappearing into the sky. A single dirty white feather drifted down. As Lorelei reached for it, she saw a coiled something on the ground, half-hidden beneath a bush of yellow gorse. She bent to pick it up.

The gorse released a waft of pale coconut perfume, and Lorelei began to smile.

"A ball," announced the Count.

"A ball," Lorelei repeated.

"A masked ball. In honor of your seventeenth birthday."

"I see," said Lorelei. "My birthday is tomorrow. When were you going to tell me?"

"This morning," her father answered peevishly. "But you ran off on me. Again."

Lorelei had tried to sneak back into the manor after her morning walk, but two of her father's footmen caught her in the gardens and frog-marched her to his study. She bore with their manhandling valiantly, but refused to speak until the Count, perceiving her entry, the disarray of her clothes, and the set of her chin, asked in vexation, "Why on earth are you wearing a noose around your waist, young lady?"

"It's a belt," Lorelei said witheringly.

The Count decided to ignore this, asked her to sit down, and told her his surprise. The masquerade did come as an unpleasant jolt to Lorelei; if there was anyone in Ash Hollow more averse to society than the Count himself, it was his daughter. They rarely entertained—and never since the death of the Countess.

"Is there some marital-minded peer currently abiding in Ash Hollow town?" Lorelei inquired. "Perhaps a nobleman with pockets to let, whose amity with opera dancers and appalling gambling habits have forced him to rusticate, who is now so bored with our northern wilderness that he has prevailed upon you for some light entertainment?"

The Count sighed. Half the time he did not understand his daughter; the rest of the time he wanted nothing but to stuff her mouth with his fist. "Something like that, Lorelei."

At the age of fifty, the Count looked tired. Three years ago he had been hale and fleshy (though slightly wild about the eyes, being married to such a succubus); now his flesh hung on his bones. His nose was purple-threaded and his hairline was receding. He looked at his daughter in her dingy lace and smeared mummer's makeup, and tried not to consider the possible travesties in store for the following night.

"You should have told me about this sooner," Lorelei said.

"Yes, well..." The Count rubbed his beaky nose. "Less time for your palpitations this way. Run along. Your maid has arranged your evening attire for tomorrow. Make sure she gives you a thorough scrubbing. I expect you to attend this masque wearing the guise of a living girl."

"*That*, I'm afraid, is beyond even Marilee's multitudinous powers!"

And Lorelei slammed out of his study.

After her bath, Lorelei threw herself into bed, drawing the curtains shut behind her. When Marilee protested, saying it was nearly time for supper and that My Lady's hair needed seeing to, Lorelei poked her head back through the drapes.

"Not another word, you treacherous, deceitful, cruel, conspiring thing! You knew about the masque! I might have been fifty miles from here by now! I might have drowned myself in the millpond three times over! I'm done with you and your hairpins! Don't say anything! If you do I swear I'll scream! I'll eat you! I'll make sure a hairpin is the father of your children!"

More annoyed than alarmed, Marilee blew a loud raspberry and ducked out of the room. Lorelei buried her head under a pile of pillows. She was trembling. Her skull was throbbing, and her mouth tasted of bark and gorse. She set her will to fall asleep, and her will accomplished her ends. She began dreaming almost immediately.

On the moor, Death stepped out of the skeleton tree. He was dressed in a long coat of closely-woven white feathers and wore the dreadful beaked mask of bygone plague doctors. When she peered more closely however, Lorelei saw that the mask was really flesh: that Death had the head of a white raven and that his eyes were mad.

"Who put you in that tree?"

Death stroked the tree with one clawed hand. It seemed a mere caress, but a moment later writing appeared on the trunk where his talon touched. The letters were elegant and silver-scored against the black trunk:

I did.

"Why?" Lorelei laid her face against his downy breast. Even dreaming, she felt worn and tired. Her eyelids burned. "Why do you keep yourself bound, when this magic holds us apart?"

Then the feathers were melting against her body, sinking back into a glimmering chill. Soon her cheek was pressed against bare skin, and she knew that Death wore a human face again. She looked up into his terrible eyes. All his long needle teeth glinted and glittered in a tender smile.

"Lorelei, Lorelei," he said. "You cannot know my hunger. You cannot know the havoc and despair and bloodshed I leave in my wake. I am hateful when I am free. Only you, of all the living, have dared to love me. You dream your death a thousand times; a thousand times my thirst is slaked in you. I am a monster in your waking world. Here, you have made me a god."

Lorelei was weeping. "I don't want to live there. I want the dead to stay dead, and I want to join them—here, with you. Do you know how living hurts me? The sunlight pierces my eyes, food is like dust in my mouth, and laughter is the grinding of rusted gears. My nerves feel exposed to every falling leaf, every brush of wind. You are my only oblivion! My love!"

Death laid her down in the moss. "Hush, dearest. I will comfort you." He drew a wide garroting band from his feathered tunic. It was a Catalan garrote—the kind with a spike for breaking the spine. Lorelei's sobs calmed when she saw it. He slipped it around her neck.

"Better?"

She nodded, but before he began working the crank, told him, "I know how to free you. The bird showed me."

"Do not free me." He wound the crank once.

"I must," Lorelei gasped. The spike was digging into the back of her neck—she felt the pain all the way to her thighs, where it was pain no longer. "There is a masquerade tomorrow, and you must attend!"

Her neck snapped in the next moment, so she did not hear his reply.

* * *

It was the shady side of midnight. Marilee woke from slumber to the thump of a chair falling to the floor. Most nights she slept on a cot in Lorelei's dressing room, so as to rise at dawn, tend her ladyship's fire, and lay out her ladyship's clothes. She was therefore a light sleeper and furious at being roused at such an obscene hour. There was rustling in the chamber beside her, soft footsteps, and a door opening. Muttering maledictions, Marilee swung her feet over the cot, shoved on her boots, grabbed her cloak, and went to see what little Lady Lorelei was up to.

At the manor gates, Marilee almost let the girl go her way. If Lorelei drowned in a bog, so be it. If she were meeting a secret lover—let her! Marilee had no business trudging all hours after an impossible heiress who was barmy as a bonesetter—her duties stopped at the edge of the Count's property. She watched from the shadows as Lorelei lit her lamp and lifted it high. She was wearing, Marilee noticed, sensible clothes for once: a dark dress and sturdy boots and a cloak with a deep hood. She had a noose thrown over one shoulder. She did not look behind her. Marilee felt a stitch of misgiving.

"Rope? Oh, lass! That's no end for ye!"

Forgetting that she had been prepared to let the girl drown, Marilee picked up her pace and followed Lorelei down the moor path. In this way, she came to the skeleton tree just a few minutes after Lorelei had darkened her lamp and disappeared behind it.

Marilee hated that tree. The moor families had stories about it. It was haunted, it had been planted over the grave of a sorcerer to keep him from rising again, it was the place where seven witches had trapped a mighty wizard; and should he ever come free of it, he would visit his wrath on Ash Hollow town. Marilee's flesh puckered up with white welts. Her hair stood up like wire.

"Lady?" Her voice quavered. "Lorelei, lass, come out from there! It's a terrible bad place!"

There was no answer. Marilee edged closer. She was afraid of the dark moor, afraid of the tree, afraid that whatever bided inside it had swallowed her mistress entire. "Lady Lorelei?"

Marilee was standing directly under the clattering black branches now. In the skeleton tree's shadow, midnight yawned and showed its blacker depths. Faint with fear, Marilee swayed; she grabbed the trunk to steady herself and felt a faint flutter in the bark beneath her fingers, like a heartbeat. The wind sighed. Marilee knew she was weak—knew that the ghouls and ghosts who had walked her childhood were bogeymen meant to frighten unmanageable cubs—nevertheless, she wept.

"Marilee."

Lorelei's voice soughed down from above, from the branches. Marilee looked up—and a noose dropped over her head. Before she could summon the wits to react, the rope tightened, and Marilee was lifted off the ground as Lorelei jumped down from the skeleton tree. She landed in a crouch, the end of the rope tight in her fist.

Lorelei watched her maid kick and buck and writhe. She was more interested than disgusted. She had, after all, been killed a thousand ninety-six times herself—though this was the first time she had witnessed a death. She wished she could have kept her lamp lit.

At last, Marilee stopped maggoting around. Her feet hung limp. There was a smell of urine and soil. Lorelei tied off the rope. She took a gutting knife out of her boot and said: "Really, Marilee, you should not have come. But I am very, very glad you did."

Lorelei's ball gown was of deep red velvet. The slender sleeves ended in points. The neckline plunged over what became—with the help of a sadistically laced corset—an ample bosom. Lorelei employed the help of a kitchen girl, saying merely that Marilee was ill or dead or had given notice or some such, because she had not been up that morning to light Lorelei's fire. The kitchen girl, glad for the promotion, executed Lorelei's every order, and was so nervous that she did not speak a word except, occasionally, "Oh, I'm *sorry*, miss!" This suited Lorelei just fine.

She scented her startling new cleavage with musk and placed a heart-shaped patch on the swell of her left breast. Her slippers were satin with tiny rubies on the heels. She wore at her throat a wide black ribbon, fastened with a large onyx broach. She had braided her yellow hair and twisted it up, securing it with a comb of starling feathers.

"What do you think?" she demanded. "Will he know me?"

The kitchen girl bobbed her head in a way she hoped was amiable and professional. Lorelei smiled at her.

"Now," she said, "I am ready to dance."

The Count had spared no expense to decorate Ash Hollow manor. The ballroom was hung in garlands of flowers: bluebells, creamy roses, baby's breath, and ferns, and the refreshment tables were canopied in white silk. In the gardens, the trees were hung in paper lanterns that rocked gently in the spring breeze. The masquerade was what society called a "squeeze;" anybody who was anybody in town and the outlying countryside was in attendance. Lorelei scrutinized each powdered and perfumed one of them in the receiving line, hoping for a glimpse of sharp teeth. By the time the dancing began, she was nearly spitting with impatience. But her spirits were still high, and her impatience was not unmerry, so she accepted the hand of a short, lugubrious-looking duke and was swept into a waltz.

Often during the evening, she caught her father staring at her with incredulous eyes. At one point he drew her free of the throng, kissed her forehead, and said, tiredly, "You are exactly like your mother. There is nothing of me in you, is there?"

Lorelei laughed at him, "Nonsense, father!" and flirted her fan and danced gaily off with whoever happened to pass by. She had danced with a baronet, two squires and once again with the duke, before she caught the glimmering in the corner of her eye.

Death, it seemed, had dressed with haste. She had left a suit of her father's second-best evening clothes at the foot of the skeleton tree, right next to Marilee's ravaged corpse. She had known that her blood offering would tempt him back from exile, that he would be famished upon emergence, and that Marilee's cold dead flesh would not appease him. He looked so rumpled, the darling! His hair was a bird's nest, his cravat was not starched, and his shoes needed polishing after tramping those five miles up from the moor. All of this, and Death needed a shave.

The first person he killed was a dowager duchess: Her Grace, the (now late) Lady Mother of Lord Lugubrious. Death ripped her throat out. It was very neatly done—just a nip, really—and she swooned to the floor and died there. Most people thought it was the heat and the prodigious layers of her petticoats and the corset wedging her not-inconsiderable *avoirdupois* into something that resembled an hourglass and her elaborate and mountainous powdered wig (its weight compounded by a veiled *chapeau* that looked something like a galleon and something like a fruit basket and just a little bit like a feather duster) that had overcome her. They assumed that Her Grace had fainted dead away, and that the dark liquid spurting out around her limp form was simply spilled punch.

She was not well-liked anyway; she had the tongue of an adder and was all too aware of her own consequence and everyone else's inferiorities.

Many of the guests politely turned their backs on the frilly heap and remarked on the heat.

Lorelei moved quickly to the main doors and shut them. She drew from her red velvet *reticule* a small golden key and locked herself, along with the rest of her guests, inside the ballroom. The orchestra was playing a flowery Wagnerian waltz from the opera *Parsifal*. It would have been better with a chorus of phantom sopranos, but the tune was pleasing. With a light, pretty laugh that drew the smiling attention of several well-dressed, well-heeled gentlemen, Lorelei flitted around the edge of the ballroom to shut and lock the tall, window-paneled veranda doors, as well. All those bodies sweating under masks and chandeliers had warmed the room to cooking temperatures; now it very quickly began to swelter. It began to smell like a steam engine that had been left out in the rains to rust. There was iron in the air.

That was when people started to scream.

The orchestra stopped playing. Lorelei unpinned her yellow hair. Complicated braids snaked around her bare shoulders. The slender blade that had held the twists and coils close to her head shone in her fist with a light that was not unlike the one emanating from Death's singular *integument*.

A hand grabbed her wrist. "Lorelei!"

The Count, her father, did not ask: "What are you doing?"

He did not ask: "For the love you bear me, will you not stop this?"

He merely smiled at her, in a painfully proud way. "It falls to this."

"Yes, dear," Lorelei told him. "I am all grown up." She put her arms around him, kissed his cheek, and, sticking her knife into his left kidney, twisted. The Count held onto his daughter and clawed the fair skin of her back with his stiffening fingers. Then, groaning Lorelei's mother's name, "Erzebet!" he breathed his last.

Lorelei laughed.

Death, meanwhile, was on a rampage. He was *amuck*, as the heathens of the Orient might say, berserk, lunatic, in a frothing-mad feeding frenzy— completely adorable! Though chandeliers blazed and mirrors laminated the walls, Death was still the brightest thing in the room. He cast no reflection himself, so there was only one of him to command the fear and attention of everyone in the room: one pair of starry yellow eyes, one graceful, slithering, glimmering, black-clad body, one wide scarlet mouth which grew wider and more scarlet as he so dreadfully fed.

The duke he hurled against one wall with enough ferocity to shatter the mirror and every bone in the duke's body. The broken corpse, strangely deflated-looking, with little fragments sticking out of the skin, was still oozing as Lorelei came upon it. Death was already elsewhere—now he was snapping the chicken-skin fan of some freckled fop with one flick of his clever white fingers—now he was shoving the ivory shards up the fop's nostrils and into his brain. Death had done this to Lorelei on more than one occasion—though never with a fan!—and the mix of the novel and the familiar moved her, quickened her, stoked her, right down to her core. Lorelei oozed too, but not the same liquids as the duke.

He was so lovely! Her love! Her hangman! He was eating the eyeballs right out of that debutante's head, even as the lucky little girl screamed for help, for mercy, for mama...

What the girl lacked in enthusiasm, Lorelei decided, she made up for in volume.

While keeping a watchful, worshipful eye on Death, Lorelei did not neglect her end of things: she stabbed anyone within arm's distance, but really gave a drubbing to whomever ran right smack into her. People kept doing it, anyway. Sometimes she stuck them in the neck, so that they would spout. Sometimes the belly, for the noises they would make. Sometimes she would only maim them, say, in the legs, so that they stumbled and fell onto the slickening, sticky floor, so that their peers would trample them dead in the pandemonium and trip over their bodies, then themselves go crashing and sprawling, and in those moments of stunned immobility, have one of Lorelei's fancy ruby-studded heels come crunching down upon their skulls.

Lorelei started humming "Komm, Holder Knabe!" to herself.

Eventually, she made her way to the refreshments tables. There she found a nicely hefty cake knife, as well as a silver spoon near the *blancmange* platter. The sweet almond-flavored confections did not tempt her for one moment; not even the dark chocolate crowning the pale puddings wooed her into considering one of them—not when such a delicious, warm, *meaty* smell was in the air.

Out of the corner of her eye, she caught the panicked gaze of a certain baronet. He had taken a spindly, little, gilt chair and was systematically smashing it into the glass-paned veranda doors. Unfortunately for him, the shattered windows were still much too small to crawl through.

The locks of the doors held, but not, Lorelei believed, for long, under such battery.

She reached him just in time, after skipping and hacking her way through a shrieking seethe of domino masks, tricorn hats, swirling silks, and jostling brocades. In the spirit of collaboration, she greeted the baronet by name, spoke to him soothingly until he put down the chair—though he was still breathing very quickly and looked glazed about the eyes—put a friendly arm around his neck, and slit his throat with her cake knife. Then she sawed him open and ate his liver with her *blancmange* spoon, which she had been longing to do ever since he stepped on her toe during the *quadrille*. His liver tasted like pâté—only without all the horrible seasonings gourmet chefs were always hurling into perfectly good food, like mustard and onions.

His liver went down like butter.

Death bowed to his lady. His lady curtsied back with a cheeky grin. There was carnage between them and carnage around them. Ash Hollow Manor was silent.

"Lorelei," said Death, "do you see what you have released?"

"I see you."

"Am I not monstrous?"

"I think you are very handsome tonight."

"You," Death told her, "are delirious."

"Do you mind it awfully? Being out of your tree?"

He did one of those little blinks; the clear membranes of his eyelids slid sideways over his yellow eyes. And he, too, began to smile. The glow of the chandeliers flashed on his needle teeth, a triple-row of them, each with the transparency, density, and luster of diamonds. She stared at them, fascinated. Her body broke out in the most delicious sweat.

"No," he replied softly. "I do not mind it at all. Which is precisely why I put myself inside the tree in the first place. Do you know what they called me when last I walked this land? You have named me Death, but I am beyond Death. I am below him. I was old when Death was born."

"I love you," she said. "You and your poetry."

"I love you, too. I did not think such shattering ardor still possible. It is a madness, is it not?" He offered his hand. Lorelei laid hers upon it. Death gave her a little twirl, icy drool ribboning from his wide scarlet mouth, and he gestured at the charnel house that had once masqueraded as a ballroom. "You have a talent for this sort of thing, Lorelei."

Shrugging, Lorelei smiled. "Not too slipshod for my coming out party, I should say."

Death folded up one of her velvet sleeves and pressed his lips to her wrist. He kissed her pulse—or rather, smashed his mouth against her veins until her blood drummed a loud protest.

"Lorelei, Lorelei. Do not torment me. Are you still quite certain you want to die tonight?"

"Well—" Lorelei shrugged again. "Offer me an irresistible alternative."

"Stay with me," Death urged her, moving closer. "Do not abandon me to my hunger."

Lorelei considered how very interesting the previous night had been, what with Marilee and the noose and all. How gutting the girl and offering pieces of her insides to the skeleton tree had been the best fun she'd had—awake—in years. And tonight—what a delight!—how splendid everything had been! No doubt it was the sort of thing she could repeat again and again without ever tiring of it—and practice and experience would no doubt improve her surgical and gastronomic skills. Not to mention her dancing.

"Very well, my love." Rising on her tiptoes, Lorelei pressed her mouth against his, deliberately tearing her lips on his fangs. Death panted after her, dripping, when she broke free.

"I will bide with you a while yet. Until you can't stand not killing me anymore."

"I will restrain myself," said Death, soberly. "For you. And now, darling thing—I believe you promised me a dance?"

Lorelei lifted her velvet skirt daintily out of the congealing blood. Death placed one hand on her waist and clasped her fingers in his. She stared up into his yellow eyes, he down into a green that was the color of grave moss. They waltzed to the sound of wolves howling on the moor.

For Five Minutes, the Deep
Jude Walter Mire

Hardy Wakowski stood on the brink of the spirit world and smiled for the first time in days. It was a flat, worm-like expression that never reached his eyes. This pathetic specimen of a smile had crawled from his tired heart all the way up to those uncooperative, invertebrate lips. It was amazing it had made it that far.

"Finally," they muttered.

He stretched out his arms, looking down at the prize he'd traveled so far to discover. The *cenote*, a natural stone water basin surrounded by thick jungle, slithered with steam. Vines and creepers hung long, languid fingers to dip into the cool recess. Above, the Yucatan sun was in the business of cooking the poor vegetation alive, and the heady aroma of plant sweat was almost thick enough to chew. The dark pond wasn't as large as the ones Hardy had first considered on the tourist maps; places with names like *Ox Bell Ha*, *Nohoch Nah Chich*, and *Dos Ojos*. He had tried the last place, because it was the only name he understood, and he too was looking for something.

But there had been too many people. The crowds of Cancun had pressed close; he left before something bad happened. Here, the closest civilization was the infrequently visited ruin of *Zack Chili* a hundred miles away. Turns out, Mayan architecture is much more exciting when located within easy driving distance of surfing, parasailing, and sunbathing. The only company was the malefic sun and the endless swath of smoldering jungle.

The inside of his wetsuit was slick with perspiration, but heat didn't bother him. Extreme weather was the invariable price of uninhabitable areas, and for that solitude, he was willing to pay the price.

The hunt had grown dangerous within him.

Hardy dropped to his knees before the pool the Mayans believed led to another land.

"Thank you," he breathed.

He stretched out his neck, closed his eyes, and kissed the surface of the water. Ripples.

Hardy stood and awkwardly pulled on the unfamiliar air tanks. He checked his dive light, took a few exploratory breaths through the mouthpiece, and gave a final look to the lush green canopy. Hardy didn't feel nearly as worried as he should have, preparing to make the first dive of his life, without any backup.

His unprotected skin recoiled at the cold water: an odd counter-sensation to the insulated body heat under the wetsuit. A curtain of bubbles rose, the surroundings revealed themselves. Where the jungle above had been a thousand shades of jade, here below, the world was stained brown with tanic acid. It was more like swimming in tea than water. The rusty shaft of illumination from the dive light cut a wide arc and circled the *cenote*. Smooth stone striped with algae growing on the sedimentary outcroppings, beams of sunlight cut angular columns off to the left. Hardy began his descent. It struck him, as the pressure began to swell in his ears, that he'd finally get his five minutes of solitude. The darkness beneath him expanded, surrounded him, engulfed him. The pain intensified as he dropped too quickly, but no amount of cold pressure or bleeding ears would be enough to make him turn back. Pressure was something Hardy endured every day.

Fortunately, the bottom came before his eardrums burst. A soft moss-looking layer of dead brown leaves was flanked by stone walls, but two narrow passages led into the rock. He glanced at the surface, a tiny circle of tan the size of a silver dollar far above, and chose the left passageway.

Any residual glow vanished as he rounded a corner, kicking gently. Everywhere his light descended, wonders sprung forth. Stalactites, like the teeth of some primordial crocodile god, hung above him. Below rested a field of stalagmites that looked like a fantasy mountain range as seen from the sky. Tiny white flashes that he suspected were cave fish darted and vanished into the gloom at his intrusion. Joining the floor and ceiling rose a massive column of mottled stone that reminded him of an orgy of mushrooms. He swam up next to it, breathing deeply, bubbles rising above him in a shimmer. The thought crept upon him that no man had ever seen these things before. It was all worth the ringing in his ears.

The city he called home was a beehive of pressure. People were everywhere, inescapable. He'd tried yoga with earplugs, but could still feel their vibrations in his backside through the floorboards. Someone was always right on the other side of the drywall. He wanted to take an axe and chop through it, to find his irritation and chop through that, too. The images of his neighbors' silent corpses dripping into the carpet thrilled and frightened him. He had thrown all his cutlery down the garbage chute. Just in case.

He was tired of being irritated, and scared of what he was turning into. He didn't watch the news, but he knew what he was becoming: the sound bite of the night. "He never said much, always paid his rent on time. I still can't believe someone could kill so many people with a toilet brush."

If he could only suckle upon some lonely silence in a dark nothingness, the rage would extinguish.

Hardy had thrown out all his cleaning products and had begun planning his trip.

He reached out to touch a bulbous stone outcropping, fingertips on smooth stone. The happiness pounded like a tribal drummer inside his ribs. Passing the column on his right, he dropped to the floor. Two strange formations, one from the top and another from the bottom, reached for one another, but did not touch. He put his flippered feet on top of the lower outcropping and reached, his extended hand just long enough to connect the two. He was grinning so much, he had to be careful of water seeping into his regulator. There were buttons on it to purge the line, but he had no idea how they functioned.

Ahead of him there was a dark portal in the wall, another passage to new wonders. He swam toward it, then pulled back in alarm.

When he shone the dive light on the opening, the light did not extend into the tunnel. It stopped on a strange vacillating wall of liquid. It looked like a sheet of lumpy gelatin, or the gobs found in a lava lamp. Cautiously, he touched it. His hand passed through without resistance, but seemed to vanish. He pulled it out. The surface jiggled slowly. Treading in place, he considered the phenomenon. He couldn't see where he was going, but he would never find better seclusion than this black doorway would provide. He swam through, vanishing from the outer world.

As he became immersed, it was evident he was no longer swimming in water. He gagged and bit hard on the mouthpiece to prevent the oily, alcohol-tinged liquid from getting past his lips. This stuff didn't support him as easily; he was losing buoyancy, dropping fast. He scissored forward, passed through the dark veil and out the other side.

Where the last chamber was vast, this room was a narrow dorm; high walls barely six feet apart arched up to a cathedral ceiling. These were carved with hundreds of shallow niches. Within each, the sunken dead eyes of an inhabitant looked at Hardy, row upon row of shriveled, mummified bodies, shoulder to shoulder, like cans on a grocery store shelf, down a seemingly endless hallway. More crowded than a subway train at rush hour. Row after row of mummies, tied and bound in the Mayan fashion, legs pulled tight to the chest with stick-like arms hugging them, skeletal chins rested on bony knees. The limbs were secured with rough black cords that sunk into waterlogged flesh.

Hardy screamed. The fulminating liquid surged into his mouth, scouring his tongue. He choked, coughed, sinking to the floor of the cavern as he gasped for air and tried to regain control of his breathing. The rancid stuff was in the line, blocking the air! Desperate, he swallowed, strange fluid burning his throat, roiling in his stomach. The chest spasms won out, and he managed to pull in an acrid breath. He panted as best he could, fighting off nausea. Minutes passed.

Recovering the light he'd dropped, he raised the beam.

There was no escaping the feeling he was inside a huge preservation jar, something out of science classroom. Kicking hard, he moved down the hall, his stinging eyes wide in fear and amazement. The formaldehyde substance buzzed in his head like the sound of traffic, and as the reality sank in, the fear was gobbled up by anger. Here—even here—he could find no peace. At the bottom of the world, as far as he could get away, there was a crowd of people waiting. This was no accident. Some immortal, feather-crowned god had played a trick, decided that he could not have five measly minutes of peace. The realization boiled hot in Hardy's veins and set loose the rage he'd so long been holding back.

He grabbed the closest mummy, gripping the slimy ribs and smashing it against the wall. Strips of muscle tore and skin crumbled to bits. After cracking loose each rib, he jerked the head free from the spine, swam to the next crevice, and used the skull as a bludgeon. From mummy to mummy he went, yanking them from their niches, dismembering them, cracking their brittle bones.

Finally, exhausted from his killing spree, he paused, sucking great gulps of oxygen from the diminishing supply on his back.

The floor of the cave was littered with pieces. If any mummies remained intact, they were obscured by the cloud of dust and body debris floating on disturbed currents. He had destroyed an archeologist's wet dream, but he would have his solitude at any cost.

Suspended above a field of bones, in the belly of the earth, he clicked his dive light off and sank into oblivion.

An odd sound came to him, lifted up on the strange water. A clicking and tapping.

He cracked his eyes; saw it was no longer pitch black. A strange sepia glow filled the room. Bones, emanating a low amber phosphorescence, were moving, joining, not always into the shapes they'd originally been. Disfigured forms; skulls crowned with ribs, feet rising from shoulder blades like wings, long tendons stretching over crossed bones like dreamcatchers of human framework. As the current swelled, they rose and fell upon the floor.

Hardy wasted no time on watching the gruesome spectacle. Kicking like a madman, he swam to the end of the corridor, thrashed through the dark oily veil, and burst back into the main chamber. He felt, more than saw, shapes moving in the water around him. Flickering yellow pulses played like lightning, flashing and moving between the stalagmites below him. Something bumped his hip roughly as the small crevice that led back to the *cenote* came into view. Something jerked his dive light. He let it go, guided by the faint light of the exit.

Pummeled and harried by unseen impediments, he slipped out the crevice and looked up to see the small disc of light above. He sprang toward the surface, but something pulled him down, the straps of his tanks tightening across his chest. He fumbled at the cords, and the tanks dropped, jerking the regulator from his mouth. Unencumbered by the heavy diving gear, he shot toward the surface. Beneath him, the glow increased. Lungs near to bursting, he breached the surface, body aching, heaving for air. As he pulled himself out of the basin, the current tried to drag him under again. He scrambled backward on the ground. It was no longer the tranquil pool he'd entered.

The glowing liquid churned in a whirlpool. Dark shapes bobbed in the rapids, skulls and limbs, fragments careening against the rock. Oversized embryos like big sunken faced raisins. Hardy screamed at the swirling stew of the dead. "I just needed to be alone! Just a little while!"

The ocher tarn rose up in a wave thick as honey, filled with desecrated bones, and crashed upon him. Shards cut through his wetsuit, cracked teeth sank into his skin, and fingers latched onto his limbs, dragging him back down to the underworld cavern. He was still struggling as his knees were lifted to his chin and his wrists bound around his legs.

He'd gotten his five minutes, and the price lay before him: his very own niche in the ancient cathedral wall, where he would always have plenty of company.

Upon the Midnight Clear
Stephen Dedman

"Y̶OU ON YOUR OWN, THEN?"

It was a question I was sick of hearing, and I guess my expression showed it, because the goth recoiled slightly. "Yes," I said, more mildly than I felt.

"On holiday?"

"Uh-huh." I stared out of the window, pretending to look at the northern English scenery, which consisted of snow and not much else, and even that wasn't easy to see in the darkness. At least it was warm in the bus, but why do I always end up sitting next to some weirdo?

"How far you going?" she asked.

I didn't answer.

"I'm getting off in Carlisle."

"Hawick," I replied.

"Got friends there?"

"No."

"Family?" I shook my head. "Then what you want to go *there* for? We're having a party tomorrow; why don't you come along? We can find you a bed easy enough."

I stared at her balefully and noticed that her earrings included linked female symbols and a double-bladed axe. I admit, since I caught Stuart in bed with one of my students, I've occasionally thought that all men should be given a choice of castration without anesthetic or the electric chair—but that doesn't mean I'm a dyke. "No, thanks."

"I mean...well, spending Christmas by yourself is bad enough, but spending it in a hole like Hawick..." she pronounced it 'Hoik.' "It'll be a great party...."

"I won't be staying there; I'm going straight to the castle," I replied.

"I'm from L.A., and I've never had a chance to sleep in a real castle before—and Christmas is just a rip-off, anyway." Ho ho bloody ho.

She smiled—and then turned even more pale beneath her makeup. "Hermitage Castle?"

"Yes."

She was mercifully quiet for a while, as though thinking of something to say. "Must be difficult, though, traveling on your own. Dangerous, even."

I laughed, probably for the first time since the plane landed. I'd heard that too often before, too. "Dangerous? This place?" She looked and sounded sincere enough, though it was hard to be sure with that makeup and accent. "I teach *jeet kune do* and self-defense. The scariest thing I've seen since I got here was *Phantom of the Opera*. I admit, I didn't actually plan to make this trip alone, but my fiancé dumped me in November, and I was stuck with the ticket. I'm enjoying it more than I expected. So, what have you got around here that's dangerous? Serial killers? Or just drunks?"

She was silent for a moment. "Are you superstitious?"

I laughed. "I'm not even Californian."

"Do you believe in ghosts?"

"No."

She stared into the darkness, and I did the same. It was easy enough not to believe in ghosts in L.A., but this was a much older world.... I shivered slightly, and then told myself I was being stupid.

"I guess you *could* call him a serial killer," said the goth, softly. "He's probably killed at least a hundred people by now—all of them lone travelers, like yourself, backpackers and hitchhikers and walkers. If there is just one of him, that is: there may be a gang, or maybe a whole murderous family. It's hard to tell what's real, and what's some sort of urban myth. Well, not really urban, not out here, but a myth, anyway."

I nodded. I'd been on a Jack the Ripper walking tour while I was in London, and I know how legends grow up around even the most unglamorous killers, thugs like Manson and Dillinger and Wyatt Earp.

"They call him Redcap, because he wears this floppy red cap, like an old-fashioned nightcap. They say he dyes it with blood, human blood, and when he's been very busy he dyes his jacket red, too, sometimes even his trousers. When he's been frantically busy he's red from the tip of his cap to the top of his great heavy boots. And this is his busy time, his favorite time—close to the winter solstice, when the nights last forever, and it's too cold outside for people to venture out, or even go stare out of a window, unless they desperately need to.

"He likes the old ruined abbeys and monasteries, and other places like the Roman roads. I suspect that's where he finds his victims, because there's not much else but ruins to attract the travelers up here. But he never travels very far from the border; maybe he's staking out a territory, or maybe he doesn't have a car. Maybe he's homeless and lives in one of the ruins...."

I shuddered again and then got a grip on myself. I'd encountered plenty of street people near Venice Beach, and worse. "Does he have a gun?"

"I don't think so."

"No problem, then."

The goth shook her head violently. "I think he uses an axe—a large axe, maybe even a halberd or something, though I've heard some say he has a machete, or a claymore, or a scythe. Anyway, he decapitates his victims, and he must take the heads with him, because none of them have ever been found. Fortunately, most of them still have their passports, or they'd be impossible to identify." Her voice sounded slightly dreamy, but terribly sincere. I stared at her, but she didn't even smile; she just looked through the window of the bus. "Carlisle," she said, "are you sure you wouldn't rather come to the party?"

The bus was already slowing. I noticed a girl standing at the stop, waiting; her head was shaved, and she carried a potted palm and a skateboard. "No, thanks," I said, snapping out of it. It had to be the best pickup routine I'd ever heard, but not good enough to make me give up on men just yet.

"Okay," she said, looking rather crestfallen and then grabbed her daypack from the overhead rack as the bus groaned to a halt. She reached into her jacket, removed a notepad and a calligraphy pen, and scrawled something on a page, which she ripped out and handed to me. "My name and number—in case you change your mind about the party. Have a merry Christmas," she said, sadly.

"Thanks. And to you."

"You'll have the place to yerself," said my host, puffing slightly as he struggled to get my backpack up the ancient stairs one-handed. "We've only done up the one tower, and there's nobody else here tonight."

The room in the castle didn't look as large or as comfortable in reality as it had in the brochure, but I was used to that. Most of the renovations had been for the sake of weatherproofing and were obviously anachronistic, even the tiny four-poster bed. I didn't really mind; I prefer a toilet to a *garderobe*, and rugs (even tartan rugs) to rushes, any day. I would have liked some electricity, too, but the fireplace near the bed was a nice touch—big enough for roasting a pig, if not an ox, and with a real fire behind the grate.

"I'll be in the cottage if you need anything," my host wheezed as he dropped the pack just inside the doorway. "Goodnight—oh, and merry Christmas," he added, a little hesitantly, leaning on the doorframe with his left hand slightly extended.

I took out my wallet to give him a tip and noticed the piece of paper. "Have you ever heard of Redcap?" I asked.

He blinked, and his blue eyes seemed to disappear into his scarlet face. "The fairy?"

"Fairy?"

"Elf...goblin would be the best name for him, I guess." He chuckled. "Scottish elves aren't like American elves—mostly, they're a bit like life in the Middle Ages: nasty, brutish, and short. Redcap's one of the worst; he's small but strong, with red eyes and big teeth, and he likes to kill travelers just to dye his cap red. Or he *did*—in old wives' tales. They say you can keep him out by leaving a sock under your bed; it always works for me." He shook his head and chuckled again. "So who's been telling you fairy stories?"

"Just a girl I met on the bus," I replied, feeling a little foolish, and tipped him twice what I'd intended. Ho ho bloody ho.

He grinned. "At least you didn't ask about the castle ghost."

"Is there one?"

He shook his head. "I could rattle some chains outside your door if you like, but no, I've certainly never seen one. Mind you, I don't believe in the Loch Ness Monster either."

"Who does? Thank you; good night." As soon as he was gone, I locked and bolted the door and began peeling off my clothes. I was too tired to go back down to the cottage for a shower; I just wanted to go to bed. Alone.

The bed was barely big enough even for one of me and as hard as it was small; nevertheless, I fell asleep immediately.

Fa la la la la, la la la la!

I was dreaming that I was Lady Macbeth, when I was woken by the sound of a voice murdering a Christmas carol; I rolled over, disoriented by the huge shadows thrown by the dying fire.

Don we now our gay apparel, fa la la, fa la la, la la la.

"'Methought I heard a voice cry, Sleep no more!'" I muttered, and tried folding the pillow around my ears. When that didn't work, I grabbed the electric lantern my host had left me and rummaged through my overnight bag for my earplugs and night mask. That muffled the noise enough for me to ignore it, and I rolled over and tried to return to sleep. I had almost succeeded when I heard creaking footsteps and something that might have been singing punctuated by laughter. I pulled one of the earplugs out and listened. The footfalls sounded as if they were coming from the room above me, but that must have been just an echo; my host had told me the room was empty....

Over the fields we go, I heard someone sing, *laughing all the way*. The voice sounded thin and stretched, rather like one of those musical Christmas cards that's been left in a box of ornaments for too long, so that the battery's gone flat and turns "We Wish You a Merry Christmas" into a funeral march.

I peeled my night mask off and stared at my travel clock. Twelve past midnight. *Bells on bobtail ring*, the singer continued, *making spirits bright...* It still sounded as though he was in the room above. Maybe it was my host, more than a little drunk, playing some sort of prank—a ghost act to frighten the tourists.

Oh what fun...

Or maybe it was the goth and her friends, having a slumber party joke, bringing the party to me after I'd refused to go to it. Ho ho bloody ho.

it is...

The voice sounded clearer, now—still harsh and unmusical, but loud, as though it were coming down the—

There was a crash, and two huge boots appeared in the fireplace, scattering the embers. Above them was a pair of red trousers. Santa Claus?

I stared as one of the boots kicked the grate aside, and a lumpy sack was thrown into the room. I'd stopped believing in Santa Claus twenty years ago, but—

The neck of the sack parted, and a human head rolled out. The fat, short elf in the fireplace stepped towards me. He was wearing red, from the tops of his boots to the floppy cap on his head, and carrying a scythe.

...to sing, he warbled and lashed out with the scythe. I tried to dodge it, but misjudged, and the blade sliced into my arm and cut it to the bone. The pain was worse than anything I'd ever experienced before, and I almost

blacked out. The elf grinned, revealing long, sharp, brown teeth, and held out his cap to catch the bright red blood spurting from my arm as I screamed. The scythe rose again, and I rolled over and fell out of bed an instant before the blade penetrated the mattress. I grabbed the first item of clothing I could to wrap around my arm, then scrambled backwards to the door and, without taking my eyes from him, reached up for the latch.

His grin broadened and he crooned *a slaying song tonight* as he walked slowly towards me. I opened the door, backed through it onto the landing, then fell down the tower's spiraling steps. He continued to sing as he followed me, his huge heavy boots ringing on the stone stairs.

I lay there at the foot of the steps, wanting to move but unable to get my legs to cooperate, as though my body refused to believe I was in any danger. The elf oozed his way down the narrow staircase. At least he'd stopped singing.

"Get away from me!" I shrieked. "You're not real! I don't believe in you!"

He seemed to hesitate for a moment, then raised the scythe. It was a clumsy weapon for such a confined space; there was no room to slice, only stab, but that would be lethal enough. I reached for the latch, opened the door far enough to squeeze out, and ran.

The ground was thick with frost, and I skidded painfully towards the cottage, not daring to look back. This isn't happening, I thought, as the pain in my feet subsided to numbness, I don't believe it, there's no such thing as—

The cottage was dark and silent. I hit the front door with a thud, but there was no response. I screamed for help and beat on the door with my fists, pausing occasionally to listen, but no one stirred. I glanced back over my shoulder, seeing my bloody footprints where the skin of my feet had frozen and peeled away, and then the door to the tower opened, and Redcap hurtled out. Despite his girth, and his nailed boots, he ran quite quickly, maybe too quickly for me to outrun him for long. I continued to pound for a few seconds, then glanced around for somewhere else to hide. There was a phone booth twenty yards away, an old-fashioned box of wood and glass; still screaming, I hurtled towards it. The elf grinned, then changed his course to intercept mine. He swung the scythe at my neck, and I dropped to the ground and slid. I shut myself into the phone booth and collapsed on the floor, panting. It smelt of piss, but maybe that was me.

For the first time, I noticed how cold I was, naked apart from a T-shirt and whatever I had wrapped around my arm—which turned out to be my Levi's. I looked around for Redcap, but he'd vanished. Hunting for easier prey, perhaps? Or just waiting behind the opaque side of the booth for me to venture outside?

I slithered into my jeans, wrapped the T-shirt around my bleeding arm, and put my hands into my pockets for a little extra warmth. I found coins in one, a screwed-up scrap of paper in the other—a name and phone number. The goth. I hesitated for a moment, then dialed 999 and asked for an ambulance. The operator wearily promised to send one as soon as possible; her tone implied that she thought I'd cut my arm myself, though that may just have been her accent. Lots of people committed suicide at Christmas, didn't they? I sat there and shivered for a moment, trying to convince myself that I *wasn't* crazy or suicidal, that I *hadn't* done this to myself, that there really *was* a red-capped elf with a scythe waiting outside to murder me if I left the booth...it was hard enough convincing myself; how was I going to convince the paramedics?

What if he killed the paramedics? Maybe I should call the cops, as well...no, British bobbies don't carry guns, they'd be walking into a trap too...*if* they came, *if* they believed me, *if* they didn't try to lock me away as a suicide.

Maybe I was just having a nightmare, but I'd never been this conscious of smells and pain and other sensations in a nightmare: my arm was throbbing, my feet were hurting more as they thawed slightly, my nipples were so tight from the cold they felt like toothaches. I'd never been able to read in a nightmare, either. I blinked, and realized I'd curled up into a fetal ball. I took a deep breath. I *wasn't* crazy, I *wasn't* trying to kill myself, I *had* seen a homicidal Santa Claus try to decapitate me, seen a head roll out of his sack...Redcap *did* exist, the goth knew about him, she knew I wasn't crazy....

I looked around, reached for the receiver again, inserted a few coins in the slot, and dialed the number on the scrap of paper. The phone rang a dozen times before someone picked it up and yelled, "Whaaat?" over the background music.

"Morgan?" I croaked.

A moment's hesitation, just long enough to wonder whether I'd dialed the wrong number, then, "Nah. Morg! Phone!"

One of the booth's glass panels shattered; I turned, but saw nothing but darkness, and screamed into the receiver. A moment later, I heard, "Hello?"

"Morgan? It's Julie—the girl from the bus. I'm at the castle and, uh...Redcap's here, he's trying to kill me!" I heard my voice rising and quavering and tried to get a grip on myself.

"What? Where are you?"

I gulped for breath. "In the phone booth outside. He's still hanging around somewhere, he has a scythe, he's cut my arm open with it, I've called an ambulance, but I don't know when they're going to get here. Is there anything I can do?"

There was a long silence. "You're serious, aren't you?"

I stared at the hole in the side of the booth. "Dead serious."

More silence. "What are you wearing?"

"*What?*"

"It's just a legend," she said, sounding flustered, "but wearing your clothes inside out is supposed to be protection against elves. Or there's crosses, or iron knives, or...I can't remember anything else. Sorry."

"Turn my clothes inside out? What's that supposed to do?"

"I don't know; act as armor, maybe. Look, I can borrow a car and drive over, just in case the ambulance is late...."

"Thanks," I said, and, unable to think of anything else to say, said, "Goodbye," and hung up. I peered into the darkness for a moment, then unbuttoned my jeans and struggled to turn them inside out. I stepped back inside them, then unwrapped the T-shirt from my arm, tore a few pages from the phone book to serve as a bandage, turned the shirt inside-out, and pulled it over my head as though it were a sack. I heard another pane of glass shatter and screamed, then heard something whisper:

Tsk, tsk. A big girl like you, can't even dress yourself properly.

Maybe it was Redcap, maybe it was just a voice inside my head, I didn't know. To drown it out, I started singing, "Silent night, holy night—"

A big girl like you, wetting herself like a baby.

"All is calm, all is bright..." Another pane smashed. How did the rest of the song go? I drew a deep breath and began a new song, "Hark the herald angels sing..."

A big girl like you, believing in fairies.

I wanted to look, but didn't dare. Seeing him out there would have been bad enough, possibly even fatal, but not seeing him would mean it was just a voice in my head.

A big girl like you, believing in Santa Claus.

"Glory to the new-born King, peace on Earth and mercy mild—"

You're going to bleed to death, you're going to freeze.

"We three kings of Orient are," I quavered. "Bearing gifts, we travel afar—"

Sorrowing, sighing, bleeding, dying, sealed in the stone-cold tomb, the voice sneered.

I tried to keep singing, but my voice had dried up; it sounded too much like his to bear. I sat there in silence for what seemed like hours, until I heard the door open.

Someone grabbed my arms, and I screamed.

I opened my eyes and saw nothing but whiteness until I managed to focus. There was no point in asking where I was; old hospitals have a stench of disinfectant that you could cut with...well, you know. I looked around; my arm was bandaged from palm to elbow, and tethered to the side of the bed. There was a little box with a button near my hand; I pressed it, and a nurse walked in a few minutes later.

Morgan visited me after breakfast and told me that the caretaker had found me in the phone booth, having wandered out after hearing the glass breaking. "They think I'm crazy, don't they?" I asked. "They think I did this to myself."

She hesitated, then nodded. "You're on your own in a strange country, you've just had a relationship breakup, it's Christmas...big-time stress. No one would be surprised if you were depressed; amazed if you weren't, really."

"I'm fine. Well, I was until yesterday...."

A shrug. "They've tried to contact your fiancé, but he didn't answer, so they got your parents, instead. Your insurance covers you for a stay in the hospital if they call it an accident. So if I were you, I'd go along with that. You'll get out of here a lot sooner that way. Say you cut your arm on something, opening your Swiss Army knife or whatever, you ran to the phone, you passed out there...they'll buy it."

"And what about Redcap?"

She blinked, then shook her head. "Better just call it an accident. Do you need anything? Books or whatever? They brought your backpack in...."

"Not now, thanks."

"I'll leave it where you can reach it. Anyway, I'd better go. It's a bit early for visitors. Would you like me to come back?"

"Yeah, thanks. What is the time?"

She smiled. "About four a.m. Merry—uh, bye."

"Bye." I sat there for a few minutes, then rolled onto my side, leaned down, and unzipped my backpack.

My ex's head grinned up at me, and I heard someone whisper, *Merry Christmas.*

Demons in His Art
Chris Kozlowski

He fights his demons through his art;
In a splash of color, one lies
Menacing on the page before him—
Divided, half red and half blue,
A mixture of anger and indifference.
A pentagram brands the beast's forehead,
And globs of paint pop the eyes out
Of its bloated, horned head.
A typical demon, really…

Almost cliche in its symbols of evil,
But disturbing nevertheless.
The paint flows over the edges
And threatens to overwhelm his fragile ego.
"I want to rip this up," he screams,
Lifting up the paper—a childish tantrum—
But all of the feelings are real, so real,
Asking me to save his art,
Some part of himself.

"I'm like an adolescent, still trying to shock people,"
He observes, in a moment of clarity—but then
That same adolescent rebellion overtakes him again:
"You know, I hold people up at ATMs;
If they give me the money, I leave them alone."
So provocative, betraying his feelings of powerlessness.
I don't bite, sensing his fear

Of the demon he has created,
Which lies yet unfinished on the page.

I ask him what his picture is about.
Halfway between tears and rage he whispers,
"There is no hope."
"For the painting?" I ask plainly, "Or for you?"
"Both," he states.
I point to an unfinished corner—"If we start here,
You can let some light in—maybe some yellow?"
The task seems huge to him,
And I see the fear in his eyes.

"You finish it," he pleads, "you put the light in."
I suggest we put it in together, but
This is as close as he will let me get today.
I see him drawing back—
He is finished being vulnerable, for now.
Perhaps we will fight his demons again another day.
Still, I marvel at his picture—
At this menacing figure which tries, (but does not quite succeed)
In masking its creator's despair.

The white corner, I think, somehow redeems the painting—
For there is hope, still, in the unfinished page.

Soul Collector
Craig D.B. Patton

THE SOUL COLLECTOR MIGHT HAVE smiled, if he could remember how. Combines were traversing the immense fields on either side of the state highway, mowing down the decaying remnants of the year's corn crop. Autumn: harvest time.

His black sedan whispered over the roads, never needing gas. The living saw and heard nothing as he passed, though their thoughts turned grey. Parents drew their children close. Lovers grabbed for each others' hands. People called estranged family members, moved to say the things they could not say before.

The soul collector's gaunt hands, the skin like rice paper drawn over a bamboo frame, stayed on the wheel except to tighten the knot of his narrow, black tie.

It was dark by the time he turned into Betty Gunderson's driveway. The house was removed from its neighbors, set back amidst a grove of trees that loomed over it. Overgrown bushes crowded the porch. The feeble glow of a lamp could be seen from a ground floor window.

He got out of the car, taking with him the briefcase that had been on the seat beside him. Shafts of moonlight poking through the canopy of trees illuminated the cracked skin stretched over his skull and the solitary bristles of white hair clinging to the top of it. A silver lapel pin of a raven in flight was the only adornment he wore. He walked across the broken, weed-covered flagstones leading to the front door.

A touch of his hand and the locks clicked aside and the door swung open. He found Betty slumped in a sofa chair in the living room, draped in a mustard-colored afghan, staring at the flickering blue light of the television. Great folds of skin hung slack from her face and neck. Her hair was the color of cobwebs and matted against her head.

The soul collector walked across the room, passing through Betty's line of sight. He stopped two-feet from her. Betty's eyes remained fixed on the television, though she did shudder and pull the afghan closer around her neck.

She could not see him yet. He would have to wait. It sometimes happened, and he had no one else to see this night. The ominous rattle in her breathing suggested it would not be long.

The soul collector stood and waited, still clutching the briefcase. An hour passed. Betty continued to stare at the television, taking occasional swallows from a bottle of vodka. Her face grew flushed. Twice, she coughed.

He grew restless and shifted on his emaciated feet.

Betty's eyes closed. Her chin dipped. She began to snore.

The soul collector stared down at her. He had never had to wait so long. His was the business of finality.

He reached inside his jacket and withdrew a mobile phone. The battery was as dead as he, and he pressed no buttons. He held it to his ear. A sound like sand hissing over rocks in a howling wind emanated from it.

"Betty Gunderson is still alive," the soul collector said in a torn silk voice. "What must I do?"

A whisper cut through the howl. "Remain."

He returned the phone to his jacket.

Betty shivered beneath the afghan. A thin sheen of sweat covered her brow. Her eyelids rolled as her eyes darted beneath them. A fever had risen in her. Progress, though perhaps only slight.

He began to notice the details of the room. Paintings of landscapes. No pictures of family or friends. Magazines spilled from a console table beneath the window. There was a couch, covered in a landslide of unfolded laundry; no place for anyone to sit. Everything spoke of a life of isolation. Another unwelcome question flared in him. Why did she live in such solitude?

It was not his to know the details of the lives of the people he visited. Nor had he ever wondered such a thing before.

Betty stirred in her fever. Formless sounds burbled from her lips, then she spoke two clear syllables, "Howard."

A name.

He'd had a name once. A mortal name. Had it been Howard? The soul collector tried to recall. He did not think so, but time is the river that wears the stones of memory smooth. He rejected the question in irritation.

The work was all that mattered now, the task appointed to him after living a life that had left the scales dead even.

The briefcase grew heavy in his hand. He carried it to the console table and spread out the magazines until he could set it on a stable shelf of them. The soul collector unsnapped the locks and opened it.

On the right side, recessed in molded black padding, was a large syringe with a thick, three-inch long needle. On the left side, also recessed in padding, were twenty-four small glass vials. Two of the vials were empty. The other twenty-two contained swirls of smoke.

On impulse, the soul collector gently removed one of the vials and held it up in the dim light. The soul inside shifted, twisting against the glass. Jorge Ramirez. The soul collector had found him in the final throes of a heart attack on a high school football field with a crowd of people clustered around him, an ambulance wailing closer. Jorge's eyes had been open when the soul collector emerged through the throng. The man had stared in terror at him and the needle he held ready. He remembered how brown Jorge's eyes were, like two decaying acorns.

It was all over in an instant.

The soul collector placed the vial back in its slot. His gaze swept across the others, remembering the names and the moment of each death.

"Oh, Howard," Betty cried out.

The soul collector recognized the tinge of panic coloring the words. It crept into voices when the living felt themselves begin to slip, began to sense that the end was near. He grasped the burnished silver plunger of the syringe. The needle gleamed in the glow of the lamp. Betty Gunderson was almost ready.

He would have only one more appointment before it was time to return to the beyond and deliver those he had collected. Then, just like his many, many peers, he would be sent out again.

Betty's eyes snapped open. Her head turned toward him.

The soul collector wondered what she had heard. He knew that, in other places, other times, there had been a sound. Ankou rolling his creaking cart closer and closer along the byways of Ireland and Britain. The goddess Mors sweeping down from the sky over ancient Rome as a screaming raven, talons bared. The storm that was Oya tearing across Africa as she ripped aside the very fabric of mortality. But the soul collector was silence itself. In this place, in this time, it was deemed appropriate by that which lay beyond. As the people of this land withdrew from wonder, lost sight of awe, that which lay beyond had withdrawn. Silence was one way of expressing the distance that existed now. Another was that the once-revered task of gathering souls had been handed down to once-mortal beings such as he.

Betty's bloodshot eyes were wide, the pupils dilating and contracting, trying to focus on him. She reached up with a trembling hand.

"I didn't…mean it, Howard." Her head dipped as she broke into a spasm of coughing. When she lifted it again, there were specks of blood on the afghan. "The…things I said. What I did. I didn't—" The coughing took her again, far worse than the first time. She quaked beneath the afghan.

He waited. Was Howard her husband? Her son? Her lover? When he delivered her soul, would whatever she had said and done weigh down the scale enough to doom her for eternity?

And what had he done in his own life that had denied him eternal bliss?

The soul collector blinked and grew rigid. He tried to push the question back into the dark from which it had come and refocus on the task before him. He failed.

Betty grew still again. "Forgive m…" The rest of it came out as a hiss of escaping air.

What had he done?

He stood there for half an hour, flailing for an unreachable answer, before he noticed that Betty Gunderson was dead.

She had said something at the end.

He could not remember what it was. The soul collector looked at the syringe gripped in his right hand. Familiar, cold reality. It was all that mattered in the end. He bent over her and placed the tip of the needle between her eyes.

It was all over in an instant.

Dad Brings A Deader Home
Yvonne Navarro

Year Sixteen

"**W**HAT ARE YOU DOING? YOU can't bring that dead piece of *shit* in here!"

Joe's father ignored him and gave the deader a little push through the front door. "Go on in," he ordered, as if it could actually hear him. Then, "Sit down, please." In sync with his voice, the older man's fingers worked hesitantly on the fingerpads of a small remote box.

Joe stared at the deader angrily. The thing moved easily enough, but a little sluggishly—as if the microprocessor's commands weren't being transmitted fast enough. Maybe that's what happened when they zinged back an eight-year-old. It looked ridiculous, sitting on his mother's paisley-print couch like some kind of oversized doll. Probably an older model, he thought derisively. But still expensive—

"Where'd the money come from? Huh? Where'd you get the money to pay for it?" he demanded.

Alex Weiland, a big man accustomed to slinging sides of beef in a meat-packing plant, couldn't meet his son's eyes. Joe felt heat rush to his face.

"You used part of my college fund, didn't you?" He slammed his fist down on the back of the couch. The deader never flinched.

"Come on, Bernie. I'll show you to your room," Alex said. He pushed a button and the deader stood obediently.

Joe's jaw dropped and he stared at his father with horrified eyes. "*Bernie*?" he whispered. "You named him *Bernie*?" His knees bent and he dropped onto the couch. "Oh, Jesus."

Alex turned to Joe, his eyes pleading. "You have to understand. Your mother *needs* this—just for awhile, until she gets her head straight. Then we'll sell him and get our money back. Okay?"

"No," Joe said woodenly. "You're wrong. She doesn't need some corpse walking around trying to replace my brother. You're even going to put him in the same room, aren't you?" Alex didn't answer, and Joe raised his face, unashamed at the tears he felt slipping down his cheeks. "Bernie can't be *replaced*, Dad. He's nothing but smashed pieces now—the monorail made sure of that. And this *thing* doesn't even look like him."

His father turned away; the deader followed.

"He can't *be* Bernie!" Joe howled.

He was alone in the living room.

Joe watched his mother watch the deader. She didn't seem surprised, so he guessed this was something she and his father had discussed, a family thing to which he had not been privy—like so many others since Bernie's death six weeks ago. Cathy Weiland was quiet during the meal, cutting her food, putting it in her mouth for a few token chews before swallowing it, then washing it down with a generous swallow of wine. The meal, Joe felt positive, was wonderful; as things were, he couldn't taste anything, and the efforts of his mother to make his favorite meal—Swiss steak—were wasted.

Speaking of waste, he saw with disgust that she had placed a full plate of food in front of the deader—he would not, *could* not call it by his brother's name—who, of course, didn't eat. After dinner maybe, his father would take the thing out to the shed and give it an injection or something, to replace the nutrients in its system. Had it come with an instruction book?

In the meantime, it just sat there, staring at nothing.

The deader had brown hair that curled a little at the ends and bloodless, rubbery-looking skin. His mother had removed the sonar glasses to reveal the deader's dark, empty, blue eyes; a tiny spear of pain went through Joe as he realized the deader *did* slightly resemble his brother.

He eyed it resentfully. It didn't move much—none of them did. Unlike living people, deaders only moved when the microprocessor or remote control told them to. A living child would have fidgeted, scratched at his neck, swung his legs under the too-tall chair. Joe wondered who it had been— where had it lived, what had killed it? Were there people out there somewhere that had loved this little boy like he and his parents had loved Bernie? If so, why had they allowed this to happen? Or did they even realize their son's body was sitting at a dining room table in front of a congealing supper with a family of strangers? The kids at school had often speculated on a black market for bodies; maybe the unknown couple slept soundly with the false belief that the boy's body was safely buried in a neighborhood cemetery.

Joe put his fork down and pushed his chair back. "I can't eat with that thing at the table."

His mother looked away from the deader for the first time. Her eyes slid down Joe like brittle shards of blue ice.

"You are not excused," she said.

Joe glanced at his father's hard face and hesitated, then settled back onto his chair and stared at his plate. He could hear the clink of his parents' utensils as they continued the meal, the tick of the old-fashioned wall clock behind him as it worked away the seconds.

"It's not going to work, Mom," he finally said in a low voice. He felt like crying again. "This thing can't even speak. Bernie was alive. He used to t-talk about th-things—"

"Shut up," his mother said.

"—going on at s-school," Joe continued. He struggled to get the words out around the salty lump of grief in his throat. "He always l-laughed—"

"Shut *up*, I said! Didn't you hear me?" Cathy's voice was strident.

He tried to be quiet, he really did, but the words found their way out on their own.

"Bernie would have hated this."

His mother's dinner plate hit him in the forehead, grinding cold meat and gravy into his eyes and brows before it fell to the floor and shattered.

"I don't want to see another scene like the one at dinner."

Joe sat on the edge of his bed, feeling the water mattress rock gently beneath his legs. The purpling bruise above his right eyebrow throbbed, the eye partially closed from swelling. He couldn't believe this was happening. His father gazed at him sternly from the doorway, like some kind of demigod ready to mete out justice.

"I bought the deader because your mother and I agreed that it would temporarily fill the void left by Bernie's death, maybe give her a chance to adjust to his being gone. I told you that when I brought him home."

"What she needs to do is accept that Bernie is *dead*, not replace him with someone else who's just as dead," Joe snapped. He got up and went to the mirror, touching his fingers gingerly to his cheek. He thought he could still smell mashed potatoes on his skin. "Look what's happening already. She's never done anything like this before—"

"That's because you don't know when to keep your mouth shut," Alex interrupted. "There are certain things *you're* going to have to accept. One is that Bernie's death has changed your mother—it's changed all of us. Another is that the deader stays until she says it's okay to get rid of him."

"Bullshit!" Joe flared. "I'm not living in this house with that corpse walking around like some kind of voiceless movie monster." He threw open his closet and jerked out his sports bag. "When he's gone, I'll come back." He tossed it on the bed and opened a drawer.

A ripping sound made him turn, and he saw with a jolt that his father's large hands had torn the carryall nearly in half. "You're not going anywhere," Alex said. His dark brows were pinched. "You'll stay in this damned house until you finish school—"

"I'm almost eighteen, remember? I can do what I want!"

"Don't *fuck* with me, Joseph!" Alex bellowed.

Joe felt his face blanch; he'd never seen his father so angry, and fear—a new experience for him—made his breath shorten. The older man lowered his voice and shuddered as he forced himself back under control.

"You just watch your manners and stay put—and mind you, I'm not asking, I'm ordering. Humor your mother, and hopefully, this will all blow over in a month or so."

His dad slammed the door behind him, and Joe's racing heart slowed a little. He sank back on the bedcovers and cradled his aching face in his hands.

"Damn you, Bernie," he whispered miserably. "Why'd you have to fall off that monorail platform?"

It was creepy, the way it was just there all the time, moving only when you made it. Joe could never think of it as Bernie—just *it*; after the first few days his mother gave up trying to get Joe to call the deader by name, and on that his father didn't push him. Every fourth word out of his mother's mouth seemed to be Bernie, but Joe noted that while his father didn't avoid the deader, Alex called it by his dead son's name as seldom as possible.

It wasn't long before Joe decided that the deader must not be functioning correctly. He'd thought for sure it would be programmed for lifelike behavior, basic tasks—but this dumbshit would stand for days unless you told it to sit. Shouldn't the microprocessor kick in after a certain amount of time and get the thing off its feet? And he'd obviously been wrong when he'd assumed they were equipped with some kind of homing device; this one didn't seem to realize it should stay with the family. Maybe that was nothing but a rumor he'd picked up, but how did you control a deader that wouldn't stay put? From dealing with his dad, Joe figured the really effective instructions were the ones given in a yelling voice with the threat of force. But you couldn't teach something that was deaf, felt nothing, and looked at you without comprehension—if it really saw you at all.

Home-life turned out to be only one of his problems. The Saturday after his dad brought the deader home, the family ran into a guy at the grocery with whom Joe had never gotten along.

"Hey, Joey! Cool," sneered Hank Beckert in his twangy voice. Beckert was an asshole with a block of concrete for a heart; Joe ignored him and kept walking. "A deader in the family." Hank laughed nastily. "Matches your brother."

Both his mother and father gaped at the boy in amazement, unable to believe the cruel words. Joe's vision glazed sudden red and he lunged at the older teen, who quickly danced around a woman and her grocery-laden cart; the woman glared at them both.

"You sonofabitch!" Joe yelled. "Get over here!"

"Better watch your new brother, buddy-boy," Hank said merrily. "Little boy's lost!"

Joe spun and saw the deader plodding mindlessly down the aisle. His father was pushing the STOP button on the remote, but the deader kept going. Joe turned back but Hank had disappeared.

"Bernie!" his mother was calling, "Come back!" She started to run after him, but Alex stopped her and jerked his head at Joe. Reluctantly, Joe trotted down the aisle and reached for the deader.

It was the first time he'd touched it. His fingers wrapped around the deader's wrist and encountered cold, dry flesh—there was no warm blood in these veins, no sir. He yanked his hand back instinctively and glanced swiftly towards his father; the look on Alex's face made him grind his teeth and take the deader by the arm.

"Come on, deader," he hissed, avoiding the eyes of the people staring at them. "Back to the group." His fingers tightened viciously for a second, then he realized how futile that was—deaders didn't feel pain. Shame filled him as he led the docile deader back to his parents; the poor kid whose body this had been had been given no choice in the matter. Joe was suddenly certain that no one would want to be like this—life force gone, nothing but a tool being used by somebody else. A malfunctioning one at that, he thought sadly.

With more of a sympathetic eye, Joe tried to approach the problem logically in the following weeks, deciding that if he had to live with the deader, he might as well make the best of it. With that in mind, he started making it do some of the things he'd wanted his little brother to do when he'd been alive.

Which just went to show, again, that it wasn't Bernie.

Bernie would never have cleaned his room for him. Joe stopped after a couple of tries at sitting on his bed and working the control pad while the deader dusted and swept around him. It just seemed too obscenely easy.

His father installed a latch on the bedroom door and began locking the deader in Bernie's room at night to keep it from wandering around the house. Lying on his stomach in the early morning darkness, Joe pulled the pillow over his head to try to block the sound of the deader's feet shuffling back and forth in the room next to his. He couldn't understand why his parents just didn't get the thing fixed.

Or better yet, return it.

"Hey, Joey. I hear your mom's gone a little crazy and named that piece of fly flesh after your little brother. Looks like I wasn't wrong, was I?"

On his way home from school, Joe glanced over as Hank Beckert slowed his convertible to keep pace with Joe. "What's the scoop, man?" Hank had a couple of bimbos in the front seat showing plenty of cleavage, but obviously no brains; both looked stoned out of their heads.

"Fuck off, Beckert," he said without slowing. "Don't you have a job to go to?"

"Touchy, touchy!" The highly-polished car glided alongside the curb like a moist red worm. "But then I would be too if my mom was nurse-maiding someone else's decomposing brat. Tell me, does she give it baths?" The girls giggled, and Hank leered at Joe over their heads.

Pissed now, Joe kicked out at the fender but missed as Hank stomped the accelerator; above the fading thrum of the car's engine he could hear Beckert's laughter. He spat in the street and rubbed his eyes to clear some of the dust and exhaust away. *Shithead needs an oil change,* he thought sourly as he shifted his books.

He poked along, knowing he'd be late for dinner but not caring. Eating with the deader at the table had stopped bothering him, though he couldn't understand why his mom had to call it Bernie. Nor could he forget the feel of the deader's flesh under his fingers at the store a couple of weeks ago. What if the deader wasn't *really* dead, just trapped in that body? He couldn't get rid of the thought; it went hand-in-hand with the restless shambling coming from Bernie's room every night. No matter how many times you remoted the deader to sit and stay, twenty minutes later it was up again.

What if a person's soul, assuming there was such a thing, didn't get to leave the body if the body was mechanically returned to life? If you could even call a deader's pitiful existence life. Joe stopped in the park and sprawled on a bench, watching the people around him. Over the past two months, he'd noticed that deaders were becoming more and more a part of everyday life—or had he just never seen it before?

His wandering gaze stopped on a couple across the walk, and he watched them idly. The two were in their mid-thirties, with stylish clothes that said money and plenty of it; several rings glittered on the woman's hand, a thick rope of woven gold encircled the man's neck. Next to them, sitting silent and unmoving on the bench, was another girl, Joe's age. She was pretty, with dark brown eyes and clean blond hair fixed in bouncy curls that framed her pale face. Joe's eyes traveled appreciatively down her shoulders and stopped on the swollen stomach; disappointed, he realized she was probably seven or eight months' pregnant. As he watched, the man reached over and pushed sonar glasses on the bridge of the girl's nose, then his wife pulled a keypad from her handbag and punched in commands; the girl responded by rising from the bench, belly distended and graceless.

Joe was stunned. He'd heard about surrogate deaders on the newscast, but that was on the East Coast—not here, in a small town a hundred miles south of nowhere. As the trio strolled away, he considered the concept, remembering Bernie as a newborn and his mother wrapping an old wind-up clock in a towel and putting it in the crib. When Joe, only ten at the time, had asked why, she'd explained that it reminded the baby of the comforting sound of his mother's heartbeat.

The idea of a deader surrogate was mind-boggling, and he could think of a hundred technical questions, such as how did the deader maintain a warm-enough body temperature and provide the fetus with oxygen? And was she given extra nutrients to support the child?

And what of the deader herself—did she know she carried a child? Surely not; if a deader couldn't feel pain, how could it feel life? But what if a soul was stranded inside, watching but unable to feel, wanting but never able to experience?

But above all: what kind of a person would the baby turn out to be, after growing in the silent womb of a dead woman?

"We're ready to leave. Go get your brother," Cathy said.

"What?" Joe blinked at his mother, and her face turned a sudden, obvious red. He looked at his father and was perversely gratified to see that for once even the old man looked shaken.

"I-I mean, go get Bernie."

"He's not my brother!" Joe said loudly.

"I know that! It was a slip, that's all. He's in his room. Go up and bring him down." She fumbled with her purse, fingers awkward.

"You mean he's in *Bernie's* room, not *his* room. He's in my *brother's* room." Sympathy for the mindless deader warred in him with the pain of loss, still fresh after four months. "*You* go get him!"

"Joe—" His father's voice cut in, sounding tired. The tone conveyed it all, much more than any lecture could have. *Are we still fighting about this? I thought your mother would be well by now, and we could get on with our lives.*

His mother slammed her purse down in frustration. "Damn you!" Cathy hissed. "Why can't you be more like—"

"Like what?" Joe screamed. His hands cut the air helplessly. "Like that poor, dead, little kid pacing around upstairs? Like your replacement model?"

"Yes!"

"Cathy, stop it!" Alex shouted. "You're going too far!"

"At least he's quiet! And he never c-causes us any tr-trouble—" She began to cry in great, struggling gasps.

Joe watched numbly as his father enfolded her in his arms and murmured soothingly; she clung to him and hid her face against his shoulder.

When they found Joe's, Alex's eyes were full of pain and regret. Joe turn away and climbed the stairs.

At the door to Bernie's room, Joe stopped and listened for a moment to the shuffling of the deader's feet across the carpeting of a little boy's red, white, and blue stars. With a sigh, he picked up the remote from the hall table, flipped the latch, and opened the door.

Inside, the Bernie-deader walked in a seemingly-endless elongated circle in front of the dresser. The window, with its open mini-blinds and bright sunshine, held no interest for it, nor did the science fiction posters on the walls or model spaceships strung from the dropped ceiling panels.

It just walked.

Around and around.

Joe's throat constricted in pity. "You're gonna wear a hole in the carpeting, kid," he said hoarsely. He fumbled with the keypad; seconds later the deader obligingly sat. Joe pulled the door shut and latched it, then retreated to his own room and sat on the bed.

In a few minutes the tears came, but he didn't know if they were for the Bernie-deader or for himself.

"Hey, Joey. How are ya?"

Joe grimaced as he heard the voice; why couldn't that weasel leave him alone? The park was his refuge, the one place he could get away from his parents and the Bernie-deader, and he didn't need hassles from Hank Beckert to screw it up. The bench, that a moment ago had been comfortable, shook his teeth as Becker flounced down next to him. Joe ran a hand through his hair and got up.

"Hey man, don't leave." Beckert grabbed the sleeve of Joe's jacket. His eyes were calculating. "I thought you and I could have a talk and you could, you know, fill me in on all the details."

Joe yanked his arm out of Hank's grip and turned his back. "I don't know what you're talking about."

"Sure you do. Like what goes on at your house? I always wondered how people, you know, dealt with deaders in everyday life. And you never answered my question about whether your mom gives that corpse his baths." Hank laughed nastily.

Joe knew Hank was testing him, seeing how far he could be pushed. Knowing didn't stop his face from flushing at Hank's implication and he whirled.

"You just shut the fuck up, Beckert!"

"What are you so embarrassed about?" Hank shot back. He stood, then waggled his fingers mockingly and took a couple of mincing steps around Joe. "Are you hiding something? Maybe you're the one who likes to give the baths, huh? How 'bout it—you like playing with dead meat?"

Joe couldn't stop himself. His fist balled up and connected with Beckert's jaw before he'd actually known what he was going to do, the knuckles feeling strong and sure as they drove into the other's flesh.

Hank gave a yelp and grabbed the side of his face as he back-stepped, then ducked as Joe leapt at him again; in spite of the wildness of Joe's swing, it missed him by only a fraction of an inch. Behind the two, a woman began shouting for them to stop; Hank ignored her and rushed the younger teenager, clutching him in a tackle that sent them slamming to the sidewalk in a lung-bruising roll.

Caught between a haze of anger and the sight of the leaf-laden trees tumbling disjointedly around him, Joe didn't think about the location of the park bench until the hard, paint-peeling wood connected with his temple.

His world exploded into blackness.

"Mr. Weiland? Hi, we're from the Free Christian Church on Sixth Street. We wondered if we might speak with you for a few minutes?" The two women on the front step gave encouraging smiles beneath pastel-tinted straw hats.

"I'm sorry," Alex said and started to close the door. Purplish shadows rimmed his eyes. "We're not interested."

"Alex, who is it?" Cathy called from the kitchen.

"Mrs. Weiland?" One of the women stopped the door with a heeled shoe, ignoring Alex's look of irritation.

Cathy came out of the kitchen, licking frosting from a spoon. "Yes? I don't believe we know you," she said. "Alex, don't be rude. Invite them in." She stuck the spoon in her mouth and wiped her hands on her apron.

Alex hesitated, then stepped back. The women entered, the older one giving him a smug look as Cathy waved them into the living room.

"We're from the Free Christian Church," the younger of the two repeated. "I'm Sister Beth and this is Sister Jessica." We just came by to extend our regards." Her gaze swept Cathy appraisingly. "I hope we didn't disturb you...you weren't making dinner?"

"Oh, no," Cathy said with a smile. "Actually, I was baking a birthday cake for Joe—he's my oldest."

Sister Jessica nodded primly. "We've heard at the church how difficult it's been for you. Terrible enough to lose a son, but to have the other boy injured in that terrible incident in the park!" She clucked. "You must be overjoyed to have him home."

Sister Beth nodded in agreement, then picked up the conversation. "We understand that after the younger boy's death, you and Mr. Weiland purchased a deader," she said smoothly. "While they seem to be accepted more readily in today's society, we at the Free Christian Church tend to be a bit more old-fashioned. But," she added hastily at Alex's scowl, "we like to think we can keep our minds open."

"Well," Cathy said as she reached for a large keypad on the coffee table, "we don't think of them like that anymore." The four of them turned at the sound of footsteps on the stairs.

Alex felt a small stab of bittersweet triumph as the stuffy expression on the older woman's face abruptly crumbled.

"These are my two sons, Bernie and Joe," Cathy said proudly. "Our speech consultant believes they'll be able to talk in a couple of years."

It had taken the rest of the college money, but there were no sons to send to college now, anyway. Alex stood in the bathroom wearily, watching as Joe followed the remote commands to wash up before bed. Joe had always worn his hair shorter than Bernie, and it crushed Alex every time he saw the seam just below the hairline where the microprocessor was embedded in his son's skull. Almost as hard to live with was the small square of synthetic skin along Joe's right temple that replaced the bone and flesh punctured by the corner of the park bench.

When the washing was finished, they went into Joe's room and Alex stood at the window while Joe obediently changed into pajamas and slipped under the covers. That done, Alex tucked the blanket snugly around him, a habit from when Joe had been small, like Bernie. Although Cathy did it all the time, he could not bring himself to kiss the boy goodnight.

Alex checked the other's room and found everything as it should be, then headed downstairs, not thinking to fasten the latch on Bernie's room—that had always been Joe's job. Alex stopped and briefly looked in on Cathy. The nightlight glowed softly in their bedroom, making her hair gleam a gentle red; she was already asleep, lips turned up in a small, satisfied smile.

He sat down at the dining room table with a bottle of bourbon and a big glass. There were no tears in him anymore, only a great empty spot where all the life had been sucked out. If only he could give that life back to the son he'd bedded down a few minutes ago...not to mention the tormented little stranger in his younger son's room.

Twenty minutes later Alex heard creaking along the upstairs landing. "Cathy?" he called softly. "You awake?" When there was no answer, he forced himself to stand, legs already trembling from the booze. He labored up the steps, remembering the unlocked door of Bernie's room as he rubbed his grainy eyes, wondering why they'd never gotten around to having Bernie fixed.

Bernie wasn't in his room. Too drained to be alarmed, Alex could see the door to Joe's room was ajar; from its darkness came the sound of slow, measured footsteps. He reached round the door and flipped the light switch.

Joe was where he should be, lying under the covers and staring sightlessly at the ceiling, his only movement the microprocessor-ordered blink of his eyelids every ten seconds.

At the foot of Joe's bed, Bernie walked in his endless circle.

A Patchwork of Poems, Reanimated into Something Barely Alive
Katherine Norem

Shopping
The clothes hang limply
at Aberzombie and Fitch
moistened with gravedirt.

Zombies 1, Know-it-all 0
Knock knock.
"Who's there?"
"BRAAAAAIINS."
"Brains who?"
(pause) "BRAAAAAIINS!!!"
(opens door) "No, you're supposed to s…"

But Not at Alinea
Brain foam, light as air.
Freshly shaved toenail garnish.
Haute zombie cuisine.

Puffy
The scalpel made delicate nips
along the sad corpse's cold hips.
Restylane's expensive,
Silicone is offensive…
So how do you like my new lips?

A Tiny Ladle
A Pharaoh of old, named Thutmose
said, "Pull my corpse's brain out through my nose!
And it will go in a jar,
to be adorned with a star."
Then…? "The Undead eat it later, I s'pose."

A Natural Progression
The newly dead always are crusty.
Then, as they age, they turn rusty.
But I like a crotch
that is aged, like fine Scotch.
Hey! You there, babe! Come fuck me dusty!

The Tatesville Curse
Andrea Dubnick

ONE FINE AUTUMN DAY, ARLENE Schultz climbed out of her grave and began to tear apart anything she could get her cold blue hands around. She had been a strong young woman, so she toppled quite a few of the oldest headstones in Tatesville's graveyard before she found the cemetery's front gate. She shambled out onto Main Street and turned north.

Things like this just don't happen every day in a town like Tatesville. But Tatesville's roots ran deeply through the centuries, and the roots of bad feelings run as deep as human nature.

As Arlene trudged along toward the Schultz home, she met not a single living soul. In almost every house she passed, however, someone monitored her post-mortem stroll. In Tatesville, the Neighborhood Watch is a committee of the whole. Always. Telephone lines all over town blazed up immediately.

"Arlene Schultz? Didn't we bury her last…Oh, I see!"

"I'm not surprised, the way she was, and all—"

"Shades of Tabitha—"

"Sheesh! Tall tales. Salem copycats—"

"Copycat crimes back then? No way!"

"Here we go again. Who was the last…uh…incident?"

"Another Reviver? Not again!"

Things like this didn't just happen every day in Tatesville, but Arlene was not the first Reviver. That was Tabitha Tate, in the autumn of 1718. Everybody knew that story.

Hounded into an early grave by a reckless husband, Tabitha had simply refused to stay there and allow him to ruin her neat dairy operation. She clawed her way back from the dead, up through the ground, and returned to her ordinary life.

Just as in life, Tabitha went to the milking shed at dawn. Months spent underground had made her stiff and clumsy. The cows would not tolerate her cold dead fingers and trampled down on the shed. Tabitha didn't even notice.

Then she gathered up dirty laundry and headed for the creek. Her grave-ravaged fingers could not keep hold of the garments, so shirts and britches drifted down the creek, one by one. To each chore she gave undivided, unrelenting, undead attention until she completed it, or completely destroyed it. By the time she finally disintegrated, her tidy homestead was a worse shambles than her no-account man had made of it all summer.

Stories may differ about the exact date of Tabitha's return, but disintegrate she surely did, six or eight weeks later. All the stories agree that she was never seen again after the night of Halloween.

Since Tabitha's time, Tatesville folks who die without making peace with themselves, their surroundings, and their successors rise up as repeat customers in the checkout line of life. Halloween night, however, remains the constant close of Tatesville's undead season.

Most folks today believe that the Tatesville Curse (or "Tabitha's Second Chance") affects only Tatesville natives who die in town. Folks buried elsewhere—Darlington, Chicago, Florida—apparently stay put. No word has ever come back about undead antics by Tatesville's émigrés, and that's just the sort of thing people talk about.

In Tatesville, a person isn't considered dead and buried, properly and permanently dead and buried, until after Halloween.

Our Lady of the Resurrection parish house lies just down the street from the Schultz home. Perhaps luck, or Our Lady Herself, saw to it that the new priest was standing at his office window just in time to see Arlene. Father Francis X. Kowalski—Father K to everyone in Tate County, churchgoer or not—had just hung another framed certificate on the wall. He stepped back to admire the effect.

Then Arlene caught his eye. *Little early in the season for a Halloween party,* the priest thought idly, watching her struggle along. *And early in the day for a costumed adult on the street.* He had to admire the costumer's attention to gross detail, though. *If I didn't know Arlene Schultz was dead and buried...* He turned back to the wall.

The certificate "attested the successful completion of all requirements and attainment of necessary proficiency for Advanced Training Intensive in

Family Grief Counseling." More importantly to Father K, it marked the beginning of his Tatesville career.

Nearly six months ago, Father K had enrolled in the six-week Advanced Training Intensive. Throughout the Grief Counseling course, however, the subject of parishioners returning from the dead never came up, either in lecture or discussion. Modern Church doctrine offers little on the subject of the undead. Post-Vatican II reforms abandoned the lugubrious old preoccupation with death, while standing strong on a purely spiritual Afterlife. They said nothing at all about dead bodies climbing out of their graves and plodding up the streets in the middle of the afternoon.

On Wednesday of the fourth week of the Advanced Intensive, Father K first heard of Tatesville and Monsignor Woods. Monsignor Woods had ruled Our Lady of the Resurrection parish for over forty years without loosening the grip of his iron fist. Apathetic complacency by parishioners and indifferent tolerance by a distant Church hierarchy had allowed him to ignore reforms mandated by the Vatican since the early '60s...until the previous weekend.

On that Saturday evening, Monsignor had gone to sleep in this life, after preparing a long and rancorous sermon ascribing the decline of morality to such things as women attending Church bareheaded, the use of birth control, and tattoos. On Sunday morning, he awoke in the next life. Presumably the sermon was never delivered.

Less than three weeks later, Father K found himself installed at Our Lady of the Resurrection. The parish house was packed to the eaves with daunting amounts of pre-Vatican II devotional equipment and supplies. Every nook, cranny, cupboard, drawer and shelf held files of catechisms, boxes of holy cards, coils of plastic rosaries, and price lists for more. Each windowsill sported plaster statues. Every inch of wall space wore religious pictures. *Holery*, Father K called the old-fashioned paraphernalia as he crated it up. *Which is proper, 'Plastic Jesuses' or 'Jesusi Plastici'?*

He wondered if he could discreetly convince the driver scheduled to deliver his new computer set-up to take a few boxes away.

He recalled his conversation with the Advanced Intensive Co-ordinator. "This parish—your parish—serves all of Tate County," the other had said, pointing out Tatesville on a map. "And it's pretty...ah...rural. Don't be surprised if they still eat fish on Fridays and try to buy indulgences from you...but I think the Inquisition is over. Old Woods never did get used to Vatican II's reforms. Poor unreconstructed old bas—geezer. May he rest in peace...though I don't imagine he does." He clapped Father K on the shoulder. "Sorry, Frank. Wouldn't have been my decision."

"Maybe you can bring them into the second half of the twentieth century. More than that might be asking too much. Good luck, Frank!"

Inside the Schultz home, Arlene's mother regarded her daughter's progress up the block. Betty peeked through the curtains and wished Tom was home. She did not look forward to this impending visit. She'd had a troublesome pregnancy with her daughter, a difficult delivery. Arlene's arrivals were never easy.

The Schultzes had loved Arlene well enough in life, but during each year of childhood, Arlene rewrote the criteria for "problem child"—acting out, truancy, underachievement, petty crime. Soon she blossomed into a "difficult" young woman—eating disorders, wild sexuality, body piercing, alcohol, tobacco, firearms, recreational drugs, prescription drugs, day trading. Not long after that, she was dead. Now she was back.

Betty would never have said she wanted to see Arlene dead, of course. But all in all, her life and Tom's had calmed down quite a bit since they had buried Arlene. Betty had lost weight. Tom's ulcer problems had subsided. They went on a cruise. They redecorated the house.

No one in his or her right mind would want to see Arlene now, anyway. Her face showed grim and pallid under the garish grave-makeup. Bits of her filthy clothes and torn skin, results of bursting through her coffin and wriggling up through six feet of heavy soil, left a clay-footed trail of crumbs of...well, *crumbs*...in her wake. Arlene, or what was left of her, stumped up the walk.

Still standing at the window, Betty allowed a tiny "Ha!" to escape her lips. This was a "Ha!" of vindication on a point that had nagged at her ever since the funeral.

"You know, Tom," she said aloud to her absent spouse, "I begged you to buy her a better casket. Something a little...well, *nicer* than that pine box." Tom had held out for the final, and at $299.95 the least costly, entry in the undertaker's long list of Luxury Eternal Rest Packages. "You know what your problem is, Tom Schultz? You're just a big tightwad! Now—*now*—look! Why, you talk about your penny-wise, pound-foolish, muddle-headed, oh, *oh*—"

—As Arlene exploded through the big oak door, banging it against the wall and ramming a doorknob-shaped hole into the drywall. She picked up the decorative table near the door, spilling the daily mail to the floor. She flung the table across the room; it smashed against her mother's portrait gallery.

"Not my authentic reproduction Sheraton gate-leg occasional table!" gasped Betty. "Fruitwood veneer. A real classic..." Broken glass and shattered family photographs sifted down on top of the remains of the table—cheap fiberboard after all, just as Tom had insisted.

Arlene made a beeline for the TV set and punched it out with one backhanded blow. The picture tube imploded with a noise like no other. Shards of glass so tiny they drifted like smoke puffed out into the room, but she paid no attention. She rocked the brand-new, Euro-style entertainment center (replacing the old California mission shelving unit from Betty's first apartment back in the seventies) back and forth against the wall. Videocassettes, CD jewel-boxes, and bric-a-brac cascaded around her. Dangling only by their cables, the electronic components hung on desperately.

Across the street, Father K had witnessed only Arlene's entrance, but already it was time to call for help. He picked up his sleek new dual-line, multi-function telephone and speed-coded the number for Tate County's Volunteer Rescue squad.

Father K starting speaking as soon as the line connected. "Hello Police Father Frank Kowalski Lady'Res Tatesville emergency situation need police Shultz Main Street breaking in destroyed door woman still here need help."

"Slow down, now," drawled the voice on the other end. "Hidy'do, Father K. Tom Schultz here, Officer Schultz today. Now give me all that again, slower, please."

Father K knew that Tom volunteered on the squad, but he was startled to reach him on duty. "Somebody's broken down the door of your house, Tom! Betty's alone. They...he's...disguised as your poor Arlene. You need to get over here right now! I'll go get Betty!" He banged down the phone and turned to his clerical closet.

Father K knew that Frank Kowalski knew better than to pit his unarmed and untrained self in defense against a home invader who was probably armed, possibly deranged, and preposterously disguised. But Holy Orders conferred a certain indefinable authority upon a consecrated priest, and he would rely on that strength.

Ducking his clerical stole around his neck, Father K slipped a hand into his jacket pocket. He found the smooth leather of his volume of Holy Rites reassuring. Always before, he'd compared the traveling missal to a businessman's notebook computer. Now, it suddenly felt...more like a six-gun. Now, Father K was Gary Cooper in *High Noon*, going out to wreak justice, whether anyone else in town cared or not. He strode toward the front door.

As he reached for the knob, his eye was drawn to something above the door. A single, tiny vial nestled behind two slender nails driven into the wooden strip at the top of the frame. Undoubtedly Holy Water, an overlooked relic of Monsignor's tenure. *A hideout round*, he thought. *A reload of spiritual ammunition.* He reached up slid the little bottle out. *Just in case*, he thought. He blew the dust off and slipped it inside his breast pocket. *It couldn't hurt.* After all, many parishioners still took comfort in these old-fashioned trappings of religion. *It couldn't hurt.*

Father K opened the door and strode into the street, mentally in step with Gary Cooper. He was ready for battle—spiritual battle—with the home invader.

The Neighborhood Watch relayed up and down Tatesville the priest's arrival on the street. Gary Cooper had an unseen Watch of Neighbors, too.

"What's he think he can do there, an exorcism?"

"Do those even work if you're not Catholic?"

"There's nothing anybody can do. You just have to see it through."

"It's still full moon tonight, I think—"

"No, silly, that's werewolves, in the movies."

"Who was the last Reviver?"

"Marie Something. 1955, I think. Maybe '56."

Looking beyond the ruined doorjamb at the Schultz house, Frank Kowalski thought even Gary Cooper would have been stumped, armed only with a single bottle of Holy Water. He stepped through the splinters of the front door. Neither Betty nor Arlene noticed.

Tom Schultz pulled up the police cruiser on the wrong side of the street. He left the engine running and the lightbar flashing, and hit the front stoop two paces behind Father K.

The priest turned quickly. "Good, you're here!" he said. "I'll get Betty." He threaded his way toward her through the rubble. "Come on, you'll be safer in the kitchen." She waved him away, without taking her eyes off Arlene.

Tom had stopped about two paces into the room. He stood there, rooted to the spot, shifting his weight from one foot to the other. "I s'pose this was bound to happen, Bet," he said softly.

Father K gave up on Betty and turned his attention to Arlene. "Hello," he said, keeping his voice low and casual. "We can help you. I'm Father K. We need you to stop breaking things. Let us help you. Just stop. Where you are. Right now."

Arlene paid him no heed.

"Tom," Father K continued in the same tone, "go arrest the guy in the mask. Grab him, or her. Or I will," he said, hoping he would not have to make good on the threat.

"Ain't much I can do," said Tom heavily. "Law enforcement's for the living."

"Tom, it's just a disguise—a mask. Look. Betty, put some water on a paper towel for me, will you, please?" Father K waved Betty into the kitchen.

Betty moved as if she were in a trance.

"Tom, go arrest that person," said Father K sternly. "Now."

Tom moved slowly toward Arlene, who was yanking the few electronic components free and smashing them on the floor, one by one. He seized Arlene's shoulders.

Her arms went slack. Tom held her stiffly, at arm's length. He locked steps with her, turning bother of them around to Father K.

Betty returned with the soggy paper towel, and numbly handed it to the priest.

The priest took a couple of very deep breaths to steady himself at the sight of Arlene's dreadful dead face. Her soul might be beautiful in the eyes of God, but the rest of Arlene was pretty icky to look at up close. "Makeup," muttered Father K, shuddering as he slapped the wet paper towel to Arlene's cheek and began to wash her.

"Don't!" wailed Betty. "No, please. It's...not what you think. I think."

Arlene shied back roughly, nearly crushing Tom into the remains of the entertainment center.

As his stomach turned over, Father K realized that the mess in the wet paper towel included a patch of skin and the tip of Arlene's nose. "Good Lord, have mercy!" he gasped.

Tom said, "Oof!" and moved away from Arlene, but the pressure from his fingers left corrugated indentations on her upper arms.

She stood there for a moment, unmoving, unblinking.

Father K quickly reached for the vial of Holy Water. Twisting open the cap, he raised both hands and spilled its cleansing essence over his own hands and onto Arlene's head. "In the name of the Father, and the Son and the Holy Spirit," he murmured.

Arlene just blinked a couple of times as water dripped down her face. Then she turned away from the appalled living, kicked out to clear her path, and staggered up the stairs. She lurched up and down the hall a couple of times before locating the master bedroom. She shambled right out again after just a cursory trashing. She was apparently after bigger game.

She threw herself into the room at the head of the stairs, slamming her body at the walls, ripping down curtains, tossing objects over her shoulder and down the staircase. The complete set of TIME-LIFE books on the Old West came avalanching down, followed by two bowling trophies.

The Schultzes speechlessly watched their Reviver daughter methodically dismantle their house.

A framed award came sailing down the stairs like a rectangular Frisbee. It shattered at Tom's feet. Two duck decoys skittered down the book-slick stairs, like real ducks racing a river's rapids.

The situation had gone beyond Father K's ability to comprehend. But the ultimate role of a priest, always and everywhere, is to pray, so he prayed. He began with the Lord's Prayer, because he always found the ritual of declaiming those ancient words a comfort in itself.

It had no effect on Arlene.

At the time of his consecration, Father K had solemnly sworn to Ever Defend Against Satan and All His Hellish Works. In life as a rational, enlightened man, he wasn't certain he even believed in a literal Satan, a distinct entity, a personality. But if there were a Satan, he would be sure to have Hellish Works, and this Work looked pretty Hellish to Frank Kowalski. So he prayed as Our Lord had prayed with He was tempted in the desert: *Get thee behind me, Satan!*

Still, nothing.

Betty almost levitated across the room with a shriek when her grandfather's antique shotgun came clanging down the stairs end-over-end. Officer Tom didn't even flinch. Father K neatly sidestepped. Arlene followed it down, half flying, half falling over the debris.

Father K recalled a few bits from the old Rite of Exorcism. That Rite isn't used much in today's Church, but it's still taught in Seminary, and now some of it just bubbled up into his mind. The old *omnium Latinum phrase-orum* rolled off his tongue sonorously enough.

Completely wasted on Arlene.

Officer Tom stood motionless, his hands hanging at his sides, but he cringed when Arlene started in on his La-Z-Boy recliner. "Nonono," he wailed softly, while she flung bits of foam stuffing around like confetti. "Nononononono…"

Father K stood quietly, waiting for inspiration; divine, if possible. By now, he was open to any suggestion.

He shifted to the comfortable language of family grief counseling. "You are not to blame for this," he said to Tom and Betty. He kept his tone gentle, firm. "The Devil's works can be very persuasive. The Devil is very good at special effects like this."

He stopped abruptly. The phrase had seemed pretty good when he thought of it, right up until he heard himself actually say the words. *What an awful thing to say to people in pain*! He was suddenly glad that the Schultzes were still engrossed by Arlene. "This um…may look like Arlene. It does look like Arlene, sort of. But this…manifestation"—*ah! much better word choice*—"is just an evil display of the Devil's work. Probably." *You are completely out of control*! his mind shrilled.

"This isn't your daughter, it cannot be. Arlene died. She is with God…probably." He sounded so hollow. So *hysterical*.

Get a grip on yourself. "Tom, take Betty in your arms. Yes, yes…like that." The couple looked at him in surprise, but did what he said. "Listen to me: this thing…manifestation…it looks like your daughter, but it's not."

Tom Schultz had never taken his eyes off the Reviver as it worked its destructive way around the house. He shook his head. "Don't know about that, Father," he said.

"Well, I do know! I know Arlene Schultz was a good person…basically. A Christian," said Father K. In his short time in Tatesville, he had picked up some stories about Arlene's adventures, but the dead were often forgiven their wild oats after the fact. "This isn't the Arlene you should remember."

Tom insisted, "Beggin' pardon, Father, but our little girl always did have some kind of a temper."

"I told you we shouldn't redo her room right away!" squawked Betty. "But no-oo! You had to have your den, your personal space. Couldn't wait for your I-love-me room, could you? Not even a decent time to mourn your daughter."

Tom had no time to reply, because Arlene chose that moment to body-slam herself into the front picture window. Blinds and glass rained down. Father K and the Schultzes scattered out of the way.

And then suddenly the rampage was over. As if someone had hit an unseen OFF switch, Arlene sat down in the midst of the wrecked sofa. She picked up one of the TIME-LIFE volumes and set it open on her lap. The book was upside-down, but she looked to be settled in for the afternoon. The only thing missing from the tableau was a cat curled up at her feet.

"Huh-huh-huh," Tom said, a sound so ragged that it took the other two a moment to recognize his laughter. "She needs a cat, a stuffed cat, our Arlene, huh-huh!"

"What's to laugh about, Tom Schultz?" snarled Betty. "It's still five-six weeks until Halloween."

Tom was still tittering on the verge of control. "Dunno if we can take it. If the house can take it."

Father K could not make himself believe that they had accepted this Demonic Manifestation as their dead daughter Arlene. But it appeared the…thing…was going to stay. So, they had to make peace with it.

Time for another approach. After all, he rationalized, when Our Lord returned from the dead, at Easter, He spent some time on earth before he ascended to Heaven. And tradition, if not Scripture, said the He stayed with his mother, although here the tradition (or at least Father K's grasp of tradition) became vague. "These can be difficult times in a family's life…The entire family must readjust a bit, when adult children come back, move in with parents."

"What did you say, Father?" Betty seemed startled. Tom shook himself.

Father Kowalski looked from one parent to the other. "You may need to—"

Betty shook her head. "We'll be all right, Father. You mean well, I know. Arlene…she's always been…well, a handful. We knew that all along."

"They don't hurt the living, Father," said Tom. "Not intentionally. If they pull down a house, you'd best be out of it first!" He made a noise between a laugh and a bark. "Ah, well," he slung an arm around his wife's shoulders, "I guess this is why Tatesvillers need homeowners insurance, eh, old girl?"

Tom's two-way radio squawked. "Break for Officer Tom!"

"Volunteers," he sighed. He yanked the radio off his belt and thumbed the talk button. "Schultz. Go ahead."

"What's the SitRep at your twenty, Officer Tom?"

Tom rolled his eyes. "Look, I've got a...personal situation here. I'm...uh...ten-seven until further notice."

"You need some backup there, buddy?"

"Nah...I will need to get hold of Ed the insurance guy, though. Schultz out."

"No, wait! Roll Patrol reports some ah...soil action. At you know...those coordinates."

"Whuh-uh—uh, ten nine?"

"Soil action, ten-four, Sir."

"Ten-four. Schultz out." Tom re-holstered his radio. He looked at Betty and nodded. "That's him, right enough."

"Him who?" asked Father K.

"Well, Monsignor, of course," said Betty.

"What? Monsignor Woods? He's dead!" spluttered Father K. "You don't think—you're not saying—"

"Now, I know what you're thinking," Tom said.

"You do?" Father K squeaked. He hated it when his voice squeaked.

"You're thinking that they have to eat meat," nodded Tom. "Living flesh."

"I am?" Father K blanched. "Who does?"

"Why, Revivers. Like our Arlene," said Tom. "It's such a kinder word than 'zombie'—Reviver. Don't you think?"

"*Zombie?*"

"Zombies, Revivers," Tom shrugged. "Wouldn't matter to our Arlene. She was always a vegetarian. Don't know about the Monsignor."

This time Father K could not keep the shock off his face.

"Tom's just yanking your chain, Father," Betty said. "Tatesville Revivers don't eat anything at all. Tom, I don't think Father knows. We should tell him."

"Tell me what?"

Betty waved them all out onto the front stoop. Arlene had left no chair unbroken, and nobody wanted to sit next to her on the sofa.

Tom stepped over to the police cruiser and turned off the motor and flashing lights. "Tatesville is an old town," he said. "There's...things we don't tell to just everybody."

"I'm sure every community has its secrets," Father K offered blandly.

Tom told him the secret of Tatesville.

Father K turned pasty-white and sat down heavily on the stoop.

"It's not a Catholic thing," said Betty, "not that we'd know much about that, of course. Revivers aren't a Christian thing at all, just Tatesville. We just thought you would've already heard," she patted Father K's arm, "because of Monsignor."

Father K felt something very nasty growing in the pit of his stomach. "Monsignor...Woods?"

"Well, he was so old-fashioned," Tom nodded. "No offense, but you're more...up-to-date, I guess, about Catholic things."

The priest did his noncommittal nod, adding a wan smile.

"Just stay out of his way, if he does come back," Betty confided. "After all, he might not make it back all the way. He wasn't very strong, there, at the end."

"On toward the end of October," Tom offered, "or whenever he's ...y'know...finished, just call the Rescue Squad. We'll round up all the parts and put 'em back in the ground, slick as that. You'll see."

But Father Kowalski did not even begin to see, until a full day and a half later. He was sitting quietly in the study, reading an old Andrew Greeley novel.

At first he ignored the scratching noises, because he knew a family of raccoons lived behind the trashcans. But the scratching continued until Father K simply had to get up to check if it really was raccoons. Would it be Monsignor Woods this time? Feeble old Monsignor, still unresigned to the Church's reforms of nearly forty years ago, scrabbling with ravaged Reviver hands at the door of his former study.

And if it was just raccoons this time, what about the next? And the next scratching noise after that?

Father Francis X. Kowalski had never before so devoutly looked forward to the Feast of All Saints...it comes the morning after Halloween night.

Children of Stone
Tina L. Jens

My parents kept me from children who were rough
Who threw words like stones and who wore torn clothes
—Stephen Spender

ANNA LOUISA AND KENNETH RAN out of the house, letting the back door slam. Barreling at top speed, they under-ducked their swings. They dodged around the first row of tombstones that sat just a few yards beyond their swing set and headed up the hill.

They were arguing about the new statue as they jogged along the border of the winding road that led into the heart of the cemetery. They stopped. Not two yards in front of them, sat a girl perched atop a tombstone, singing and swinging her legs in time to the music. She was about Kenneth's age, but Anna Louisa had never seen her before.

Anna Louisa frowned as she noticed the girl was sitting on Elizabeth Fromlich's tombstone. Born 1882—Died 1894. Anna knew it well; this grave belonged to Mr. Fromlich's great-aunt. How rude! Anna thought, she's scuffing the stone with her heels!

Anna Louisa crossed her arms deliberately and studied the girl. She was dressed funny. In a beige wool skirt, much longer than any Anna Louisa wore, and a long blousey top that came almost down to her knees. She looked like she had walked out of Grammy's scrapbook. But the girl was too busy staring at Kenneth to take any notice of her, Anna thought crossly. Then she spied the girl's black, high-top, buttonhook shoes. You couldn't buy those in any of the stores around here.

The girl still hadn't taken any notice of her. Anna stepped in front of Kenneth. "Who are you?" Anna Louisa demanded.

"Who are you?" the strange girl said coyly in a thick Swedish accent. She spoke to Kenneth, but Anna answered her.

"I'm Anna Louisa, and this is Kenneth."

"Hello, Kennet," the girl said, accenting the *t* like Mother did. She held out her hand to him and bobbed her head.

Anna bristled as Kenneth stepped out from behind her to grin stupidly at the girl. Kenneth never talked to girls, so Anna Louisa went on. "Father owns this cemetery."

"Jonathan Wunders is your father?" the girl asked. Still she spoke only to Kenneth.

Anna Louisa stepped in front of Kenneth again before correcting the girl. "That was Grandfather. He owned it first."

The girl was still kicking her heels against the stone. The "Beloved" was almost covered up by her black heel marks.

"I don't think it's very nice of you to sit on that little girl's stone," Anna told her. "And you still haven't told us your name."

The girl giggled and hopped off the tombstone. "You should call me Lizzie, and I don't think she minds." She dropped a mock curtsy to Kenneth, who shyly took her outstretched hand.

Anna Louisa stared as they waltzed up the path, swinging their arms wide. She paused to look at the marker again, then, not wanting to leave her brother alone, she ran after them.

"Let's go meet the new girl," Lizzie called back.

"We were going to see the new statue," Anna said.

They rounded the long mausoleum that held the remains of those who were cremated. Lizzie led as they threaded their way through the tombstones. Anna didn't like it; it was *their* cemetery.

At last they came to the brick walkway that led to the garden of statues. The garden held only the graves of children. Most families chose to erect a statue rather than a traditional tombstone. Anna Louisa looked about the brick-paved circular garden. Most of the statues were children, but there were some angels and an odd assortment of gargoyles, all molded or cut to the finest detail in bronze and stone.

Anna Louisa didn't like the gargoyles and angels much—they weren't doing anything. The angels stood stiffly, arms at their sides or held out in an awkward reach. The gargoyles hunched down, squatting on their pedestals. But the children were alive! It was like Mr. Fromlich had poured the mold over a bunch of kids at play. Anna liked to come to the inner circle and pretend she was playing with them. There was Nancy Morgan, Born 1891—Died 1902. Next to her was Keith Jensen 1920—1929. And across the way, Beret Andersen, 1960—1966.

Lizzie stopped in front of the newest statue and made a wide, sweeping bow. "Allow me to introduce Katie. She is most pleased to make your acquaintance." Lizzie's eyes danced, daring them to contradict her.

Anna Louisa decided she didn't like the girl's singsong voice, she didn't really like this girl at all. "That's not her name." Anna read the plaque aloud, "Ruth Ester Swanson. Beloved daughter, 1981—1988."

Kenneth stood quietly examining the statue, then reached to stroke the face of the stone girl. "Not Ruth. Katie."

Lizzie took Kenneth's hand and turned him away from Anna. Kenneth didn't see it, but Anna saw the girl's mean smile.

* * *

A chill ran down Anna's back as she remembered that day. She wished they had never gone to the garden with Lizzie to meet the Katie-statue. But she wished even more they had never met Lizzie at all. She searched through her bed covers for Emily, her best friend—next to Kenneth. Emily had been a gift from Mr. Fromlich on her eighth birthday. The china doll had once belonged to Mr. Fromlich's great-aunt, Elizabeth.

At last, Anna found the doll. Hugging the prize tightly to her chest, she flounced back against her pillows. She hated being confined to bed. Dumb old knee! It wasn't ever going to heal!

Anna Louisa had moped all morning. All she could do was watch the snow fall. But this afternoon had been worse. She had had a nightmare, and she couldn't get it out of her head. It had been all misty, and she was floating in the statue-garden, petting and crooning to the statues. She was carrying her doll, Emily. Somewhere behind her, Anna heard a rusty-iron *squeak*. She whirled around. Tears were flowing from Katie's bronze eyes. Anna touched the tears. They felt like baby oil. She heard another *squeak* and twisted around to see the little cherub boy's head turn. She backed up against Katie.

Too late, she realized Katie was alive! Her bronze arms wrapped around Anna and snatched Emily away. Then the other statues moved, the pedestals sliding toward her. Hundreds of bronze arms, grabbing at her. Bronze fingers clutching at her mouth. The statues were trying to pull her apart...

Anna Louisa had woken up screaming. Mother had come, but she couldn't calm Anna down. When Mother left the room to get a cold washcloth, Anna heard the girls giggling again. And that awful singing.

Kenneth falls down.
Kenneth, Kenneth, Kenneth falls down.
Kenneth falls down.

The singing wasn't part of her dream, Anna was sure. They were singing Kenneth's name, were they going to hurt him, too?

...It was still early in October; the trees in the cemetery had turned to bright red, but enough had dropped their leaves that the children could make loud scrunchy sounds as they marched between the tombstones.

"Where do you live?" Kenneth asked Lizzie.

"It's a secret."

"But we can call you sometime."

Lizzie shook her head no as she leaned against a tombstone and kicked at the leaves.

Kenneth looked for Lizzie every day after studies, Anna trailing behind him. Sometimes they would come upon her sitting on Elizabeth Fromlich's tombstone, or find her talking to the statues in the garden. But many days she was nowhere to be found. Anna Louisa didn't mind. She didn't understand why Kenneth was so interested in the girl. They had never needed other playmates before. When they did find Lizzie, they only played the games *she* wanted to play. Anna liked to play on the swing set, but the older girl refused to go so close to the house. Instead, they would play follow the leader, winding around the tombstones, or leapfrog, jumping over the markers.

Today, Lizzie had let Kenneth pick the game; American legion; they would march up to the grave, blow "Taps" on a pretend bugle, then shoot a make-believe twenty-one-gun salute, like the soldiers had done over one of the graves last year.

They were hunting under the oak trees, looking for sticks suitable for rifles. Anna Louisa had wandered farther up the hill, where the graves and trees were older, and she could find a better stick. It was darker up here and colder. The old Larsen mausoleum, where they sometimes played house, gave off a grim air, but Anna was used to it.

She sang to herself as she searched for her make-believe weapon. "Ring around the rosy. Pocket full of posy—"

Anna, Anna, Anna, falls down.
Anna falls down.

Anna Louisa whirled in a circle, looking for the hollow, childish voices that echoed off the marble stones. Kenneth and Lizzie were far away and took no notice.

She thought she heard giggling—and footsteps running away.

Anna, Anna, Anna, falls down.

Anna falls down.

"Come out!"

More giggles, or just the wind kicking up the leaves? She stood stock-still, hands clenched in fists at her side. She looked once more all about her. Then she ran.

Kenneth and Lizzie were still halfheartedly beating the bushes for their make-believe props. "What's wrong, Anna? Did you find a stick?"

Lizzie just giggled.

"I—I couldn't find one." She didn't want to tell Kenneth about the voices in front of Lizzie. It could wait til they went in to supper.

"I don't want to play legion, anyway," Lizzie said, carelessly. "I know! Let's play freeze-tag."

"I don't want to play tag. I want to go home!"

"Come on, Anna. Let's play something! Please?"

Anna wasn't in the mood. "Let's go in."

"No, Anna." Kenneth shook his head stubbornly.

"Let's play by the statues," Lizzie said.

Anna Louisa dragged her feet, lagging behind. She didn't like how Lizzie was always giving orders. She didn't want to play in the statue garden. She wanted to go home.

"Who's going to be It?" Lizzie asked, leaning up against the Katie statue in that disrespectful way of hers.

"Not me!" Kenneth yelped.

"I don't want to be It," Anna insisted.

"I'll count," Lizzie said, bending down on one knee.

Of course Lizzie would count. She didn't do it fair. But Anna stuck her foot in the circle, anyway.

"Eenie, meenie, miney, moe, catch a girl by the toe, when she hollers don't let go, this means—that—you—are—It." Lizzie was pointing at Anna's foot, just as Anna had known she would be.

Lizzie smirked. "Come on, Kenneth, this baby can't catch us."

Lizzie and Kenneth darted off, dodging Anna's outstretched hands. They laughed so hard at the funny poses they struck that it only took Anna three turns to tag Kenneth. It took him four to tag her back. She and

Kenneth would always slip, or have to sneeze, just as the other one yelled, "Freeze!" And they couldn't help giggling if It came and stood nose-to-nose while they were 'frozen' and blew in their face.

But try as they might, they couldn't catch Lizzie. No matter how fast they were running or sliding about, she could stop instantly—always in the same pose, her arms reaching out, hands turned ever so slightly inward, and her head tilted as if listening. She didn't pant or twitch a muscle. Not even her eyes moved. She could stand that way for minutes at a time. It wasn't really fair, you were supposed to strike a different pose each time.

Anna tried to stand as still as Lizzie, but finally, she couldn't help turning her head just a little bit to watch the other girl. It was all right; Kenneth didn't catch her.

He was intent on making Lizzie move this time. He walked up to the taller girl and stared at her with a lopsided grin, trying to make her laugh, as he had done with Anna. Lizzie didn't move. He circled her, chugging faster and faster around her, and roared like a motor. Lizzie didn't make a sound. He clasped his hands behind his back and marched away, then whirled around and shouted, "Gotcha!" Lizzie didn't seem to see.

"She looks like one of the *real* statues, Kenneth!"

Anna flinched as Kenneth gave her a dirty look.

Then a horrible look crept across his face as he realized she was right. He turned back to study the still-motionless Lizzie. Kenneth reached out to touch Lizzie's cheek. He jerked his hand back like he'd been burned. He backed away.

"What is it?" Anna whispered.

"She's cold!"

Anna felt ridiculous when she realized she still held her pose. She dropped her arms, then tiptoed over to Kenneth. She touched Lizzie's face, stared at her hand, then turned to stroke the Katie-statue's cheek. They felt the same.

Anna Louisa and Kenneth stared at each other for a long time.

"Say it, Kenneth."

He called out, "Unfreeze!"

Lizzie blinked and moved.

Anna Louisa rubbed her fingertips together; they still felt cold and tingly.

Kenneth said quietly, "I don't want to play anymore." He backed away from Lizzie, keeping his distance.

But Lizzie wasn't ready to quit. "Oh, don't be a party pooper, I'll be It now." The words were playful, but her voice sounded menacing.

"We don't want to play anymore."

Lizzie turned on Anna Louisa, scowling. "I *said* I'd be It. It's my turn! You can't quit until I've had my turn!"

"That's only fair, Anna," Kenneth said out loud. Behind Lizzie's back he whispered, "Just once, then we'll go in."

Anna didn't care about being fair right now, but she consented to her brother's secret message.

Kenneth had walked off to get a good starting position. Lizzie crept up to Anna and hissed in her face, "*Once* is all I need."

Anna backed away.

Lizzie screeched, "Go!"

Anna and Kenneth took off running, dodging behind the statues, one step ahead of Lizzie. It wasn't a game to Anna Louisa anymore; she knew she mustn't let the older girl catch her. She darted behind the statue that Lizzie had nicknamed Michael. But she hadn't seen that Lizzie was right behind her.

"Freeze!"

Anna Louisa struck a pose like the ballerina on her music box, but her fingers were still moving when Lizzie's hand closed around her knee. Anna gasped. An icy chill passed through her wool skirt and sunk into the bone. She tumbled to the ground.

Kenneth was at her side. Anna saw her brother's lips move, but his voice sounded like it was far, far away. She heard laughter. She thought she saw the lips of the Katie-statue move. Then there was only darkness.

* * *

Anna never told Mother about the dream, or the voices, just like she didn't tell Mother what happened in the statue garden. Mother wouldn't believe her, and Kenneth kept insisting, "It's not Lizzie's fault!" But Anna Louisa knew it was.

It was almost time for Kenneth to come home. Maybe they'd throw bread crumbs out her window and watch the birds hop in the snow. Anna heard the kids shouting in a snowball fight out on the street.

Finally, Anna spied Kenneth trudging up the drive. But rather than come inside to sit with her as he usually did, he just waved, then ran into the cemetery.

"Kenneth! Come back!" Anna yelled, but he couldn't hear her through the window. She knew he was going to look for Lizzie.

She stumbled out of bed and grabbed at her crutches, twisting her knee as she came around the corner. She tried to ignore the pain as she pulled on her boots and slipped her coat over her flannel nightgown. At the last minute, she grabbed Emily and shoved her into a coat pocket.

She'd never catch Kenneth in time.

Once outside, she hurried toward the statue garden as fast as she could; her crutches kept slipping on the ice and snow as she hobbled along.

She could see Kenneth ahead, just reaching the stone walk. Lizzie was waiting.

Lizzie took Kenneth's arm, pulled his glove off, and stroked his hand.

Anna yelled, "Kenneth! Don't let her touch you!"

Lizzie's voice carried back over the snow. "You haven't been out to play with me in a long time...I've made new friends, Kennet—meet Katie."

A pale-looking girl crept out from behind a tombstone. It was the statue Lizzie had introduced them to.

"Meet Michael."

As Anna struggled closer, she saw something crawl out from behind another tombstone—the cherub that stood on Tom Andrews's grave. Lizzie had nicknamed him Michael. Michael didn't leave a trail behind him as he walked through the snow.

Lizzie continued her introductions, "Meet Marissa—and Kim—Miguel—Dana—Josh—"

Each child looked like one of the statues.

And Kenneth was the only one in the group whose breath left a cloud in the air.

Anna Louisa wanted to help him, but she was stuck. She had fallen in the snow, and one of her crutches had slid, like a toboggan, to the bottom of the hill.

Anna swiped her sleeve across her face to clear away the snow and tears, then crawled, using her elbows and her one good knee.

Finally, she collapsed behind a tombstone not ten feet away from her brother. As she watched, the gang of statue-children began to circle him, walking slowly round and round.

"Kenneth! Get out of there!" Anna whispered hoarsely. But Kenneth stood frozen.

The statues were walking faster and faster. They joined hands and began to chant, each child beginning the rhyme a few beats later.

Ring around the rosy.
Pocket full of posy
Ashes, Ashes

The statues broke into a run. Kenneth began turning, too, twisting in the opposite direction with his arms flung out like the spokes on a revolving Maypole.

Kenneth falls down.
Kenneth, Kenneth, Kenneth falls down.
Kenneth falls down.

As the statue-children shouted Kenneth's name, they darted in, poking him, taunting him. Each time they touched him, Kenneth would cry out, his body jerking in pain.

Lizzie sat atop one of the tombstones, kicking her heels and laughing.

Anna knew that each spot they touched would freeze, never to move again.

Anna Louisa sputtered hysterically and scuttled out from behind the tombstone. "Stop it, Lizzie!"

Kenneth stumbled about the circle, trying to stay on his feet as his body slowly froze up. Anna could see the muscles twitching wildly in his legs and face—the few muscles the statue-children hadn't touched yet. A wheezy lisp came from Kenneth's throat as he tried to breathe. Still the statue-children ran circles around him, taunting him, jabbing him, slowly turning his body—his hands, his stomach, his ribs—to stone.

Anna Louisa could feel Kenneth's pain as he took one deep gasp and tried to scream. Before any sound came out, Lizzie reached out and touched his throat. His words died there.

Only Kenneth's eyes moved now, darting back and forth. The children began to widen their circle; the chanting died down to a whisper.

"It's big sister!"

Anna shrieked and rolled over, her bad leg twisting beneath her. Lizzie kicked a patch of snow in Anna's face. She reached down and plucked Emily out of Anna's pocket.

"Give her back!" Anna shouted, grabbing for the doll.

Lizzie stood straddling Anna, fussing with the doll's clothes. Then she leaned down and sneered, "She's mine! She's always been mine. And her name is *not* Emily!"

Anna batted at Lizzie's legs. "She's mine! Mr. Fromlich gave her to me!"

Lizzie skipped back and dangled the doll just out of reach of Anna's flailing hands. She hissed, "Want to trade my doll for your brother?"

"Give me Emily!" Anna screeched.

Lizzie laughed and tossed the doll into the snow. Anna Louisa crawled to rescue Emily. She barely noticed Lizzie turn on her heel and head toward Kenneth.

Anna groaned as she inched nearer her doll; finally, she could just reach the delicate little arm. Anna Louisa gently brushed Emily off and tucked her safely inside her coat.

Then she looked up to see what was happening to Kenneth.

Lizzie stood in front of him, their noses almost touching. A grin crept over Lizzie's face. "Hey, whoever heard of a statue that could see?"

She blew a puff of air that closed Kenneth's eyes for good.

The truck from Fromlich's Figurines had arrived with a new statue. It was Mr. Fromlich, himself, driving today. But Anna Louisa didn't care. Kenneth hadn't come home last night, and she couldn't tell Mother and Father why. She heard Father and Mr. Fromlich talking outside.

"From!" Father exclaimed. "You're early. I did not expect this for two weeks more."

"Yah! I surprise myself, too." Mr. Fromlich said. "I didna expect this one to be so easy."

Finally, curiosity got the best of Anna; she limped outside to stand on the porch, rubbing her arms to keep warm. Mr. Fromlich sat in the truck cab, his window rolled half-way down.

"Still no news about your son? Tch, tch. Perhaps you find him today."

Anna shivered as she watched Father sign the papers for the newest statue, then walk up the drive to open the gate.

"Anna Louisa, you'll catch a cold death without a coat." Mr. Fromlich smiled at her. The ice crystals on the glass distorted his lips. He was singing to himself as he shifted the truck into gear and pulled away.

Anna turned to go inside, then stopped, as the words to his song drifted back to her.

Ring around the rosy.
Pocket full of posy.
Ashes, ashes—

The Cemetery Plant
John Peel

"MOTHER, ARE YOU STILL CARRYING on that ridiculous feud with Cordelia Oshansky?"

Julia Gordon glanced up sharply from the carpet where she was playing with her grandson and his Hispanic playmate. Francis gave a whimper at the loss of her attention, but then set about trying to steal one of the toy cars from Juan. Julia's only son, Richard, was looking down at her with an odd, amused expression on his face.

A *feud*?

Julia would never call it a feud. It hurt too much for that. She could still bitterly recall the smug look of victory on Cordelia's face as her roses took first place in the Maine Garden Club finals.

And Julia's took second place.

For the fourteenth year in a row.

No, it was no feud.

It was war....

Richard had inherited Julia's passion for flowers and turned it into a stunningly successful career. At the age of thirty-two, he was in charge of his pharmaceutical company's research branch here in Central America, charged with discovering potential new cures in the botanicals from the various jungle plants.

"It's not a feud," she protested.

"You brought me up to always be truthful—can't you follow your own advice?"

Richard was very dear to her, but the half-smile on his face now annoyed his mother. "I'm certain she cheats with her roses. I wish I could expose her, destroy her reputation with the club."

"I can do better than that for you." Richard grinned fully now.

"Leave Francis here with Juan and his mother and come along with me."

Julia followed her son from the residential part of the house to the research side. Richard's company had invested a great deal of money into this venture to pry potential cures from the native plants, and her son was working brilliantly to that aim. Here in the laboratories, he and his team were taking apart many of the local plants to extract the often complex compounds within and examine their potential medicinal uses. Richard led her into one small room and gestured dramatically at the flower in a small pot on the table.

The first sight took her breath away.

It was *black*. The petals were long and thin, opening at the bell to reveal a long, yellow-tipped stamen. The flower was only an inch and a half long.

"The only truly black flower in all of nature. It's unique and quite a puzzle."

Julia stared into the jet depths. "How so?"

"Nobody knows how it's pollinated. Insects can't see black as a color—red looks black to them, and red is a whole lot easier a color for a plant to produce. Why would evolution go to all the effort of growing a black flower unless there was something to be gained by it?" He shrugged. "Just about the only creatures it attracts are humans—and *we* certainly don't pollinate it."

"It's the most beautiful flower I have ever seen." Julia didn't want to take her eyes away from it.

He waved at the pot. "It's yours."

"You mean that?"

"Be careful with it, and don't be surprised if you hear some stories about the plant from the locals. Its scientific name is *Lisianthius nigrescens*, but they call it *la flor de muerte*, 'flower of death.' They plant it near the graves of the recently deceased. They're a rather superstitious lot."

"Thank you, Richard—I shall treasure this and tend it carefully." She picked it up gently and carried it back to her room.

Maria, the maid her son had assigned her, was dusting when Julia entered, bearing her treasure. She placed the *Lisianthius* on the end table below the window.

The maid paled and crossed herself. "*Madre de Dios!*" she exclaimed. "Señora Gordon, take that thing away!"

Julia frowned. "It's beautiful." She could annihilate Cordelia at the next show! Everyone would then have to admit that Julia Gordon was the true genius of the Garden Club. Seeing that smug look wiped from Cordelia's face would be worth almost anything....

"Sometimes beauty hides the deadliest sins," the maid replied. "It is evil. It is dangerous, Señora."

Julia laughed. "Come now, child—that's simply superstition."

"Return it to the cemetery, where it belongs."

"I shall do no such thing."

"Then promise me you will move it to another room when you sleep, at least." Maria gripped Julia's arm. "Please, Señora—I would not ask this if it were not important!"

Julia was starting to get annoyed with the maid. "I promise I will not sleep in the same room with this plant. Now, are you happy?"

"Think me a simple peasant if you will—I do not care. But *listen* to me, and keep your word."

As the day wore on, Julia found that she couldn't ignore the warning. She had moved the *Lisianthius* into the empty room next to hers to placate Maria, but she returned time and again, entranced by the black flower. She couldn't resist it, nor could she forget the intensity of Maria's fear.

The natives might know something her son didn't. He believed so firmly in his science that he sometimes dismissed others who were less educated than he. It was a touch of arrogance his late father had also possessed. It was her son's one flaw.

Curiosity and apprehension warred against her son's science, and by the time night had fallen, Julia knew she had to do some research of her own. She had to *know*.

On her way back to her room after dinner, she met Paco in the hallway. Paco was a good-natured youth, but with a strong weakness for the local tequila. He staggered past her, heading for his small room, an almost-empty bottle clutched in his feverish hand. He hadn't even seen her.

She could test the *Lisianthius* on Paco.... He would be stretched out in his room in a few moments, and she could bring the plant...Maria said it was only dangerous if you slept in its presence. *She* would watch and stay awake. If anything looked like it would happen, all she needed to do was to pick up the plant and remove it from the room. There would be no *real* danger to the young man.

Her desperate need to know fought her conscience, but it was an extremely one-sided battle. Nothing could possibly go badly wrong—and, besides, Maria's fears were probably just a folk legend with no basis in the truth.

But she had to know...had to know *everything* about her wonderful new specimen.

She hurried off and collected the plant and then retraced her steps to Paco's room. She found she was feeling absurdly guilty, but she knew that was foolish. What was the worst that might happen? Perhaps the flower produced some lethal gas that would slay a sleeping person—but she would be awake, and at the first sign of trouble, she could act. This would be a perfectly safe experiment. Perfectly safe.

Paco had indeed fallen face-down on his bed, snoring softly. The now-empty tequila bottle lay on the floor beside the bed. The servant hadn't bothered (or, more likely, been able) to get undressed, which was a good thing. She wouldn't have felt comfortable in a room with a naked youth. She set the *Lisianthius* down beside the bed and then settled into the small chair close by and prepared to wait.

She sat there, watching by the thin light that shone in the room's one window, for less than an hour. Every five minutes, punctually, she leaned over Paco and checked that he was breathing regularly and that his pulse was still strong. And each time there was no change.

She was starting to feel stupid for even thinking that there was any substance to Maria's ridiculous fears.

Then Paco's breathing pattern altered. He'd been snoring gently, but suddenly the sounds broke and then stopped. He gave a faint choking sound. Julia leaned forward, eager, excited. Was something happening? She glanced at the black plant, almost invisible in the faint light of the room. It had shown no evidence of doing anything. She sniffed, but detected no odor. She herself felt perfectly fine.

But Paco gave a gasp, and even in the darkness, she could see that his body convulsed slightly. What was happening? She leaned forward, alarmed, and reached for the boy's throat. Placing two fingers over the jugular, Julia gave a start.

There was no pulse.

Julia jerked back in her chair, shocked and confused. The boy had been quite healthy—merely drunk. What had happened to him? She glanced at the *Lisianthius* on the dresser.

Why had the youth died? She felt a growing certainty that *somehow* the plant had done this to him. Well, the plant—and her. Despite her resolve, despite her best intentions, the boy had died. And she was to blame. She felt a growing guilt, but overriding that, she felt a burning curiosity. Since there was now nothing she could do for the boy—she had never learned CPR and doubted it would help even if she had—she managed to bury her feelings for the moment, all but her curiosity. She stared at the flower, wondering what it truly was.

She felt a sudden chill flowing across her skin. A vague movement from the bed had caught her eye. But Paco was definitely dead! What could possibly…

The body was as still as it had been, but *something* was happening. She stared at the dead boy, spellbound, unable to look away. A thin mist was forming over the youth. She peered closer. It seemed to be rising from the corpse. Some atmospheric condition, perhaps? The body was, after all, still warm. But—if it was something to do with the atmosphere, shouldn't mist be rising from her also?

The mist rose, but didn't thin. Instead, it seemed to coagulate. It should have been dissipating, but it wasn't—it was growing thicker and more distinct.

She shuddered as she realized it was taking form. The pale mists writhed and moved, shaping into…

Paco.

Or, rather, a copy of the boy. Julia was breathing shallowly, her eyes focused on what was happening. The mist was thin and the light indistinct, but the features were clearly that of the dead boy. The shape was unclothed, and its masculinity was without doubt.

A ghost, Julia realized. The boy's spirit had risen from the fallen body and was standing beside the bed.

She gave a faint whimper, her hands shaking. Did the thing know she had been responsible for his death? Was it after revenge? Or was this what happened naturally after death, and the spirit was simply departing this world? She barely breathed, watching the faint form. Perhaps, if it was here for revenge, she deserved such retribution.

It simply stood there, the dead eyes firmly fixed. But not on her. The ghost didn't seem able to see her—or, perhaps, it wasn't interested. It might have more important things on what was left of its mind. Julia couldn't move, could hardly think.

Then she realized that its eyes were fixed on the *Lisianthius*. Staring at the black plant, it seemed enthralled.

That was exactly the right word to describe it: enthralled. It was focused on the plant as if nothing else existed in the entire universe.

The ghost finally made a movement. It raised its right hand, wispy, transparent, and reached slowly for the plant. Paco's spirit was insubstantial. The hand reached *through* the wood of the small dresser as if there was nothing in its path. It cupped the flower, as if striving to hold it and failing. For the first time, some expression crossed the shadowy features of the ghost's face. Paco looked anguished, pained. The hand reached again, but could touch nothing.

Or, rather, very little. As the hand moved through the bell of the flower, Julia could see small dots of substance that appeared to cling to the misty form of the fingers. Curiosity overcame her fear and guilt, and she leaned forward again, peering closer. It was pollen! Pollen from the flower was somehow being carried by the almost-nothingness of the ghost's hand....

Pollen...light, almost insubstantial itself! The material that composed the ghost was so thin it could interact with virtually nothing—except the pollen....

Julia shivered again as she finally understood the truth. The *Lisianthius had*, as scientists suspected, a rare pollinator. But they had no idea just *how* rare.... The *Lisianthius* had evolved a symbiosis with humans. It used their spirits to carry its pollen. The spirits of the dead had little use for anything—except, perhaps, they could still feel the tug of beauty.

A thrill of discovery coursed through her, driving out fear and shock. She knew what none other did—that the *Lisianthius* bred by killing people, and then capturing their ghosts to act as unwitting pollinators....

Fascinating!

Wonderful!

And...useful...

Julia had been raised in a Catholic household and had attended church until she had drifted away in her teenage years. She knew, almost unconsciously, the beliefs in temptation. That the Devil could plant within the souls of the unwary desires that would be very hard to ignore. Only through the grace of God could such temptations be fought, for human frailty made other battle impossible. And the Devil knew *precisely* what one's darkest, deepest desires were and played upon them.

It *had* to be true, or else how could she explain the next thought that came into her mind? She was not a bad person, not one who held grudges, not one who envied other people. Whatever her feelings about Cordelia Oshansky, surely she didn't *really* hate her.

Then *why* was she thinking that she could use the *Lisianthius* to eliminate her rival—simply, silently, undetectably? She wasn't the sort of person to wish evil onto anyone.

Except, perhaps, Cordelia....

No! She tried to shake the temptation from her mind. But it was rooted now, and growing.

A small gift of a delightful plant, one that Cordelia would find it impossible to refuse.... A single night, and then...

She would be unrivaled in the Garden Club. She, alone, would be the queen bee. No more Cordelia and her smugness at every competition. No more of whatever cheating she performed to win.

No more second places—ever!

No more Cordelia: the thought was becoming irresistible. No matter what the source of the thought, the idea was growing stronger.

She also knew that she lacked the will and the strength to fight this temptation. The God she no longer believed in couldn't save her from her own nature.

In that awful instant, Julia peered into her own soul, aided by the beauty of the *Lisianthius*—and she saw the same darkness within as the petals of the plant possessed.

She clutched the potted plant to herself and stared down at the dead youth. Guilt still stabbed at her soul, but she could control it with the new strength of purpose she had. "I am sorry," she murmured to the boy. "Truly, I am sorry. I did not mean this to happen. I did not know it would. But I cannot turn back time, and I cannot give you your life back. I take what small comfort I can from knowing that the tequila would have killed you eventually. And I shall bear the guilt as long as I live." With a final nod, she fled the young man's room, afraid to look back.

In the morning, his death would be assumed to be an accident. Nobody would ever suspect that she had been involved. She was safe from retribution.

She returned the *Lisianthius* to the spare bedroom next to hers and then hurried into her own room. As she prepared herself for bed, she couldn't stop herself from reflecting on what she was planning to do.

She knew that her plans for Cordelia were evil. There was simply no other word for it. Evil. And she was shocked at herself. She had always believed that she was a good person. She donated to charities, she had raised her son well, and she had sympathy for those less fortunate than herself. She wasn't an alcoholic, didn't do drugs, didn't sleep around.

But to discover the hatred within her soul that would allow her to contemplate—no, *plan*—murder...that shocked her. She had always disliked Cordelia, but it was a long fall from *dislike* to murder. And yet, here she was, aiming to kill her rival.

And, worse, she didn't feel bad about it. She felt *good*. This world would be better off without Cordelia Oshansky in it. *Her* world would be better without that bitch.

Julia took her sleeping tablets and changed into her nightgown before slipping between the comforting covers of her bed. Killing Cordelia would be something she would enjoy—in anticipation, and in the act.

Never again would she be second.

Richard Gordon moved through the silent house, aching a little. It had been a long day, but a good one. It was always so pleasant when his mother came to visit, and it had been a joy watching her playing with her grandson. And then, when he had sprung his surprise on her, he had really loved seeing the enraptured expression on her face. He had known she'd love that odd flower. It had been a great idea to give it to her.

He passed the empty room next to his mother's and saw that the door was ajar. As he moved to close it, he saw the *Lisianthius* plant on the table by the window He frowned. How had it come to be there? He was certain his mother wouldn't let it out of her sight.

Then he realized what must have happened. Maria, with her ridiculous belief in the dark magical powers of the plant, must have taken in from his mother's room and moved it here. He shook his head in disgust. Superstitious claptrap! His mother would be annoyed and worried in the morning if she awoke to find her beloved plant missing.

Richard picked it up and moved quietly to his mother's room. He rapped softly on the door, but there was no reply. Opening the door, he saw that his mother was in bed, asleep. Well, the poor darling needed her rest. Without making any noise, he slipped into the room and placed the *Lisianthius* on the bedside table. When Julia awoke in the morning, the first thing she would see would be this enthralling plant.

Smiling, Richard left the room and shut the door behind him.

It Ain't Much to Brag About But It's All Mine
Bill Breedlove

MY MOM WAS SCREAMING AGAIN, somewhere in the vast house, or maybe outside on the verandah (it's much too large to dare call it a "porch"). I couldn't make out the exact words, but I knew it went something like: "Audrey, for Christ's sake, stop running in and out so much!" or, "Audrey, for the love of the Holy Christ, stop making so much noise!" or, perhaps the all-time favorite, a drawn out "Auuudddddrrrrreeeee!"

In my defense, I would be neither running in nor out and not even making any noise. But I know, even at my tender age of twelve, that when Mother is sitting on the verandah at ten-thirty in the morning drinking a gin and tonic out of a pitcher, any behavior I might exhibit is bound to get me into some kind of trouble.

Normally, I can manage to stay out of Mom's and Charles's hair. He usually fiddles on his laptop computer, looking at stock market numbers until the afternoon, when he eventually joins my mother for pitcher-emptying duty on the verandah. This week, though, I am caught in a weird kind of limbo—all of the summer people have pretty much left the island, so most of the places I used to go hang out at are closed, but school hasn't quite started yet either, so I am pretty much without anything to do. And, just ask my mother, *that* is *always* the recipe for disaster.

Next week, when I start taking the ferry back to the mainland to school every day, I don't know who'll be happier.

So far today, I've tried reading my latest issue of *Smithsonian* magazine, the one the island doctor started saving for me after I got caught looking at the drowned body of little Tommy Beringer, who had the bad luck to fall overboard off his family's Chris-Craft on Memorial Day weekend, and then had the colossal bad luck to try to swim up to the back of the boat where the dual propellers are. As a service to the Beringer family, the doctor listed cause of death officially as "drowning," but from what I was able to see, it looked like it sure would be hard to hold any water inside your body with all those extra openings. When the doctor flicked on the light in his makeshift morgue, and caught me with my flashlight peeking under the sheet (how was I supposed to know about silent alarms and motion detectors? I'm only twelve!), he was alarmed at first, but then when I confessed my curiosity about medicine (true), death (especially true), and science in general (whoops, false), he took me into his office, and we had a long talk about science, appropriate methods of gathering data, and the repercussions of breaking and entering. I think he was just relieved I wasn't after the Valium and Tranxene stashed there. Although he declined to give me a job helping clean up at the clinic, the doctor did promise to pass along books and magazines which might satisfy my "abundant curiosity."

I guess it's that curiosity which got me banned for life from the Beaver Island Public Library. Or maybe it was my smuggling in scissors and cutting passages, which I knew to be false, out of the already-thin selection of books available there. I'm not allowed in the butcher shop due to the time I went behind the counter and tried to trim pork chops on my own (I was only ten, then). The hardware store should be self-explanatory, as should the construction site where they are developing new "water view condos."

In short, I am a little girl pariah, trapped on an island with small-minded people.... Actually, most of that last sentence I stole from some book I read, but it's close to right, so why not?

After I finished *Smithsonian*, I kind of wandered around the house, trying to stay out of Maribel's—our housekeeper—way. (Does she hate me? What do you think?) Unfortunately, I happened to pass in front of the back parlor window, and my mother saw me briefly.

"For the sweet love of Christ, Audrey! Can't you stop running through the house like a herd of buffalo? Can't you go play somewhere?" She frowned into her glass and tinkled the ice impatiently. "Maribel, I am absolutely *parched* out here! Did you get lost on the way back from the kitchen with that pitcher?"

I grabbed my Windbreaker and headed out the side door. As I was leaving, Maribel bustled past me with a sloshing pitcher of clear liquid with some limes floating on top. She paused long enough to fix me with a sour look that I couldn't decide was for me on general principles, or for disapproval of my mother's lifestyle.

Since the town was pretty well dead, and most everywhere else I was banned from, I decided to go exploring in the vast woods behind our house. Living on a small island off the northernmost tip of Michigan, the woods are alive with colors in early September. I thought maybe I could find some pretty leaves for my scrapbook. According to the tree book I stole from the library, I was still short a Chinese Elm and a White Birch leaf; both trees which were supposed to be indigenous to the island, but neither of which I had ever seen.

The Chinese Elm was especially interesting, because island history had it that the original inhabitants of Beaver Island—the Cree Indian tribe—had been involved in a particularly-bitter war with pirates (yes, pirates) who came to the island to steal trees for the lucrative lumber trade on the Great Lakes. The story is that the Cree placed a curse on the trees, making them worthless. Well, the curse turned out to be Dutch Elm disease, which Chinese Elm trees are immune to, so the pirates supposedly planted acres of them, just to spite the Cree. Chinese Elm also have particularly aggressive roots, which tend to strangle other trees, so there was a short but nasty "war" until finally the Michigan National Guard chugged all the way up here in a new iron warship to sink all the pirate boats and relocate the Cree into Canada.

Of course, the island history doesn't exactly say that, since admitting to forcibly relocating Native Americans isn't politically correct anymore. That's why I was tearing the lying pages out of the book when I got caught by the librarian. Anyway, I was hoping to find a Chinese Elm leaf, which would at least lend some truth to the old pirate tale.

The woods are well kept near my family's house, but they soon turn tangled and difficult to navigate. Experience has taught me to follow the property line between our house and Mrs. Bissel's up to the base of Whiskey Hill, and then head due north.

It was a pleasantly chilly day, and in the deeper parts of the forest, the parts completely shaded over by leaves, where the sun never penetrates, I could even see my breath. It was enjoyable crunching through the leaves that had already fallen and turned brown. I was lost in thinking about the propeller marks on Tommy Beringer, when a voice startled me.

"Hey! What the hell are you up to now!"

I let out a little yelp of surprise, and then I saw it was our neighbor, Mrs. Bissel. If my mother had a sketchy lifestyle, Mrs. Bissel was an out-and-out juicer. She typically spent her days in a wrinkled housecoat, drinking what my parents said was ridiculously expensive pinot noir from sunup to sundown. Since she was living on her widow's pension, her only companion was a mangy housecat (unfortunately named Maurice) with a faggy pink collar. She carried Maurice everywhere with her, including her drunken ramblings across the island. Even though Mrs. Bissel hated me, she probably should've been grateful for my presence—since she certainly would've been the resident who was banned from the most island establishments, if not for me.

The reason she had a special hatred for me stemmed from an incident where she yelled at me for taking some rock samples from her rock garden when I was only ten. She yelled at me so ferociously that I started crying, and then she hooked her old claw around my wrist and dragged me to my house, where she accused me of defacing her property and stealing. My mother, also in the bag at that stage of the afternoon, gladly accepted her version of the events and also gladly took over punishment activities.

Needless to say, I never forgot that incident. So, I took it upon myself to begin collecting Mrs. Bissel's old pinot noir bottles. This task was especially daunting, since she would empty two or three each day. I stored them in the old, abandoned roundhouse until one day when she was having a sort of get-together for a bunch of her church buddies. The night before, I snuck out of the house and took the gardener's wheelbarrow. Considering I had been saving the bottles for almost eight months, I had to make a lot of trips. I placed them all in her front yard in a giant pyramid with a hand-painted sign that said, MAYBE YOU SHOULD RECYCLE THESE. Unfortunately, since there is only one store on the island that sells Day-Glo orange paint, I was discovered to be the culprit.

Ever since then, she has hated me more than an early frost at a pinot vineyard.

Now, here she was, startling me while I was minding my own business, just strolling through the woods. She came clomping up through the leaves, and I had time to notice that, held by her crossed arms in the folds of her housecoat, was none other than Maurice, the cat.

"What the hell are you doing on my property, you little hellcat?" she shrieked at me. "I could have you arrested for trespassing, you know! I should!"

"Sorry, Mrs. Bissel," I said when I had recovered from my fright. "I was just looking for some...recycling."

"*Ahhhh!*" she screeched and tried to grab for me, but her bony old hand slid off my Windbreaker, and I danced away. As if on cue, Maurice the cat hissed at me from his place clutched to her scrawny bosom.

"Fuck you, too, Maurice," I said, throwing a handful of leaves at him. I skipped away, up Whiskey Hill, to the sounds of ongoing curses and threats of prosecution from Mrs. Bissel.

I had only gone a little way when I realized I was not following the northern face as I had intended to. In fact, I had never seen this side of the hill. Soon enough, I came to a chain link fence that ran along the rise of the hill, seeming to go on for miles. I figured that if someone put up a fence, it had to lead somewhere, so I wouldn't get too lost. I began to follow the fence. All of the sudden a tremendous *ka-boom* echoed in the air and shook the whole hill. If I thought I was startled before, this time I yelled out loud and fell down in a pile of damp leaves. I could hear debris raining down through the trees and the frightened cawing of crows.

At first I thought the marina gas station had blown up, but then I realized that this explosion was much closer. I started making my way toward the sound of the explosion, when there was another one, a little further off. This time I didn't fall down or even yell. After I got past some trees, I saw a sign on the fence. It said:

DANGER!

No Trespassing

Property of Burnside Developers

Construction Site

Dynamite Usage

DANGER!

So, the developers were dynamiting away part of old Whiskey Hill so they could put some condos in the side. At least, that's what I overheard Charles saying to my mother one night at dinner. Usually, I don't give a lot of credit to dinnertime conversation, given that it has been, more often than not, marinating in gin all day, but anything about Whiskey Hill I listen to carefully.

Because Whiskey Hill is the tallest point on Beaver Island, it has always had important strategic value. Looking out over the cold and choppy waters of Lake Superior that flow into the island's only harbor, Whiskey Hill might as well be a fortress.

Supposedly the Cree and the pirates fought their bloodiest battles on Whiskey Hill. In fact, legend has it that the name came from the night when the Cree had captured several of the pirate captains and were torturing them on the side of the hill. The other pirates were so upset they hauled great barrels full of whiskey to the top of the hill, stuck rags in the sides for fuses, and sent the barrels tumbling down the hill ablaze. This also set the woods ablaze, which revealed the Cree's hiding places, allowing the Indians to be picked off at will by the pirate marksmen.

Ironically, the developers were doing a similar thing close to three hundred years later, except this time there weren't any Indians left to chase away.

I had a sudden thought that maybe the dynamiting would unearth some type of artifact, or maybe a souvenir, even some pirate booty long since forgotten. I scaled the fence and dropped down over the other side. I tried to walk in a big circle around where I thought the booming had come from— I wanted to find pirate treasure, not get blown up. Huge sections of the side of the hill were gone, and twice I almost went tumbling down the side when some loose dirt gave away. From my vantage point, I could see the bulldozers and dump trucks way down in the valley below. I watched to see if any of the men would leave the work site and come up to see how the dynamiting had gone, but they seemed content to stay by the heavy equipment and talk. I made a mental note to sneak onto the construction site one night and see if I could drive a dump truck.

I was about to skirt around the other side of the hill, when the dirt started sliding underneath me. I frantically tried to keep my balance. I must've looked like a cartoon character, comically running in place until I finally fell headlong down the hill.

I never thought someone could fall so long and so far. It was like doing somersaults, except when you're doing somersaults, you're usually in a gym or maybe a backyard, and you're not bouncing off of trees and rocks. Dirt was sliding down my pants and my shirt, and my Windbreaker had come partway off, pinning my arms, which I suppose is one reason why I didn't break any bones. I had lost all sense of which way was up. I thought I had stopped skidding and was safe, when I was suddenly falling through nothing but air. That made me scream, but before I could get going, I landed hard on the ground with a *whuff* that knocked the air out of my lungs.

I was lying on my back, looking up at dirt and sky. I realized I was in some sort of pit or hole. It wasn't very deep, and it was kind of canted sideways into the ground. Slowly, I moved my arms and legs, expecting to find one of them broken. Miraculously, except for some scrapes and bruises, I was fine. This pit was large, but I could easily heave myself out of it. The dirt on the side of the walls was dry, and there was an awful, funky smell.

I grabbed a tree root to hoist myself out. There was something familiar about the thick, twisted root, and just as it hit me, I noticed all of the leaves which had blown into the pit. I picked one up. Chinese Elm.

I was studying it so intensely that it took me a minute to realize there was a weird noise. A soft, insistent scraping sound, like a persistent scratching.

In the other end of the pit, the earth was moving. It looked as if a hand was kneading the earth from underground.

I don't know why, but the moving dirt gave me bad case of the creeps. "Come on, Audrey, get a hold of yourself," I whispered. Immediately, the moving stopped. I cocked my head and took a step closer. A furious thrashing broke out, like something was trapped underground. I wildly thought that maybe a worker was caught in a landslide, but then a small thing broke out of the dirt and waved madly around.

I stared at it for a few seconds before I realized it was the index finger of a skeleton.

It was wiggling around, trying to enlarge the hole and unearth more of itself. The wiggling was a hideous parody of the "come here" gesture people typically use their index fingers for—and curiously effective, because I crept closer. The scrabbling was intensifying, and soon a skeletal thumb broke through. Now the finger and thumb clicked together like pincers. I took a step back, ready to vault out of the pit. The finger and thumb worked for awhile, but were only able to uncover a bit more of the hand. It appeared that the rest of the fingers had been broken off, either earlier, or during the explosion, leaving only the index finger and the thumb.

Enough of the hand was now visible that it had gone from one parody to another—this one the cliché of someone sunk down in quicksand, their questing hand the last remaining piece of humanity visible.

I walked closer and squatted down. The three missing fingers were broken off at various places and dangled limply. I picked up a stick and gingerly poked the hand. Immediately, the thumb and forefinger closed around the stick. The quickness of it startled me. The stick was torn from my grasp and swung around by the mystery hand, which was now shaking violently again.

As I was watching it, another thought occurred to me. This hand had to be attached to something. If I dug a little, or perhaps loosened the dirt that was imprisoning it, what would I uncover?

It sure beat the hell out of the *Smithsonian*.

I clambered out of the pit and looked around. Even though I was still pretty banged up, my bruises were forgotten. I found a broken-off branch that was nearly as big around as my thigh. The end was tapered to a sharp point, which was the important part. I threw the branch into the pit and let myself carefully down into the hole.

The hand had apparently lost interest in the stick and had flung it across the pit. I was pretty sure it couldn't wrest the big branch away from me, but I didn't want to take any chances.

I knelt down close to it (but not too close) and whispered, "Look, I want to help you get out, but you need to promise me you won't get me or anything. Click your thumb and finger together twice for yes."

As soon as I had started speaking, the hand resumed its violent movements. Patiently, I waited until the shaking subsided. "Hey, I'm still here, but like I said, there's no way I'm helping you until you promise me you won't do anything nasty to me."

Again; the violent tremors as it struggled to free itself. I waited until it stopped and repeated what I had said. We went through this many, many times, until finally there was no reaction at all when I spoke.

"All right, that's more like it," I said. "Now, promise me you'll behave yourself. Click your fingers together twice for yes." Aside from wanting it to at least make a token promise not to attack me first thing, I wanted to see if, in fact, it could understand—and communicate—with me.

There was no response, no movement at all for quite a long time. I was starting to wonder if whatever I had seen had been some sort of involuntary reaction, maybe a muscle contraction of some sort, when, very slowly, the finger and the thumb bones clicked together twice, quite distinctly.

"Oh, man," I whispered to myself, then raised my voice and spoke. "Tell me again." There was another shorter wait, and the signal was given. This thing could understand me! My heart was racing as I grabbed the branch and wedged it point-first deep into the ground next to the hand. I leaned my weight on it and broke open a large clump of dirt. Yanking the branch out of the earth, I jammed it into the ground a few inches away from the first spot. I repeated the process until I had tilled a small circle around the hand.

"Okay, can you do anything?" The hand straightened and began to shake itself back and forth. Soon enough, a good portion of the forearm was visible. When it was clear nothing else was happening, I stepped forward with the branch again. "Hold on, don't move, I'm going to dig some more. Do you understand?"

Again, the two clicks.

I did the same trick. As soon as I gave the word, the arm renewed its efforts, looking like nothing so much as a macabre butter churn. At one point, the wrist straightened, and the entire thing slipped down into the earth. I was alarmed, thinking it had retreated to wherever it had come from, but suddenly there was a burst of dirt exploding upward. I involuntarily yelled and fell back.

When I looked again, the entire arm and most of the shoulder was free. I could see part of a rib cage, but there was more to it than just bones. Dirty, grey stuff that looked like flesh clung here and there. Some remnant of clothing was still attached. Laying there, with the ball of its shoulder and part of its torso exposed, and the rest still buried, it looked like a picture you would see in *National Geographic*—or maybe *Smithsonian*—about an archaeological excavation in progress.

I crept back over. "Can you hear me?"

With a speed faster than a striking cobra, the arm shot forward, and the hand grabbed the front of my Windbreaker between its two digits. It gave a huge tug, whether to yank me closer I don't know, but the result was that still more of the body came free. I lurched back, and in doing so, pulled it from the ground which had held it prisoner. I hit the ground on my back, and it landed on top of me. I was staring right into, for lack of a better word, its face, which was actually resting on mine.

This time, I didn't yell, I screamed.

It reared up on its spine like a hideous inchworm. I grabbed it by its bony shoulders and threw it off me, across the pit, where it landed, writhing, in a pile.

I skittered away until my back was pressed against the far side of the pit. I hadn't realized it, but I was crying. Right then and there, I made a decision to smash it.

Giving the pile of bones a wide berth, I retrieved the branch, raising it over my head in true caveman-with-a-club fashion, and prepared to bash the monster into harmless bone-splinters.

The thing had landed on what would have been its stomach and was trying to flip itself over. It was not having an easy time of it for several reasons. First of all, the creature had no legs. Its body consisted of a trunk that ended in a partially-crushed pelvis. The pelvis twisted and gyrated in an attempt to gain a purchase in the dirt in a futile manner that still would have made Elvis Presley envious. Furthermore, its other arm was missing, meaning the only limb it had was the original arm with its reduced supply of fingers.

The trunk of the body was mostly covered in grey, papery-looking flesh. Here and there, there were sad little holes where pieces of dirty bone could be seen—a rib or maybe part of the clavicle. Parts of the collarbone stood out clearly, although I could detect the remains of what apparently had been some sort of vest which still clung, tattered but stubborn, to the torso.

But the true wonder was the head; a true horror-movie skull. The cheeks and forehead had some flesh, but there was no nose, only a gaping hole. And the eye sockets were as empty as Old Mother Hubbard's cupboard. Perhaps most dramatically, the jaw was still affixed, and it moved rhythmically, grinding together the upper and lower sets of yellow teeth.

At last, it succeeded in raising itself up with its arm and whipsawing around to flip over. For what reason, I don't know, since then it began writhing helplessly on its back.

I lowered the branch. This thing was pretty ugly, but it looked pretty harmless, as well, though the clamping jaws were creepy. I watched its twisting pelvis drawing bizarre figure-eights in the dirt.

I knew I had to have it.

What it was—or what it had been once—wasn't important. What was important was that I could have it all for myself, that I could take it out of this hole in the ground, take it and make it mine.

Maybe I could tame it, like the wild raccoon my uncle Charlie found near his fishing cabin. He raised it from a baby, and it used to stand on its hind legs, begging for potato chips that it would hold in its paws like hands and munch. Uncle Charlie kept the raccoon around his fishing cabin for three or four years until the summer there was a rabies scare, and the old man up the way shot it and made a bicycle seat-cover out of its hide. No more munching potato chips.

The corpse had quieted its movements now, just twisting calmly in the dirt, arm waving weakly, head turning slowly. I crept over and knelt near the head—well out of reach. I knew it could hear me, even though it didn't have any ears.

"Hey, hey you…do you remember me? I'm the girl who pulled you out of the ground. I'm your friend."

Immediately the head whipped around, and the arm made a grab in my general direction, but I was anticipating this, and I brought the branch down hard—really hard—on the thing's skull. If it couldn't play nice, I didn't have any qualms about bashing it to pieces.

"No!" I scolded, as if speaking to a naughty puppy who had just wet the carpet. "Bad thing! Bad!"

It craned its bony neck back and snapped at where I had struck it with the branch, no doubt hoping I had been foolish enough to leave my hand there. This time, I stood up. "Fore!" I yelled and used a modified golf swing, smashing the branch against the head so hard that the thing spun halfway around. I jumped over it and used the branch to pin it down by the neck. With my left foot, I stepped on its arm, and gradually let my butt sink until it was resting on the moldy rib cage. As a leveraging tool, its pelvis was now useless; the thing was immobilized.

"Well now," I said, pleased with my efforts. "It looks like Mr. Bones is in a little pre-dick-er-ment." I giggled, and it echoed off the walls of the pit.

The thing finally stopped thrashing and fixed its empty eye sockets on the place in the air where my voice was coming from. That was what I wanted—its attention.

I leaned so close I could smell the slightly-overripe smell coming off the thing—kind of like a bag of apples left way too long in the cool dark of a basement. "Listen to me, Bonesy, listen to me real good. I like you. You're kind of cute. I think we can be friends. But, in order for us to be friends, you have to stop trying to get me. If you try to grab me again, I am going to take this big old axe I have with me and break you into tiny bone chips and you'll end up in somebody's hot dog. Do you understand me? Click your fingers twice for yes, once for the hot dog."

It seemed like an eternity, but finally, the thing slowly brought its thumb and forefinger together twice.

I had already known it could hear and understand me, so what really pleased me was the discovery—just as I suspected—that it couldn't really see out of those empty eye sockets. Big old axe, indeed.

"Okay, Bonesy, I am going to get up slowly now and take my foot off your arm. If you try anything funny, you know what's going to happen. It's up to you." I waited to see if there would be some reaction, but it just lay there, still and unanimated.

Using the branch as a crutch, I gingerly rose to my feet, keeping my foot firmly planted on its arm. When I was once again standing and could jump out of the way if I needed to, I removed my foot.

The thing turned its head slowly from side to side, and made a comical gesture flexing its wrist where I had been standing on it.

I knew then we were going to get along just fine.

"Good job!" I said, trying to reinforce the positive behavior. I looked around the pit. "Okay, I'm going to wrap you in something and get you out of this hole," I said, looking at my Bugs Bunny watch, which said it was almost lunchtime. "Then I have to go away for awhile, but I'll leave you somewhere safe. Okay?"

I had already started removing my Windbreaker when I noticed the thing was slowly shaking its head from side to side. That was surprising.

"No?" I asked, a little irritated. After all, who was the pet here? "What do you mean 'no'?"

The thing stretched out its long index finger and began drawing in the dirt. For a moment, my breath caught in my throat, and the only sound in the pit was the rasp of the dirt against the old bone. I leaned over, no longer mindful of keeping a safe distance, and looked at what symbols it was making. It was writing. The letters were shaky and oddly shaped, but still legible. The thing was only writing one word, and, due to my high intelligence and keen perception, I was able to figure out where it was going long before it completed the last letter. When it was finished writing, it turned its head to me, as if waiting for my reaction. I stood there, staring at the one word looking up at me from the bottom of the pit.

HUNGRY

While I was eating my tuna sandwich, watching my mother draw figure-eights in the ring of moisture left by her glass on the table, my mind was turning furiously. There was a September wind blowing across the porch, and I was chilled without my Windbreaker. Of course, the knowledge that Bonesy was nestled in it snug and warm in the hayloft, made me feel a little better. I wondered if Bonesy would like some tuna sandwich. What does a girl feed her pet monster?

Maribel bustled onto the porch with another pitcher for my mother, and I asked sweetly if I could have another sandwich. The maid nodded once, curtly, and disappeared into the house.

My mother's head snapped up from the condensation drawing she had been working on. "Another sandwich? For the love of the holy, merciful Christ, Audrey, where do you put all that food? If you're not careful, you're going to end up fat and lonely, like your aunt Jessica."

Aunt Jessica weighed about 140 pounds and had never married, due to the fact she was a confirmed lesbian. This didn't stop my mother, who weighed all of 110 pounds soaking wet, from attributing aunt Jessica's singlehood to a chronic weight problem.

I knew my best strategy was to sit there quietly until Maribel returned with my tuna fish, so instead of replying, I busied myself wrapping up some slices of honeydew melon and cantaloupe in a linen napkin, on the off-chance Bonesy was vegan.

When I'd wrapped my sandwich and was fully outfitted with supplies, I excused myself from the table and dashed off to the old barn, which we had been meaning to convert into a guesthouse for years, but had never gotten around to the actual converting. When there's just three people banging around in a twenty-seven-room mansion, guesthouses don't seem real important.

I went through the side door and stuffed the rolled napkins in my shirt so I could climb the wooden ladder up to the hayloft. I liked the hayloft as a spot for old Bonesy, since a) I knew no one—especially our old and lazy "caretaker" Herman—would ever venture up there, and b) I knew even if Bonesy thrashed around to his heart's content, he couldn't get into any mischief up there.

I had reached the top of the ladder and was about to shout a sunny greeting of "Hey Bonesy, guess what, it's luunncch time!" when I froze.

I had left him—it—the thing—in a little alcove wrapped in my Windbreaker, but he had tossed it aside. The thing was up on its elbow, head lowered, leaning forward, looking for all the world like a nightmare version of a cat stalking its prey.

I followed its line of sight and, sure enough, there was a large field mouse, sitting on a block of hay, munching on some scrounged piece of something.

With infinite patience, the corpse pulled itself forward a centimeter at a time, dragging its body with that one arm. It moved so slowly, the hay underneath it barely whispered. The broken pelvis it dragged behind twitched periodically like a tail. Perhaps most amazingly, even though I had taken him for a dried-up old husk, Bonesy was drooling like Niagara Falls as he closed in on the unsuspecting field mouse.

At the last moment, the mouse must've sensed something was amiss, because it turned suddenly and dropped whatever it had been chewing. But then—and at the time I thought it was the most horrible thing I had ever seen—Bonesy pounced. With that same terrible speed the creature had used when it grabbed me, the arm shot out and snared the poor mouse between the thumb and forefinger.

The mouse had time to squeal, but only once.

In a horribly fluid motion, the arm bent and delivered the mouse to the drooling mouth, where it stuffed half the squirming body in, and then clamped its jaws down. The mouse's hind legs, sticking out of the mouth, went absolutely rigid, and blood splashed in an amazing flow. The thing worked its neck once, presumably swallowing the first half of Mr. Mouse, and then tossed the back half in. It again gave one mammoth chew and swallowed.

The entire mouse had been disposed of in less than five seconds.

I looked down at my napkin-wrapped gifts of melon and tuna fish and felt sick to my stomach.

The thing was banging its head against the floor in some kind of happy rhythm, clearly pleased. Even more than when it grabbed me, I wanted to smash its filthy skull to pieces.

Well, part of me did. The other part was fascinated by such a monstrosity; especially that it was mine. All mine. It could only catch mice as long as I let it. It could only live as long as I decided. If I wanted to bash its head in, I could, and no one would be the wiser.

It lay banging its head on the floor, blood and drool staining the large teeth and running freely off to soak in the hay. I tossed the linen napkins. "Here ya go, Bonesy, some extra chow. Not as tasty as a mouse, but what the hell, huh?" I sat down with a sigh and watched it tear into the napkins, greedily masticating the tuna fish and shoving huge pieces of melon into the whole mess. There I was, less than two feet away from this abomination, but I had no fear. I knew deep in my heart that it wouldn't hurt me.

We were pals.

The next several weeks were pretty uneventful. Since I spent most of my time in the barn, I stayed pretty much out of my mother's hair, so I think she actually began to forget about me altogether. Maribel frowned even more severely than usual about my odd pilfering of food from the kitchens, but apparently decided not to risk infuriating my mother by squealing on me.

I tried feeding all types of things to Bonesy, and—without exception—he ate every single thing I put in front of him. Including, on one memorable occasion, an entire Swanson's "Hungry Man" Double Salisbury Steak Dinner—meat, potatoes, corn, green beans, apple fritter, and microwavable tray. He could eat as much as I could provide, and his appetite was never satiated.

Even more disquieting to me, though, were the traces of unfortunate animals I found in the hayloft. Mice, rats, barn swallows, and even a raccoon, all appeared to have met untimely ends at the singular hand of Bonesy.

Like any pet owner, I was indulgent toward his little quirks. I would chide him for what he had done, but nonetheless, clean up the mess, and try to find a way to keep animals from getting into the hayloft.

It was a pleasant few weeks, right up until I climbed the ladder and saw Bonesy chewing on a certain tattered pink collar that still legibly read, *Maurice*.

I swooned, actually swooned, like those women in bad old movies do, except they weren't twenty feet off the ground clinging to a rickety wooden ladder. Bonesy was banging his head against the floor in what I now knew to be his post-kill celebration. There was less blood than usual, but some very incriminating tufts of fur that had not been ingested.

"Oh my god, what did you do…what did you do, Bonesy?" Like a dumb mutt, the head swiveled around at the sound of my voice, no doubt expecting food. The collar slipped from between his jaws, and the bell on it made a forlorn little *ping!* as it struck the floor. The first thing I could think to do was grab the collar and stuff it in the back pocket of my jeans. "Bonesy, you dumb ass, don't you know who the first suspect is going to be? Me! And if they come looking around the grounds for that damn Maurice…" Well, I would have a difficult time explaining Bonesy.

The thing flipped itself over and gave me a mouth-slightly-open, expectant look; like I should throw a ball for it to fetch, or something. This was getting out of hand. "Bonesy, that's it. You have to go. That old witch from next door is going to know for sure, somehow, I'm responsible for this. I'm going to get in so much trouble! All because of you!" I sat down and started to cry. Bonesy heard me weeping, and began to clump and scratch to where I was sitting. He cocked his hideous head at me curiously, then tentatively reached out its bony hand and gently squeezed my shoulder.

That only made me cry harder. "Why did you have to kill Mrs. Bissel's cat? Now she's going to get me in big trouble, and I'll have to get rid of you forever." Abruptly, I realized what exactly it was that was giving my shoulder a comforting squeeze, and I fiercely batted the arm away. "Get away from me you monster!" I shouted. "You freak!"

The empty eye sockets regarded me for a moment more, and then Bonesy turned and clumped his way back to the little nest he had carved out, looking like nothing so much as a dejected hound dog from Hell.

I thought I was home free when it came to the matter of Maurice. I could leave Bonesy in the hayloft for the time being, since nobody would ever look for Maurice up there. I did tell Bonesy to bury himself in hay if he heard strange voices, but I'm not sure he understood me.

I disposed of the incriminating collar as part of what I thought to be a highly seasonal and chummy bonfire that I made for the whole family. My mother was so impressed, she even ruffled my hair the way she had undoubtedly seen a sitcom mom do to a precocious sitcom tyke.

All was quiet for a few days, so needless to say I was quite surprised when my mother yelled, "Audrey, for the love of the eternally-vigilant sweet Christ, get down here right *now*!" and I went downstairs to find the sheriff and two deputies sitting in our second living room.

All three of the lawmen regarded me coolly. That old harpy, Mrs. Bissel, must've given them an earful about me.

"Audrey, these police are here about—" my mother began, but the sheriff neatly cut her off.

"Hello, Audrey. I am Sheriff Thompson, and these are two deputies, Deputy Kyle and Deputy Simmons. We're sorry to bother you like this, but we had heard from some of the other neighbors that you often had...disagreements with Mrs. Bissel, the lady who lives the next house over."

"Yeah, sometimes we got into it, but it was no big deal." I was thinking: "Boy, I'd love to pan-fry that old battleaxe over a big bonfire."

"Well, Audrey, we understand. But, with the disappearance and all, we need to gather as much information as possible." Sheriff Thompson was giving me his "let's-all-play-ball-with-the-nice-lawmen" routine, but I wasn't having any of it. I mean, really, I know crime is slow on the island, but three cops for one faggy kitty? Come on!

"Look Sheriff, I'm sorry, but these things happen. If people took more care, they wouldn't happen as often. I know it might offend you to hear me say this, but I'm sort of glad. I mean, everybody hated that smelly old thing, anyway."

I thought that sentence might shock them, but in no way was I prepared for the reaction it garnered. There were indeed satisfyingly-shocked expressions on the faces of the lawmen, but my mother went, "For the love of the merciful sweet Christ!" and fainted dead-away, *thump* on the floor.

There was a moment of silence in the room before the deputies jumped up to revive my mother. Sheriff Thompson never took his eyes off me. Under that level of scrutiny, I felt my comments needed to be amended, so I added, "I mean, it was just an old cat."

The sheriff continued to gaze at me with unflappable concentration. "I think we need to talk some more, Audrey. We don't know anything about a cat disappearing. We came to see if you knew anything about Mrs. Bissel's disappearance."

After I got home from the sheriff's office, I changed out of my dress-clothes and raced out to the barn. Even as I climbed the ladder, I knew what I would find. Under the harsh light of the lantern, I could see the hay piled up in the corner, partially covering the loose boards that allowed Bonesy to sneak out on foraging expeditions; the little pelts and body parts from scores of animals; pet collars; and, finally, a thoroughly-gnawed ankle, still encased in an old lady's slipper.

"This time is finally it, Bonesy! Did you know the sheriff suspects me in Mrs. Bissel's disappearance? Nice going! All they'd have to do is find *this*." I picked up the slipper with its grisly contents and flung it at the thing, which was shifting and cringing in the corner. "I'd be in jail for the rest of my life. *The rest of my life!* Do you understand that?"

It was no use. I knew what I had to do. What I should have done a long time ago. Again, that rebellious part of me rose up against the thought of abandoning Bonesy, especially now that he had become so tame and used to being fed. But I knew it was the only answer.

Before I could change my mind, I opened the old blanket I had brought with me and flung it over him. He writhed and struggled, but I used my weight on his chest and my foot to pin down his flailing arm. Twice around with the twine I held in my other hand, and he was secure. The bundle flopped around, Bonesy thumping his head on the floor. Seeing him all tied up like that made me sad, and I knew I had to act before I lost my nerve.

I grabbed Mrs. Bissel's foot and shoved it into the folds of the blanket. I threw the whole package over the ledge and heard it thump on the floor below. I took a deep breath and climbed back down the ladder.

He was still thrashing. I shoved Bonesy (and the foot, which had gone rolling behind a cider barrel) into a large trash bag, the kind that the groundskeeper uses for leaves every fall.

I could easily drag the bag on the ground. When I reached the old well, covered by boards and marked with a red kerchief, I stopped to rest. Dragging Bonesy was hard work.

Still, I knew I had to finish before I changed my mind. I hunted around for a few heavy rocks and put those in the bag, too, although I knew Bonesy would have a heck of a time floating to the top of this deep well. Just, with him, I knew it was best not to take any chances.

I figured I had thrown in enough rocks, and I tore the boards covering the well away. Spiders and centipedes came crawling out of the darkness, perhaps seeing the night sky for the first time. I felt bad sticking Bonesy in such a horrible place, but what was I supposed to do? I couldn't have him eating the neighbors all winter, could I?

Everything was ready, but I still felt horribly guilty. I owed him some explanation. I sat down next to the bag. "Bonesy," I began softly, and at the first murmur of my voice, the bag began to flop about wildly. "Bonesey, I'm sorry. But, it's better this way." That sounded lame. I decided to try a different approach.

"Bonesy, believe me, if it was up to me, I would keep you. But, it's my mean, old mother and her boyfriend, Charles's, fault. They already promised to send me to military school next semester, just because they know I'm guilty of something." This part was true. "So, my mom and Charles are making me get rid of you. They want to hurt me, and they know the best way to hurt me is by making me get rid of you." This part wasn't exactly true, but it sounded good, and, more importantly, for some reason it made me start crying, which made the rest of my speech even more heart-wrenching. "So, Bonesy, this is it. Just remember, remember…" I was really bawling now. "Remember I'll love you forever, Bonesy." I hugged the bag tightly, and then tipped it into the darkness and it plunged to the bottom of the well. I heard a muffled splash.

"Goodbye, Bonesy," I said, and hastily dragged the boards over the hole. I wanted to get back inside before I was missed.

Of course, no one had even noticed my absence. I changed into my PJs and lay on my bed, trying not to think about poor old Bonesy, stuck in the cold water of that well. Still, he must've been partially encouraged by my speech. All in all, I thought, a job well done…

* * *

That was just a little over six hours ago, and now I realize how wrong I was—about everything.

Because I know so much about the island history, I think Bonesy must've been one of the pirates who tossed flaming whiskey barrels on the Cree Indians. Except, maybe he's one of the guys who gets caught by the justifiably pissed-off Indians. So, maybe they torture him for awhile, no biggie, but maybe also the medicine man lays some big curse on him, you know, the "you'll suffer and suffer, but never die" kind of curse, just like in the movies, but this time the curse actually takes. So, there's Bonesy, all shut up in his little prison, until the developers come along and dynamite him, not only out of wherever he was, but also into pieces.

Then, here comes this snotty little girl who takes him in and shows him some affection, perhaps the first affection and human contact he's had in a couple hundred years. Then, this little girl, his only friend, tells him about the mean old lady next door. Well, what do you suppose happens next?

But, then, it gets better. Instead of helping, he just gets the little girl into more trouble. And now the little girl's mean mother and guy pal are making the little girl miserable and making her get rid of her friend, Bonesy. What do you think happens next?

It's four a.m. My mother is screaming. Not *For the love of the benevolent sweet Christ* this time, just screaming. It doesn't go on for long. Charles makes some kind of noise, but that doesn't last long, either.

Their bedroom is all the way across the great hall, but I still hear sticky chewing sounds and the familiar banging noise of a certain bony head bounding off the floor in pure pleasure.

I close my eyes, believing when I open them again, everything will be okay. The trouble is, with my eyes closed, I hear even better. I hear the thump and drag as that one arm drags the rest of its eager body forward toward my room. I hear the dry clicks as the finger and thumb creep up my door and turn the knob. I hear the rustle of the duvet as the thing climbs onto my bed and lies comfortably against my leg, completely contented.

Death, Dying & 3 Credits
Ken Goldman

*From the Swatmoore County Community College
Fall 2006 course catalog*:
Death & Dying: (3 cr) Instructor: Dr. S. Byron Hoffner
A study of historical attitudes, customs, and myths surrounding our culture's various perceptions of death and dying. Professor Hoffner has written extensively on both the psychology and physiology of the dying process in his book *Exploring the Fear of Death*. (Please note: This course is open to a limited number of senior students pending written staff approval.)

S WATMOORE'S LECTURE HALL FILLED QUICKLY, the auditorium's atmosphere unusually somber for college students fresh from summer vacation. One might think some powerful figure lay in state near the podium onstage. The cloak of mystery surrounding Dr. S. Byron Hoffner's unorthodox teaching methodology and his unconventional field of research demanded that kind of respect—and that kind of fear.

Melanie Cerra selected her seat alongside an attractive blond girl. The two exchanged polite smiles while each set up her laptop. After Melanie's other morning classes, during which social interaction seemed practically a course requirement, this unwritten code of silence felt especially awkward. If she were going to remain awake during the next ninety minutes, she would have to change that. She turned to her seatmate.

"I'm Melanie. Does this place feel like a funeral, or what?"

The blond smiled but kept her voice low. "Bobbie. I need the three credits to graduate, and this was the only class I could fit into my schedule. I haven't seen this course listed before, so I don't know much about it or the instructor. It *does* seem kind of creepy in here, doesn't it? But what would you expect from a course about death?"

"Do you believe we had to sign a release form just to get in? I hear the instructor won't allow anyone under twenty-one to register for this class. What's that about? Does he plan on having Happy Hour here after this wake?"

"Maybe the college doesn't want any lawsuits. This guy Hoffner is new here, but I hear he's quirky. His questionnaire sure was. He wanted an essay about how I felt watching my mother die last year. I wrote the paper, all right. But I added that I didn't feel it was an appropriate question to ask. I guess that was okay, because here I am."

Melanie busied herself with her laptop's cursor, opening a new file for her class notes. "My father died last winter, three days before Christmas. Pancreatic cancer. It was awful. I'd never experienced grief, not like that, like I was being choked. So that's what I wrote. Maybe Dr. Hoffner prefers his class filled with orphans."

A bookish-looking guy wearing thick, Coke-bottle glasses, turned in his seat. Melanie felt certain he would ask them to shut their mouths, but he wanted to talk, too. "With me it was about my Labrador, Skank. I wrote how I felt really upset when I had to put him down last summer. I don't live in the safest neighborhood, and you need either a dog or a gun. But Skank was old and kept shitting everywhere in my apartment, so I couldn't keep him. Hoffner just wrote 'Good enough' on my answer sheet then apparently signed my class slip. I never even met the guy."

"I don't think anyone has," Melanie said. "His book jacket mentions his methods are a little unorthodox. His course is like some big campus secret."

Bobbie said in an ominous voice, "More like this is some clandestine secret society, and we three are among the select few to be granted membership. Knights of The Living Dead. *Hoo hah!*"

Melanie studied the other students. She didn't doubt that everyone in the lecture hall had a nodding acquaintance with death.

Bobbie nudged her to turn around when Dr. Hoffner took the platform. She hummed the *Addams Family* theme until Melanie poked her in the ribs.

Melanie had expected some rumpled old academic with uncombed hair and a cheap tweed sports jacket with elbow patches. But this guy was young and wore a fashionable, olive green, corduroy sports jacket covering a chest more thick than his facial features suggested. Hoffner seemed the youthful professorial type right out of central casting, cute in an Opie-from-Mayberry sort of way.

He paused at his podium, studying the crowd, giving his students time to check him out, too. Mutual scrutinizing completed, Hoffner began his lecture, offering no wooden introduction of himself or even a "good morning." With his first words, the man went for the gut.

"Let's clarify two things at the get-go. I have no intention of being politically correct today, and no one leaves to pee. Them's my rules. *Capice? Comprende?*"

He smiled when he didn't receive a response.

"This course is about death and dying, just like your catalog says, and I'll start with my basic premise: no person has ever passed away nor gone to his eternal reward. No hospital patient has ever expired, nor have any of your loved ones played the harp in Heaven. Those expressions are lies, tacky euphemisms intended to make death palatable because, throughout history, dying has scared the living bejeesus out of everyone. The truth is, when you die, you're fucking dead, not deceased nor resting in peace. I won't sugarcoat death for you in this class. I won't even embalm it. Death is ugly, and it smells bad. Someday you'll be rotting inside your coffin, and you will stink. My purpose is to teach you to accept death with all its hideousness and grossness intact, just as nature intended."

A few students laughed, although the man did not seem to be joking. Melanie typed Hoffner's objective into her computer: *Lesson Goal: To accept death for what it is. (Real)*

"All right, then. So, how many of you in this room are dying? Hands?"

Dumbfounded students turned to one another, then stared back at their instructor. The room fell silent. No one ventured to raise a hand.

Hoffner grinned and leaned forward on his elbow. He seemed about to reveal the answer to an elaborate riddle.

"Well, gang, here's your wake-up call. All of you—and me too—are dying. Being born is your death sentence, and you're ten minutes closer to that expiration date than when you walked into this lecture hall. Even as I speak, your brain cells are shorting out, your internal clock is ticking. Death is real, and it's out there waiting. Your date of death is as real as your birthday, and it's coming, you can be absofuckinglutely certain of it. Does that thought frighten you? Does it make death any more real? Probably not, so I'll demonstrate my point."

In three minutes Opie had transformed into Vincent Price. Melanie tapped her keyboard: *From the moment we're born we begin to die.*

Back at the podium, Hoffner held a small fishbowl. Inside swam a tiny, gilled creature with long and golden fins.

"Anyone here from PETA or the ASPCA? I'm hoping not. Class, this is Ariel, like Disney's *Little Mermaid*. Beautiful, isn't she? I found her in a mountain stream last spring, fed and cared for her all summer. She's pretty plump now and seems happy just lolling inside her little bowl all day long. Ariel, she doesn't ask for much, just a few daily specks of food and some clean water. I've grown rather fond of her."

Melanie distrusted the professor's sincerity, but this class could take it. Seniors could comprehend life's sudden horrors better than their younger cohorts. Back in high school, she had to chloroform a hapless frog before dissecting the poor creature's innards. Now she found herself mouthing the words *it's just a stupid goldfish*. Expecting the worst brand of histrionics, she unconsciously typed the same lip-synched words into her computer.

"...Do I detect a reaction from the crowd, an uneasy stirring in your seats?" The smile never left Hoffner's face. "Don't be afraid to think it. You're expecting me to kill this helpless little fish to prove my point, to bring to the forefront your aversion to death. It's not a bad idea, for the purpose of demonstration, wouldn't you agree? Just like reality television, eh?" He spilled some water from the fishbowl to the floor.

Bobbie gasped, quickly covering her mouth, others murmured.

"I heard that!" Hoffner's dark eyes drew a bead on Bobbie. "This young woman expressed her revulsion, even though two hours from now she'll be inside the cafeteria ordering the tuna salad without thinking twice." He continued to stare at her, and Bobbie turned crimson. "Am I getting through? Have I made a splash?" He spilled more water.

"I think I want to leave," she whispered to Melanie.

"No pee breaks, remember?"

The goldfish named Ariel struggled to remain below the diminishing supply of liquid. As the bowl emptied, the little fish began to flop inside.

Melanie's finger thumped upon one key of her laptop. ? ? ? ? ? ? ? ? ? ? ? ? ? ? ? ? ? ? ?? ?

"I'd say our finned friend is having some difficulty breathing. It would be a simple matter to refill her bowl, if I chose to do so. But that would be giving in to my fear of death, demonstrating how the thought of it repulses and terrifies me, wouldn't it? And I have a point to prove. So I'll ask you to indulge me while I do this...."

Hoffner reached into the bowl, grabbed the squiggling fish by its tail and held it up for the class. "I'll refill her bowl if someone requests it right now, perhaps some naturalist who is willing to receive an *F* for this course by asking me to spare little Ariel's life. Any takers?"

The instructor waited. No fish saviors sat in this classroom.

"All right, I think we can begin." Hoffner dropped the fish to the floor, allowing it to flop about for a moment, then he chased it around the platform, stomping at the fish like he was performing a river dance, until a thick golden paste clung to his shoe.

He walked to the podium. "Can you believe I did that? Did it anger you, depress you? That little goldfish, so alive and content a moment ago, is now jelly. Death is one fast bastard, eh? Ariel was here, and now she's not. Can you accept that simple fact? Is it real to you now?"

Melanie stared at her keyboard. She had no idea what to write.

Bobbie whispered, "That man is nuttier than a Snickers bar."

"Three credits," Melanie whispered back.

Hoffner stepped from behind his podium, sat on the edge of the platform, and removed a handkerchief from his pocket. He wiped the sticky fish goo from his loafer. Without missing a beat, he continued as if he were discussing whether it might rain.

"Elizabeth Kubler-Ross. Does the name ring any bells? She was a woman who made a lifetime study of death, if you'll excuse the seeming contradiction. Old Liz has since bought the farm herself, but while she was with us, she believed the process of dying occurred in five significant stages, something to remember when the Grim Reaper crosses your path or a loved one's." He walked to the chalkboard, wrote *DENIAL* in large case letters.

Melanie tapped the word into her computer, but Bobbie snapped her laptop shut. For her, this lesson was over.

"There's this old joke: Mr. Smith's doctor tells him, 'I have some good news and some bad news. The bad news is you're going to die in six months.' 'Six months?' cries Mr. Smith. 'What could possibly be the good news?' The doc answers, 'See that luscious receptionist out front? I'm fucking her!'

"But that's not the punch line. See, Mr. Smith goes home and assures himself, 'I'm not going to die, nope and nuh huh, not me! Dying is what happens to the next guy.' Smith goes for a second opinion, maybe a third. Then one day, six months later, Mr. Smith keels into his mashed potatoes.

"...Is that funny, or what?"

No one in the lecture hall seemed to think it was.

"Let's bring it closer to home. If I informed you that someone in this room was going to die before this morning's class is over, you would tell yourself, 'That's total bullshit!' You would deny it. Deny, deny, and then deny some more."

"That *is* total bullshit," the guy with the thick glasses mumbled. "What's with this sadistic fuck?"

"...Of course, little Ariel probably awoke this morning believing all she had to worry about was when her breakfast was coming. Who could know that before noon she would be scraped off the good professor's loafer like a wad of Juicy Fruit? Death? Hell, that only happens to other fish!"

If the man were batshit crazy or some Marquis de Sade wannabe, it still wouldn't hurt to score some points with him. Melanie raised her hand and identified herself.

"Suppose a person is terminally ill, and his doctor tells him he's got six weeks? He starts feeling sick, sees in his mirror some skeletal imitation of himself, becomes weak and tired. He can't keep denying his death is inevitable."

Bobbie whispered, "Brown-nosing 101, that's down the hall." But Hoffner seemed impressed with her question. He scribbled a second word on the chalkboard.

BARGAINING

"Miss Cerra, your terminal patient is about to go through a process. 'Please, Mother Mary-Jesus-Allah-Bozo,' he begs. 'I'll do anything. *Just don't let me die!*' It's another form of denial, of course. Your bony patient, maybe he suddenly finds religion, tells himself, 'I'll be good so God won't let me croak.' So he begs, pleads, prays...

"Think of it like this. If I tell you there's a bomb under one of your seats right now, something I disguised that looks like a dropped pen—and if I get you to genuinely believe it, wouldn't you beg me not to set the fucker off? If you'd like to play God for a while, put someone's life in your hands, then watch them plead with you not to let them die. Hallelujah and amen! I promise it'll be good for a few laughs."

Melanie turned to Bobbie. "See any pens under my seat?"

"He's just fucking with us, making us paranoid," Bobbie said, but she took a quick peek under Melanie's chair. "Does a pencil count?"

Melanie checked for herself. Nothing was there. "Bitch!"

Bobbie leaned close to her seatmate. "Paranoia...the game the whole family can play!"

Hoffner's death rant continued. "Death makes no bargains. When it comes to your mortality, you're betting against the House, and the House always wins. You lose, and losing pisses you off. So..."

He wrote *ANGER* on the board, and Melanie dutifully typed the word. She felt pretty angry herself that Hoffner was getting his rocks off playing with their heads, first stomping some poor goldfish, then planting crazy suspicions about bombs beneath their seats. Still, she had to admit, Hoffner knew how to make his point.

"...Of course, anger burns itself out pretty fast. You can only rant for so long before you realize it's not doing any good. So you're left with a mess o' the blues, emotionally busted. Good for creativity maybe, not so good for your mental health." He added another word to his board, separating it from the others.

DEPRESSION

"I'd like to share a little secret with you people, okay?"

"Anyone mind if I smoke?" Without waiting for a response, Hoffner lit up. The cigarette shifted in his mouth as he spoke. "I know, I know. These things will kill you. Well, let's say I'm past that denial stage, and I no longer give a rat's turd. 'Smoke-free environment,' my ass. Smoke 'em if you got 'em, gang!" No one took him up on his offer, but Hoffner didn't appear to notice. "Up your ass with a Marlboro, Mr. Death!" He inhaled a mouthful of smoke like some defiant, pimpled adolescent, but now the instructor's bravado seemed forced and unconvincing. Something odd was going on, some lunatic shift in tone that exceeded eccentricity. "Oh hell, I almost forgot. About that secret I wanted to share..."

Hoffner's smile twitched, then disappeared. He was soaked in sweat. For the first time, he seemed unable to find the correct words. He sat on the edge of the platform smoking. He stubbed one cigarette out, lit another. Sixty students waited for whatever demonstration of insanity he planned next.

"I have lung cancer. Stage four, I'm told, advanced enough to kill me very dead and very soon." He took another long drag, pretending to savor the smoke filling his lungs, but he wasn't that good an actor. He didn't say another word.

The room fell silent. Someone dropped a book. Several students flinched at the sudden crack of noise. Given the tenor of Hoffner's lecture, Melanie half-expected the man to jump up shouting, "Gotcha!" and chortle like a maniac. That didn't happen.

Finally, he got to his feet and said, "There's more." His voice had the tone of a man at confession. "See, I wasn't kidding about someone in here dying before this class is over. There's no death denial going on in my classroom, kids." He walked to the chalkboard and scribbled the fifth word.

ACCEPTANCE!!!

Melanie didn't bother typing. "Christ, the man is having some sort of nervous breakdown."

Bobbie nodded. "I think he's planning on sharing it with us."

Hoffner was losing it, but he didn't appear about to slow down. "I know I'm going to die, so I'm giving the Reaper his due today. A man can't get more accepting of death than that, can he? The House always wins, but I still get to choose the game."

Sopping sweat, the instructor removed his corduroy jacket. Beneath it he wore a thick black vest. Melanie's brain didn't immediately register what she saw. Wired tubes, maybe a dozen of them, adhered to the vest and were lined up like little soldiers. Suddenly, she gulped for air.

"That's right, sports fans. It's a bomb, homemade and ready to bring the house down on each and everyone in here, enough explosives to spatter the four walls with the dripping remains of your arteries and intestines. All I have to do is pull this little cord here, and today's class will be summarily dismissed. See, I've worked out a way to make today's lesson a genuine exercise in show-and-tell."

A boy in the front row left his seat. Hoffner raised a hand, then quickly returned it to the thick cord dangling from his side. "Nuh uh! No piss breaks! Sorry!" Another beefy student pulled the kid back into his chair.

"I'm not going to blow the place up just yet, don't worry. That is, unless anyone here is thinking of using their cell phone, of course." His eyes scanned the lecture hall. "That's good, kids. Real good. Now let's shut those laptops too, shall we? Wireless access at Swatmoore is state of the art, and we wouldn't want any IMs upsetting the outside world." He waited while two dozen laptops snapped shut.

A girl in the back row started crying. Another student shouted curses.

"You're faking!"

"You crazy prick!"

Hoffner ignored them. He reached into his pocket, withdrew a small revolver.

Several young women whimpered. Hoffner ignored them, also. Instead, he beelined to Melanie's seat. He held the gun out to her.

"Go on, Miss Cerra. Take it. It's only a .22, not much more than a cap pistol, really, and you seem reliable enough to use it."

She stared at the weapon in his hand as if the instructor were offering her a steaming turd.

"I don't know what you want me to—"

"Take the fucking gun!" some guy shouted.

"He's crazy! Can't you see that?"

Melanie rose from her seat and took the .22, gazing at her hand as if the revolver might suddenly, on its own, blow her head off.

"What do you want me to do with it?"

Hoffner smiled. "I want you to point it at me and shoot me, of course. I want you to stand right here, take careful aim, and put a bullet right between my eyes. See how well I accept death? Hell, the Grim Reaper and me, we're old pals."

"I can't do that! I can't—"

"That's denial, Miss Cerra. You *can* and you *will,* or I bring the house down right now, *Boom, Boom, Ka-boom!"*

"Please, don't…"

"Yes! And there it is, bargaining! You're going through the stages well, so, let's cut to the chase, okay? Unless you're angry enough to throw that .22 right in my face. Of course, that would defeat your purpose entirely, wouldn't it?"

"Shoot him!"

Melanie's hand shook, but she pointed the revolver at him.

"He's bluffing!" the guy wearing Coke-bottle glasses shouted at her. "The gun isn't loaded! There's no bomb! It's a setup, all of it! He's fucking with you!"

The tears came quickly. Melanie swiped one hand at them, trying to hold the gun steady in the other.

"I can't do this…don't make me do this.…"

"Good, Miss Cerra. We've hit depression, now. Let's take it home.…"

"I…"

"Shoot him!"

"Do it!"

"The clock is ticking, Miss Cerra. Ten…nine…"

"Please. Oh, God…please!"

"…six…five…four…"

"Kill him!!!"

Melanie's hand was shaking badly. She aimed the pistol at Hoffner's head. Her finger twitched on the trigger.

"...two...one..."

A single shot rang out, one quick, unimpressive pop in the expansive lecture hall. But it did the job. A small red hole appeared dead center above the man's eyebrows, and Dr. S. Byron Hoffner crumpled like a sack. On the floor his legs kicked, and the image of that damned goldfish replayed inside Melanie's brain. The professor didn't kick for long. Melanie looked at the gun she still held.

"I didn't...I didn't shoot him!" She turned to Bobbie. "I swear, I didn't—"

"*I* did," the guy with the glasses said. He held his own gun up for all to see, some toy-like thing that could have passed for a cigarette lighter. He approached Melanie, touched her shoulder. "I hoped he was bluffing, but I couldn't take the chance." He turned to the students surrounding them. "I'm licensed for it. I swear!"

Murmurs all around.

"He's dead, isn't he?"

"He isn't moving! Someone call 911!"

"There's a bullet in his brain, asshole. 911 can't do shit!"

"Does this mean the course will be canceled?"

Melanie turned to the guy with the gun.

"You may have saved our lives. I don't even know your name."

"It's Henry. And I guess I'm the new marshal in town."

Bobbie pointed at the professor's body. One of the tubes attached to his vest had broken with his fall. She climbed from her chair, pulled the tube from the vest.

"It's empty. There's nothing inside...no powder." She tore away another tube, shook it, then broke it open. It was empty, too. Bobbie looked at Melanie. "It's fake. Just a hollow, plastic tube. There's no bomb here."

A girl who had been hysterical managed to ask, "Do you think that cancer story was just...?"

"...Bullshit?" Melanie asked, and now she too was drying her eyes. "How could that man be so intent on making his point? Who would do something so completely insane just to create this whole scenario?" She remembered the notes she had written into her computer earlier.

Lesson Goal: To accept death for what it is. (Real)

[I won't sugar coat death for you in this class.]

Bobbie managed some composure. "There's only one way to find out what's bullshit here and what's not." She reached for the gun, and Melanie handed it to her. Running her fingers through her curly hair, she raised the hand holding the revolver. "I never fired a gun before. We're in this together, everyone in here, right?" She turned back to Melanie.

"Three credits," Melanie said.

Bobbie managed half a smile.

Henry stood by her side. "Go ahead. The first shot is free."

That almost earned a grin. Bobbie tightened her grip on the weapon's handle.

"Here goes…"

She aimed the .22 at the professor's body that lay crumpled on the floor. Struggling uncertainly for a moment, she pulled the trigger.

A little red flag popped from the gun's barrel.

It read, "BANG!"

The Mud, The Blood, and The Bones
Christopher Fulbright & Angeline Hawkes

1880, Callahan, Texas

A CLUNKY TUNE WAFTED FROM the piano in the noisy Red Gap Saloon. Smoke curled around the heads of the men at the tables. Dust blew in through swinging doors that opened onto the unpaved street.

The sound of clanking glass and the rustle of taffeta caught John Wesley Harding's ear. He looked across the room toward the dancing woman on the bar and then refocused on his hand.

"You gonna play or ya gonna sit there grinnin' at that dancin' whore all damn day?" the old timer across the table said.

Harding frowned and studied his hand. A laugh echoed above the din of the room breaking his concentration once again. He stared towards the ruckus, recognizing the man.

"Mister, you playin'? If yer still in, I call," a player said, tossing his cards for all to see. *Full house.*

Harding placed his cards face-down upon the table, his eyes focused on a man standing in front of the saloon whore.

The impatient player reached out to turn over Harding's cards.

With a flash of silver, Harding's hand darted—a knife drove through the back of the nervy gambler's hand. The blade sank deep into the wood tabletop. The handle quaked as blood welled up around the wound, the card player howling in surprise. The player next to the injured man helped him yank the blade free and wrap the bleeding wound in a dirty shirttail. The knife was dropped with a solid *thunk* onto the table before the two men backed away into the crowd.

Harding reached over the cards and reclaimed his knife. He wiped the blood onto his coat sleeve, saying nothing. He eyed the other players with a cool stare and then turned his cards face up. *Straight flush.* Curses traveled the circle of players as the men quickly paid up. They dispersed just as fast. Harding absently scooped the money into a pile, his eyes again upon the laughing man running his paw up the leg of the dancer.

The old man had stayed behind. "What's got yer eye, boy?"

Nodding toward the laughing man, Harding said, "That there be Buckskin Cooper. Them two guns strapped to his belt have killed twenty-one men."

"White men or Injuns?"

"White men. He don't count Injuns."

The old man laughed, then saw Harding was serious. He coughed. "What's yer interest in him?"

"He owes me money. Cheated me in Abilene, 'bout six months back. Left me with this," Harding's fingertips traced a jagged scar across his cheek. "Bullet grazed me. Could've been my eye." Harding paused. "I aim to get what's comin' to me."

"What's that hangin' from his coat?"

"Scalps. It's a little hobby of his." Harding stacked the coins and folded the bills, sticking the wad into his coat pocket.

The old man grimaced. "Injuns?"

"Yep. Buckskin double deals the Injuns. Trades with some, kills for others."

The old man laughed. "Well, from what I've heard tell you ain't no better, son. I heard you killed four men jest for snorin'."

Harding smiled. "Don't believe everything you hear, old timer." His face grew serious. "I only shot *one* man for snorin'—and I gave him fair warnin'." He stood, hitched up his sagging gun belt, and crossed the room toward Cooper. The old man quickly left the saloon, anticipating the unfolding events.

Buckskin Cooper turned around and spied Harding standing before him, hands resting on the butts of his revolvers. "I know you?" Cooper spat toward a spittoon. The clump of black chew missed, splattering onto the floor.

"Think hard."

Realization crossed Cooper's face.

"You owe me money, Cooper."

Cooper laughed. "Go away, Harding. Cain't you see I'm entertainin' a lady?"

The "lady" had crawled off the countertop and stood trembling near the table. She was hesitant to stay, but didn't want to lose the possible customer.

Without warning, Harding belted Cooper in the nose. A crimson fountain gushed over Cooper's scalp-laden buckskin coat.

The woman screamed and jumped.

"You damn—"

Before Cooper could finish his sentence, Harding pounded his fist into the man's face twice more, knocking at least one tooth from Cooper's mouth along with a string of unintelligible obscenities. Cooper went for his gun, but Harding's hands were quicker, and two shots fired in rapid succession caught Buckskin below each knee. The man collapsed onto the dirty floor, rage and expressions of pain exploding from his lips.

"You sunabitch!" Cooper scrambled for the gun that had fallen from his grasp. He wallowed in the pools of black chew that covered the floor around the spittoon, his fingers coiling around the trigger of the gun.

Harding fired off another bullet, sending Cooper's revolver spinning out of reach. Cooper's hand spouted blood, a jagged hole through the center of his palm.

"Looks like you and the good Lord got somethin' in common now, don't it?" Harding laughed and gave his revolver a twirl. He stood over Cooper, who lay panting heavily, blood pouring from his legs and hand.

"Come on, you bastard. Finish me and git it over with."

Harding laughed again.

The saloon girl's hands flew to her mouth. "Don't!"

Harding frowned and turned an angry face to the dancing whore. "You want that I should shoot you, too, lady?"

She quickly shook her head.

Harding flicked his wrist, his gun pointing toward the stairs. "Then go on and git."

She fled in terror up the steep stairs.

He turned his attention back to the groveling man on the floor. "You got my money?"

"What if I don't?"

Harding leaned over and pressed the barrel of his gun against Cooper's forehead. "I might have to do this...." He pulled the trigger, and Cooper's brain, deficient as it was, decorated the wood floor beneath and behind him in a crimson spray of gore.

The saloon filled with shouts and the sound of running boots as the more fearful patrons cleared out.

Harding knelt, tugged at Cooper's coat, and dug through the pockets.

He noticed the boots on the dead man's feet looked new and about the right size, so he pulled one off and was tugging on the other when Miss Sadie, one of the soiled doves that worked the rooms upstairs, came to a halt beside him, one hand on her hip. She surveyed the grisly scene, shook her head, and with a sigh said to Harding: "Long as yer takin' everything, I've got some more property of Buckskin's up in my room that yer entitled to."

Yanking the boot from Cooper's still-warm foot, Harding straightened himself up as the dead leg hit the floor with a thud. He gave Sadie a crooked smile. "You don't say?"

"I do say. Buckskin were my beau. Seeing how you gone and shot him dead, you might as well have it all." Sadie turned, her curls shaking as she sashayed up the stairs.

He followed her, one hand on the rail, visions of Sadie's long, ivory legs straddling his shoulders crowded his thoughts. She stopped before her door and twisted the key in the lock.

Entering the room, she was turning toward the armoire when Harding scooped an arm around her waist and swept her to the bed. She feigned to push him away, but laughed.

"Ain't you 'posed to be sad? All broken up o'er the death of yer beau or somethin'?"

"Buckskin Cooper was low down, but sometimes he sent money. I kept him around because I didn't know no way to git rid of the sunabitch."

Harding laughed. "So you ain't got no qualms about doin' me some favors then?"

She gave him a damn pretty smile. "Not if you ain't got no qualms 'bout *payin'* for them favors."

He had her drawers off, her clothes strewn across the floor, and his pants around his ankles faster than a cowboy could spit, and sure enough those long, ivory legs looked just fine clasped around his shoulders. The brass bed beneath them squeaked louder than a buckboard on a rutty road after a rainstorm.

After he was spent, they lay on the bed gasping for air, when a loud thump sounded from the armoire.

"What's that?" John Wesley asked, lunging for his gun belt.

Sadie stood, hair tousled, naked as the day she was born, and strode toward the armoire. She yanked open the door, and an Indian woman not much bigger than a sack of grain tumbled to the floor, hands and feet bound, mouth gagged.

"What in the hell is that?" Harding jumped from the bed.

"*That* is Buckskin's property that *yer* takin' with you." Sadie pushed the woman back into the armoire.

"She alive?"

"Course she's alive. I've been giving her belladonna to keep her asleep. The little savage was Buckskin's plaything. He jest about wore out every hole she's got. I was s'posed to be watchin' her while he played cards. Now you went and shot Buckskin dead, so the Injun's all yours. Her name's Tonacey."

"What am I 'posed to do with an Injun woman?"

"None of my concern. She's well broke in by Buckskin though, so she might prove entertainin'. In any case, you got to leave."

"I ain't takin' no Injun squaw with me."

"Yes, you are. You done killed Buckskin, now this here Injun's yer problem." Sadie stepped forward suddenly.

Harding backhanded her. She dropped to the floor with a shout.

"Whatcha go and do that fer?" she said, blood breaking the pink flesh of her lips.

"Thought you was goin' fer my gun."

"I don't want yer goddamn gun, you idiot." Sadie struggled to stand.

A thunder of fists knocked on the door. "Sadie? Sadie? You good in there?" a booming male voice sounded through the thin door.

"Cooper's got friends, don't he?" Harding asked.

"Yep. I 'magine they'll be wantin' a piece of yer hide more sooner than later, but he ain't one of 'em." Sadie pulled her blouse on.

The door exploded in a splintery gust as a hulking man charged through. He stood there, panting like an angry bull, gun drawn. "You the ass that dropped that man downstairs, ain't ya? Old Willie said he saw you go up here with Sadie."

"He was jest leavin' Edgar." Sadie tossed a large burlap bag to Harding. "You put the Injun in the bag and git out of here."

"My horse is round front, Cooper's friends will be watchin' fer me." Harding tossed a large stack of bills on the bed.

Sadie eyed the money angrily, then turned to Edgar. "Git his horse from round front, bring it to the back. Git supplies and water from Dora in the kitchen, and put them on the horse. He can sneak out of town the back way."

Harding said, "Don't forget the bullets."

"We ain't got none to spare. Go on, Edgar."

Edgar shook his head. "Whatever you say, Sadie." He left.

"Yer takin' the Injun with you." Sadie stood, hands on her hips, near the broken door.

Seeing no other choice, Harding yanked up his britches and snapped his suspenders into place. He rolled Tonacey into the bag. She stirred slightly. Slinging her over his shoulder, he headed downstairs.

He went through the kitchen onto the back porch. He flopped the bagged-up woman over the horse's haunches. Water and supplies were roped to his saddle. The narrow street behind the saloon was deserted.

"You better git. Gonna be dark soon. Place gits mean once the sun goes down." Sadie watched as he leapt into the saddle. "If you git out of this alive, don't you ever come back to this town, John Wesley Harding."

"Ain't got no reason to." He pushed his hat down and led his horse over the dirt road leading out of Callahan and into the desert beyond.

He rode under the pale light of the moon. The horse was a sturdy ride, and it kept a steady gait. The desert sands, speckled with sere shrubbery, cactus, and the occasional tree, angled down into a valley ahead of him. The slope ended at the base of a mountain range that rose high and dark against the purple velvet sky. All would've been fine to keep going, except the Injun was waking. He could feel her stirring, draped over the back of the steed, throwing the horse off balance.

The steed snorted and danced sideways as the Injun woman struggled.

"Whoa there," he muttered and patted the horse on the side of the neck.

They'd just come to the foothills, so he found a level spot, concealed from the open range by a copse of trees. He pulled the wriggling, bagged form off the horse. As soon as she felt his arms around her, she went rigid and kicked out. She almost got him pretty good once, but he chuckled and tossed her hard to the earth. She landed with a thud. He heard a sharp intake of breath through her nostrils. The bag had slipped halfway down. Her long black hair shone blue in the moonlight. She was pretty for an Indian woman.

He set up camp, unfurled his bedroll, and started a small fire with tinder and scattered limbs. He got the horse tied up and the rest squared away. He figured he was far enough away from Callahan not to worry about pursuers. If anyone did come up, he'd have them in plain sight on the horizon.

Harding picked the girl up, carried her to his bedroll, and yanked the burlap bag from her feet. Her hands were bound behind her back and her wrists bled, the ropes crusted with blood, hands looking pale. Her bare ankles were tied tight, and her mouth was still gagged. Her calico dress was torn up the front. He parted the fabric with a dirty hand to reveal her nakedness beneath.

He smiled.

The girl's black eyes reflected the moon with fear.

"Well, now," he said with a grin. "You'n I 're gonna get ta know each other a little bit better...."

He undid his pants and forced her knees apart, despite her best efforts to keep them closed. Her legs were deep tan and smooth, shapely all the way up to the treasure in the middle. She squirmed as he climbed atop and held her down, but there wasn't much she could do the way she was. Black eyes wild, she began to scream against the gag. She thrashed, making it difficult for him to hold her and take care of his business at the same time. He smacked her sharply across the cheek to shut her up while he had his way with her. By the time he was done, she had resigned herself to her fate and was unmoving, head turned away. Her eyes were open, but stared sightlessly into the night.

Harding snapped his suspenders against his chest and went to boil some coffee. He let her lie there. The coffee was done soon enough, and as he sipped a mug of the murky swill, he double checked that his pistols were reloaded. His eyes scanned the horizon before he said, "I think you an' I could get along real well."

Tonacey's head lolled toward him. She looked at him calmly. Like she was already dead. She watched while he cooked a little food and choked down a couple cups of coffee. He followed his meal with a shot of whiskey and then went over and removed her gag to give her some water. He didn't know how long Cooper'd had her tied, but she seemed pretty close to gone, like she used up her last reserve of energy to put up her feeble attempt of resistance. Her dress was still hitched around her shoulders; she made no effort to wiggle it back into place.

Harding looked toward the mountains. Lights twinkled there, floating and disappearing in an eerie, unnatural way. In all his travels he'd never seen anything like it. A look of awe was spreading over the woman's face.

"What are them lights? In the mountains? You see 'em?"

She smiled slightly. "I see," she said, in English, a thick accent forming her words.

"You ever seen 'em before?"

She shook her head no. "They come." Her voice was hoarse and parched.

"*They come?* Who's they and why they comin'?"

Tonacey lay still. "They are *Noyukanuu*. They are wandering souls of those that seek justice."

"Justice, huh?"

Tonacey continued to stare at the fading lights.

"What did you say they were called again?"

"*Noyukanuu. Taibo* call them ghost lights."

"Aw, you speakin' too much Injun talk. Now what's this tay-boo?" Harding poked the fire with a stick. Sparks flew up into the black of the night.

"*Taibo*. White man."

"Hmm. Well, I don't believe in no ghosts or wandering spirits or *No-kan-oo* or whatever Injun hocus-pocus you got goin' on." Harding watched her, still laying there motionless, still staring into the mountains. The lights were very faint now. Almost gone. Something akin to pity washed over him, and he pulled her dress over her nakedness and fixed her with a clean gag, then put out the fire before he laid down to get some rest. He slept with one ear tuned to the sounds of the woods for any sign of pursuers.

They made it through the night unmolested.

At daybreak, he broke camp; fixed Tonacey so she sat upright behind him for balance, saddled up, and headed toward the foothills. He wasn't much wild about totin' her around but hadn't yet figured out what to do with her—maybe he could sell her to a brothel, recoup some more of what Cooper'd owed him.

The morning ride started off cool in the shade. An invigorating breeze rolled over the hillside. His ears pricked at the slightest distant sound, and his eyes caught each shifting shadow. Their horse made its way along a traversing path. It did well throughout the morning, but as noon approached, the horse's legs trembled as the grade of the slope steepened. All it would take was for the woman to make one sudden move to throw the steed off balance, sending them plunging down the hill into trees, sharp rocks, and cactus. He marveled that she hadn't thought of it earlier. Perhaps, he figured, she was plenty beat down after her travels with Cooper, and his show last night taught her she weren't gonna get away with nothin' with him, either.

In any event, he woulda been better off without her. He set his hopes on gettin' something for her in Eastland, the next county over.

Midday stretched into afternoon. They rode over the first low set of hills that gave way to a higher ridge of mountains known as the Callahan Divide. They weren't mountains like in Arizona or New Mexico, but the sun made 'em feel just as tall and foreboding.

They paused before heading up the next slope, watered the horse, and let it graze on clumps of vegetation. He gave Tonacey some water and a once-over. Her hair was damp from sweat. Her sharp eyes regarded him with loathing.

"Ain't me that put ya in this mess, missy," he growled. She said nothing and made no attempt to fight him as he gagged her again. He admired the sensual curve of her leg, the exposed skin of her bronze breasts, chocolate nipples straining through the thin, torn fabric of her dress. He thought that he might take a longer break and—

A tingling at the nape of his neck coincided with the slight catch in the corner of his eye of a shifting shadow at the base of the valley.

Harding's hand went to the grip of his Schofield .45 as he scanned the brush with squinting eyes. He paused, watching like a hawk, knees half-bent, ready for action.

All was still, except for the stirring of a breeze that came through the valley, hotter now in the afternoon. He watched the trunks of trees, the swaying grasses that hissed, and wiped a drop of sweat from his eyebrow.

Damn woman was makin' him paranoid.

He swung onto the steed and spurred it uphill. Hooves dug into the crumbling dirt, pluming up clouds of dust. Rocks and gravel caught the horse's steps, kinked its ankle, as the extra weight of the woman made the climb difficult.

Harding paused at the edge of the trees. He could see the top of the divide—probably a mere twenty minutes away—where the trees thinned out into open territory from here to the rocky peak. Nothing but scattered grasses, cactus, deadfall, and rocks. He pulled on the reins, looking behind them. The horse stopped.

"C'mon," Harding grunted as he spurred the mount. It stumbled, almost spilling them. The Injun woman made a noise—a peep of alarm as her bound hands gripped his belt.

They righted just in time. Heart thrumming in his chest, Harding took them on a longer traverse across the wide-open hilltop.

Wind kicked up dust. The Texas sun shone down like a molten eye. Sweat ringed his hat and crawled along the back of his neck. His throat was dry as the dirt beneath their feet.

They had almost reached the crest of the hill when Harding looked up. The tan face and long black hair of an Indian brave stared down a notched arrow, aimed at him from a cluster of rocks just this side of the peak.

"Damn it!" Harding tried to rein the horse back, but the grade was too steep. The horse reared and almost fell backward, stumbling on its rear legs. Tonacey was thrown from the back of the horse.

He ripped his pistol from his holster and fired at his attacker. The shot ricocheted in a chip of rock and whined off into the distance. Too late, he heard a sailing hiss from behind and felt the sudden push and tug of a broadhead arrow that pierced and stuck in his shoulder. The shot hit the flesh between bone and cartilage and went clean through. Yelling in pain and rage, he yanked it the rest of the way through the flesh. He cast the shaft to the ground and spun in the saddle, firing off another shot behind him where the arrow had come from.

"You should have left woman behind, *taibo*," the voice echoed across the rocks. "We wanted Cooper. You take Cooper's life, but take his burden as well."

Harding spat, "You want the damn woman, Injun, you can have her!"

Tonacey's eyes grew wide. She lay curled on the ground, bloodied and bruised. Harding sneered and fired his pistol. The bullet pierced her forehead, exploding blood and brains over the rocks. Those black eyes went blank. A ruined skull lolled on her limp neck.

The act drew howls of Comanche fury from the hills, and he realized he must have been trailed all the way from Callahan by the small band of braves, waiting for his weakest moment to attack. Two of the Injuns above rose from their positions behind the rocks. One let fly an arrow, and a second fired off a couple shots from a rifle, both braves missing him.

Harding charged, one gun blazing, the arm of his wounded side held close to his chest. An Injun fired a wild shot at Harding and missed, instead blowing one arm from Tonacey's corpse that lay behind him. It jerked as the limb was torn loose at the shoulder. A second shot ricocheted from a rock with a whizzing sound. Harding leaned forward on his horse, killed the Injun holding the rifle and, with a second shot, sent the bowman sprawling. Harding's horse—lighter now—ascended quickly to the top of the hill.

Harding jumped from the horse, firing well-placed rounds into the pursuing group of Comanche. He saw two of them hit for certain, and the others had fallen back into the foliage, but he knew the Comanche and knew their pause wouldn't last long. They wouldn't wait him out—they'd already be moving to encircle him, to come around behind and take his life.

Weren't no way he was gonna be killed by the red man. Not now and not here. Not after he'd outgunned gunslingers that never been outgunned before.

He drew back the barrel catch with one hand and threw the barrel out with a flick of his wrist, jamming cartridges into the cylinders, reloading quickly. Hopping back onto the horse, he urged it down the other side of the divide. He spotted a plateau the next range over. Atop the mountain was a flat expanse of land, trees skirting a natural wall of rock around the upper shelf, it seemed too good to be true. Dark clouds gathered in the skies above, rolling in like the distant anger of a forgotten god. Lightning flashed, and tufts of grey hung ominously from the cloud. Looked like a heavy summer rain.

He would beat them to the plateau, take the high ground first, and fight them off. He knew he couldn't outrun them with his worn-out horse and bleeding wound, and they sure wouldn't grant any mercy if he surrendered. It'd have to be a fight to the death. He swore he wouldn't be the one doin' the dyin'.

While his horse ran at a full gallop across the next valley, he thought how much Cooper *really* owed him now.

By the time he crossed to the next range and started up the base of the plateau, rain began to fall from the darkening skies, pocking the dusty earth. The higher he climbed, the heavier it fell, until at last, reaching the lip of the plateau shelf, the skies let loose with a downpour that echoed with rolling thunder.

Harding yanked his horse to the right, leading the beast towards a craggy overhang barely visible now in the slashing rain. The rocky protrusion was a godsend, and Harding tugged the nervous mount closer to the mountain, slid off, and slung the reins around a boulder.

He crouched, hugging the mountainside, listening through the wind and rain for the fury of approaching hooves. He heard none. He scowled in the darkness until his horse gave a dusty snort. He flinched in the noise's direction. Still, he waited.

When his knees began to lock from the crouch and his joints protested at the hunkered down position, Harding stood and stretched—still alert, clutching his gun, waiting for his pursuers. With one hand, he scraped together the dead wood and bramble collected under the overhang and built a small fire. He sat beside it, welcoming the heat that permeated his wet clothes.

An owl hooted eerily in the distance. The rain continued in a constant patter over the rocks, over the shrubby plants, over everything. Through the constant fall of the rain, Harding saw the flicker of floating lights. Some touched the ground behind rocks and shrubs, like giant lightning bugs. Some hovered, fading out and then burning bright again.

If the Comanche were hot on his tail, and then abruptly vanished, there had to be a damn good reason why. Little rain weren't gonna scare off a war party. Shivers ran up his arms, causing the wet hairs there to prick up. Uneasy, he searched through the dim shadows illuminated by his flickering fire and the occasional haunting burst of floating light.

Around him, on every side, were the rocky telltale mounds of Comanche burial pits.

Not one, not two, but more than his eyes could see in the darkness. Littered atop the wet mounds were broken arrows, defleshed horse skeletons, and saturated feather-sewn quivers. The Comanche weren't afraid of the rain, or of a lone, life-hardened gunslinger. The Comanche were afraid to cross onto the sacred soil of their burial ground. Maybe they were afraid of those avenging spirits the woman had talked about. What did she call them?

Noyukanuu.

Harding's heart pounded in his chest, thrashing against his rib cage. Uncontrollable fear seized him and made his trained hands quake. He stepped into the shadows to see if he could tell how far the burial pits spread across the plateau.

crunch

He peered down at his boot. The jaw of a bleached skull had shattered beneath his heel. The remains stared up at him with vacant eye sockets. He gulped and jumped at the lone howl of a coyote somewhere in the darkness. Turning his gaze, he caught one of the fleeting lights as it touched down upon one of the burial pits. Two other glowing orbs drifted through the wet night to land upon other mounds and disappear into the rocky piles that covered the dead.

Just some lightnin' bugs, he thought, not entirely convincing himself of its truth.

He made his careful way back to the fire and resumed his watch, a restless hand planted on the butt of his revolver. His ammunition was low. Only a few rounds left.

Rain washed over tawny rocks. Above, a blood red moon peeked through clouds in the black night sky. Panic welled up. He fought to remain composed. His hands shook and teeth chattered—not from cold, but from a creeping terror that had worked its way up from his guts. Hell, he didn't even know what he was afraid of. All he knew was there was something unnatural about this place. Something wrong. Something even bloodthirsty Injuns feared.

Shivering, Harding dug into the recesses of his mind and recalled broken verses of the Psalm his grandma used to quote. "The Lord is my shepherd. I shall not want. He maketh me lie down, he maketh me lie down, he..." Harding racked his brain. Where did the good Lord make him lie down? And why the hell was he lyin' down in the first place?

Something shuffled to his right. Harding jumped.

It sounded like feet scuffing rocks and dragging through mud.

Harding pulled his gun, wincing at the pain from his wound, and with a shaking hand, aimed into the darkness.

shuffle, shuffle

There it was again. On the other side of him this time. He spun, prepared to face his attacker. Across the plateau he could see a lumbering figure dragging something behind. Then, three or four bright flashes of light over burial pits and suddenly three or four stooped figures, only shadows from where he stood, emerged, pushing their way out of the burial mounds. A moan emanated from the collective group. They seemed drawn to his sputtering fire.

"Stop right there!" he hollered into the rain. The low moans continued as the lurching band came nearer. Behind the oncoming figures, more of the hovering lights soaked into distant mounds.

He squinted into the dark. He couldn't tell who the men were or what they were dragging. All he could do was stand there and wait for them to enter the faint illumination of his fire.

The lead figure shambled into the orange glow from the flames. Its skin was a tepid pallor, greyish pale and slick with rain so that it looked almost covered in slime. Long black hair hung in patches from the figure's skull. Its eyes were shriveled pits with blackened sockets, lips stretched too tight across a gap-toothed grin. The worst part: the neck of the man—if it could be called such—was cut wide open, nearly in half, and jagged flaps of skin hung limp, exposing the gaping wound of severed veins, shriveled muscle, arteries, and throat.

Then his horrified gaze locked onto the broken body being dragged behind the gruesome figure—Tonacey.

Dragged by one leg, her ruined head bounced and smacked on every rock and indentation on the ground, causing her limp corpse to jerk like a demented marionette.

The figures behind these two were a grim band of men, more dead than alive. Putrid, half-decomposed. Scraps peeled from bones in ribbons of flesh, flapping in the gusting rain. Open chest cavities crawled with worms and dripped with hunks of mud or ruined innards, festering wounds that had likely ended their lives many moons ago were black with rot, hands with fingers that were mere skeletal claws. From within each of the figures, vaguely luminous through bones and cavities, came the faint glow of the lights he'd seen land upon each of their burial mounds.

Harding choked and sputtered, backing instinctively against the mountain's side.

In the dying light of his fire, he watched as another of the ephemeral, luminous globes fell upon a group of rocks nearby, which were thrown up from the ground and scattered; a grasping skeletal hand emerged from the burial pit beneath. First the hand, then the arm, and finally the entire half-defleshed body of a former Indian brave. Matted feathers hung from braids. All over the plateau, Indian corpses crawled from shallow burial pits that had been touched by the magical lights…and, as one, they turned to stare in Harding's direction.

The rain beat down hard. Lightning raked the sky in ragged flashes, scraping the ebony like white skeletal hands of death.

The smell of rot was gut wrenching. He struggled against the urge to vomit, gagging, dry retching, and covered his mouth and nose with his handkerchief. The other hand, quaking, fired his revolver in rapid succession into the lumbering crowd of dead Injuns.

"What do you want? Huh?" Harding shouted, terror seizing him. "Go away! Jest go away I tell ya! I got no quarrel with you!"

The moans grew louder.

He fired the last of his cartridges and watched a few of the Indians knocked to the muddy ground scramble onto unstable legs, resuming their course.

Their course: straight toward him.

Harding slung the heavy revolver into the oncoming horror and made a run for it. Through the blinding rain, he ran until he realized he had nowhere left to go. He backed himself onto the edge of a rocky precipice and knew, too late, that he had made a fool's call in judgment.

The Indians closed in. Closer they came until they surrounded him. He scrabbled back in a crab walk on hands and knees until his hands slipped off the edge of the cliff. He tried to throw himself over the edge, realizing at some point that he was screaming, but their hands snagged his clothing. Tearing the fabric. Pulling him closer.

They dragged him toward an open pit, holding him, struggling in their grasp. Harding was pulled to a sitting position and watched as a sad trio laid the broken body of Tonacey, missing one arm, into the pit, straightening her dress respectfully. They caressed her as one might caress a loved one, a sister, who had passed.

Empty eye sockets raised to survey him, then returned to the limp form of the woman in the grave. Shredded bloody fabric hung from Tonacey's dress. The decaying skulls turned back to Harding.

From out of a tattered leather vest, a long dead brave pulled a tomahawk. He moved purposely toward Harding, who slowly realized the monster's intent. Kicking and flailing, he vainly attempted to break free from the rotting hands that held him. Two shambling braves held his arm out from his side.

Without warning, the hatchet sunk into his flesh, cleaved his bone from the socket. Blood spurted from his shoulder, from the stump of his dismembered limb. Harding screamed and felt blackness engulf him.

When he came to, it was only moments later. He was still lying near the pit that held the lifeless body of Tonacey. His severed arm was tucked into the shredded fabric of her dress. His arm had been used to make her whole. Harding felt the blood pumping from his side, felt life draining into the mud beneath him.

His cloudy vision beheld a handful of the monsters as they were consumed by the ghostly lights and then faded away in a glorious fireball. A few remained behind.

Harding prayed to his grandmother's god to save him, but the blood continued to pour from his wound in a thick jet with each waning beat of his heart.

The remaining monsters hovered over the woman as if praying. One of them reached down and lifted her head to add a few moldy feathers to her tangled, muddy hair. It beheld the gaping hole in her skull, the back blown away, the contents spilled.

A rotting corpse of a brave shuffled over to Harding, hatchet in hand, and seized him, jerking his head to one side. Terror gripped his weakening heart as he realized the monster's goal—to make Tonacey whole for burial.

The stinking Comanche hand gripped his hair and wrenched his head forward. Harding hardly had enough life left in him to emit one final cry before the hatchet split open the back of his skull. The undead brave removed a hunk of bone, clawing deep into the new cavity, digging out Harding's dripping brain. As the rotting figure transferred the grey matter in gruesome bits to their destination, a gathering of lights swarmed the new pit and the broken body of the Indian girl.

The *Noyukanuu* made Tonacey whole.

As the supernatural glow completed its work, the animated corpses of the braves slowly moved to pile new rocks upon her body, reverently completing her burial mound. When finished, the figures dissolved, presumably returned to their former resting places, in coronas of light that illuminated the plateau in a flash before being swallowed by the darkness.

Harding's body was left behind for the scavengers of the night.

Frankenstein
Jo Fletcher

Snip and sew
From head to toe
A new torso,
Says Frankenstein

Glue and patch
The latest batch;
To mix and match
Tries Frankenstein.

Blood and bone,
Then flesh fresh-grown;
The seed is sown!
Cries Frankenstein.

The brain is next—
The doctor's vexed:
A psycho's fixed
For Frankenstein.

A high IQ
He couldn't do
And that he'll rue,
Will Frankenstein.

The lever's yanked,
The dials cranked,
The power's banked
By Frankenstein

Now watch him rise
And blink his eyes—
The Monster's size
Dwarfs Frankenstein.

His doubts assuaged,
The Monster's made—
Now be afraid,
Dear Frankenstein.

For what's created
Can't be sedated
And hope's outdated—
Pray, Frankenstein.

The Monster walks
And sort-of talks,
But his brain baulks—
Poor Frankenstein.

The storm's amuck,
The lightning's struck,
The doc's in luck—
Oh, Frankenstein!

And when he's killed,
The town is stilled,
Then Hell's revealed
To Frankenstein.

I guess 'tis best
That theories rest,
For damned the test
Of Frankenstein…

Jimmy and Me and the Nigger Man
Scott A. Cupp

IT WAS REALLY DARK OUT that night when Jimmy and me made the Nigger Man. It was dark as a black hole in Hell where the fire don't blaze nor glow, but burns just the same. The thunder crashed over the hills, but the lightnin never come, nor did it rain. Heaven was not pleased. Within a day, neither was we.

It begun as simple as anything. Jimmy and me'd had to read about Huck Finn and Nigger Jim for Miss Johnson, her being the English teacher around here. I thought as it was a good enough story, but Jimmy just seemed to go kinda weird on it.

When he read it, his eyes would start to glaze over, and you could hear his mind cogs clickin all the way over to Raymond's Blacksmith Shop. I should have known then that it was trouble.

It durn near always is when he gets that look.

He looked at me with that shit-eatin grin on his face. "Bob," he says, "We got to get us a good nigger just like ole Jim from the story, so's we can go raftin down the mighty Mississip and fight pirates and be heroes and the like. I can be the Captain and you can be the First Mate. We'll keelhaul anyone who don't agree with us, and"—there was this hesitation in his voice, and the gleam in his eye begun to sparkle—"there won't be no more school!"

Well, I got to say, I weren't quite sure how Jimmy was gonna pull this one off. I mean, he has had some of the most consarndest schemes ever to lay rest in a mortal mind. There was that time that we was gonna make wings outta bird feathers and fly away to Araby to be sheiks and have us a harem and genies. I durn near broke my neck when I fell out of that tree. And, I had to work for old Farmer Harris for two months on account of them chickens we plucked for their feathers. And there was the time that we was gonna dam up the river and charge all the people for their water. We both got good and soaked over that one.

Now, I thought, how's he gonna get a nigger? Lincum done freed 'em all, and lots of people around here are still sore over that mess. Jimmy's unk done died in that war. His mama never would talk about it. When she died, we finally found out that he'd fought for the Blue. Most folks round here took to the Gray, so I guessed as how I could see why she didn't want to talk much about it. She were only three when he went and left. The note tellin the family that he was dead come just a week afore her sixth birthday. He weren't but seventeen at the time. I forget the place he died, but I'd never heard of it before, and I ain't heard it since. Jimmy found the cap that they sent as a part of his stuff and took to wearin it around town until Bully Bentley and six others took it off his head and burnt it. Three of them boys ain't been the same since, and Bully still can't hear out of that one ear.

Anyways, Jimmy says, "We gotta get us a good nigger. That means we got to make our own. That way, he'll be owin to us and'll do whatever it is that we wants him to do. If I was to say, 'Nigger, jump in the water and go get us that big catfish,' why, he'd do that very thing. He'll be our personal slave and friend."

Now, I may not be the smartest thing that ever walked the streets of Fairfield, but I knowed that you didn't just up and make a nigger, and I told Jimmy so. He just stood there lookin at me with that grin never movin, and he says, "You remember Raoul the Magnificent?"

How could I ever forget Raoul? We'd seen the Amazing Travelling Magic Man the week before. He'd amazed us with pullin rabbits out of his top hat and makin fire appear at his fingertips and such. Me and Jimmy had waited days to get the chance to see his show. One of these days I'm going to take the time to learn the magic arts and travel the world just like he done. I'll be Robert the Wonderful, and I'll entertain kings and queens in Europe and walk through the walls.

"Yeah," I said. "I remember the show."

"Well, Raoul the Magnificent is over to Waterton on Saturday. I figure that you and me need to go over and see him."

I was beginning to get lost. "Why does we need to go see Raoul the Magnificent?"

"We need to see him on account of his magic wand. You remember the one with the big star on top that he used to put the lady he'd done sawed in half back together with? I figure that we can use that to help build us our nigger."

I turned for the house. I didn't hold no truck with stealin no magic wands from magicians who might saw you in half and leave you that way wheres you can still talk and breathe, but you couldn't walk, or who might turn you into a toad so's you'd have to eat flies. No sir, I didn't want nothin to do with that. And besides, who'd ever built a nigger?

Jimmy was callin to me as I was walkin, but I weren't listenin. I'd done that too many times in the past.

Saturday, we was standin in Waterton, Jimmy starin like he ain't never been in the city before and me tryin to avoid stepping in the cow shit, there havin been a trail drive through there two days before.

We found the saloon where Raoul was to perform. Jimmy snucked around back to see if he could get in. That boy has got a way with locks that ain't mortal. He can just ask one to open and—*clunk!*—it falls at his feet.

He weren't gone five minutes when he come hotfootin it up the street, wavin at me to follow and fast. When dealin with magicmen, I make it my business to get the hell out when someone says it needs to be got out.

I hit one of them cow turds full speed and slid into another. There'd be Hell to pay when my ma smelled my pants. But that was tomorrow, and I was tryin to avoid a mad magicman today.

When Jimmy finally stopped runnin, we was a good mile from Waterton. He was kinda laughin, kinda gaspin for air. But, from under his shirt, he pulled the wand, and he begun to wave it over his head and dance.

That was the beginning of the end.

For a while, I'd done forgot about the magician. I guess I thought that he had so many magic wands that he might not miss one. I hoped I was right. Anyways, if we got the nigger made before he found us, I would give him the wand back just fine.

It was Monday at school that Jimmy give me the plan for makin our nigger. I was to meet him that night at the cave. "And," he said, "be sure to bring a freshly dead cat. One that's got blood on its paws!"

I found Mrs. Riley's cat under the front stoop. It were a Siamese, and I hated that egg-sucker almost as much as he hated me. We'd had us a disagreement some time back over who owned this dead mouse I'd found near his bed. I wanted it so as to make a potion to ward off swamp demons, and I reckon as how he'd wanted it for lunch. We'd both ended up with somethin less than half, there bein this other cat that et the head whiles we were fightin over the whole mess. My potion wouldn't work with only half a mouse, so I'd left him with it and the hopes of stomach cramps leading him on up to Kitty Heaven.

He weren't that hard to catch. I brung a dead fish, and purty soon he was shinin up to me like it was money, just a-purrin and tryin to go for that fish. I dropped the fish to the ground and, as he went for it, I grubbed him by the tail and lifted him high 'bove my head. "You gonna die now, you bastid!" I screamed as I swunged him by the tail over my head. He'd done forgot the fish and was hangin on to me with them claws, a-yowlin like the Saints comin on in. When I could feel the blood starts to flow down my wrist, I swunged him hard against the side of the buildin, never lettin go of that tail. He let out one more yelp and then sorta collapsed.

He was fresh dead with my blood on his paws. I hoped he would do.

I was to meet Jimmy at the regular hideout down by the caves near the river. We usually met behind this dead tree and had some of our secret potions and spells hid down among the ruts. It was there that we dreamed about pirates and knights in armor and damsels in distress. It was Jimmy's favorite spot in the whole damned world. It was there that we was gonna make our nigger.

When I got there, Jimmy had done been at work for a while. I could see that he'd made a man out of river-mud clay for his head and legs and this old tree trunk for his body and arms. As I got there, he added two berries to the face, for eyes I guess.

It was dark out, but Jimmy didn't have no trouble at all recognizin the cat. "That's Mrs. Riley's cat, Herkyles, ain't it?" he said, knowing right well that I hated to acknowledge that damned cat's name. It seemed sinful to name such a cat after a god of strength and valor and golden fleeces.

I just held it out to him. "It's freshly dead, and it's got my blood on its paws." The damned thing had done started to go stiff on me. Just like it to start trouble even when it was done dead. I shoulda just burned it and found me another one to kill.

"Put him in here," Jimmy says, pointin to the tree trunk that was the chest. "Stuff him in there real deep. It'll give the nigger cunnin and the ability to see in the dark more'n me and you."

I put the cat in there deep. He was so stiff that I kinda had to force him in a little, but I reckon he didn't mind too much.

I reckon that it must have been around midnight then. Jimmy said that these things was best done at midnight. Neither of us had a watch, so we had to guess. I bet that that's where things went wrong.

Somewhere Jimmy had found this jacket of bright red, and there he stood, with that grin on his face, with that jacket hangin loose on his back (it were too big, but he didn't seem to notice), and that wand in his hand. He was wavin the wand all around. Or maybe it was wavin him. I couldn't tell.

All of a sudden, he jumps around, that coat a-swirlin behind him with a mind of its own. The star on the wand begun to glow, just a little at first, and then it got brighter. Jimmy, he starts to howlin like a dog and sayin words that weren't never part of the secret ceremonies we'd done before. They weren't English, and I couldn't hardly recognize any of them. They sure didn't sound like none of the made-up words that he'd used before. They was words like Yuck Succotash and Shubby Niggerath and Cruel Loose. I didn't like the sounds of them words, and I sure didn't like the way that wand's star was shinin. It was a white star on the wand, but then it begun to glow in lots of colors—red, then blue and green. Finally, it shone in black. I passed out then. You cain't imagine the horror of seein your best friend traipsin around like a crazed gypsy with a magic wand that was glowin black as a dark night in Hell.

When I come to, there was thunder rollin through the hills, but I couldn't see no clouds.

Jimmy let out a scream that made me want to go join old Herkyles. And then he fell over. The wand continued to glow.

I run over to Jimmy. Just as I got there, there was a flash of black light from the wand to the nigger.

Then, the berries begun to move on that black mud face. They looked like eyes. Jimmy rose up, took the wand, and slammed it into that black mud head. "Live!" he screamed.

The wand stuck in the mud, and the berries was gone. In their place was eyes. Black, evil lookin eyes that didn't have no whites around them and that seemed to stare into your very soul.

Jimmy had hung on to the wand and wouldn't let go. I tried to pull it out of the Nigger Man's head, but I couldn't get it to come. Jimmy finally let go.

The Nigger Man started to rise. He used them tree-limb arms to push hisself up. Parts of him were still mud and tree then. But as I watched, they seemed to get real smoky, and suddenly they wasn't mud nor tree. They wasn't quite flesh, neither. What they was, I didn't want to know. Dreams of raftin down the Mississippi no longer bothered me. We had made our Nigger Man, and all I wanted to do was be shut of it.

Jimmy started to become hisself about then. The Nigger Man was startin to stand. He weren't quite sure on his feet, seein as how they were two pieces of not-quite-wood that didn't really match. He fell down once, maybe twice, before he seemed to get the hang of it.

Jimmy just stared and kept sayin, "We done it! We just damn well done it!" like there was ever a doubt in his mind. He stood up and raised his body to his full height. "Nigger," he said, "I am your Master and Creator. This here is Bob, your Co-Master and Co-Creator."

The Nigger Man didn't seem to hear. Then, as I looked at his not-quite-mud face, I noticed that Jimmy hadn't made him no ears. I don't know how he expected the Nigger Man to be followin orders when he couldn't hear em none.

But the Nigger Man turned kinda slow-like and begun to walk over to Jimmy. He still didn't have the walkin down so good, but I figured he'd get better as it got along. He just stood there—not movin, not talkin, not doin nothin. Jimmy reached up and grabbed one of them tree limbs that was sort of a hand and begun to lead the Nigger Man away.

"What you doin?" I asked.

"I'm gonna put him into the cave until we can come out and work on teachin him the things that he's got to know. How to talk, how to fetch. He's a big one, ain't he? And he's our nigger."

We packed the Nigger Man into the cave. He didn't fight us none. I was tired and ready for sleep when I got to home. This week had already been more than a saint could bear, and I weren't no saint.

I don't know how I slept that night. If I'da known what was comin…well, I don't know as I would have done nothin different. I like to think I would, but sometimes you just don't know. And with Jimmy, it was hard to do things any ways 'cept the way he wanted em done.

Anyways, the things that was done was done and nothin I can say or do now is ever gonna change that one bit. It went like this—

The next morning, when Jimmy and me got to the cave, we was astonished to find the Nigger Man weren't there. You could tell that he'd been there cause everythin inside were all scuffed up and the like, and you could see where he'd uprutted some bushes when he'd left the cave. So at least there was a trail to follow.

It seemed funny trackin someone through the woods without callin for them. Jimmy had started to, but since he didn't have no name other than the Nigger Man, and we hadn't even called him that, Jimmy didn't figure it would do no good to yell it. I pointed out to him that he didn't give our slave and friend no ears, so it weren't no wonder that he didn't stay put like he ought, but were out wanderin around.

The Nigger Man had just crawled out of the cave and had went wherever he wanted to. Sometimes it were in circles over and over again. Sometimes it were through bushes that didn't want nothin to go through them. He were persistent though, and often as not them bushes weren't planted no more when we found them.

It took a while, but finally we caught up to him settin by the river, throwin flowers in it like he had some good sense. Jimmy went up and pulled him on his arm, him not having a sleeve (nor any clothes as it was) to tug on. The Nigger Man turned around and looked at us with them dark eyes.

Jimmy started in on the lecture I knowed he'd been rehearsin all durin our hunt. All about the Nigger Man's responsibilities to his Masters and Creators, and why was he runnin off like that, didn't he have the sense God give a crawdad?

I'd done heard most of it durin the hunt, so I was starin into space, watchin the birds fly by. The Nigger Man weren't doin much of nothing. I still don't think he could hear nor think.

He finally stood up, and I spied a piece of cloth on the ground under him. It weren't much, just a piece of blue gingham just like all the girls wear. It weren't even much of a scrap, but it also weren't supposed to be there. A glance to the right brought my eyes to the river. I found the rest of the gingham.

Out there in the current, there was something hooked onto a limb of a fallen tree. It were a blue gingham dress, filled with Mandy Spencer. I remembered as how she liked to come down to the river and throw flowers into it. I guess she found the Nigger Man and musta started to scream, she bein noted for that. I remember once she screamed for thirty minutes when Harry Allison shoved a garter snake up in her face. And...I guess...the Nigger Man done went out and killed her.

My eyes was suddenly filled with tears, and I was lookin for something heavy. I found a rock and begun to beat on the Nigger Man with it. For a while, he didn't even seem to notice. The rock kept makin a kind of boomin noise on the tree-trunk chest.

Finally, he turned. I dropped the rock, sorry that I had ever seed it. There was hate in them eyes. And on the left side of his face there was a small white ear with a pierced earring in it, just like Mandy always wore.

The Nigger Man stretched his arms out towards me. The tree limbs that was his arms started to move. They was growin and headin towards me. I tried to run, but them arms growed fast. First thing I knowed, I was on the ground, wrapped in the arms of the Nigger Man. Then the limbs started to shrink, drawin me back towards him.

I didn't even think about Jimmy whiles this was goin on. I guess I forgot he was even there. Suddenly, he's standin behind the Nigger Man with the rock I dropped, and he's smashin it into the head as hard as he could.

The tree limbs finally released me after what seemed like forever. My ankles was red and sore as hell. I began to rub them.

Jimmy was yellin at me, but I wasn't listenin. He finally dropped the rock and grabbed me, half carryin, half draggin me with him. The Nigger Man's head was a mess, all kinda squished up. It didn't quite look like flesh all messed up. Then the muck started to ooze back together, and his head was reformin right before my eyes.

We ran into the woods. I'm sure we musta run in circles. There was one rock I'm sure we passed three times. But it was hard to notice where we was goin when the Nigger Man was a-chasin us, his head reformin as he run, that magic wand still stickin out the side. As his head was fixin itself, the wand was glowin; this time it was a green color.

We run like bats out of Hell. The Nigger Man never was far behind. He didn't move fast, but he didn't dodge much neither. If somethin got in his way and was smaller than he was, it got runned over. Jimmy and me occasionally had to run around things, like trees.

Sometimes Jimmy was in the lead, sometimes it was me. Neither of us had a plan. I don't guess that we'd have made one if the Nigger Man hadn't chunked a boulder at us. Big thing just come crashin through the air and on through some mesquite and made a path where there hadn't been none before. Jimmy decided we better hole up somewhere.

"Make for the cave!" he shouted, not carin if the Nigger Man heard us or not. "We'll hide in there until someone can find us."

"All right," I said. "But remember, if someone finds us they also gonna find him, and that may not do us no good."

But we run for the cave. And barely made it. There was another boulder come swishin through the air. That one nearly took off Jimmy's head.

Tree limbs may be good for holdin ankles but they cain't pitch rocks for shit. Thank God!

Then I saw it.

The mouth of the cave was glowin blue! I didn't want to go into no shiny blue light, but fear of the Nigger Man drove me into the unknown.

Jimmy hadn't even noticed the glow. He was still lookin glassy eyed from seein the ear and dodgin the boulders. He was also twitchin and jerkin from side to side, like a dog that's been partial run over by a wagon.

"So!" boomed a voice. "The thieves return at last to meet their fate."

I died. This was for sure the voice of Doom and it was right here in the cave. It was the voice of Raoul the Magnificent, wizard to kings and emperors. Jimmy just sorta twitched. I think one of them boulders musta grazed his scalp a little 'cause I could see some blood on his ear. His blood. His ear.

Raoul increased the glow. I saw it was comin from another of his fabulous wands. "So, my boys, let's us talk about magic and thieves."

Jimmy moaned.

"Did you know that in the court of Charlemagne, thieves had their thumbs cut off, and had to serve the Queen's lapdog, which licked the stump if it was thirsty? Or that, in Argo, thieves had flaming embers placed inside their stomachs and were used as ovens to roast potatoes in? Now, what do you suppose I have planned for you?" The glow begun to change from blue to a dark red or purple. Raoul seemed to glow. His long mustache begun to writhe like snakes that was attached to his face. Lightnin flashed from Raoul's eyes and hit the walls of the cave. "Where's my wand?"

"Well, sir, Mr. Raoul, it's outside stuck in the head of the Nigger Man that's done got Mandy's ear and killed her and now wants to kill me and Jimmy and please don't turn us into toads. I don't like flies and couldn't eat a one and then I'd die. We didn't mean no harm!" There was tears in my eyes and my mouth was runnin faster than my mind coulda ever thought. I told him everything, from readin Huck Finn and Nigger Jim and stealin his wand (his eyes glowed fire red at that) and the killin of Herkyles and the buildin of the Nigger Man and Mandy and the tree limbs. I think I told him everything, maybe not quite in the order that it happened, but he got the idea that things wasn't goin the way that Jimmy had seed it.

All the time that we was talkin, the Nigger Man was still comin. He'd found the cave and begun to come in, them tree limbs growin fast and explorin the walls of the cave lookin for us. Finally, the limbs crawled into the part of the cave where we was. I didn't see them as I was still runnin off talking to Raoul. He'd lost most of his fearsomeness and seemed to be interested in just exactly what it was that we had done. I was telling him what I could of the stuff Jimmy said at midnight, but the words didn't make much sense to me then, and it's real hard to remember nonsense words. But Raoul knew what they was all about.

He got a funny look on his face when them tree limbs circled round his ankles, like it didn't quite hurt, but he sure didn't want to do it again. Then the tree limbs tried to pull him outside. They should never have tried that. He rose up to his full height (about ten or twelve feet I believe) and begun to mumble some funny soundin words, like Jimmy had done. The wand was movin around like it had a mind of its own. Suddenly, there was this blaze of light and a scream of tortured agony. The tree limbs was on fire, and the Nigger Man was fryin away. Raoul sent another ball of fire down the cave mouth. There was another scream.

Raoul run to the mouth of the cave. The Nigger Man was burnin just like he was in Hell. His arms and chest was blazin. The clay mud of his face was beginnin to harden. The berries oozed out juices. It was horrid, and I watched ever second of it. Finally, I could smell the fur on Herkyles begin to burn. I knowed it was over then. The Nigger Man just fell over into some heaps. The head stayed in one piece, Raoul's wand still there, not even fazed by all of the fire and stuff.

Raoul waved to me. "Get the wand, boy! You two put it in, it has to be you that takes it out. Smash the head and bring me that wand!"

I grabbed the head. It was hot to touch. Raoul had fired the clay-mud head into a pot. I raised it over my head and flung it into the ground. "Take that, you bastid!" I screamed. "Breakin's too good for you!" The head broke into a zillion pieces. Only two parts was whole—the wand and Mandy's ear.

The wand weren't glowin no more. It was cool to the touch. "Do you surrender this wand to me of your own free will and renounce all claims to it?" he asked, lookin at me first, then back at the wand.

Somethin struck me. "What if I doesn't?"

That weren't the thing to say to Raoul just then.

"Why, I'll raise the Nigger Man up right where he lies and have him eat you up like a squash." The mustache started movin again.

"You can have the wand on two conditions," I says.

"Conditions! You are hardly in the place to be making conditions!"

"Still, I has two. The first is for Jimmy and me. I want's you to fix up Jimmy so's he don't moan and twitch like he's been doin."

"Well, I guess that can be accomplished. What is it that you desire for yourself?"

"Let's talk about the second condition first. I wants you to bring back Mandy and fix her ear so's it's right and she ain't dead." I figured that I owed it to her, since Jimmy and me had made her dead.

Raoul looked at me and shooked his head. "It can't be done, my boy. There are rules to all of this. That's why you have to surrender the wand. I can't take it from you. You could take it from me, because you don't know the rules. Me, I know them and, at times, they are very constricting. With the wand, I can make things that weren't ever alive appear to live. But I can't make something live that has died. I wish that I could. There are a great many people besides Mandy that I would bring back." Tears began to form in his eyes as I could see him rememberin someone who was now gone.

"Now, again I ask, what is it that you want in return for my wand?"

My voice caught in my throat. Here goes. "I want to travel with you and learn magic and entertain kings and queens and learn to walk through walls. I always wanted to, so I'm askin now. Take me with you."

Raoul looked at me with his eyes beginnin to glow again.

"So, you want to learn magic and walk through walls?" He stared at me some more. "Give me the wand and it's done."

"And you'll take care of Jimmy, too?" Makin sure that he didn't get out of that part.

"Done!" he said. I gived him the wand. He went to Jimmy and laid the wand upside of his head and whispered stuff into his ear. Jimmy's eyes began to unglaze, and he started to smile.

Raoul lifted out his hand to me. "Now, my friend, let us go."

And we walked out through the walls of the cave.

The Horror of No Beer
Richard Gilliam

PEOPLE SOMETIMES ASK WHAT'S a world-famous author like Lawrence Larkin doing working as a night clerk at the Lambeau Inn. I tell them it's mostly so I can laugh at the drunk Packer fans when they try to get their plastic room keys to work. There are other reasons I don't tell. Natasha, the bartender at the lounge, lets me run a tab between paychecks. Plus, she stocks some of those really good, Eastern European beers it's tough to find here in the land of Old Style and Miller Genuine Draft.

Something else I don't mention is that a hotel is a great place to observe people. Writing is much easier if you don't have to make stuff up. After a while, you have a reservoir of people-stories floating around in your head, and before you can say Vicki Baum, you've got yourself a novel.

Things occasionally get weird in ways that would freak the *X-Files*. Halloween at a hotel is often strange, and Halloweens when there are Packer home football games are among the strangest. It was way past midnight a few years ago when this poor guy dressed like a swan from *Swan Lake* calls on the house phone and says his plastic thingee won't work. So I head down to his room and find him and a duck and a vampire looking real bloodshot and angry.

"You seen anyone dressed like a hotel clerk?" snarls the vampire, and then he starts to lecture me about all the stuff he doesn't like about Green Bay. Real nasty fellow, and I mark him to be a mean drunk of the worst kind, the petty sort of person you don't want to be around. There's nothing wrong with any of the three keys—they're just too drunk to put the magnetized strip in the slot the way the picture on the door shows them to—so I let each of them into their room, and I don't even wait not to be thanked. It's maybe an hour later when the phone rings again, and this time it's Tasha saying please come to the bar, that there's a real vampire passed out in the storage cooler.

"No beer," says Tasha as I enter. "We ran out."

"It's okay," I reassure her. "I don't drink while I'm on the job."

"No, you don't understand. It's the vampire. He needs beer," she says.

"So do I, but I can manage to wait til my day off."

"No. He *needs* beer. Like most vampires need blood. He's a friend. From the Old Country. Helped my parents get out of Europe when it mattered. I owe him, plus he's a decent guy and one of my best customers."

"Beer," mutters the vampire. I hadn't noticed him shivering on the floor. I suppose I had been expecting the drunk in the vampire costume. This vampire had an aura around him, the sort of thing you feel and know he's authentic. There was a good feel to the aura, as if he was the kind of person who made the best out of whatever strange cards he got dealt.

"He needs *Brasov Select*," Tasha says. "From the waters of his home in the foothills of the Transylvanian Alps. We ran out about an hour ago. The guy in the vampire costume was buying rounds for the swan and the duck, and I forgot to set some back in the cooler."

"Give him a Pilsner Urquell. Close enough in taste he'll never know the difference."

"Won't do. Has to be brewed from his home city," she said, glancing towards the window as if to check on the status of the sun.

"We still have a few minutes," I said, hoping the vampire would stay calm. "Does he have fangs?"

"Yes, of course. He's a vampire. That's why he drinks from cans rather than from bottles. Easier to sink his fangs into a can."

"I know what room the guy in the vampire costume is in."

"What?"

"He's got fangs. Let him drink the Brasov Select out of the guy in the vampire costume."

"I don't drink...blood," moaned the vampire, obviously in some distress.

"Will it hurt the vampire? I mean, the one in the costume?"

"Who knows?" I said. "What's the worst that could happen? That the guy wakes up with an unnatural craving for beer? He's an alcoholic already. Besides, it might help him. A vampire would be a big step up from what he is now."

"I've never had blood before," said the vampire, still a bit scared.

"About time you did," I replied, lifting him to his feet. "About time you did."

* * *

I saw them both the next evening, having dinner together with a couple of Brasov Selects on the table, so I guess it worked out. They were both just kind of picking at the food, pretending to eat, so I was pretty sure what had happened. Tasha was happy because Brasov is a really expensive beer, and now she has another regular customer.

So, at last you know the real reason, the one I don't tell to people when they ask why I work at the Lambeau Inn. It's a great place to find stories.

But Somebody's Got to Do It
Edo van Belkom

IT'S A SHITTY JOB, BUT somebody's got to do it.

You hear a lot of that around here, and for the most part it's true. The shitty job in question is fireman at one of the biggest crematoriums in the country. The bodies come in at a rate of about thirty an hour, and they go out just as fast, or perhaps I should say they go up just as fast...up, as in smoke.

It's a bad joke, I know, but bad jokes are a reality here, they help you get through the day, through the weeks and months and years. The bodies became a blur a long time ago, and they aren't really human to me anymore. Meat, that's how I look at them, or at least that's how I think of them. I don't like to look at them too much because I like to keep my lunch off my shirt and down in my stomach where it belongs.

The fresh ones aren't so bad, the ones they rush over after car crashes and heart attacks. Sure they're bloody and all, but they don't look or smell too bad. The ones they find in the bush, that have been seasoned a week or two in the sun, or at the bottom of a lake, are the ones that make my skin crawl. They're the most dangerous too, the ones most likely to cause trouble.

Of course there aren't too many zombies around anymore, not like in '98 and '99 when the plague swept across the country and infected three-quarters of the population with the virus. It was war in those days, war on the unarmed masses of walking deadheads. The Zed Squad was a million strong, then, and heavily armed. Okay, so maybe it was really more like shooting fish in a barrel, but the papers and television made it sound like a war. That was then.

It's all changed now. Ever since they banned cemetery burials in '01, they've been able to keep the zombie problem pretty much in check. Sure, there's still the odd one that gets loose now and then, but the Zeds usually make short work of them.

The Zed Squad, The Zeds, Zedders. Their official name is The Zombie Squad, but how many people call the cops the Police Force? The Zeds got a whole set of nicknames and slogans of their own, probably make all kinds of bad jokes too, just like us. I guess it's the same, whether you work with dead people or living-dead people, you gotta have fun with it, or you might stop for a minute and think about what's really going on. It's a shitty job, but somebody's got to do it.

I didn't grow up wanting to be a fireman, at least not the kind that burns dead people in ovens. I went to college, even graduated with honors. But what do you do with a B.A. in geography besides teach high school? So, I applied for a job at the government offices, and waddyaknow, I got offered a job at the province's new creamery. That's one of the nicknames we have for the place. It's another bad joke, but what else can you do?

I don't say much on the job. I don't like to come off sounding conceited or full of myself. I'm the only guy in the place with any sort of education, and the conversation here isn't what I'd call stimulating. (Correction! The conversation *is* stimulating, it just doesn't stimulate any part of the body remotely connected to the brain.)

Anyway, Fernando says more than enough for both of us. He's my partner, Don Montalban Fernando. He's part Mexican, part Spanish, part Irish, part Navajo, part Canadian. At least he says he is. I never challenge him on anything he says because that would mean speaking to him like I was interested in his personal life. And, I'm not sure if he'd know how to handle a regular conversation. Check it out.

"Hey, man," he says in surprise as a fresh corpse comes down the chute.

He usually prefaces his comments with that phrase, or a subtle variation on it. "Hey, hey, hey, man..."

I look down at the body. It's a woman. She looks like she died on the delivery table; she's naked with a long straight incision across her belly. My guess is she was having a baby by Cesarean, and something went wrong. I don't like to speculate on these kinds of things, but Fernando does.

"Hey man, I think I slept with this chick last week. Yeah, I remember riding the hump with this bitch." He cups one of the corpse's large, milk-filled breasts in his hand and squeezes. He's gentle at first, but then his grip gets tighter.

I wait patiently til he's done. He doesn't play with each body for very long because he knows there'll be another one along in a minute or so.

Shit happens and people die: another of our slogans. It's not as good as: Life's a bitch and then you burn, but you get the idea.

When Fernando finishes fondling the corpse, I undo the straps holding it onto its transport slab and send the slab down the rollers. When it hits the fortified frame around the furnace entrance, the body slides off the slab and shoots right into the fire.

Fernando hits the button that controls the gas, and the flames burn orange-white for a moment then die down. The heat inside our little hell machine tops off at around five-thousand degrees Fahrenheit. The body is gone in less than a minute. It gets burned so clean that the residue only has to be scraped off the inside of the furnace once a month.

They say that in few months, the creameries will have put more bodies through the ovens than the Nazis did more than sixty years ago. I don't like to think about that much either, but when I do, I console myself by thinking there's a big difference between firemen and Nazis—at least our customers are dead before they arrive.

Fernando and I take the slab off the rollers and put it on the hoist that takes it back upstairs.

Another body comes down the chute.

"Oh shit, man, this one's *tender*."

By "tender," he means it's one of those bodies that's been sitting in the sun. It's grey and blue and there's some sort of green-yellow pus oozing out of a hole in its chest. And maggots, lot and lots of maggots. We both put our masks on in a hurry and take plenty of care unstrapping this one. The grey ones with maggots are the ones you've got to worry about.

I remember one time, about a week after I started, a corpse came down the chute looking a lot like this one. Harrison, the guy I was working with at the time, didn't seem to be too concerned. He put his mask on, but didn't bother being too careful about the rest of it. And wouldn't you know it, once he had the straps off, the grey-green corpse rose up off the slab and took a bite out of his neck. I can still remember the sound—like someone biting into a crisp green apple.

I watched Harrison grab his neck, and then I screamed for help, and Carbonneau came running out of his office with the standard issue sawed-off and blew that zombie's head clean off its shoulders. I sent the slab down the rollers as quick as I could, and then I dared to take a look at Harrison. He was writhing around on the floor like a worm that's just been cut in half. Wet, gurgling sounds were popping up out of the bloody, red hole in his neck. A few maggots had made the jump from dead to living flesh and were crawling all over the gaping wound. Harrison reached out like a drowning man, but nobody moved to help him.

"Turn around if you don't want to see this," Carbonneau said as he pumped a shell into the gun's chamber.

Everyone else turned around but me. I stayed put and watched Carbonneau point the gun and close his eyes. "Forgive me, Harry," he whispered, then pulled the trigger.

The meaty pulp on the floor steamed hotly for a few minutes before it cooled. I helped Carbonneau get the pieces of Harrison onto a slab, and we both made the sign of the cross as we slid him down the rollers.

"One strap left," Fernando says, bringing my head back to the job at hand.

I nod numbly and tense my muscles. He unsnaps the final strap, and we begin to push the slab toward the fire.

The maggoty green head turns in my direction. Pieces of grey skin fall away from its face as its mouth opens, and black, rotting teeth snap dangerously close to my hand.

The head prepares for another bite. Already Fernando has a length of pipe in his hand. He is swinging. The zombie's mouth is open, then closed. I feel something hot on my fingers. The pipe glances off my arm and connects with the hellish green head, splitting it in two.

"Hey man! Are you all right?" He swings the pipe again and smashes the zombie's head into roadkill.

"I'm okay. I'm all right. Just nipped my glove, that's all."

The pain in the end of my finger is incredible. There is a slight tear on the outside of the glove, and I know the bastard got me. The skin on the tip of my finger has been broken. There's no doubt I'm infected with the virus.

Fuck! I scream inside my head. *Shit! Damn! Fuck!*

"I don't feel so good, though. I got quite a scare. I think I'll go home, if it's okay with you."

"Hey, man, sure," Fernando says. "Take it easy. I'll cover for you."

I nod thanks and leave.

In the change room I remove the glove slowly because a) it hurts and b) I'm afraid of what I'll find. I drop the glove on the floor and try to hold my infected hand to stop it from shaking. Already the tip of my finger has turned green. And already, it's starting to smell—bad!

I walk home with my hand in my pocket, deep inside my pocket. The night is cool, but I'm sweating like a cold beer on a hot day, and I'm freezing. I don't look up. Don't want to risk looking anyone in the eye, afraid they might notice something…different about me.

I remember one time I was walking home from work when I turned down Main Street. I was nearly blinded by the Zed Squad's spotlights. They'd set up barricades at both ends of the block, and in the middle of the street was this zombie stumbling around in circles, all grey and maggoty. There were plenty of film crews and newspapermen—zombies making it that far into town is big news. It's also a good photo opportunity for both the newsies and the Zeds.

After they let the zombie walk in circles for the benefit of the cameras, the Zeds at one end of the street took cover, and a guy said over a loudspeaker—"Prepare for termination!"

Everyone ran for cover, but there was just this little *Kirack!* of a gunshot. That's all it took, one shot, and this zombie's head exploded like an overripe melon with explosive charges inside, where the seeds should have been. I hung around to watch them scrape body parts off the pavement. The Zeds didn't take too much care while they bagged the zombie, they just shoveled it up and put it into a bag like dog shit off a sidewalk.

My stomach spasms at the thought as I walk along Main Street. I lean against a building and retch. My stomach is empty, and all I can manage are a couple of dry heaves.

At last I'm home. My finger doesn't hurt anymore. The pain has moved up my arm, and now it's my wrist that feels like it's on fire. I look at my hand under the light of a desk lamp. It's stone-grey in places, green like moss in others.

The tip of my finger where the infection started is dripping some kind of green liquid. It drips onto the scattered papers on my desk and splatters in uneven splotches like a Rorschach test. One blot looks like a dog, another like a cat, yet another like a close play at the plate. I squeeze the tip of my finger and the green stuff flows out like sludge. I look down at the paper and think: a broad and two guys fucking their brains out.

I laugh.

I wrap my finger in a towel and walk over to the bed. I lie down. I expect the room to spin, but it does not. Instead the walls and ceiling bend and curve, as if the room is turning itself inside out. I think I see a light open up above me, but I fall asleep before I can be sure.

* * *

I wake up and roll onto my side. It's three in the afternoon—time for work. I feel hungry, but I can wait til lunch break. I walk into the bathroom and look in the mirror. I don't look too bad really, a little pale is all. My finger is healed over now with a hard, green-black scab. I tap it against the rim of the sink and feel no pain.

I look myself over and see that I'm already dressed. I leave the house for work. I walk slowly, like I'm dragging my feet. I try to walk faster, but I can't.

Because I can't walk so good, I get to work late. Everyone looks at me strangely—I guess I'm paler than I thought.

"Hey, man," says a voice. "You look like shit!"

"Where you been the last two days?" another voice says. "We've already been interviewing for your job."

I try to answer. My jawbone works, but I can't move my tongue well enough to form a word. I try to say "I'm back," but it ends up sounding like "Ugh-huh."

"You back to stay?" a voice asks.

I nod, yes.

"All right, then. Get back to work."

I nod.

"Hey, man, we thought you were a goner. We thought we'd hear about you gettin' offed by the Zeds. I'm glad you're back, my wife will be glad to hear it too. When I told her what happened to you, she started gettin' all worried about the same shit happenin' to me...."

I nod when I think I'm supposed to. This seems to be enough.

"...Hey, man, not talkin' too much today? Must be feelin' just like your old self again, huh?"

The first body comes down the chute. Its clothes are torn in places, and the bits of exposed meat smell delicious. I put a hand on its chest. It's still warm. I want nothing more than to sink my teeth into that soft pink flesh, but something at the base of my skull tells me, *Not yet. Wait!*

We unstrap the body and I send it into the furnace. Pangs of hunger begin to rip through me. I want meat, I *need* meat.

"Hey, man, I'm goin' for a coffee. Want one?"

No, I shake my head.

"Okay. I'll be back in a few minutes. I got to take a crap too."

I nod.

A body comes down the chute. It's black and blue and bruised and rotten. Bad meat. I unstrap it and send it quickly into the fire.

Another body. An old man. Heart attack, maybe. He is lukewarm. I bend over him. My teeth open wide and dig deeply into his belly. Delicious. I take three more bites before I send the body down the track.

Another body is before me. A young woman. Half of her head is missing. Car crash. Her blood-blackened blouse is open. A tittie is exposed. Peekaboo! I chomp down on the breast. It is soft and warm in my mouth. Good meat. I quickly eat the other breast and parts of her neck.

I hunger for more, but I unstrap the body and send it into the flames.

"I'm back."

I nod. I continue working.

"Hey, man. Gettin' back to work is doin' you good. You already got some color back in your cheeks. You'll be your old self again in no time."

A body slides down the chute. A woman. Another car crash, or perhaps the same one.

"Hey, man. I know this bitch. She gave me the best blowjob of my life a couple years back."

I nod.

"Oh, shit," the voice says. "I forgot to take a crap. You don't mind if I take off for a second, do ya?"

I shake my head.

I am alone again. A warm tender meal lies before me. I remember something...words, a phrase.

It's a shitty job, but somebody's got to do it.

Yes, I think. And thank god it's me.

I Fuck the Dead
Sukie de la Croix

He'll buy you a bike,
Yes, he'll buy you a bike,
He likes to buy things for the people he likes,
He's twisted.

His mother said Johnny was really a girl,

His mother said Johnny was really a girl.

She made him wear dresses and forced him to twirl
In front of the mirror,

Just like a girl.

His little girl shoes and his hair up in curls.
His mother said Johnny was really a girl.

But he'll buy you a bike,
Yes, he'll buy you a bike,
He likes to buy things for the people he likes,
He's twisted.

Now his mother is dead and Johnny's grown up,

His mother is dead and Johnny's grown up.

Now Johnny just wanders the streets of his town
Wearing his mother's shoes and his mother's gowns.
Saying, "My mommy is dead,
My mommy is dead...."

People say Johnny is not all there.
He's sick in his brain.

Johnny's insane!

He ought to be locked away somewhere.

But Johnny's a good boy,
Johnny's not bad.
Johnny had things other boys never had.

...Like dolls...

No, Johnny's not bad!

He plays with the children in the park,
He gives them candy,
He says he's their sweetheart.

But at home all alone in his room
The curtains are drawn,
And deep in the gloom,
Johnny sees the corpse of his mother,
Lying on the bed, exactly where he smothered her.

Johnny kisses his mother's cold lips,
He kisses her thighs and he kisses her hips,
He kisses the holes where she once had eyes.

Then he opens her legs,
And pushes inside.

Saying,
"I fuck the dead, I fuck the dead,

The dead don't come back to fuck up your head,

I fuck the dead, I fuck the dead,

The dead don't come back to fuck up your head."

But Johnny's a good boy,
Johnny's not bad.

No, Johnny's not bad!

He'll buy you a bike,
Yes, he'll buy you a bike,
He likes to buy things for the people he likes.

Blood of the Rose
Karen E. Taylor

THE FIRST TIME ADAM SAW Marie, she was seated by the side of her husband's casket. She made an oddly composed widow, dressed all in black, complete with hat and gossamer veil that did not quite hide her somber smile or the predatory gleam in her eyes. Her hands rested, smooth and reassuring, along her gently expanded abdomen, and she held court with visiting relatives and friends like a queen.

He knew all about her, of course; her age, her address, even her credit rating. But the neatly completed information form she had given the funeral director days before had not prepared him for the utter shock of her menacing beauty, the black eyes and perfect olive complexion that seemed to shine through her veil. The sharpness of her gaze was like the cold whisper of a scalpel against his skin and slashed him where he stood in his obsequious pose in the far doorway.

"Maintain the distance," his boss, Louis Bowe, owner of the Bowe Funeral Home, always said. "Think of yourself as a highly paid and valued servant, because that is what you are. Comfort should be offered, but with dignity and grace. We are the detached, sympathetic voice of reason in an insane world."

But Marie's eyes beckoned him into her insanity, and he fell, moving across the distance of the outer room, propelled through the inner room, almost as if dragged through the crowd of mourners and the overwhelming display of funeral roses to a suddenly vacated space at her side.

"Mrs. Zenos?" His ordinarily composed, detached voice cracked slightly, to his embarrassment. "I'm Adam Rose. Allow me to express my sincerest condolences on your bereavement."

She held her hand out, and he touched it briefly. Her skin was smooth, hot. "Mr. Rose," her voice was a rich deep contralto with a faint touch of a

Greek accent, "thank you. I understand that you did the work on my Stephen."

So much meaning was encompassed by her words "my Stephen," a love and devotion almost beyond his comprehension. But the eyes that considered him through the veil were dry and eager. He cleared his throat. "Yes, I hope you are satisfied with our results, Mrs. Zenos."

"Indeed I am, most pleased." She reached over and tenderly stroked the cold arm of her husband. "We have all been saying that he looks so well, so alive." Her hand lingered caressingly on the corpse, and Adam blushed, thinking suddenly and unavoidably of that hot skin pressed against his own. "You have done well."

He nodded briefly. "I'll be here for the remaining days of viewing, and of course for the funeral service. And if there's any other way I can be of assistance, please ask for me."

Marie smiled at him, exposing perfect, tiny white teeth. "You may be sure I will do that, Adam."

The next two days of viewing Stephen Zenos's body seemed to Adam to fly by in a feverish rush. Surrounded by a throng of mourners, swathed in black, and shrouded in the heavy scent of the flowers, Marie watched him as he tended to his duties. Her black eyes continually followed him as he played escort to elderly women and men, steering them to vacant chairs and whispering dignified words of comfort; her eyes studied him as he pressed endless glasses of cool water into reaching hands; and sought him out as he delivered and rearranged the continual onslaught of bouquets.

The flowers were all roses; he'd thought that a coincidence on the first day, but with each new arrangement, an odd and ominous symmetry was being established. The other attendants laughed about "The Rose Funeral" in hushed, but irreverent tones, speculating on Marie's apparent interest in Adam. "Maybe we should put you into a vase, too, Adam, and deliver you to her."

And he would blush, and they would laugh even harder. But he didn't laugh, couldn't laugh. Everywhere Adam went, she was there, her rich voice rising over the other voices, her hands either caressing the dead skin of the corpse or clasped possessively over her stomach, where Stephen's child rested. Over those two days, he grew to hate the corpse and then even the child, jealous for the touch of those hands.

The last night of viewing he lingered in the office, waiting for the mourners and family to depart. Mr. Bowe was present that night, and Adam had made himself as unobtrusive as possible, fearing his fascination with the widow might be noticed. When Bowe finally entered the office, he smiled at Adam. "Good job, son. I'm going home now. Close up for me, will you?"

Adam nodded. "Yes, sir." The front door opened, then shut, and the faint sound of Bowe's car faded as it pulled out of the parking lot. Silence descended on the rooms. Adam shuffled some papers, then put them aside and stood up, stretching and yawning slightly. Turning out the light, he closed the office door and started down the hall to the viewing rooms, to put them in order before the morning.

He gasped when he entered the room where Stephen Zenos's body lay. Marie stared up at him from where she sat cross-legged in the middle of the floor, her dress fanned around her, surrounded by a circle of flickering votive candles. She had removed her hat and veil and was reaching into the basket positioned next to her, pulling out several dark round objects and lining them up carefully in front of her. "Adam," her smile sent an anticipatory thrill through him, "I know this is most likely a little unorthodox, but it is an old family tradition. Humor me. In fact," she smiled deeper, her eyes boring into his, her small hands beckoning, "do more than that. Join me, Adam."

"But," he hesitated at the edge of the candles' circle, "I shouldn't, or you shouldn't...be here, I mean."

Marie laughed, "Ah, but it is only you and I and Stephen here, now, and he won't tell a soul. Join me, Adam."

He stepped into the circle and sat down, overwhelmed by the aroma of the roses, the candles, and her. "It is a beautiful scent, isn't it, Adam? Stephen loved my candles. I mold them myself, mixing the wax and the essences according to very old customs. My mother taught me when I was just a girl." She picked up one of the objects in front of her, held it up to her face and inhaled, then handed it to him. It was a plum, the outer skin so dark it seemed black in the candlelight. "Stephen's favorite fruit." Her eyes, no longer hidden by the veil, were beautiful and reflected the flicker of the flames. "Eat," she urged him, selecting a plum for herself and biting into it. The juice ran over her chin, and she wiped it away with the back of her hand, laughing.

Adam sat on the floor and stared at her, lightheaded from the scented air. The plum rested in his palm, forgotten and uneaten, until she gave another laugh and guided his hand to his mouth, pressing the cool skin of the fruit to his lips. "Eat, Adam."

His teeth burst through the surface of the plum; the skin was tart and crisp, but the center so sweet it brought tears to his eyes. He rolled the fruit in his mouth, savoring its texture, its flavor. He saw, as he pulled his hand away, that the plum's flesh was colored a deep red, as red as the roses, as red as blood, as red as Marie's lips as she urged him to eat more. Adam finished, sucking the last shreds from the pit, embarrassed by the sticky juice that now coated his fingers and his lips.

Marie laughed again and pulled his hand to her mouth, licking the fingertips, then leaned into Adam and kissed him. His head reeled with that kiss, with the heady scent of the candles, the roses and Marie, with the cloying taste of the plum and her tongue. And when the kiss was done, she held his head between her palms. "Ah, my dear, do you know how long I had to search for you? How many funeral homes I had to call to find a Rose like you?"

He shook his head; he felt drunk, drugged with her presence. She smiled, stood up within the circle of the candles, and slowly began to unbutton her black widow's dress. Adam could only stare as she slid it from her shoulders, as she shed her bra, her hose, her black satin panties. When she stood naked in front of him, she reached her hands down to pull him up to her. He rose on unsteady legs, his eyes still fastened to her, admiring the swollen breasts and the soft curve of her stomach where the child rested. She was beautiful, the most beautiful woman he had ever seen, and she wanted him, she said she'd been searching for him.

He opened his mouth to speak, to say that he loved her, but could only produce a strange garbled sound. "No, don't try to talk," she reached down into her basket again, pulling out something long and shiny. "It won't help. Old family traditions, Adam, are so important. So very important. The candles, the roses, the plums, all prepared especially for you. My mother was a powerful woman and bequeathed that power to me. Power over life and death," Marie laughed as she brought the knife to his throat, "Yes, even power enough to bring back the dead. All is ready now, but for the final step. To bathe my Stephen's body in the blood of a rose."

Louis Bowe was surprised early the next morning to discover Marie Zenos waiting for him by the locked doors. "Mr. Bowe," she smiled sadly and touched his hand, "I have decided that I do not wish a final viewing this morning. All my goodbyes were said last night, and I do not want the coffin opened again. Let him rest now, safe from prying eyes."

"Whatever you'd like, Mrs. Zenos; we are here to serve your needs."

"And that you have, Mr. Bowe. I have been satisfied." Marie's voice dropped lower, "Most satisfied."

Bowe shook his head slightly when a man emerged from the Zenos car and came to stand next to Marie, gently cupping her elbow in his hand. Such an uncanny resemblance to her late husband, he thought briefly as he unlocked the doors and escorted them inside. But he didn't give it much consideration, thinking only how glad he'd be to see the end of this funeral; the smell of the roses was stronger this morning, made his eyes water and his head ache. He hoped that Adam would arrive soon. It was not like him to be late.

White of the Moon (A Lullaby)
Jo Fletcher

In sleep, my child,
Dream deep, my child,
Forsake now all your ghosts.
Though bright the moon,
So white the moon,
My arms will hold you close.

By day, my child,
At play, my child,
Human as any you seem.
But come bright the moon,
Come white of moon,
In your eyes a twisted gleam.

Insane, my child,
No game, my child,
Your innocence cannot last.
In bright of moon,
In white of moon,
Derangement grips you fast.

Be still, my child,
Don't kill, my child:
The temptation's all to blame
When bright of moon,
That white of moon
Draws you like moths to flame.

Though dear, my child,
I fear my child,
When Diana rides the sky
And bright of moon,
The white of moon
Lights the madness in your eye.

Don't cry, my child,
Don't sigh, my child,
But pray my arms won't fail.
In bright of moon,
In light of moon—
A mother's loving jail.

My only child,
My lonely child,
Come nestle against my breast.
Through bright of moon,
Through white of moon,
Now gently laid to rest.

The Alberscine's Vigil
Thomas J. Strauch

THE WHOLE PLACE REMINDED MADDY of Stateville. She taught eighth grade for three semesters near Stateville Federal Prison.

Or Alcatraz. She'd seen it last year from a tour boat when she was in California for the Catechism Ecclesiology Seminar; though why a conference on that outmoded dogma was held in San Francisco, she never knew. Maddy remembered how frustrating it was to know every other nun with one foot in the twentieth century was finagling her way to Rome for Vatican II, while she endured lectures on new ways to teach young minds the finer points between Actual and Sanctifying Grace.

She'd heard about Fort Leavenworth from Sister Mary Gerianna, her roomie at Five Blessed Martyrs. Gerianna had part-timed in that federal prison's administrative office while she saved for convent school. Told some hair-raising stories about life on the inside. Or at least, the life on the inside that a seventeen-year-old bookkeeper could observe from the warden's office.

Gerianna's real name had been Julie McDermot. But she gave that up once she finished her novitiate. Maddy missed Sister Gerianna. Missed Julie McDermot even more. They'd done some good work at Five Blessed Martyrs, the two of them. But then, Sister Mary Gerianna hung herself in the band room in '61, and took Julie McDermot with her.

The fact was, the Good Sisters of the Alberscinian Order were doing that sort of thing all the time.

Stateville.

Alcatraz.

Fort Leavenworth.

The Alberscinian Retreat House out in the Minneapolis boondocks outdid them all.

The Alberscines favored bad pastiches of faux-Gothic for their facilities, like the Mother House in Cleveland, where Maddy'd done her obligatory four years. She took her final vows there in '58, but in the five years since, this place, this "retreat house," had only been a rumor, rarely mentioned by the more sensible nuns, and only in hushed whispers by the hardliners. It was someplace they sent you if you really messed up. If you were really bad.

Really, *really* bad.

The Alberscine Retreat House Prioress perched behind her boat-sized desk, pince-nez barely clinging to her skinny nose, her head bowed over a pile of reports. Maddy shifted in her wooden chair, her eyes roaming the Priorate, even though there wasn't much to linger on. White-washed walls. Rugged stone floors oozing a damp chill right through Maddy's shoes. There was the Prioress, her desk, the crucifix on the wall behind.

And one portal-sized window leaking September sun, and just a feeble strip of light at that.

Boredom, impatience, nerves—Maddy juggled the emotions as she gazed out the little window, watching Minnesota prairie winds whip the last leaves across browning grass, then kick them up and over the retreat walls. Quarry-stone walls, ten feet tall at least, ringing the entire compound, and crowned with rusty spikes: they were intimidating enough to keep anyone from prying into the cloistered world of the Alberscines. And just as sure to keep the cloistered from going over the wall into the real world.

Out there, one last, little brown leaf lingered in the breeze too long. It fluttered, fell, and was spiked on the wall.

Maddy checked her watch, glanced at the Prioress, and waited to be sentenced.

Half an hour, an hour, all silent in that spartan office, except for two women's breathing. She watched the sun hover above that quarry-stone wall, watched a nun cross the grounds, carrying a large cross as the wind lashed her layered robes. The nun was dressed, like the Prioress, in the old-fashioned Alberscine vestments. A voluminous floor-length shift, cinched at the waist with a knotted rope and a wood bead rosary. A black chasuble layered over that. A rigid white cowl encased the nun's head like a knight's helmet. A long, black veil topped it all.

Maddy'd switched to the new vestments as soon as word came down from the Mother House after Vatican II that they were approved.

Grudgingly, but approved. A crisp A-line dress, black, wool, and long sleeved, but so liberating and *normal* after five years of dressing like a pilgrim. Sensible, low-heeled pumps, nothing too shiny or spiky, even regular nylons. And just a short, simple, black veil, pinned loosely over her hair like a scarf. It let Maddy's whole face show, let her ears poke out from under her hair, let her unruly, red bangs tickle her forehead and eyebrows.

The spot of henna color seemed a rude intrusion in the Priorate's austerity.

Out there on the grounds, that nun trudged through unmown grass, a leather-bound missal tucked under one arm, still dragging the heavy cross. Finally the nun disappeared behind leafless trees as the sun sank below the wall.

Maddy turned away from the window to find the prioress staring at her with pinched eyes. Intimidation 101. House Mothers all interned in the death camps, or so the novitiates always said.

"Sister Mary Madalena." The prioress's face barely moved inside the starched white cowl. Only her thin lips wiggled, wrapping themselves in a sneer around each word. "You know why you've been sent to us?"

"I was told I'd been transferred to the order's retreat for a short stay, which would afford me an opportunity to reflect on my role as a Bride of Christ."

The Prioress smirked, then produced a manila envelope from her desk. Two books slid out on top of her neat stack of reports. "Sylvia Plath," she read off a paperback with a torn cover. "You've read this book, Sister?"

"*The Bell Jar*? Yes, I have."

"And yet, having read it, a book condemned by your diocese's Archbishop and by the Mother Superior, you still felt it was appropriate to assign to your students?"

Maddy had gone over this a hundred times back at St. Basil's—with the principal, with the parents, with the Holy Name Society officers. "I assume those reports document everything," Maddy said, doing her best to maintain the defiant edge in her voice. "If you've read them, you know I didn't assign the book. I simply recommended it to a couple of bright girls with inquiring minds."

The Prioress nodded. "And this one as well?" She held up a hardbound Baudelaire. *The Flowers of Evil*. "This also was suitable for seniors in a Catholic young women's high school? An Alberscinian school?"

Maddy sighed. "I don't mean to be impertinent, Prioress, but again, I didn't assign Baudelaire to anyone. A group of girls were working on a literary project—"

"Whore!" The Prioress leaped on top of the desk and flung the paperback at Maddy. "Filthy Whore of Babylon!" She hurled the hardbound Baudelaire. Maddy dove to the floor, but the book caught her at the edge of her mouth.

"*Sister* Mary Madalena," the Prioress shrieked, crouching on her desk. "Madalena. Oh, how very appropriate, just like *Magdalene*, whore of Jerusalem. Our Lord Jesus Christ may have saved *her* soul, but you, Sister, you are beyond redemption for your sins." She snatched up the report. "Impertinence is the least of your transgressions." She showered papers down on Maddy, one by one. "Obscenity. Corruption. Debauchery. A thousand good women have worked and bled and died for over two hundred years for this sacred order. And you—you think you will shame us now? It's not so very long ago that you'd have been flogged for even bringing this wretched trash into one of our holy convents."

Maddy grabbed the chair and started to drag herself up off the rough stone floor. Her knees were bruised, her nylons shredded. She tasted blood in her mouth. But she swallowed it and fought back the tears welling up in her eyes "With all due respect, Prioress, this is 1963. The order can't dictate what we read or—"

"*Cannot?* The Holy Mother Church is not a republic, Sister Madalena. The Good Sisters of the Alberscinian Order are not a democracy. Forget whatever vile blasphemy you've adopted from the Twenty-First Ecumenical Council. Vatican II never happened inside these walls." The Prioress climbed regally off her desk. "Those books are only a small sign of your true wickedness, Sister Mary Madalena. Your Mother Superior's reports tell the whole story, don't they? You know why you're really here, don't you?"

"Y-yes, Prioress."

"Get up off the floor, then, Sister Madalena. Get out of my office. Sister Ursillina will escort you to your chambers. Get used to them, Sister. I think your stay with us will be a long one."

Maddy got up and tried to salvage some of her dignity. She turned to go, pausing by the Priorate door to straighten her veil, to brush some grit off her dress.

"And you will hand those whore's rags over to Ursillina as well, Sister," the Prioress said. "We'll burn them along with these vile books of yours."

* * *

Maddy dragged her wooden rake through another mountain of dead leaves. The handle chafed her broken blisters, and her back spasmed with each stroke, but it was better to keep raking. If Ursillina or the Prioress caught her resting, they'd just dream up a new torture. The little bit of autumn sun that had appeared earlier was fading. Ursillina and the Prioress were almost certainly on their way to vespers.

Anyway, if she continued to rake, she stayed warmer. A dreary September had chilled into a frigid October. Maddy longed for her black topcoat, the nifty one with the zip-in, zip-out lining she bought at J.C. Penney last year. And her black wool gloves. Gerianna knitted those.

But they were gone, of course. The gloves, the coat, all her things. Even her wristwatch. Ursillina made her toss them in the incinerator that very first evening. Maddy had stood there, stark naked in the basement, her embarrassment painted orange by the firelight, watching her few possessions consumed by the flames.

They made her walk back to her room like that, naked, shivering, mortified when the other Sisters filed past on their way to dinner. She found her new clothes waiting for her on her bed: the traditional Alberscine vestments, along with clunky, grandma-style shoes, some coarse, greyed underthings, and black cotton stockings she had to roll over her knees to keep up. There was a pile of white rags there too, rank with the stench of lye soap and bleach. At first, Maddy couldn't even guess what they were for. Then she remembered that her period was due in a few days. She'd raced back down the hall to the communal bathroom, naked as she was, to throw up.

"We'd better hurry with this section, Sister Madalena." It was Sister Sidiellus, raking a huge leaf pile a few yards away. Maddy barely heard Sidiellus's whisper. It was the first thing the young nun said in their three long days raking the grounds together.

"Why are you whispering, Sister?"

Sidiellus glanced over her shoulder. "We're not supposed to…"

There was no talking in the retreat. Only with the Prioress herself, or with one of her minions. The good Sisters could only lift their voices in prayer, before sunrise, at the noon Angelus, at vespers: each prayer a plea for absolution.

"No one can hear us out here."

Sidiellus shook her head. She raked some more, then spoke again, louder this time. "How long will you be here?"

Maddy shrugged her aching shoulders. "I don't know. I suppose that's part of the punishment. Not knowing. It's been three and a half weeks. Feels like forever."

"I've been here a year."

Maddy stopped raking. "A year?" Sidiellus didn't look old enough to have taken her vows a year ago. A skinny figure lurked under the layers of robes. She had a scared teenager's face wrapped up in that starched cowl and veil, the kind of face Maddy had seen on dozens of girls back at St. Basil's, the ones the popular girls picked on. "What did you do?"

Sidiellus started to answer, then shook her head and clawed her rake through the leaves.

Though it was getting dark, Maddy was in no mood to hurry. She knew if she missed vespers, she could forget about dinner, but she'd already had enough of the kitchen's mystery soup and rye bread. Anyway, there were another three acres waiting for tomorrow. It was better than scrubbing the bathrooms. She'd done that for the first two weeks.

Maddy wondered what the Prioress had in mind for winter.

Out of the corner of her eye, Maddy spotted a nun crossing the grounds, missal in one hand, dragging a huge cross with the other. It was the same every day, just around dusk, though not always the same nun.

"Sister, where's she going?"

Sidiellus looked up, saw the nun vanishing into the darkness by the walls, and looked back down at her leaves. "Vigil."

"What's that?"

"One of the Sisters sits Vigil each night."

"What is Vigil?"

"I'm not sure, but it lasts all night, and it's the worst punishment."

"How do you know?"

"I *don't* know. And don't ask. Quit talking, Sister. I want to finish and get my dinner."

Maddy leaned on her rake and looked where the nun had gone through the gnarled trees clinging to the west wall, their dark trunks merging with the shadows.

"Sister, please, let's just finish. All I know is that some are chosen to sit Vigil. Sometimes it's just for one night. Sometimes for many. And sometimes…"

"Sometimes?"

Sidiellus stopped raking. She looked around. There was no one.

"Sometimes they sit Vigil and never return."

Maddy thought about Kevin.

There wasn't much else to do during the long nights in her room. The first few nights, she was so bone-tired that she fell asleep before she hit the bed. But now she was getting used to the gulag hours, the regimen, her room.

Room? Cell, more like it. An oversized closet, really. A low bed, lumpier than the floor. A wall-mounted hurricane lamp, lamp oil refilled only once a week. Two books left with her vestments that first night: a 1920s vintage Bible and the Alberscinian Press's own edition of *The Life of St. Alberscine*. Maddy knocked off the Bible, cover to cover, the first two weeks. She was saving the biography of the order's founder til she was really desperate.

Mostly, it was like tonight. She undid the Alberscine combat boots, freed her head from the helmet cowl, dragged her fingers through her hair, and rubbed her ears til they bent back into shape. Then she curled up on the bed, drew her knees up to her chin, and endured the minutes dragging like hours through the dark.

Father Kevin O'Connell, Assistant Pastor at St. Basil's Parish, coach of the girl's volleyball team, occasional sub in civics class.

Father Kevin, with the curly black hair of the dark Irish, with eyes bluer than the royal blue cardigan he wore so casually over his clerical shirt. Kevin, with the perpetual grin on his unlined, thirty-year-old face. A smile for everyone, especially the girls, who giggled and blushed when he made inappropriate jokes. Those girls sometimes flirting with him. Kevin sometimes flirting back.

Maddy thought about the day he drove her in his very own Pontiac—priests could *own* things, after all—downtown to pick up new textbooks. Treated her to dinner at a real restaurant afterwards. He had a 7-and-7 before the meal, and ordered a bottle of Burgundy with dinner. Played the radio in the Pontiac on the drive back, folk songs, the Lettermen, the Righteous Brothers, rock-and-roll.

Maddy barely heard the knock on the door.

"Sister?" It was more a breath than a whisper. Maddy knew it wasn't Ursillina or the Prioress. They never knocked.

Maddy opened the door as quietly, and Sister Sidiellus tiptoed in, bare feet silent on the stone floor, standing there with a bewildered look on her face, like she'd just leaped into danger with no clue what to do next.

"If they catch you in here, they'll make us scrub the floors with our tongues or something."

Sidiellus turned back towards the door.

"No." Maddy touched her arm. "Stay. It's okay."

"You're not like the other Sisters." Sister Sidiellus crept over to Maddy's window and looked outside. A half-moon lit the grounds. "Why don't you seem scared?"

"Of what? Of them?" Maddy plopped down on her bed and tucked her legs under herself, Indian-style. It took a little doing with the tangle of chasuble and robes.

"What did you do, Sister? I mean, to get sent here?"

Maddy shrugged. "Broke the rules, I guess."

"I heard, that is I overheard, Ursillina say you were selling pornography to your students."

Maddy laughed, too loud she suddenly realized, and slapped her hand over her mouth. It was the first time she'd even cracked a smile since the bus dropped her off at the retreat's gates. "Yes, well, there just wasn't much money in bootlegging, and I don't have the figure for the burlesque. So it was pornography for me." She laughed again, but quieter this time.

Sidiellus glanced at the door with a worried look.

"I'm kidding, Sister. Don't you remember how to joke?"

Sidiellus smiled half a smile, as much as her starched cowl would allow. She looked at Maddy's red hair, wavy and free. Touched trembly fingers to her own cowl, nodded, and her smile widened. She pulled a long pin out of her veil and unclasped her cowl. Long blond hair tumbled out, and Maddy could see she'd been a pretty girl before a year 'on retreat' drew dark circles under those innocent eyes.

Sister Sidiellus tossed her veil and cowl aside, plopped down on the bed beside Maddy, and tried to arrange her legs like Maddy's too, but three days of raking in the autumn cold wouldn't let her. "Please tell me, what did you do?"

So Maddy told her. Told her how it wasn't *The Bell Jar* or even Baudelaire. Maddy had weathered flaps like those before; five Alberscine schools in five years since her final vows.

Maddy told Sidiellus about Kevin.

Told her about the Burgundy wine and the songs on the radio and the wide seats in Kevin's Pontiac. Told her about the feel of the summer breeze blowing in the car's open windows, about Father O'Connell talking about how the world was changing and how the clerics had to change with it. How he talked about the protests down South, the beatnik clubs downtown, the Peace Corps, and the books the kids were reading on the college campuses.

Maddy told how Father O'Connell kissed her, and how she didn't tell him to stop, even though she knew she should, knew it was wrong. How she didn't tell him to stop when he kissed her again, but kissed him back instead. Didn't tell him to stop when his hand slid under her dress, that brand new just-below-the-knees uniform that showed off her legs. It was scandalous, Mother Superior said, and would make men think about sex when they looked at a nun, and that was wrong, and there she was in the front seat of a Pontiac with beautiful, handsome Kevin, with his hand under her black wool dress, with his hand rubbing across her bare thigh just above her stockings, and Maddy knew she had pretty legs, she just hadn't thought about them for years. But she thought about them then, thought about them as Father O'Connell's hand slipped higher, as he took her hand and placed it between his legs, where she found his pants undone. And there she held him and squeezed him and stroked him while Kevin's hand still crept higher up her bare thigh, crawled under her drawers and slipped inside to where it was so warm and so moist and so...

"I should have stopped him, Sister. I knew I should have stopped." Maddy sat on the lumpy cot, staring straight ahead at the patch of moonlight reflected on her whitewashed wall.

"Y-Yes," Sidiellus said, her voice breathy, tense. "It was a sin. The sin of fornication."

"That's not what I meant. It wasn't a sin. It was stupid. He was so... Only I didn't know then."

She didn't know that old Mrs. Kolinsky was peering out from behind her two-flat's chiffon curtains, late as it was. Mrs. Kolinsky, treasurer of St. Basil's Mothers Club and head of the Ladies Sodality.

Father O'Connell denied it all at first. But Maddy stood up to the Mother Superior and told the truth, even when Kevin accused her of leading him into sin, said she'd tempted him with lewd words and actions. "The banned books were just gravy."

"What about Father O'Connell?"

"*Father* O'Connell's teaching U.S. history at a college in Vermont, last I heard. A girl's college. He should be very happy there."

Neither of them said anything for awhile. Maddy could taste that Burgundy wine like it was yesterday. She wished she had a glass right now.

"What about you? Who'd you murder?"

Sister Sidiellus hopped off the bed. "I...I didn't..." She ran for the door, stopped, ran back and scooped up her veil and cowl. At the door again, she paused. "What was it like?"

"What was what like?"

Sidiellus slipped through the door.

Since Maddy and Sidiellus managed to earn all the worst chores over the next two months, they spent less and less time with the other Sisters. Which was just as well, they decided. The other nuns rarely spoke.

They had separate duties this day. Maddy had to wash the stained glass windows on the retreat's tiny chapel. Inside and out, with vinegar and water that kept turning to ice. Snow flurries fell in the late afternoon, speckling the glass, and Maddy suspected the Prioress would have her back on the rickety ladder washing them again tomorrow. Her hands were still numb during vespers, and she had trouble gripping her spoon at dinner. She assumed Sidiellus went through something similarly barbaric. She saw Ursillina leading the girl across the grounds with a broom and a bucket in the afternoon.

Sidiellus didn't knock anymore. She'd just slip in through Maddy's door most every night now, around midnight. Knocking was too risky.

"It's a graveyard," Sidiellus said, leaning against the door.

She stood on tiptoe, dancing one black stockinged foot, then the other off the cold stone floor. With winter looming, the cells could be iceboxes at night. Sidiellus never wore her veil and cowl to Maddy's room anymore. Tonight, dank and chilly as it was, she only had on her white cotton shift, the shapeless slip the nuns wore under their habits; rough, but not as coarse and scratchy as the thick robes.

"What's a graveyard?" Maddy sat on her bed, her blanket wrapped around her legs. "And get over here before you freeze."

Sidiellus scampered across the room and jumped on the bed, snuggling up close, shivering. Maddy wrapped the blanket around the both of them.

"Vigil. It's in a graveyard under those old trees."

"The Alberscine cemetery is at the Mother House. I've seen it."

"I had to go clean it up today." Sister Ursillina told me it's where they bury the Sisters who die while they're...staying here."

Sidiellus's cold feet wormed their way under Maddy's thighs. "The Sisters buried there died before they could complete their penance. They haven't atoned for their sins, yet. So they can't be interred in consecrated ground."

"The Church would never go for that. Not anymore."

"That's what sitting Vigil is for. A nun must sit Vigil every night to pray for the souls of the Sisters buried there. She said sometimes even she and the Prioress take their turn. To beg indulgence, so the sinners can leave Purgatory."

"It doesn't sound like such a harsh punishment. Sitting Vigil, I mean. At least, not for this place. A little cold in the winter, maybe, but it could be kind of nice in the warm weather. Course, it is a graveyard." She felt Sister Sidiellus's feet tucking further under her legs. Felt Sidiellus's head lean against her shoulder. She thought about inching away. It felt funny. "What's with the big crucifix? You see them dragging it over every evening. It's big enough to..."

Sister Sidiellus giggled. "They're not all in Purgatory."

"Where are they then?"

Sidiellus shrugged, still smiling. "Some of the nuns who've died were sent here because they were very bad. Very, very bad. Ursillina told me. The Sister sitting Vigil needs the crucifix."

"Angels and miracles—the Church is trying so hard to sweep all that business under the carpet. Demons and devils—it's an embarrassment—witches and exorcisms. That went out with the Inquisition. I didn't buy all that stuff in Saturday matinees, and I didn't buy it in Catechism classes, I'm sure not going for it now. Not even here." Maddy got off the bed. She looked out the window, but the afternoon's flurries had turned into real snow, and the grounds were veiled in windblown white. "That does it."

She turned away from the window. "I've been thinking it over for a few days now. I suppose I was thinking it over even before I was sent here. I'll do my time 'on retreat,' I'm not going to let them think they broke me. But then...I'm leaving the Order."

Sidiellus sucked in her breath. "Don't even say that. You can't leave the Order. You took vows. You're a Bride of Christ. You'll be excommunicated—"

"*My* God wouldn't send nuns to concentration camps. My God doesn't care about Angeluses and vespers and all this ridiculous ritualism and all these inane rules. That can't be all there is, Sister, it just can't."

"That's paganism. It's blasphemy."

"You know it's not." Maddy plopped down on the bed and took Sidiellus's hand. "Come with me. There's a whole world out there. It's changing, it's happening without us."

"I couldn't. It's a sin."

"We're all sinners. Especially us, right? That's why we're here, isn't it?" Maddy was tempted to ask Sidiellus again what she had done to be sentenced to the retreat. Sip the sacramental wine? Whistle a banned tune in the convent? Sneak a peek in the boys' locker room?

But Sidiellus always evaded her, and Maddy didn't really care anymore.

Sidiellus shook her head. "I'm not as brave as you are."

Maddy didn't press her. She'd let the nun wrestle with her own demons. Let her snuggle there on the cot, with Sidiellus's feet tucked under Maddy's legs, and her head on Maddy's shoulder. They sat in the dark for a long time, saying nothing.

Sidiellus finally said, "You've still never told me."

"What?"

"What it was like."

"What was what...oh."

Sidiellus lifted her head. With her face just inches away, only their fogged breaths hovered between them. "Was it...was it like this?"

Sidiellus closed her eyes, leaned forward, and pecked Maddy's lips.

Maddy was too stunned to react.

Sidiellius kissed her again, longer this time. She wrapped her skinny arms tight around Maddy. Her tongue probed at Maddy's lips.

And familiar bells rang warning in Maddy's head: *No, stop, it's a sin, this is wrong, no, Kevin, we really shouldn't do this...*

But it felt good.

Wrong, but good. The touch of another person, so human, so real, so forbidden here in the hellish underworld of the Alberscine retreat. It was the front seat of Father O'Connell's Pontiac all over again, only the air was chillier, the lips were trembly and unsure and softer. But the pounding in Maddy's chest and her temples and her belly—that was the same. Sidiellus started to ease Maddy down on the lumpy mattress.

"No." Maddy pushed the girl aside. She leaped off the bed. "I don't want to."

Sidiellus whined, "Oh God, Oh my God, what have I done? You'll tell. I'm damned now, damned for good."

"No, Sister." She reached for her, but Sidiellus slipped away. "It's okay. Really. It's just...I don't want to do this. Not with—"

"With me, you mean," Sidiellus sobbed. "I'm wicked and evil and ugly, and you're repulsed by me."

"You—you're beautiful. But very young, I think, and very confused. There's nothing wrong with what you did. It's just...not for me."

"I'm going to burn in Hell. For all eternity." Sidiellus made for the door.

"You're not," Maddy said. But the other nun cried uncontrollably. Sidiellus flung open the door...

...and shrieked.

The Prioress stood in the hallway.

Maddy didn't see Sidiellus for days.

Didn't see anyone. Though she was ready for the Prioress or Ursillina to rip into her that very night, nothing was said. Sidiellus had skulked out of Maddy's room, and the Prioress had glided away behind her. The next morning, and the two mornings after that, Maddy never even saw the Prioress or Ursillina. No toilet scrubbing, no gutter cleaning, no jobs at all. So she kept to herself, hid in her room, mostly. They'd get to her once they were ready. They were probably too busy browbeating Sidiellus over a wash bucket or worse. It made Maddy cry when she thought about that frail, frightened girl down on her knees, dodging slaps and worse from Ursillina and the Prioress.

It was late afternoon, the third day after the big scene. Maddy sneaked into the kitchen and wolfed down some bread and milk. She passed no one on her way back to her room, concluded the other nuns were all busy on their various duties, and hoped the showers would be empty. She hadn't bathed in three days.

She showered quickly. Drying off, she wondered if she should sneak back to the kitchen and load up on more food. Maybe today was as good a day as any to leave this place. She'd said she wouldn't let the Alberscines think they'd beaten her, but maybe they had beaten her after all. Maybe today was the day to escape.

She had no money. They'd taken all her things. She didn't even have a coat. The bus had driven an hour out of the last town before it dropped her in front of the retreat's gates. Could she walk all the way to town, or would she wind up frozen to death along a wintry Minnesota back road?

What about Sidiellus? She couldn't just leave her here, could she? Could that wisp of a girl hike through the snow? Would she?

Hair still damp, cowl and veil in hand, Maddy crept down the hall to Sidiellus's room.

The door was wide open.

Inside, it was emptier than Maddy's own cell. The bed was made. There was nothing in the room. Maddy crossed the stone floor to the window, stared across the grounds to the band of leafless trees and the quarry-stone walls. To the dark shadowy spots there. Was that where Sidiellus had been these past nights? Sitting Vigil?

"She's dead."

Maddy whirled around. The Prioress stood in the doorway, Ursillina hovering in the hall. "W-who's...?"

"Your whore," the Prioress sneered. "Sister Sidiellus."

"When? How?"

The Prioress removed her pince-nez and polished them on her robes. "Sitting Vigil last night. The worst sin of all, the most hideous transgression against God. Took her own life. Ursillina found her this morning. We only finished burying her before the noon meal."

"It's a good thing," Ursillina chimed in. "The weather's turning colder by the day. The ground will be frozen soon." There was a trace of giggle in her voice.

"You're lying. She can't be dead. She wouldn't have killed herself."

"Perhaps if you weren't so determined to lead another soul down your own sinful path, the poor girl would still be alive. But no, not you, Sister Mary Madalena. You're not content to fornicate with priests, you'd see our holy retreat turned into another Sodom, laying with other women, doing things with your sinful mouths and your wicked hands."

"It wasn't like that," Maddy sobbed, "Mother, it—"

"Enough!"

Sister Ursillina stepped into the room, dragging that cross, that four-foot-long metal cross. She thrust it at Maddy. Stuck a missal in her hand.

"Sister Mary Madalena, we have no intention of listening to you heap one sin on top of another. You can confess your evils while you pray to God for mercy, pray for Sidiellus and for the others. All the others." The Prioress grabbed Maddy by the neck and pulled her towards the door. "It's growing late, Sister. *You* will sit Vigil tonight."

The grey sky grew greyer still as Ursillina and the Prioress led Maddy out of the retreat house. Maddy's crying didn't stop as the two nuns dragged her through snow that was already blowing into low drifts.

"You're surprised your little whore killed herself? You knew her sinful past. You were drawn to it, like a moth to a flame. All sinners cling to one another."

Maddy tripped and tumbled in the snow, but they hoisted her up and dragged her along. "What are you talking about?"

"Your little whore's done this before. Don't pretend you don't know that's why she was here. I'm sure you two shared your filthy little secrets. She'd done it before, with a student, no less. Caught in the act in the supply room in her school."

Across the grounds. Into the trees. Closer to the quarry-stone walls.

"The girl's father was so ashamed, of course he beat her. The girl died. But who could blame the man?"

Maddy moaned, "Poor Sidiellus—"

"The whore tried to kill herself then," the prioress screamed over the wind. "Sick without her vulgar little slut, shamed by what she'd done. Your Sidiellus stood right in the blessed Sacristy of her church and slit her wrists. Shed her tainted blood all over the altar. Sacrilege! But the other Sisters found her. Saved her. Sent her to us. Like all the sinners, they sent her to us."

They threw Maddy down into the snow—cross, missal, cowl, and veil scattering.

"Now pray, Sister Madalena, pray for the souls of the wicked and the damned. Pray for your precious little Sidiellus, pray for all of them." She and Ursillina turned to go. "And pray for yourself. Pray, so some other Sister will have the goodwill to pray over you, when your sinful flesh wastes away here under this heathen dirt."

The wind kicked up stronger, whipping a curtain of snowflakes off the ground between Maddy and the two nuns. "Keep the cross close, Sister," Ursillina called as they disappeared into the dark and the snow. "You may find you'll need it before morning." Maddy distinctly heard Ursillina giggle.

And then they were gone.

By the time Maddy finally pulled herself up out of the snow, the little copse of trees was shadow dark. She stood up and wiped her face, her tears falling in flakes of ice. She brushed the snow off her robes, then clutched them tight around her. The cold snaked its way right up under her billowing robes.

To the west, under a low blanket of grey, she saw a ribbon of orange hovering along the top of the wall, pierced by jagged silhouettes of the spikes. The sliver of light was shrinking fast.

Maddy didn't pray. She knew she should, should pray for Sidiellus. But somehow, Hail Marys and Our Fathers and Glory Be's seemed almost ...silly now. She left the cross half-buried in the snow. Left the missal where it fell, its black cover dusted white. Let her cowl and veil blow where they would.

There was a bench, a rough old stone thing. Maddy sat down. Snow was piled over low mounds. The graves of the poor girls and women who took sick and died "on retreat," who couldn't take the punishments the Prioress and her minions handed out, who gave up and died. No markers, no tombstones. Nothing to mark who was there, good women who couldn't—or wouldn't—buckle under to the Alberscines.

But one of those mounds wasn't quite covered with snow. The dirt was dark and moist looking, fresh black dirt, blackening as the shadows buried the graveyard.

Maddy screamed.

Screamed one curse after another. Screamed at the darkening sky, screamed at the Prioress and Ursillina and all the Alberscines, screamed in rage at Father Kevin and the whole Church, and at Heaven itself. Screamed until her throat was too dry and frozen to scream anymore. Then she pulled her robes tight around her, curled up on the bench, and cried.

The cold finally made her stop. Shivering uncontrollably, Maddy sat up. Her vision was blurred, and the stinging snowflakes made it worse.

Her eyes were playing tricks on her.

White snow curtains twirled into shapes above those mounds. Gossamer sheets of white, twisting...

Maddy ground her fists into her eyes.

The snow, the wind, the frozen tears, they were playing tricks on her.

Shapes hovered above the mounds.

Above their graves. Hovered there, then glided right over to the newest mound, the freshest grave. Now the wind played tricks on Maddy's ears, too. It howled with each gust, whined in the leafless trees, moaned over the shifting drifts.

"*Sister, come out.*"

Maddy shouted hoarsely, "This isn't real!"

The snow swirled into gauzy robes, crystalline veils. The figures knelt beside Sidiellus's grave. *"Come out, it's time."*

Maddy dove behind the bench. "Leave her alone!"

"Join us."

Maddy clamped her hands over her ears.

"M-Maddy?"

"This can't, just can't." It was Sidiellus's voice. It sounded hollow, part-wind, part-words. Maddy dropped her hands and raised her head. Peeked over the top of the bench.

Sidiellus stood on top of her grave. Flanked by six figures, white as the snow, but solid and real, and frighteningly close.

"You've come to sit Vigil for me, haven't you?"

"You're not real," Maddy shouted. "You're just a dream."

The Sidiellus-thing looked down, touched herself, then looked back at Maddy. "No, not a dream, Maddy. Don't hide, not from me."

Maddy backed away from the bench, back til she bumped into a tree.

Sidiellus and the other figures giggled, the sound like broken-glass and crystal wind chimes. Her feet floated over the snow.

"I've been bad, Maddy." Sidiellus stroked Maddy's cheek.

The touch was frigidly cold, but it burned, too, burned like the touch of dry ice.

"Sidiellus, did you really take your own life?"

"I tried, Maddy. Oh, I tried. Hung myself, with my rosary beads. Right from that tree you're leaning on. I was really very, very bad."

The figures began to prance. Maddy glanced at their faces—white faces with hollow cheeks and black, dead eyes.

"The worst sin. The worst..."

"It's the worst of sins, suicide. Despair. Forsaking God's greatest gift. Worse than anything you and I did, Maddy."

"We didn't...I didn't..."

"They saved me. My sisters came out of the snow and saved me." Sidiellus leaned close. Maddy's nostrils wrinkled at the scent: dead flowers and sticky sweet cordials and burning incense. "You were wrong, Maddy. Angels and demons. Miracles. It's all true. I had to sin the worst of sins to find out, but they showed me." Pale fingers danced across Maddy's chin, traced a line down her throat, and stroked the pulsing skin there. "They showed me everything I ever wanted to know."

The Sidiellus-thing smiled her frightened, little-girl smile. It widened, red lips on a pale face, red lips parting, leering open around a mouth full of ugly, white sin. The vulgar smells of death and Hell washed over Maddy.

Sidiellus's tongue lolled out and rolled over those lips, flicked at the tips of her short, sharp fangs. She reached both hands to Maddy's throat. She pulled Maddy closer.

Maddy screamed and twisted away.

"Join us, Maddy. It will be so much nicer than Father Kevin."

Maddy stumbled and fell face first into the snow.

"Join us on Vigil, join us."

Sidiellus glided closer. "You're already one of us. A sinner, just like us. Sit Vigil with us, Maddy." Sidiellus's robes brushed Maddy's legs.

Maddy clawed through the snow, face scraping across a frozen drift. Her hand bumped something hard and metallic.

"It's not your prayers we want. Just your blood. And your soul."

Maddy clutched the four-foot-long crucifix and whirled to face Sidiellus.

Sidiellus's eyes flickered—hungry-red to frightened-black—just for a flash, Maddy saw those same, innocent, little-girl eyes she'd known before, pleading. The look vanished, and Sidiellus's eyes glowed a thirsty, sinful-red again, and her white-fanged mouth plunged down.

Maddy thrust the crucifix as hard as she could, deep into Sidiellus's chest. Sidiellus flopped backwards, the huge cross sticking out of her. The snow sizzled and steamed all around her.

Maddy's hands were burned raw. The other figures were approaching, their red mouths gaping, drool running over their fangs.

Maddy grabbed the missal and flung it at the figures. They shrieked and dodged the book. Maddy was at the quarry-stone wall in a flash. Her fingers clawed the mortar, hands wrapped around those jagged spikes, her feet pawed at the stones.

Cold fingers tore at her robes, that rancid, dead-flower smell drenching her.

She flipped over the top of the wall, didn't stop to catch her breath, just scrambled on all fours across the snow, then ran flat out down the dark road.

Even with her heart thundering in her ears and her breath blasting steam out her mouth, she swore it wasn't the wind, swore she still heard Sidiellus's voice.

Pray for me, Maddy.

Carting platters of ham and eggs to truck drivers was a lot different from teaching English Lit. at St. Basil's.

She just about laughed her head off the first day on the job, when they handed her the uniform: a black shift and a white apron. A private joke, she told them, the colors were so familiar.

Her walkup apartment was only a few blocks away from the diner, just off the main exit for Duluth. It was a dump—cramped, drafty, radiators clanging like cathedral bells all the time. But it was hers.

Tips were pretty good at the diner, once you caught on to the routine. Shorten the hem a few inches on the uniform, bend over a lot so they could see you real good, bat your eyelashes, and laugh at their jokes. There was always an extra dollar or two beside the plate when they were gone.

Tips were pretty good, enough for the apartment, even enough for a down payment on the old Pontiac. It was more rust than metal, and if she didn't bring in twenty-five cash every Friday afternoon they'd take it back, but it was hers, too. The radio worked, anyway. And the music was good these days.

Her landlord never asked, but figured she had family downstate, seeing as she subscribed to the Minneapolis papers. She'd scour them every morning before heading off to work, even the mornings when Jeff slept over, and that was getting to be more and more often, now that his route took him through Duluth twice a month.

Jeff never asked either, not about the mounds of newspapers cluttering the apartment, not about the articles she clipped out and kept in a manila folder locked in a drawer, not about the crucifixes she had nailed all over the walls and the doors and hanging over the windows. He'd asked once, asked her if she was the church-going type, and how could she be such a tiger in bed if she was so all-fired-up religious. But he only asked once, because a laugh was the only answer he got, and it was kind of a scary laugh, so they went back to their original agreement of 'no questions, no talk, just sex.'

So Jeff sure wasn't going to ask when she said she'd be away for a couple of days, heading downstate, and that was okay anyway because Jeff knew he should be spending more time at home; the wife was really getting on his case about the kids. He just told Maddy to be careful, just because it was springtime didn't mean the roads weren't still slick. Minnesota back roads were tricky in the spring; they could go from wet to ice in a blink.

Maddy sipped little brown bottles of Stroh's and drove with the windows wide open, even though it was kind of chilly. Sipped Stroh's and lit one Kool Filter King off another. It was Jeff that started her smoking. But she preferred the menthol to his filterless Luckies. She had the radio blaring all the way, rock-and-roll and Motown. The sweet smells of green things sprouting up alongside the road reminded her of summer breezes sifting in another Pontiac's window, with those same songs lilting out of the radio, and the sweet touch of insincere lips and hands.

The wind was crisp this Friday afternoon, crisp and cool as it blew in her window and tugged at the manila folder beside her on the front seat, blew the cover open and rifled newsprint. The clippings blew all over the interior of the Pontiac, some right out the window. "The Alberscine Mystery" one article was titled. "Brutal slayings discovered at rural convent," it went on to say. "Sheriff's Office reports no leads on mysterious disappearances at Alberscine Retreat House," another said. "Services tomorrow for Alberscinian Prioress and assistant."

Maddy pulled the Pontiac to a stop right alongside those quarry-stone walls. She downed the last of her Stroh's and shut off the radio, staring ahead at the gates. Then she stepped out of the car and lit another Kool. Smoked it, still staring at the gates. They hung open, quivering in the wind. Yellow and black striped sawhorses were overturned in the brush beside them. Official investigations had ended months ago.

Maddy ground out the Kool with her tennis shoe, then reached inside the Pontiac. She pulled a little crucifix from the visor. Brushed aside whatever newspaper clippings hadn't blown away and pulled out a missal. She'd bought it at a religious store in Duluth, and Maddy read that missal every night, even when Jeff stayed over, once they were done and he would be snoring away. She read it while she sipped beers and chain-smoked Kools, read it over and over again.

With the sun dipping low across the farmland to the west, it was cold and getting colder. Maddy zipped up her jacket. She tucked the missal under her arm, shoved the crucifix in the back pocket of her jeans, and headed for the gates.

It was almost time.

Almost time, and she wanted to read from that missal, read over Sidielius's grave. Maybe the Prioress's and Ursillina's, too.

She was going to sit Vigil tonight.

Sent Down From God
Randy Miller

VERA TRUESDALE UNDERSTOOD THAT A pastor's wife had few rights in the public presence of her husband. The church's teachings made that clear enough. Women were to be submissive to men in this life. When she'd attended a seminar on the evils of pornography last month, the leader had shown bondage pictures to the crowd, and Vera Truesdale had thought, for an instant, that's just what it's like to be a preacher's wife: silent, bound, and supposedly loving every minute of it. And then she fell into the role of proper spiritual outrage.

In the parsonage, however, Vera ran the show. The two-story house was kept in immaculate condition and was free of religious kitsch. Every time some parishioner gave her husband a carved scripture verse or a sculpted pair of praying hands, Glenn Truesdale either kept it at his office or consigned it to the attic.

Vera made her stand after the grits and cantaloupe had been finished and the coffee had been replenished. "I still don't understand why you'd want to be vice president of the denomination, Glenn. You've never had the political bug."

Reverend Truesdale simply could not believe his wife had doubts about his glorious meting with Ridley Brown and the others yesterday. "I've always wanted to be whatever God wanted me to be, Vera. Ever since I met you at that pep rally thirty years ago, we've followed His lead."

Vera thought back to those days at the small southern religious college when the shy young coed held hands with the handsome boy she never thought would notice her. True, they'd both had dreams in their eyes then. But, she thought, this didn't sound like the life they'd discussed. She wasn't even sure this sounded like the father of her children, the man who prayed for her after a miscarriage, and the love of her life. She wondered when he had changed.

"And now, Vera, He's leading me into an important position within the denomination. Ridley Brown himself confirmed it."

"And all you have to do is stab your friend in the back."

"Tom McKee hasn't been my friend for a great many years, Vera. Maybe once we liked each other back at the seminary. But that was before he lost his way." Glenn Truesdale didn't need to add that his Faith Center church and McKee's Harmony church had been at odds for several years.

"Liked? We were the three musketeers, Glenn. Don't you remember the ski trip to Breckenridge? Don't you remember drinking root beer half the night at the A&W in Trinidad, Colorado when Raton Pass was closed? How about the Friday night cookouts at his house?"

"Yes, I do remember those. But that was long ago when we were young. That was a different Tom McKee. You don't remember the things he's said at conventions? You don't remember that quiet Scottish voice with his loud attacks on our theology?"

"Those weren't meant personally, and you know it. You two used to get along great—until his church began growing, and he got that television program."

"The better to spread his lies with."

"He was terribly hurt when you didn't visit him after the heart surgery last year."

"And I wasn't hurt when he mocked my preaching in front of the Ministerial Alliance? Remember the line about packing a suitcase for a guilt trip?"

"Is that really what this is all about? I thought Clairmont was your dream, Glenn. I thought you were perfectly happy here. We went through four other towns, and you told me all the while that this is what God wanted. I wouldn't want you to jeopardize it just because you're jealous of Tom McKee."

The reverend stared blankly, then stood and walked from the breakfast nook. He opened the door to the garage, stepped out of the house and said, "When you're ready to discuss this rationally, then we'll continue.

"Many are called, but few are chosen, Vera. Will you pray with me before I go to work?"

Vera Truesdale had noticed for a few months that disagreements were officially closed when he left for church. There, she had to play the good, silent, supportive wife. This prayer was just home delivery of her public role. She declined.

"Well, I'll pray for you anyway, Vera, that you'll see God's providence more clearly."

She was afraid that she was seeing things all too clearly already.

Only twenty-four hours ago, in a spacious but impersonal airport hotel suite, in the presence of his denomination's spiritual giants, Glenn Truesdale had believed completely that God would send down His wisdom. The five men stood, heads bowed in silent prayer.

Truesdale had developed a method to maintain his concentration through long prayer sessions: the more fervently he prayed, the deeper he dug his manicured thumbnails into the ridge between his eyes. Prayer, he frequently told his congregation, is worth a little bit of pain, and one should always pray with hands held high on the forehead to catch the Holy Ghost.

To his right stood Derrick Reid, Olympic wrestling champion turned youth evangelist. To his left, Lloyd Langenkamp, the arms millionaire and deacon, and Milton Eams, the firebrand television preacher. And straight ahead was Dr. Ridley Brown, the right-hand man of the Reverend John Jacob Jernigan himself, the man considered the second-most powerful non-Catholic preacher in the nation, just behind Billy Graham.

To actually consult with these men, the leaders of the denomination's conservative wing, was clearly the highlight of the Reverend Truesdale's thirty-year career in the ministry. He had hoped his suit didn't look too cheap or his shoes too rustic.

Brown had explained why he'd been summoned so secretly: "We have invited you here today, brother, to ask you to serve as our nominee as second vice president of the denomination, an appointment which, as you know, will lead to your eventual candidacy for president. We have prayed about it. We have studied your record. The Lord has led us to you. I know you'll want to pray about it, but I'm sure that you'll follow His call."

Truesdale lowered his eyes. "I will take this up in our next prayer meeting back home."

"Let me suggest, Brother Truesdale, that you pray on it rather more quickly than that. We'd like a decision before you leave. And, let me emphasize, the Lord has great need of you for the most important battle in the 168 years of our blessed church."

Truesdale had expected the discussion to touch on this most important battle—the denomination was gearing up for next year's election at the convention. The liberals, not as so-called moderate as the media would believe, had lost the last three elections. One more victory for the conservatives and the liberals might as well hand over the keys to the seminaries and the denominational offices.

"We know that the liberals are going to have to run one of two candidates," Brown said. "They owe Van Lambert a chance—he's done a lot of organizing for them—but he's too much of a nice guy for his own good. Down deep, he's still hoping for a compromise."

"So I'm afraid they're going to offer it to Tom McKee. And he's trouble for us. He's known, and he's popular with even a lot of our own folks."

Truesdale had studied the faces of the committee. Eyes were assessing him, his will, his very commitment to Christ.

Brown said, "The Reverend Jernigan and I agreed yesterday to offer you a position within the elite, brother. God wants us to pay the price. These men have paid the price. And your price, brother, is to stop Tom McKee."

Reid added firmly, "When I wrestled against those commies in the Olympics, I knew I'd have to wrestle on their level."

Eams said, "The man is against us, Glenn."

Truesdale asked if he could pray about it—in his church, the order of services often included six or seven prayer sessions. He knelt and adopted his lightning-rod pose again. He felt Reid's massive hand grip his skull and then other hands were laid upon his shoulders.

After three minutes, he stood and addressed these men of God. "Gentlemen, I hope the only thing Tom McKee will be running for is the border. However, in dealing with him, I've found only one Biblical passage can apply... 'If thine eye offend thee, pluck it out'."

Truesdale needed a rumor, and he had learned in fifteen years at Faith Center exactly which of his congregation were adept in the fine art of gossip. One of the deacons could spread the good word at his barbershop, and two of the women were connected with more than half of the social clubs in town. He had private conversations with them, as well as with a caterer who handled most of the men's service clubs' banquets.

He also needed an impersonator, and he knew he wouldn't find a Tom McKee look-alike in his church. Truesdale would settle for a university drama major if necessary, but he decided to check the local comedy clubs first. He found a suitable candidate at the second club, Laugh Til You Stop: a five-foot-seven performer named Bert Drummond desperately looking for a gig. Drummond, blond and thin with a remarkably unnoteworthy face, was unsteadily gripping a gin and tonic.

Truesdale was wearing a purple baseball cap, an old yellow leisure suit, and red sneakers—he'd decided an eye patch was too obvious—but he had to be certain no one would recognize him in this den of ill-repute.

He asked, "Can you imitate this man? You won't be under close scrutiny so no one will be able to see that you're not quite the same body type. All you have to do is fool someone at ten to twenty yards."

"I can impersonate anyone for money, pal. I've done Jerry Lewis, Jimmy Cagney, Kirk Douglas. For enough money, I'd try Kareem Abdul-Jabbar. I don't exactly have a lot of options open right now. Maybe if I could get to Orlando. Try to crack the tourist crowd. You know, I got a family routine. No profanity. What's the deal?"

"What's your going rate for this kind of performance, Mr. Drummond?"

"Hell, if you're paying and you're not drinking, I figure about fifteen hundred will cover it." Drummond stared at his well-chewed fingernails and figured the guy would talk him down to five hundred, which would cover back rent.

The preacher took out a roll of John Jacob Jernigan's money and peeled off two C-notes. "The rest you get after the job."

With shaking hands, Drummond reached out to take the money. In the process, Drummond managed to spill some of his drink on the preacher's sleeve. The preacher recoiled as if it were sulfuric acid.

"Just my luck," Drummond said, rolling his eyes. "You'd have paid five thousand, right?"

"Maybe, maybe not," said the preacher, dabbing at the liquor with a napkin.

Truesdale reached into a bag and pulled out a burnt-orange sweatshirt with the words TEXAS FOOTBALL imprinted on it—Tom McKee had actually worn such a shirt in his casual Sunday night services during the autumn. "This is what you'll need to wear. Now, this is what you'll do and when you'll do it...."

Later, the Reverend Truesdale discarded his disguise in a Goodwill box and stopped at a self-serve Exxon, making sure to spill some fuel on his wrist. Preachers couldn't afford to smell like a gin mill, and gas fumes could cover a multitude of smells. He drove home in the muggy darkness with all four windows of the Lincoln rolled down.

The Reverend Tom McKee had long refused speaking engagements and other tasks on Thursday nights in order to spend the evening at home. While he and his wife, Margaret, watched NBC comedies and snacked on pretzels, a group of protesters assembled outside the town's most notorious gay bar.

The protesters included members of a Faith Center Sunday School class that included three of Truesdale's primary gossip hounds. It had been presented during last week's class as a "unique opportunity to put your faith into action." The Reverend Truesdale, through his Sunday school director, had suggested the proper time and place for such an enterprise. He also made sure that other Clairmont churches were represented in the group. After all, other churches read the Apostle Paul; their members knew the score on gays.

Truesdale was conveniently visiting a new deacon and his wife across town. Despite his praise of his weight room and her decorating, the preacher couldn't help but sneak frequent looks at the couple's Christian clock that spouted a different Bible verse every hour on the hour. Vera would have heaved it into the trash can.

The clock was telling Truesdale that in God's Heaven there were many mansions at the very moment when Bert Drummond, hair dyed grey, false nose in place, and wearing the burnt-orange sweatshirt, bolted from his chair where he'd downed three gin and tonics, pushed through the door, and dashed for a nearby yellow cab. In plain sight of the protesters.

Sure enough, voices from the crowd yelled, "Hey, that's Tom McKee!" as the cab raced away.

When Truesdale met Drummond behind the comedy club at eight-thirty that night, he handed the poor sot his money and told him, "A word of advice, seek God and be on the next bus out of town. Perhaps He will lead you to greener pastures elsewhere."

Truesdale went home and waited for the storm to envelop Tom McKee.

By Monday, the storm was over.

Tom McKee had died of heart failure in his sleep, after what must have been the longest weekend of his life. He had fielded phone calls from the press, the Ministerial Alliance, several deacons, and finally, a secondhand source said, from the liberal wing itself. He had denied rumors about his sexual preference, but the whispers wouldn't stop. They'd asked him to pray about whether to continue as a candidate. Sunday, he'd had to defend himself from his pulpit.

When the cameras showed up at Faith Center church that Monday afternoon, the Reverend Truesdale stood in his best grey suit, with the faint turquoise line in the weave, and the silk tie with the turquoise crosses and proclaimed: "God has sent down His lightning and taken away one of the spiritual leaders of our city. I respected Tom McKee even when I did not agree with him. He's in a better place now, of that I am sure."

It was a shame Tom had died, Truesdale thought. He really hadn't meant for things to go so far. Still, as these things go, heart failure in your sleep wasn't a bad way to go. Glenn wondered if God would call him home in such a painless manner.

He received proper, respectful calls from Brown and the rest that afternoon. Brown told him, "It was a terrible thing that God had to call Tom McKee away, but the Lord has cleared the path for a convincing victory for us next year. You've been a true blessing, brother."

He'd taken his wife to the church for a Youth Department dinner and returned home to find a message on the phone recorder: "Glenn, this is John Jacob Jernigan calling from Jerusalem where I'm on a holy tour. I just heard some news about our brother preacher, and I want you to know that I feel for his family. I also wanted you to know that I appreciate your fine work for the Lord. May He bless you in the coming year."

When they buried Tom McKee on Thursday, Truesdale stood well behind the crowd. He owed himself a glance at the casket going into the ground. He knew his rival would get a good sendoff—Van Lambert had flown in from Tennessee to do the honors.

As a fellow eulogizer, Glenn Truesdale recognized a good service when he saw one. This one had a decent mixture of sorrow and hope, he had to admit, but the service was far too much like a wake for his liking. Wakes, he knew, were of the Catholic Church and, therefore, unsuitable for his denomination. Too much humor in the reminiscing. Not enough sobriety.

There'd been one angry look, though. Margaret McKee had spotted him and given him a vicious stare.

The Reverend Truesdale would pray for God to relieve her pain, he decided. Vera, who had actually wept with her, told him later that Margaret would visit her sister in Oregon for a month.

When he returned home, the message light on the answering machine was flashing. He punched the Play button and bent over to hear the soft, whispery voice. "Be in your sanctuary tonight at midnight," the voice said with a trace of Glaswegian lilt. Truesdale couldn't believe his ears; it sounded like Tom McKee! "...or prepare to suffer for eternity."

And the line went dead.

The fingernails were gouging into the ridge between Truesdale's eyes. He'd been praying, knees bent before the altar in the Faith Center sanctuary, for an hour now, waiting for a ghost. He tried to concentrate on appropriate Scripture verses, but found himself remembering a foggy morning in Edinburgh thirty years ago. He'd been attending an international missions conference—he and Vera, newly graduated from college, were praying about serving overseas—and had planned to take a night train down to London. With some free time, he'd walked past a castle and old buildings until the fog descended. He'd leaned against a lamppost on an unfamiliar street and heard the sound of bagpipes wafting out of the mist. For a short, blessed time, Truesdale had imagined a regiment of Christian souls marching forth to claim victory over Satan's hordes on an eerie moor. It was invigorating.

When the fog cleared, though, he'd walked into a small park and found an old man rehearsing the pipes in an ancient bandshell. He learned not to believe in ghosts on that foggy afternoon. He didn't think he believed in them tonight, either.

Truesdale opened his eyes and glanced at his Seiko; three minutes after midnight. Glenn Truesdale resumed his prayer stance. He heard footsteps softly advancing down the center aisle.

His last prayer was that the tripwire, carefully looped between pews, would catch his ghost. He did not dare to look. He heard a sudden gasp and crash, followed by a low moan.

When the Reverend Truesdale unfolded himself and walked cautiously to the body, he found Bert Drummond, makeup in place but wig askew, grimacing, with both hands around his left ankle.

"You bloody bastard," the actor hissed. "You bloody bastard."

The reverend stood in genuine surprise. "Brother, why are you doing this to me? Why call me here at midnight?"

"You killed him, you bastard," Bert said through clenched teeth. His ankle must have been sprained pretty badly. "And you got me to help. I didn't even know what I was doing, but I figured it out quick enough. One of the comedians had a joke in his routine about the guy Friday night, and I figured it out. Even went to his church Sunday. Saw the man's eyes and knew I had helped drive him to the edge."

"You don't understand, brother," Truesdale said. "I, or I should say, *we*, had nothing to do with his death. Don't you understand that God called that man home to Heaven? Don't you understand that the man apparently had a bad heart? It was his time, plain and simple."

"Well, you damn well pushed him. And you don't have an ounce of sorrow about it, do you?"

"There's not anything to be sorry for. It was God's will..." Truesdale's voice stopped.

The sweet, discordant sound of bagpipes began to fill the sanctuary, and the ghost of Tom McKee drifted slowly toward the two men.

It said, "And what would you know about God's will, Glenn?"

Truesdale turned and ingloriously stumbled over his own tripwire. From the thick, silver carpet, he craned his neck.

The ghost said, "Don't go fainting away on me, Glenn. We're going to have a fun time, you and I. I'd better untie this wire before you break your little neck." The ghost turned to the fallen Drummond. "And you, my friend, need to go to the hospital. Stop worrying about the past. I don't blame you a bit."

The actor, face frozen, stood shakily and limped as quickly as he could out of Faith Center church and into the night.

In the meantime, Truesdale had twisted onto his back and was crawling on his elbows up the aisle. The ghost, at once visible yet somehow less than visible, began crawling up the aisle right next to the reverend.

"Aren't you going to ask me how I've been, Glenn? Aren't you going to inquire about my health?"

"How you've been, Tom?" Truesdale asked uncertainly. He climbed to his feet.

The ghost snorted, and the sanctuary shook. "Never better, Glenn. That's the funniest thing. Your heart goes out on you, and suddenly you're never better. Of course, you can imagine my surprise when I learned about your little meeting at the airport. And I know about your deal with our friend Drummond. You've been very busy, Glenn." Then the ghost smiled.

Truesdale feared the smile more than the words.

"Vera's expecting you, and I wouldn't want to keep you out late," the ghost said. "When you return here tomorrow morning, we'll talk again.... And, Glenn, you'll want to have that political bumper sticker off your fancy car."

When the Lincoln pulled into the Faith Center church lot, the sticker supporting the mayoral challenger—who had made a generous donation last month—remained squarely on the left back bumper.

When the Reverend Truesdale, eyes laced with Visine, walked into his pastoral study, the ghost of Tom McKee was waiting.

"I prayed through the night until dawn," Truesdale said. "And God told me that you couldn't touch me. That's true, isn't it? You can't lay a hand on me, can you? Can you?"

"I can't."

"So you can't levitate me above the ground or devour me like some beast or anything like that, can you?"

"Have you been reading Stephen King, Glenn?"

"You can't even physically attack me in any way, can you?"

"Well, if you've been talking to God, you would know what I could do, wouldn't you?"

"That means you can't make me do anything. Not anything. I have a pre-wedding counseling session with a young couple in ten minutes. I want you out. In the name of God, I command it!"

"You're wrong, Glenn. I intend to make you do a whole lot of things. Just remember one word of warning: I'm no Banquo's ghost."

"What is that supposed to mean?"

"I knew the schools were weak, but I'd have expected you to know *Macbeth*."

"Shakespeare? Maybe *Romeo and Juliet*...*Julius Caesar* in high school. Unlike you, I preferred to read more scriptural stuff in my college days, as I'm sure you will remember."

"I can understand that you'd know about Brutus, but you'll wish you'd had a more thorough education by tonight."

The ghost vanished.

Vera Truesdale had taken a group of women to a weekend retreat, so the pastor, faced with a freezer of frozen dinners, met some of his deacons for lunch at Paranelli's, where they met weekly to talk football, politics, and church business, in random order.

The reverend had just bitten into his piping hot spaghetti carbonara when he sprayed it onto the fresh bread sticks. He'd glanced at the TV screen over the bar, and the reporter was showing a protest site—some people in wheelchairs down at city hall. And then it showed Tom McKee shouting into a bullhorn.

His deacons stared at him.

"I must've swallowed wrong," Truesdale said, rubbing his eyes. "Just had one of those nights when I couldn't get to sleep."

The phone was ringing when he returned to the office. Suzanne DeWalt, a Faith Center member connected with the Junior League, was calling. "This man—I swear it was Tom McKee—brought a group of those homeless people into the Plaza, and they absolutely ravaged the buffet. Then he whipped out a wad of money and handed it to the manager, and the whole bunch of them walked out singing 'Dropkick Me, Jesus, Through the Goal Posts of Life'."

The reverend reached into his top desk drawer and pulled out four Tylenol, and then he went home to try to sleep.

When Truesdale awakened, the bedside alarm clock read 11:39 p.m. He stumbled into the kitchen, put on the coffee, and checked the answering machine. "You have five messages," the voice intoned.

"Hi, honey, it's Vera. We arrived at the campground safe and sound. Call you in the morning. Love you."

Beep

"Glenn, Calvin Brooks here. A guy in the barber shop just told me he thought he saw Tom McKee playing basketball down at the Y."

Beep

"Reverend Truesdale, this is Lynnette James at the Dispatch. Look, I just talked to a doctor who swears he saw Tom McKee delivering supplies to an AIDS hospice and that McKee referred him to you. Please call me at 555-8901."

Beep

"Glenn, Deacon Terry here. Some Harmony church people are saying that they went to the Buddy Guy concert down at the arts center and—you won't believe this—saw Tom McKee dancing and high-fiving on stage during the concert. I don't have to tell you that Blues is the Devil's music. That's hardly an appropriate concert for a minister. Give me a call, will you?"

Beep

"Reverend Truesdale, you don't know me, but my name's Stan Carbo, and I own The Place, a bar south of town where bikers hang out. This guy who looks like Tom McKee came in here and began to pal around with them. He said you should be sure to call him here when you wake up. The number's 555-2563."

Beep

They met one hour later in the Faith Center parking lot. Truesdale arrived in his Lincoln, with a freshly-scraped back bumper. McKee's ghost arrived in a convoy of Harleys driven by the most disreputable crew of humans Truesdale had ever seen. The ghost was wearing a black leather jacket and a black T-shirt emblazoned with a neon skull.

The ghost waved to them. The group waved back and revved their engines.

"A fine group, Glenn. The leader's name is Diamondback, and he's a fine fellow. By the way, I see your car's a little cleaner."

"I looked up *Macbeth* like you suggested. Apparently, only Macbeth could see Banquo's ghost, nobody else. Not even Lady Macbeth. So I get the point. Evidently anybody and everybody can see your ghost, if you want."

"Do you understand the lesson for the day, Glenn? I can be anywhere I want, whenever I want. So let's forget this commanding-in-the-name-of-God bit. At any rate, I had a talk with God. She doesn't care at all whether your friends or my friends take control of the denomination."

Truesdale blanched. He knew when he'd been beaten. "I apologize, Glenn. For a lot of things, I guess. You know that I didn't intend for this to happen."

"I'm happy to accept an apology. I should apologize to you, too; I could have reined myself in at times, but didn't. By the way, you can expect my friends the Road Dukes for Sunday services, as well as my friends from down at the AIDS hospice. You'll need to put in a sturdy ramp for my friends in the wheelchairs, too."

"What? I'm not going to do that." He might be beaten, but he wouldn't be battered.

"Oh, yes, I'm afraid your attendance rolls will decline, but you'll be so much happier in the long run. It's either that, Glenn, or the *National Enquirer* will send a reporter down to ask if you're going to hire Elvis as your new music director."

"There's no way I'm going to let you take over my church!"

"But I'm not taking over. You'll be preaching every Sunday. Do you think your fundamentalist friends are really going to keep you around after today, anyhow? When they see bikers and homosexuals here Sunday, they'll forget they knew you."

The ghost began to describe changes: a food kitchen for the homeless, work with ghetto churches, ordaining women as deacons. "You know, it's about time you let Vera share in your ministry a little bit."

"Why are you doing this to me?" the preacher asked, nearly sobbing.

"Because, Glenn, God and I think you'll make an excellent denomination presidential candidate for the moderates. You see, I wanted that nomination as much as you wanted to stop me. No offense, but I just never figured that they'd use you. Or that you'd be willing to go so far.... The thing is, I'm actually kind of grateful. I really like this disembodied stuff. There were a lot of chains on me when I was living, and there's just as many on you. Don't you think it's time to loosen some of them?

"Did you know I'd never ridden a motorcycle before last night? Never played pickup basketball anywhere except a church gym? Never been inside a real bar? I think you're going to like trying new things. I know Vera's ready to stretch her wings, too. We'll be the three musketeers again. Be seeing you soon."

Glenn Truesdale crouched by the altar and placed folded hands to his forehead. He wondered just who would be invited to Dr. Brown's next meeting in the impersonal hotel suite.

He wondered if it were possible that he could win a presidency with the help of Tom McKee's ghost.

And he prayed desperately for God's guidance.

After a long while, he heard the click of the sanctuary door. He straightened slowly and turned to confront the apparition, but saw his wife, wearing her plaid flannel pajamas and a black leather jacket, clutching a motorcycle helmet.

He ran up the aisle to embrace her.

She seemed to glow with excitement. "The ghost told me that you needed me, and that he'd take me to you! That rascal Tom McKee got me on a Harley in the middle of the night roaring down the interstate picking bugs out of my teeth."

Vera Truesdale stopped talking, stared at her husband, rubbed the palm of her hand against his brow.

When she removed it, there was small smear of blood from her husband's forehead.

The Midnight El
Robert Weinberg

Cold and alone, Sidney Taine waited for the Midnight El. Collar pulled up close around his neck, he shivered as the frigid Chicago wind attacked his exposed skin. With temperatures hovering only a few degrees above zero, the stiff breeze off Lake Michigan plunged the wind chill factor to twenty below. Not even the usual drunks haunted the outdoor train platforms on nights like these. Fall asleep outside in the darkness and you never woke up.

Taine hated the cold. Though he had lived in Chicago for more than a year, he had yet to adjust to the winter weather. Originally from San Francisco, he delighted his hometown friends when he groused that he never realized what the phrase "chilled to the bone" meant until he moved to the Windy City.

A sly grin and dark, piercing eyes gave him a sardonic, slightly mysterious air. An image he strived to cultivate. Like his father and grandfather before him, Taine worked as a private investigator.

Though he had opened his office in Chicago only fourteen months ago, he was already well-known throughout the city. Dubbed by one of the major urban newspapers as "The New Age Detective," Taine used both conventional techniques and occult means to solve his cases. While his unusual methods caused a few raised eyebrows, no one mocked his success rate. Specializing in missing-person investigations, Taine rarely failed to locate his quarry. Although, he had his doubts about tonight's assignment.

Before leaving his office this evening, Taine had mixed, then drank, an elixir with astonishing properties. According to a famous grimoire *The Key of Solomon*, the potion enabled the user to see the spirits of the dead. Its effects lasted until dawn, which was more than enough time for Taine. If he failed tonight, there would be no second chance.

The detective glanced down at his watch for the hundredth time. The glowing hands indicated five minutes to twelve. According to local legends, it was nearly the hour for the Midnight El to start its run.

No one knew how or when the stories began. A dozen specialists in urban folklore supplied the detective with an equal number of fabled origins. One and all, they were of the opinion that the tales dated back to the first decades of the century, when the subway first debuted in Chicago.

A few old timers, mostly retired railway conductors and engineers, claimed the Midnight El continued an even older tradition – the Phantom Train, sometimes called the Death's Head Locomotive. Despite the disagreements, several elements remained constant in all the accounts. The Midnight El hit the tracks exactly at the stroke of twelve. Its passengers consisted of those who had died that day in Chicago. The train traversed the entire city, starting at the station closest to the most deaths of the day, working its way along from there.

Taine waited on a far south side platform. Earlier in the day, twelve people had died in a flash fire only blocks from this location. There was little question this would be the train's first stop.

Slowly, the seconds ticked past. A harsh west wind wailed off the Lake, like some dread banshee warning Taine of his peril. With it came the doleful chiming of a distant church bell striking the hour. Midnight—the end of one day, start of another.

The huge train came hurtling along the track, rumbling like distant thunder. Emerging ghostlike out of thin air, dark and forbidding, blacker than the night, it lumbered into the station. Lights flashed red and yellow as it slowed to a stop. Taine caught a hurried vision inside a half-dozen cars as they rumbled past. Pale, vacant, *dead* faces stared out into the night. Riders from another city, or another day, he wasn't sure which, and he had no desire to know. Young and old, black and white, men and women, all hungering for a glimpse of life.

Hissing loudly, double doors swung open on each car. A huge, shadowy figure clad in a conductor's uniform emerged from midway along the train. In his right hand he held a massive silver pocket watch, hooked by a glittering chain to his vest. Impatiently, he stood there, waiting for new arrivals.

The conductor's gaze swept the station, rested on Taine for a moment, then continued by. The ghost train with all its passengers was invisible to mortal eyes. There was no way for the conductor to know that the man on the platform could actually see him. Nor suspect what Taine planned to do.

Once, the conductor had been a ferryman; the ancient Greeks knew him as Charon. To the Egyptians, he had been Anubis, the Opener of the Way. A hundred other cultures named him a hundred different ways. But always his task remained the same: transporting the newly dead to their final destination.

They came with the wind. Not there, then suddenly there. Each one stopped to face the conductor for an instant before being allowed to pass. The breath froze in Taine's throat as he watched them file by. Those who had died that day.

His hands clenched into fists when he sighted three pajama-clad, black children. Today's newspapers had been filled with all the grisly details of the sudden tenement fire that had resulted in their deaths. None of them had been over six years old.

Wordlessly, the last of the three turned. Lonely, mournful eyes stared deep into Taine's for an instant. The detective remained motionless. If he reacted now, it might warn the conductor. An instant passed, and then the child and all the other passengers were gone. Disappeared into the Midnight El.

The conductor stepped back into the doorway. Raising one hand, he signaled *continue* to some unseen engineer. Seeing his chance, Taine acted.

Moving with the grace of a stalking tiger, the detective darted at, then around, the astonished doorman. Before the shadowy figure could react, Taine was past him and into the subway. Ignoring the restless dead on all sides, the detective headed for the front of the car.

"Come back here," commanded the conductor, stepping aboard. Behind him, the doors swung shut. An instant later, the car jerked forward as the engine came to life. Outside, scenery blurred as the train gained speed. The floor shook with a gentle, rocking motion. The Midnight El was off to its next stop.

Taine relaxed, letting his pursuer catch up to him. Surprise had enabled him to board the ghostly train. Getting off might not prove so easy.

"You do not belong on the Midnight El, Mr. Taine," said the conductor. He spoke calmly, without any trace of accent. Listening closely, Taine caught the barest hint of amusement in the phantom's voice. "At least, not yet. Your time is not for years and years."

"You know my name, and instant of my death?" asked Taine, not the least bit intimidated by the imposing bulk of the other. Six feet, four inches tall, weighing a bit more than two hundred and thirty pounds, Taine resembled a professional football player.

Surrounded by the shadows, the ticket taker towered over Taine by a head. His face, though human, appeared cut from weathered marble. Only his black, black eyes burned with life. "Past, present, future mean nothing to me. One look at a man is all I need to review his entire life history, from the moment of his birth to the last breath he takes. It's part of my job, supervising the Midnight El."

"For what employer?"

"Someday, you'll learn the answer," replied the conductor, with a chuckle. "But it won't matter much then." He reached into his vest pocket and pulled out the silver pocket watch. "Thirteen minutes to the next stop. This train, unlike most, always runs on time. You shall exit there, Mr. Taine."

"And if I choose not to?"

"You must." The conductor frowned. "I cannot harm you. Such action is strictly forbidden under the terms of my employment. However, I appeal to your sense of compassion. A living presence on this train upsets the other passengers. Think of the pain you are inflicting on them."

Darkness gathered around the railroad man. He no longer looked so human. His coal-black eyes burned with inhuman intensity. "Leave them to their rest, Mr. Taine. You do not belong here."

"Nor does one other."

The conductor sighed, his rock-hard features softening in sorrow. "I should have guessed. You came searching for Maria Hernandez. Why?"

"Her husband hired me. He read about my services in the newspapers. I'm the final resort for those who refuse to give up hope.

"Victor told me what little he knew. My knowledge of the occult filled in the blanks. Combined together, the facts led me here."

"All trails end at the Midnight El," declared the conductor, solemnly. "Though I'm surprised you realized that."

"It was the only possible solution. Maria disappeared three nights ago. Vanished without a trace off of an isolated underground subway platform exactly at midnight. No one else recognized the significance of the time.

"The police admitted they were completely baffled. The ticket seller remembered Maria taking the escalator down to the station a few minutes before twelve. A transit patrolman spoke to her afterwards. He remembered looking up at the clock and noting the lateness of the hour. But when he looked around, the woman was no longer there. Somehow, she disappeared in the blink of an eye. Searching the tunnels for her body turned up nothing."

Taine paused. "Victor Hernandez considered me his last and only chance. I promised him I would do my best. I never mentioned the Midnight El."

"My thanks to you for that," said the conductor, nodding his understanding. "Suicides cause me the greatest pain. Especially those who sacrifice themselves to join the one they love."

"She meant a great deal to him," said Taine. "They were only married a few months. It seemed quite unfair."

"The world is unfair," said the conductor, shrugging his massive shoulders. "Or so I have been told by my passengers. Again and again, for centuries beyond imagining."

"She wasn't dead. If I don't belong here, then neither does she."

The conductor grimaced. He looked down at his great silver watch and shook his head. "There's not enough time to explain. Our schedule is too tight for long talks. Please understand my position."

"The Greeks considered Charon the most honorable of the gods. Of course, that was a thousand years ago."

"Spare me the dramatics," said the conductor. A bitter smile crossed his lips. He nodded to himself, as if making an important decision. Slowly, ever so slowly, he twisted the stem on the top of his watch.

All motion ceased. The subway car no longer shook. Outside, the blurred features of the city solidified into grotesque shapes, faintly resembling the Chicago skyline.

Taine grunted in surprise. "You can stop time?"

"For a little while," said the conductor. "Don't forget, the Midnight El visits every station within the space of a single night. On a hot summer night in a violent city like this, we often need extra minutes for all the passengers. Thus my watch. Twisting a little more produces a timeless state."

"The scenery?" asked Taine, not wanting to waste his questions, but compelled by the alieness of the landscape to ask.

"All things exist in time as well as space. Take away that fourth dimension and the other three seem twisted."

The phantom conductor turned and beckoned with his other hand. "Maria Hernandez. Attend me."

A short, slender woman in her early twenties pushed her way forward through the ranks of the dead. Long brown hair, knotted in a single thick braid, dropped down her back almost to her waist. Wide, questioning eyes looked at the detective. Unlike all the others on the train, a spark of color still touched Maria's cheeks, and her chest rose and fell with her every breath.

"Tell Mr. Taine how you missed the subway two weeks ago," said the conductor. He glanced at Taine, as if checking to make sure the detective was paying attention.

"There was a shortage in one of the drawers at closing time," began Maria, her voice calm, controlled. "My superior asked me to do a cross-check. It was merely a mathematical error, but it took nearly twenty minutes to find. By then, I was ten minutes late for my train."

She hesitated, as if remembering something particularly painful. "I was in a hurry to get home. It was our six-month anniversary. When I left that morning for the bank, my husband, Victor, promised me a big surprise when I returned. I loved surprises."

"Yes, I know," said the conductor, his voice gentle. "He bought you tickets to the theater. But that is incidental to the story. Please continue."

"Usually, I have to wait a few minutes for my train. Not that night. It arrived exactly on schedule. When I reached the El platform, the conductor was signaling to close the doors. The next train wasn't for thirty minutes. So I ran. I would have made it, too, if it wasn't for my right heel." She looked down at her shoes. "It caught in a crack in the cement. Wedged there so tight I couldn't pull my foot loose. By the time I wrenched free, the train had already left."

"Two weeks ago," said Taine, comprehension dawning. "The day of the big subway crash in the Loop."

"Four minutes after Mrs. Hernandez missed her train, it crashed head-long into another, stalled on the tracks ahead," said the conductor. "Fourteen people died when several of the cars sandwiched together. *Fifteen* should have perished."

"Fate," said Taine.

"She was destined to die," replied the conductor, as if explaining the obvious. "It was woven in the threads. A mistake was made somewhere. Her heel should have missed that crack. There was probably a knot in the twine. I assure you her name was on my passenger list. Maria was scheduled to ride the Midnight El."

"So, when she didn't, you decided to correct that mistake on your own," said Taine, his temper rising. Mrs. Hernandez stood silent, as if frozen in place. Her story told, the conductor ignored her.

"I thought a living person on board disturbed the dead?"

"With effort, the rules can be bent," said the conductor. He sighed. "It grows so boring here. You cannot imagine how terribly boring. I desired company, someone to talk to. Someone alive, someone with feelings, emotions. The dead no longer care about anything.

"The Three Sisters had to unravel a whole section of the cloth. They needed to weave a new destiny for Mrs. Hernandez to cover up their mistake. Meanwhile, Maria should have been dead but was still alive. Her spirit belonged to neither plane of existence. It took no great effort to bring her on the train as a passenger. And, here she will remain, for all eternity, neither living or dead, but in a state between the two. Immortal, undying, unchanging—exactly like me. Forever."

Taine's fists clenched in anger. "Who gave you the power to decide her fate? That's not your job. You're only the ferryman, nothing more. She doesn't belong here. I won't allow you to do this."

"Your opinion means nothing to me, Mr. Taine." The conductor's left hand rested on the stem of the pocket watch. "There is nothing you can do to stop me."

"Like hell," said the detective, and leapt forward.

A powerfully built man, he moved with astonishing speed. Once tonight he had caught the conductor by surprise. This time, he did not.

The phantom's left hand shot out and caught Taine by the throat. Without effort, he raised the detective into the air, so that the man's feet dangled inches off the floor. "I am not fooled so easily a second time."

Taine flailed wildly with both hands. Not one of his punches connected. Desperately, the detective lashed out one foot, hitting the conductor in the chest. The phantom didn't even flinch.

"In my youth I wrestled with Atlas and Hercules. Your efforts pale before theirs, Mr. Taine."

Neither man nor spirit noticed Mrs. Hernandez cautiously reaching for the silver pocket watch the trainman held in his other hand. Not until she grabbed it away.

"What!" bellowed the conductor, dropping Taine and whirling about. "You…you…"

"Just because I obeyed your commands," said Mrs. Hernandez, "didn't mean I no longer possessed a will of my own. I was waiting for the right opportunity." She gestured with her head at the crowds of the dead all around them. "I'm not like them. I'm alive."

She held the pocket watch tightly, one hand on the stem. "If you try to take this away, I'll break it. Don't make me do that."

Taine, his throat and neck burning with pain, staggered to Mrs. Hernandez's side. "Let us go. Otherwise, we'll remain here forever, frozen in time."

"Nonsense," said the conductor. "I told you the rules can only be bent so far. Sooner or later, the strain will become too great and snap this train back to the real world."

"But, if Maria breaks your watch," said Taine, "what then? You admitted needing its powers. Think of the problems maintaining your schedule without it."

"True enough." The conductor paused for a moment, as if in thought. "I am willing to offer this compromise. Maria cannot leave this train without my permission. The Fates will not spin her a new destiny as long as she remains on the El. Return the watch to me, and I'll give her a chance to return to her husband. And resume her life on Earth."

"A chance?" said the detective, suspiciously. "What exactly do you mean by that?"

"A gamble, a bet, a *wager*, Mr. Taine," said the conductor. "Relieve my boredom. Ask me a question, any question. If I cannot answer, you and Mrs. Hernandez go free. If I guess correctly, then both of you remain here for all eternity—not dead but no longer among the living—on the Midnight El. It will take a great deal of effort, but I can manage. Take it or leave it. I refuse to bend any further."

"Both of us?" said Taine. "You raised the stakes. And what about disturbing the dead? A little while ago you were anxious for me to leave."

"As I stated before, the rules can be bent. After all, I am the ferryman. And," continued Charon, the faintest trace of a smile on his lips, "what better way to sharpen your wits, Mr. Taine, than to put your own future at peril?"

"According to your earlier remarks, there's nothing in the world you don't know."

"There is only one omniscient presence. Man or spirit, we are mere reflections of his glory. Still," he added, as an afterthought, "the universe holds few mysteries for me."

Shadows gathered around the phantom. He extended one huge hand. "Make your decision. Now. Before I change my mind."

His eyes burned like two flaming coals. "No tricks. An answer must exist for your question."

"Give him the watch," Taine said to Maria.

"You agree?" asked the conductor.

"I agree," replied the detective, calmly.

The conductor twisted the stem of his great silver watch. Immediately, the scenery shifted, and the subway car started shaking.

"We arrive at the next station in a few minutes," Charon announced smugly. "You have until then to frame your question."

Maria gasped, raising her hands to her face. "But...that's cheating."

"Not true. I promised no specific length of time for our challenge." The conductor glanced down at his watch. "Your time is ticking by quickly. Better think fast."

Taine took a deep breath. Not all questions depended on facts for their answer. He prayed that the ferryman would not renege on their bargain once he realized his mistake. "You trapped yourself. I'm ready now."

"You are?" said the conductor, frowning.

"Are you prepared to accept defeat?"

"Impossible."

"Then tell me the answer to the question raised when I first boarded the train. When is the exact moment of my death?"

"You will perish..." began the conductor, then stopped, mouth open in astonishment. Slowly, the fire left his eyes. He shook his head. "Caught by my own words."

Maria Hernandez turned to Taine. "I don't understand. Caught? How?"

"The conductor bragged earlier that he knew the date of my death," said Taine. "If he answers correctly, then he wins our bet."

"And," continued Maria, comprehension dawning, "by the terms of the agreement, you must remain on the Midnight El forever."

"Thus making his prediction false," finished Taine, "since I cannot die when he predicts. On the other hand, if he says I will never die, then he does not know the date of my death. Which means he cannot answer the question. So, whatever he says, I am the winner. The bet is ours."

With a sigh, the conductor pocketed his watch. "You would have made good company, Mr. Taine."

Metal screeched on metal as the Midnight El pulled into the next station. "This is your stop. Farewell."

They were alone on a deserted subway station with a cold wind blowing.

Tears filled Maria Hernandez's eyes. "Are we really free?"

Taine nodded, his thoughts drifting. Already, he searched for an explanation for Maria's disappearance that would satisfy both the police and her husband.

"As free as any man or woman can be," he answered somberly. "For in the end, we all have a date to keep with the Midnight El."

Heart Beat
Sèphera Girón

"IT'S *MY* TURN TO BE the mummy!" Mary said, her hands on her hips. Tiny blond braids bobbed on the sides of her head like little antennae as she jumped up and down.

Janet grinned from where she was lying with her arms crossed on the long, grey stone bench. She sat up, running her hand through her short red hair, picking away the crushed leaves that were mashed into the back of her head.

The autumn wind was picking up, spinning dirt and twigs in little vortexes around the children, wafting dust and debris along the many rows of old tombstones in the graveyard.

"Okay, but then that means I get to be Sylvia!" Janet said, grinning at Laurie.

Laurie frowned. "No. I'm still Sylvia."

"No fair, you're *always* Sylvia," Janet pouted.

Mary slipped an arm around Janet and nodded. "Yeah, how come you always get to be Sylvia?"

"Because I do such a good job!" Laurie smiled smugly. She adjusted the tattered white netting that she had draped over her head. Laurie remembered when she found the piece of gauze in one of her mother's old boxes in the basement. She had run up to her bedroom and wrapped it around her head, watching herself in the mirror. It had been so perfect for the game. Her mother had come in as she was fiddling with it.

"Are you playing dress up?" her mother had asked.

Laurie nodded. "Can I have this? I found it downstairs."

Mother touched the netting, arranging it along her daughter's long dark hair. "Sure. It's just scraps from some theater piece I was working on years ago."

"It's perfect for Sylvia!" Laurie beamed, staring at her own dark eyes in the mirror. She could imagine herself as the long-dead bride.

"Sylvia? Who's Sylvia?"

"You know! The mummy's wife."

Mother shook her head. "The mummy's wife?...Oh, you mean the Thompson story."

"Yes, Sylvia."

"You still play that silly game?"

"We love that game." Laurie stared at herself, feeling the romance of the story surging through her. Her heart raced, and she put her hand up to her chest, feeling the pulse against her fingers.

Thump-thump, thump-thump

She sighed dreamily. "It's so romantic. How he's been waiting forever for her, for her heart...."

Mother patted her on the head. "Aren't you getting a little too old to be playacting such nonsense? You're nearly eleven now."

"I love that story. It's so sad. How he waits and waits and she never comes. You know, I think she wanted to be with him, too, but was afraid...."

"It's a terrible, horrible story. You'd be better off putting it out of your mind."

Thump-thump, thump-thump

"Laurie?" Janet was punching Laurie's arm. "Are you still with us?"

Laurie's hand was over her heart, and she could feel it beating. Beating so strong. Searching, searching for...

"Laurie!"

It took a second to recognize Janet's freckled face staring at her with a weird look. She looked over at Mary, who was also watching her with a strange expression.

"Huh?...Oh, sorry. I was just...lost in thought, I guess."

"I'm bored with this game," Mary complained. "Let's do something else."

"Oh, one more time, come on," Laurie pleaded, spinning in a circle, her long, dark hair tangled along the makeshift wedding veil. "It's so much fun."

"All right. One more. Then we do something else."

The three ten-year-old girls organized themselves into their starting spots in front of the monstrous crypt that bore the name THOMPSON. It belonged to a mysterious and wealthy family who had lived in the town for several generations. A scandal from decades earlier, in the thirties, had haunted these children and their parents before them. It was a story of love and tragedy, horror and the occult. It was a story that wouldn't die.

Janet stood in front of Mary and Laurie. She hung the large silver cross that they used for this game around her neck. The girls giggled and shuffled until, at last, they were able to control their laughter.

"I now pronounce you man and wife," Janet/Priest said solemnly, raising her hand and bringing it down in the sign of a cross. A gust of wind blew through the graveyard, and leaves fluttered around their ankles. Mary faced Laurie, her face flushed as she tried to control her laughter, her jutting pigtails making her an unlikely groom. Laurie stared at her solemnly with dark eyes through the veil, and Mary didn't feel like laughing much any more. Mary lifted the veil to reveal Laurie's face.

"You may kiss the bride."

Mary leaned in and pecked Laurie quickly on the lips. She knew that if she didn't, Laurie would be upset, and then they would never get out of here.

"I now pronounce you Mr. and Mrs. David Thompson." Janet/Priest bowed.

Mary/David took Laurie/Sylvia's hand, and they skipped around the crypt, scooping up handfuls of crackling leaves and flinging them in the air. After a moment or two of celebration, they settled on the stone bench that faced the crypt and pretended to be driving.

"Look out!" Laurie/Sylvia screamed, and they mimed hitting a tree.

Mary/David flung herself on the ground, moaning and groaning. "Help me, help me...." she cried, writhing in the grass.

Laurie/Sylvia dragged herself over to Mary, holding her hand. "David, don't die. Don't..."

"Remember our pact," Mary/David gasped. "Remember the promise you made...."

"Of course, I will. I'll never forget. Never," Laurie/Sylvia vowed, kissing Mary/David's hand.

Mary/David moaned and pretended to expire.

"No!" Laurie cried. "You can't leave me, David. I love you, I love you." Tears ran down her cheeks as she threw herself on Mary. Laurie lay sobbing on the grass, waves of sorrow undulating through her ten-year-old body with such heat and intensity that she didn't think she could ever stop. Mary opened her eyes and looked at Janet as Laurie continued to cry.

"Now the next part!" Janet said sternly.

Mary got up and went over to the bench. She lay down on it, her arms folded across her chest.

Janet shook Laurie. "It's time for the next part," she whispered.

Laurie got up, still shaking, and rubbed at her tear-streaked eyes with the palm of her hand.

Janet stood holding the cross, her head bowed, as Laurie acted out the next part of the story.

"You see, we made a promise," Laurie/Sylvia explained to Janet/Mortician. "He wanted to be mummified. All his parts taken out and preserved, except for his heart."

"That seems like a strange request in this day and age," Janet/Mortician mused, tapping her chin.

"He loved the Egyptians. He loved their customs and their legends." Laurie's eyes glazed over as she stared up at the mausoleum. She traced the hieroglyphics with her hands, digging into the cold hard granite crevices with her short little fingers as she had hundreds of times.

"He is to be made a mummy, and when I die, I too will join him! *Our love will be forever, our hearts will beat as one!*"

"Very well. You have the money!" Janet/Mortician said as Laurie/Sylvia handed over an imaginary wad of cash.

The two girls pretended to be cutting open Mary/David and removing her organs. They busily put them into pretend jars as Janet then doubled as a priest to say the required prayers.

"It is done," Janet/Priest stated after they prayed for a while for David's soul to find peace in the afterlife.

Laurie looked at Mary, who lay still. She knelt beside her. She trembled, afraid of what she had to say. "I have something to tell you, David. I have fallen in love with someone else. I just got married."

The mummy lay quiet.

"I'm not going to be a mummy with you. I'm going to be buried in Neil's family plot. I'm sorry. I hope you aren't angry."

Laurie walked away, feeling another wave of heat surging through her. Putting her hand to her forehead, she felt a headache pulsing to life behind her eyeballs. She sat down on another bench on the other side of the crypt and stared up at the grey sky. The clouds were heavy and low today, pregnant to bursting.

Mary roared, startling Laurie from her reverie. Mary/Mummy sat up slowly, her arms outstretched in front of her, eyes opened wide, but unseeing. She shuffled around the crypt to where Laurie sat. Mary crept up behind her and groaned, wrapping her hands around Laurie's long hair and tugging. "You will be with me…always!"

Laurie mock-screamed in fearful delight as she broke loose from Mary's clutch. Soon the girls were running from Mary/Mummy, who walked stiff-legged with her arms outstretched. Her moans echoed through the graveyard as the wind blew harder.

Before long, the girls collapsed giggling into a heap, and the first drops of rain began to fall.

Laurie shook her head and wiped away her tears. Daydreaming again.

It seemed like only yesterday she had been here, playing that silly game with her friends. Now they were all grown up, the childhood games nearly forgotten. Janet was married and had two little red-headed children, and Mary fell out of touch years ago, after the family had moved during high school. Laurie herself had only just returned to town after spending the past four years in University.

She stared at the large stone monument; it was beautiful. All the carvings and details, the whole Egyptian flavor, in the center of this traditional burial ground was so odd, yet so perfect. The years had weathered the crypt, heavy clumps of moss clung to the sides, and ivy looped and wound along the pillars, up across the top and down the other side of David's resting place, as if trying to anchor it to the earth.

It was fall, and for the first time in sixteen years she wasn't getting ready for school. It felt odd; like a ritual she needed to perform, but didn't know how. She had returned to her hometown in hopes of taking a year off to write before settling into some sort of day-job.

Her fingers clutched the pen, the notebook blank on her lap. How she wanted to capture the haunting sadness of this story, the story of the lovers prematurely parted by death. But the words would not come.

She opened her notebook and fingered through a sheaf of papers she had printed off the Internet. Headlines screamed out at her: "Young Groom Mummified," "Million Dollar Crypt Erected," "Love Pact Broken," "Eccentric Family Harbors Occult Secrets…"

There were pictures, too. She held up the wedding photo scanned from a newspaper. The couple in wedding attire stared out at her from the black-and-white photo. The groom, tall and slender, had a face bright with joy, a strong jaw, and dark hair. The bride, barely reaching his shoulder, had a face radiant even in the murky reproduction, with dark eyes and long dark hair. Their hopes and dreams for the future flooded through her. Laurie sighed and shuffled the papers until she found another photograph: one of David.

She stared at his penetrating gaze, his smoky eyes clouded with mystery. She traced her finger along his face, stroking his cheek, following his jaw. A warm tingle ran up her arm, and she smiled.

Laurie had found the picture by chance, at a garage sale when she was a teenager. She remembered how she nearly didn't pay the quarter for the old, worn photograph, but something told her to do it. The girls had long ago stopped playing the game, but some sense of nostalgia had taken root in her when she saw the picture at the old woman's house.

"Crazy as a loon," the old woman had said as she took the quarter with trembling fingers. "The whole damn family. All of them nuts as each other. No wonder that poor girl got out as fast as she could."

Laurie nodded. "But why would they expect Sylvia to stay, if her husband was dead?"

The old woman shook her head and tsked. "It was much different in those days, dearie. Especially if you married into wealth. A widow was set for life so long as she was discreet."

Laurie had been too young to really understand what the woman meant by that, but as she grew older, it was all too clear. Poor Sylvia was expected to wait out the rest of her life in that family, having affairs but never able to give her heart, for her heart had been promised to David. It was a tragedy for all of them: David, taken too soon; Sylvia, left behind and ruined by scandal. Even though she married her new lover and died in his arms, the family never forgave her.

On Halloween, the local kids would dress as the doomed couple, the mummies shuffling down the street, moaning and giggling, searching for their missing lovers. As the years passed, the story faded until it was nearly forgotten.

David's sister, Evellyn, never married, and when she died a crazy old spinster, there was no one left to tend the mausoleum. Vulturous relatives divided up the house and the goods, but the crypt was forgotten.

Laurie touched his picture again, looking into his eyes. "Poor David," she sighed, "I won't let them forget you."

She set her pen to paper and started to write.

* * *

Thump-thump, thump-thump

The sound was pervasive, flooding her senses, enveloping her dreams. She could feel her body swaddled tightly, warm and secure. She could not move her arms and legs, she could not open her eyes. All she could do was listen to the sound of a heart beating.

Thump-thump, thump-thump

She was back in the womb, the soothing pattern lulling her back to sleep. Something was stroking her face, but her eyes were tightly bound. Something gently ran along her body, exploring the swell of her breasts, her arms, her thighs, right down to her toes.

Thump-thump, thump-thump

The touch was warm and strong, and she pressed into it.

When Laurie woke, she was lying on the bench in the graveyard. She jerked up, startled by the scream of a crow perched above her. She rubbed her eyes and gazed in amazement around her. How did she get here?

It was dawn. The sun splintered through the multi-colored trees, nearly blinding her. She stared at the new blanket of red and orange leaves scattered along the ground. Why wasn't she in bed?

She stood up, and an icy wind surged through her. The warmth and comfort of the dream was lost as she trudged her way home, hugging herself, partly to conceal the fact she was wearing her nightgown.

"What do you do there all day?" Janet asked as she refilled their cups with steaming black coffee. Laurie watched Janet put the coffeepot back, still seeing the freckle-faced, red-headed girl she used to play with, although now Janet had dyed her hair a rich auburn and wore it down to her shoulders in a stylish bob. Laurie poured in cream and several spoons of sugar.

"That stuff'll kill you," Janet said as she sipped her bitter brew.

"I like it sweet. Besides, I need the rush. I haven't been getting any sleep lately."

"Join the club; two kids with a third on the way. What's sleep?" Janet laughed and patted her swollen belly.

Laurie looked at the little girl playing with blocks on the floor beside them. "I wonder if I'll ever have kids?"

"First you need to have a boyfriend." Janet grinned. "Have you *ever* had a boyfriend?"

Laurie smirked. "You mean, have I ever had sex?"

They laughed.

"Of course I have," Laurie said, staring into her cup.

"But have you ever had a boyfriend? Been in love?"

"I don't know if I'd recognize love if it came up and bit me on the butt. I have never found anyone I really…I don't know…had a feeling for. Not like I've heard about."

"No one ever?"

"There have been crushes. But passion? Real heart-pounding, 'I'll just die without this person' passion? I don't think I have it in me. Maybe I'm just a cold fish."

"Maybe you just haven't met him yet," Janet said softly, sipping her coffee. "Some people have higher standards than others."

"How did you know Stephen was the one for you?"

"My heart went zing when I saw him, that's how." Janet laughed.

"Hmmm. I wonder if my heart'll ever go zing?"

"But you never answered my original question. What do you do in that creepy old graveyard all day? God, it was bad enough hanging out there as kids."

"Creepy? It's beautiful, and so rich with history. The way the ivy has wrapped itself around the Thompson crypt, hugging its secrets, rustling with mystery…."

"As I hear tell, it's going to take more than ivy to hold that thing shut." Janet winked.

"Huh?"

"You know, the stories."

"I haven't heard. I've been away."

"Just a lot of weird stuff going on the past few years. People seeing things…" Janet said softly, not wanting the baby to hear.

"Like?"

"Remember the game?"

"Of course."

"Well, the legend lives on. People claim to see ghosts wandering around at night."

"That's not so unusual."

"How many North American graveyards have mummy spottings?"

Laurie laughed uneasily. "Everyone in town knows there's a mummy there. So why wouldn't overactive imaginations take flight?"

"I suppose…but graveyards aren't the places they used to be. They're pretty dangerous now. People get hurt, killed even."

"So they say." Laurie shrugged.

"I'm just telling you. Be careful when you go there. And stay in the light. You just never know who's hanging out. There's a lot of crazies in this world."

"That's for sure."

Laurie held her pen, trying to force the words, but the words wouldn't come. She didn't know where to begin the tale. She didn't know how to describe the love and loss. Was it, she wondered, because she had never loved and lost?

She pulled out the picture of David and Sylvia. She remembered the grief that had overwhelmed her when she played the game as a child, how she had always insisted on playing Sylvia, and how she always cried at David's death. She had played the part quite well. Perhaps she should have been an actress. Even now, remembering pretend-David lying in the grass, his body twisted and broken from the car wreck, brought tears to her eyes.

The day was dull and grey, and a light snow began to fall. There was a teenage couple over the far hill, lying between the tombstones, hands and lips roaming each other, lost in passion. Would there ever be a day when she was so consumed by passion she didn't know what was around her?

Maybe that was how the car had crashed.

Maybe Sylvia had leaned over to give David a kiss, a little hug, a squeeze on his thigh, and the car had jerked out of control and into the tree. Maybe the passion that had brought them together had torn them apart in the end. Perhaps that was why Sylvia couldn't stay with his family. Her guilt had gnawed at her, eating her alive.

Her pen started to scrawl frantically across the pages.

The first thing she smelled was rotting fruit, or maybe it was musk. Whatever it was, it snapped her awake. But she couldn't be awake; she was floating. No, she wasn't floating, she was being carried. She must be dreaming.

Laurie opened her eyes. Her face was pressed into someone's chest, she was being carried, and she could hear the steady beating of a heart.

Thump-thump, thump-thump

The smell was overpowering now. Decay and mold, dirt and dank. And the steady beating of that heart.

Laurie looked up to see who was carrying her. In the dark moonlight, she could see no face; it was blank and smooth where the features ought to be. The body was the same. There were no joints, no discernable limbs. It lacked definition. She struggled, and the smooth blank face looked down at her. Now she could see clear blue eyes. She began to scream.

But she did not wake up.

He held her tighter as she tried to pry his hands away. His fingers were swathed in yellowed strips of material. His whole body was wrapped head to foot.

Laurie screamed again, but the nightmare would not end.

The mummy moaned, his mouth moving beneath the bandages. Laurie felt the rumble of sound vibrate through his body as he shambled forward.

Her legs kicked uselessly as she saw the crypt glowing before her like a small mountain in the moonlight. The mummy squeezed her tightly, cradling her head against his shoulder as he slipped a hand across her face, blocking her mouth and nose. The fetid stink of the rotting cloth gagged her. Even with two hands, she could not budge his grip. She choked on her screams until, at last, she slipped into unconsciousness.

When she woke, she opened her eyes, grateful that the dream had been just that: a dream. She was shivering, it was so cold, and her bed felt so hard. She sat up quickly as she realized she was not in her room. It was much too dark, and the air was thick, smoky, stale. Putting her hand to her mouth, she gasped as she stared around the small room. Candles flickered all around her, casting long, drawn-out shadows on the grey stone walls. The ceiling and corners were veiled in darkness. Arranged around her on little shelves there were statues and ornaments, jewelry and books, jars and vases filled with liquid and floating chunks of meat. And photographs.

Many photographs, some framed, some just paper...

Of her.

Laurie stifled a shriek as she saw the mummy move from the shadows. He shuffled closer, his face expressionless from the many layers of bandages wrapped around his head. But she could see his vibrant blue eyes sparkling in the candlelight.

"Who are you?" she stammered.

The mummy stood still, watching her. His eyes were wide, the pupils large. The mystery and sadness that resided there stirred her. She looked around and saw nothing but darkness beyond the candles.

"Let me go."

The mummy stood watching. Just watching.

A growing fear that she would never feel the warmth of sunlight again rushed through her. She jumped off the stone slab where she had been laid to rest, her bare feet hitting the hard, cold floor. Her arms outstretched, she tried to find the doorway in the near-darkness. Her fingers frantically scratched at the smooth granite walls, searching for a handle or release.

The mummy watched as she pounded and screamed.

Her nails ripped and her fingers bled as she clawed at the stone, painting the walls with her blood. Her mind swam with the images of hundreds of horror movies. Surely there was a secret passage, some sort of spring release that could be triggered. They had to have gotten into this tomb somehow.

The mummy groaned and approached her, his hand outstretched.

"Stay the hell away from me!" she cried out, slapping at it. She stumbled and fell into a pile of framed photographs. The glass shattered, shards cutting into her leg. Blood poured from the wounds. The gashes were deep; she could see the flesh parting, exposing the bone below.

She moaned and reached for the nearest picture. It was not her, at all. It was Sylvia.

But how alike they looked, she suddenly realized: the long dark hair, the burning brown eyes, the crooked smile. She tore the paper from the frame and pressed it against her leg to try to stop the bleeding.

"I'm not her!" Laurie screamed. "Sylvia is dead. She died years before I was even born!"

The mummy stood over her, staring at her, piercing her with his gaze.

In that moment, she saw the man, the man he had once been in life. Her heart twinged. She took a deep breath as fear dropped away in a moment of clarity.

"David, I'm sorry she left you. *She* was the one you loved. Not me. *She* was the one who didn't keep the pact."

David's eyes welled up, and Laurie saw tears dripping down the bandages. Her heart ached as she watched him cry.

He slumped to the ground, pressing his face into his hands. Laurie struggled to her feet and limped over to him. She stood beside him, staring at this strange creature. Nervously, she reached out and touched him, patting him on the arm. The bandages were rough and yellowed, sticky with dirt and rot.

David let out an unearthly howl that echoed in the tiny chamber. The candles sputtered and flickered.

"It was so long ago, David. It's over. Nothing can be done." Laurie stroked his back. "You have to let me go."

David's eyes widened, and he roared. With amazing speed, he leaped to his feet. His strong hands reached out and grabbed her by the shoulders. Laurie sobbed as he lifted her high into the air and brought her face close to his. She looked at the mummy's face. She knew that jaw by heart, the cheekbones, the forehead.

Her cries echoed through the room as he threw her down on the slab so hard she heard a loud snap. As she sucked in great gulps of air, he stood above her, staring down. Her leg felt like it was on fire from the cuts, the blood still surging into puddles on the ground. Her bones were blazing; whatever had snapped was throbbing along her back.

She was too weak to protest as David touched her face with his rough cloth-covered hands. She squeezed her eyes shut as his fingers traced her body through the nightgown; those strong, rough fingers stroking her neck, cupping her breasts, lingering along her thighs, trailing down to her feet.

He returned to her chest and pressed his hand against her heart. She could hear the steady beating in her ears as it pumped what blood remained in her through her body. David took her hand and forced it against his chest. With his other hand, he covered her mouth and nose. She smelled the horrible rot, but was too weak to fight. Slowly, she drifted away.

Laurie dreamed deeply. She dreamed of chanting and moaning, of strange words muttered quickly and quietly, the scent of incense and musk, of wine and fruit. She dreamed of cold. She was so cold that she was frozen, so stiff she would never move again. She dreamed of something long and sharp inching up her nasal cavity, worming its way into her brain. She felt it hook into the tender tissue, felt a pinch, a tug, a thousand bursting lights exploding behind her eyes....

Laurie opened her eyes. Every bone in her body ached. She felt hollow and violated. She felt like everything she had ever been was sucked away, and she was just an empty shell.

She was swathed in bandages, from head to toe. As she opened her mouth to scream, she realized it was bound shut. Her arms, her hips, her breasts; all tightly wrapped. She could see, but she didn't breathe. There was nothing more to be afraid of, she realized; she was dead.

Laurie forced herself to sit up. It was painful agony that made her head spin. There were new vases and jars holding hunks of meat in them. The photographs had been rearranged, a large reproduction of the wedding photo in the center.

David shuffled from the corner, his bandages streaked with smears of blood. Strips of linen, hanging ragged from his fingers, needed to be rewound.

His eyes glowed as he watched Laurie look around.

She stared up at him, her brown eyes burning pits of darkness in the white of the bandages. He reached out, and she shrank back. David gently placed his hand on her chest.

She felt her heart pulse against his fingers.

Thump-thump, thump-thump

She sighed, tears brimming in her eyes. Her body shuddered. She slid her hand up along his body, rubbing his belly, his chest, trying to get used to the sensation of linen against linen, until she found his heart. She moaned as she felt it beating, pulsing up her fingertips and through her body, heat burning her from the inside out.

Thump-thump, thump-thump

Their hearts beat together, and Laurie knew that she was home.

The Dead Boy at Your Window
Bruce Holland Rogers

IN A DISTANT COUNTRY WHERE the towns had improbable names, a woman looked upon the unmoving form of her newborn baby and refused to see what the midwife saw. This was her son. She had brought him forth in agony, and now he must suck. She pressed his lips to her breast.

"But he is dead!" said the midwife.

"No," his mother lied. "I felt him suck just now." Her lie was as milk to the baby, who really was dead but who now opened his dead eyes and began to kick his dead legs. "There, do you see?" And she made the midwife call the father in to know his son.

The dead boy never did suck at his mother's breast. He sipped no water, never took food of any kind, so of course he never grew. But his father, who was handy with all things mechanical, built a rack for stretching him so that, year by year, he could be as tall as the other children.

When he had seen six winters, his parents sent him to school. Though he was as tall as the other students, the dead boy was strange to look upon. His bald head was almost the right size, but the rest of him was thin as a piece of leather and dry as a stick. He tried to make up for his ugliness with diligence, and every night he was up late practicing his letters and numbers.

His voice was like the rasping of dry leaves. Because it was so hard to hear him, the teacher made all the other students hold their breaths when he gave an answer. She called on him often, and he was always right.

Naturally, the other children despised him. The bullies sometimes waited for him after school, but beating him, even with sticks, did him no harm. He wouldn't even cry out.

One windy day, the bullies stole a ball of twine from their teacher's desk, and after school, they held the dead boy on the ground with his arms out so that he took the shape of a cross. They ran a stick in through his left shirtsleeve and out through the right. They stretched his shirttails down to his ankles, tied everything in place, fastened the ball of twine to a buttonhole, and launched him. To their delight, the dead boy made an excellent kite. It only added to their pleasure to see that, owing to the weight of his head, he flew upside down.

When they were bored with watching the dead boy fly, they let go of the string. The dead boy did not drift back to earth, as any ordinary kite would do. He glided. He could steer a little, though he was mostly at the mercy of the winds. And he could not come down. Indeed, the wind blew him higher and higher.

The sun set, and still the dead boy rode the wind. The moon rose, and by its glow he saw the fields and forests drifting by. He saw mountain ranges pass beneath him, and oceans and continents. At last the winds gentled, then ceased, and he glided down to the ground in a strange country. The ground was bare. The moon and stars had vanished from the sky. The air seemed grey and shrouded. The dead boy leaned to one side and shook himself until the stick fell from his shirt. He wound up the twine that had trailed behind him and waited for the sun to rise. Hour after long hour, there was only the same greyness. So he began to wander.

He encountered a man who looked much like himself, a bald head atop leathery limbs. "Where am I?" the dead boy asked.

The man looked at the greyness all around. "Where?" the man said. His voice, like the dead boy's, sounded like the whisper of dead leaves stirring.

A woman emerged from the greyness. Her head was bald, too, and her body dried out. "This!" she rasped, touching the dead boy's shirt. "I remember this!" She tugged on the dead boy's sleeve. "I had a thing like this!"

"Clothes?" said the dead boy.

"Clothes!" the woman cried. "That's what it is called!"

More shriveled people came out of the greyness. They crowded close to see the strange dead boy who wore clothes. Now the dead boy knew where he was. "This is the land of the dead."

"Why do you have clothes?" asked the dead woman. "We came here with nothing! Why do you have clothes?"

"I have always been dead," said the dead boy, "but I spent six years among the living."

"Six years!" said one of the dead. "And you have only just now come to us?"

"Did you know my wife?" asked a dead man. "Is she still among the living?"

"Give me news of my son!"

"What about my sister?"

The dead people crowded closer.

The dead boy said, "What is your sister's name?" But the dead could not remember the names of their loved ones. They did not even remember their own names. Likewise, the names of the places where they had lived, the numbers given to their years, the manners or fashions of their times, all of these they had forgotten.

"Well," said the dead boy, "in the town where I was born, there was a widow. Maybe she was your wife. I knew a boy whose mother had died and an old woman who might have been your sister."

"Are you going back?"

"Of course not," said another dead person. "No one ever goes back."

"I think I might," the dead boy said. He explained about his flying. "When next the wind blows…"

"The wind never blows here," said a man so newly dead that he remembered wind.

"Then you could run with my string."

"Would that work?"

"Take a message to my husband!" said a dead woman.

"Tell my wife that I miss her!" said a dead man.

"Let my sister know I haven't forgotten her!"

"Say to my lover that I love him still!"

They gave him their messages, not knowing whether or not their loved ones were themselves long dead. Indeed, dead lovers might well be standing next to one another in the land of the dead, giving messages for each other to the dead boy. Still, he memorized them all. Then the dead put the stick back inside his shirtsleeves, tied everything in place, and unwound his string. Running as fast as their leathery legs could manage, they pulled the dead boy back into the sky, let go of the string, and watched with their dead eyes as he glided away.

He glided a long time over the grey stillness of death until at last a puff of wind blew him higher, until a breath of wind took him higher still, until a gust of wind carried him up above the greyness to where he could see the moon and the stars. Below he saw moonlight reflected in the ocean. In the distance rose mountain peaks. The dead boy came to earth in a little village. He knew no one here, but he went to the first house he came to and rapped on the bedroom shutters. To the woman who answered, he said, "A message from the land of the dead," and gave her one of the messages. The woman wept and gave him a message in return.

House by house, he delivered the messages. House by house, he collected messages for the dead. In the morning, he found some boys to fly him, to give him back to the wind's mercy so he could carry these new messages back to the land of the dead.

So it has been ever since. On any night, head full of messages, he may rap upon any window to remind someone—to remind you, perhaps—of love that outlives memory, of love that needs no names.

Five Places You Must Visit After You Die
Tom Barlow

AFTER MY HUSBAND, C.B., WAS left with no choice but to beat his dad to death with a shovel, we finally agreed the time had come to get our kids away from Storm Lake. C.B. pulled out his atlas of cities rumored to harbor enclaves of Cleans.

"The kids are going to freak out if we tell them we're planning to leave," he said.

"Then we don't tell them," I said. "We tell them we're going on a vacation. We'll visit famous historical sites near the places on your list."

As he laughed, his front teeth wobbled. "Who in their right mind takes a vacation in the middle of a plague?"

"Watch your attitude. The kids pick up on our moods, so keep it light."

"Honey, if I kept it as light as you, I'd float away."

Our daughter, Brianna, whined when I told her we were leaving Storm Lake, but our son, Little Charley, couldn't wait to start.

"She's got a boyfriend," he explained as he crawled into my lap to study the map spread out on the kitchen table. "Where are we going?" His chubby fingers wandered across the map.

I'd marked the nearest famous sites we could use to disguise the true intention of our trip. "First stop, Mark Twain's hometown." Hannibal, Missouri topped C.B.'s list, based on a rumor passed along by his cousin Tim. "Doesn't that sound like fun?"

I heard Brianna snort from the couch.

By bedtime, we had the sleeper cab of C.B.'s Peterbilt semi packed, and we were ready to roll at first light.

* * *

1. Mark Twain's Home

We got a late start the next morning, though. As we were finishing breakfast, Brianna announced she'd invited her best friend, Zara, to join us on vacation. Before we could "discuss" it, Zara showed up at the door with her suitcase in hand.

"This is, like, so nice of you!" she said, hugging me and handing me a permission slip from her older sister.

C.B. and I almost swallowed our tongues to keep from shouting, but eventually decided that Zara's presence might soften the bitterness that had begun to color our daughter's personality. Besides, Zara had been vaccinated at the same time our kids were.

Hannibal was not all that far from our home in Iowa, but the decaying road system required numerous detours. We didn't arrive until early evening.

Hannibal proved a disappointment in both respects. C.B. and I didn't see any sign of human activity, much less a working enclave. And the Mississippi must have flooded that spring, because the downtown was still covered in shit-brown mud and smelled like a sewer.

We pretended to have sufficient enthusiasm for Twain to slog through the muck to the museum. But when Zara said, "I'm sorry, Mr. and Mrs. Bascomb, but I don't think I can walk through that without throwing up," we were relieved for the excuse to gracefully give up on the idea.

2. Central Park

It took us the best part of three days to pick our way from Missouri to New York City. On the bright side, there were thousands of abandoned trucks along the road, so we had no problem finding diesel fuel.

The NYC rumor had sounded crazier than most—an enclave set up in the subway tunnels? But we figured if there was anything left of the country, it would probably involve the Big Apple. We told the kids we wanted to show them Central Park.

We parked on the Jersey side, rather than risk the fragile bridges into the city. We had a great view of Manhattan's rubble. Brianna and Zara didn't believe me when I explained to them that, since the plague was supposed to have originated in a bio-lab there, the rest of the world had taken turns bombing the "zero vector." Not that it did any good.

We found an old ferryman to row us across the Hudson in return for four cans of beans and a deer that had run in front of the truck as we entered the outskirts of town. He set us on shore at Pier 83 by the old Javits Convention Center. From there we cut east across the island. When we reached Broadway, we found a steady stream of people lurching north toward the park.

"Why Central Park?" Charley asked.

I explained that his granddad had brought me to New York for the first time when I was about fifteen, twenty-five years before, back when the world still functioned. We'd taken a buggy ride through the park, and I still remembered it as the most magical moment of my life; lush greenery, towering buildings in the background, and a greater variety of people at a glance than I had seen in my entire Iowa childhood.

We took a break at 49th Street by the Rockefeller Center in the heart of the barbecue district. C.B. swapped a quart of clover honey for some country ham. It didn't taste like the pig back home. C.B. speculated it might be Puerto Rican.

I saw Zara wince as she bit into a bit of bone. She turned her head from me, but not far enough, and I could see her pull a loose tooth from her lower jaw and flick it into a pile of trash.

As we rested, C.B. wandered the square, offering cigarettes in return for answers to his questions about the rumors.

"Nobody knows nothing about an enclave," he reported when he returned. "They say the subways are still full of poison gas from back when the army first tried to contain the plague. But a couple of them claim that there is still a shadow government in D.C."

Disappointed, we led the family over to Central Park as he and I talked about what we would do next.

"This is it?" Brianna said, stopping and putting her hands on her hips. "This is, like, your great Central Park?"

The park had been stripped bare, nothing remaining but stumps. Old, plastic, crowd-control fencing haphazardly divided the ground into compounds, each one holding its own herd of goats and guarded by men with staffs, swords, or shotguns in their laps.

"I can just feel the pride flowing through me," Little Charley said. I'd told them that this trip would prove to them that America was too great a place to stay down for long, and he was throwing it back in my face.

We found another ferry at the 79th Street basin and made it back to our truck just before dark.

* * *

3. Lincoln's Monument

As we crossed the Potomac into Washington, we could see blackened rubble where the Pentagon had stood. C.B. parked the truck in the middle of 17th Avenue, next to the tip of the Washington Monument.

Zara had been acting increasingly eccentric since New York. During a potty stop in Delaware, she'd wandered off toward a gang of ex-soldiers standing around a bonfire on the overpass. C.B. had to wrestle her back.

"I'm worried about her," Brianna had said later, after Zara fell asleep.

"You think the bug has her?" I said, trying to keep my voice calm.

"I never told you, but she caught her dad and mom eating her older brother a couple of weeks ago."

"And now you think she has it?" I was suddenly furious. "How could you have put you and your brother at such risk? You know the vaccine doesn't always work. Different people, different bloodlines. You and your brother are blessed."

She stuck out her lower lip. "I figured, since you and Dad have stayed okay for so long since you died, she would be, too."

"You damned fool." I walked away to keep from slapping her.

After the kids fell asleep, C.B. and I made our plans.

As soon as we reached the mall, I dragged Brianna and Charley toward the Lincoln Memorial while C.B. asked Zara to help him locate his grandfather's name on the WWII memorial. Once out of our sight, he was to zip-tie her to a flagpole.

The children were unaware Zara was gone until she started to scream from the other side of the monument. Her voice was quickly drowned by a crowd of late-stage Japanese tourists, who joined in her screams like a pack of howling wolves.

C.B. came running back from behind the memorial, pursued by two women. Both seemed to have lost toes, though, and couldn't move fast. They gave up quickly, but the fact that C.B. was now far gone enough to draw their appetite tore at my heart. Terminal victims began to emit an odor that other end-stage zombies found irresistible.

I'd anticipated difficulty getting the kids to abandon Zara, but all they wanted to do was run back to the safety of the truck. Once inside, I handed them each a shotgun and we held them at ready until we cleared Washington. None of us said a word until we were beyond the outerbelt.

"You must feel terrible," I finally said to Brianna, "losing a friend like that."

She rested her head on my shoulder. "She's not the first I lost. I've gotten pretty tough."

I stroked her hair, drinking in the clean, healthy smell. "I'm sorry you need such a thick skin. I'm afraid loss is going to be a big part of your lives. You have to keep looking ahead, not behind."

"All I see ahead is more of the same."

"Then we need to find a place where the view is better."

We spent the night at a deserted pull-off near Albany. C.B. wandered off to look through the abandoned trucks for supplies, while Little Charley and Brianna helped me open cans for dinner.

"I want to go home," Brianna said. "If I'm going to die, I want to do it at home, not with a pack of strangers, like Zara." She crossed her arms on the picnic table and rested her forehead on them.

"I don't want to go," Charley said as he popped one Vienna sausage after another in his mouth. It looked like he was eating a can of fingers.

"No more Little Miss Negativity," I said. "Let me tell you something."

"Here comes the Zombie Plague speech," Little Charley said.

"Damn straight," I said. "When the bubonic plague hit Europe in the 1300s, people thought it was the end of the world. One in three people died. Anyway, that's the way evolution works; something comes along and wipes out the weak, but the ones that live through a disaster are stronger. Some of you are going to survive. There is still a reason to hope."

Unfortunately, it was at that moment that C.B. returned holding an almost empty bottle of Cuervo Gold.

After I got him settled into bed, I gave the kids their weekly inspection. To my relief, the bruise on Little Charley's shoulder was simply a bruise and healing fast. I didn't find any other signs of disease.

I gave Brianna an extra careful look-see, since she'd spent so much time with Zara. Not only did she continue to show no symptoms, but she was showing definite signs of maturing into a young lady.

After the kids fell sleep, I stepped outside and gave myself the same exam by the fading light of our campfire. The open sores on my knee had definitely grown. The entire left side of my face was purple.

I found the rum bottle I'd taken off C.B. and took a long pull. My father had shown the same symptoms shortly before his mind went to pot.

* * *

4. Niagara Falls

We reached the enclave at Syracuse too late.

The warning signs were still up on the fence of their compound near the university. A double-row of FEMA trailers sat neatly in the parking lot of the stadium, surrounded by miles of razor wire. But the people were gone. C.B. laid on the Peterbilt's horn, but no one, except one very fat German shepherd, showed his face.

Nearby Niagara Falls was the biggest disappointment of the trip, attraction-wise. We hadn't known that it had been bombed, turning the cliffs into rock jumbles through which the water flowed like ants crawling through a picnic.

The stop wasn't a total loss, though. We ran into another functioning family, from Alabama, traveling in a big motor home.

We eyeballed one another from opposite ends of the observation area for a long time until the husband, an extremely tall black man, sidled up to us. He kept one hand on the pistol strapped to his waist.

"You folks, uh...?"

"Still in our right minds?" I said.

He smiled sheepishly. "Hard question to ask, isn't it?"

"Hard to answer, too."

After we confirmed that we were all still sane, he invited us over to his rig for coffee.

He described his family's trip up the Natchez Trace, through the Ohio Valley. They were headed to Montreal, hoping to find his brother, a hardcore survivalist, still alive.

"You ever run across any towns that looked like they still functioned?" I eventually asked.

He rubbed his jaw. "Functioned? You mean like, law and order, schools, medicine? No, we haven't seen anything but destruction. Makes me sick. You?"

We described our experiences.

"I did hear one rumor," he finally said. "Just a passing conversation, really, a while back, with some folks we bought food from in Ohio. We were talking about great fishing spots we used to visit, and somebody mentioned Lake Michigan. Then somebody else made a comment about Mackinac Island, that a bunch of Coast Guard families had hijacked a load of vaccine and quarantined themselves there, shooting anybody that came around that wasn't healthy."

He poured another round of coffee. "Supposedly, they have a school going and a radio station running off the solar panels on the roof of the Grand Hotel. That's the first open school I'd heard of since the plague hit. I figured, since the vaccine was discovered nearby at Michigan State, maybe there was something to the rumor."

"So why aren't you headed that way?"

He pulled back the collar of his shirt, revealing a seeping sore.

C.B. and I talked that evening after the kids went to bed.

"I thought we were going to Mt. Rushmore next, look for that militia camp supposed to be outside Sturgis," he said, sipping on the cold coffee he'd been nursing all day.

I stretched out on the picnic table bench. The air felt cooler there near the falls, laden with moisture. "There weren't that many people in the Dakotas even before the plague," I said. "I don't know what we were thinking. What's the chances we'd find a functioning town out there? I say we give Mackinac a try."

He took off his ball cap, and I was shocked to see how much of his skull was exposed through his scalp. "I'm thinking we'd be better off heading home. I'm with Brianna; I'd just as soon die at home."

"Personally, I can compost as easy here as anywhere else. But the kids, they have a chance. They're healthier than anybody we've seen in fifteen states. We can't give up now."

He touched the crown of his head. "Truth is, I don't think I'm going to last. I've been getting these cravings..."

I closed my eyes and tried to lose my thoughts in the sound of the ruined falls. It didn't work.

Finally, I got up, went back to the truck. When I returned, I took a big swig before handing C.B. the pint bottle of Old Granddad my uncle Jim had given me before we left home.

He smiled as his fist squeezed the bottle. "You're the best wife I could have ever hoped for, you know that?" He stood up, kissed me hard, then chugged the entire pint without stopping to breath.

When he passed out, I picked up the shotgun and blew his brains out.

I tossed him over the fence of the observation deck, praying there wasn't a zombie stupid enough to risk the river below for a meal. I watched my husband until he disappeared in the gathering darkness, then spent another couple of hours watching the darkness. I put his wedding band on my thumb, glad to find it so tight I'd never be able to get it off.

I drove through the night. By dawn, we were circling Cleveland. As soon as Charley woke, he asked, "Where's Dad?"

I swallowed the lump in my throat. "Your Dad got real sick," I said. "He had to stay behind."

There was silence in the cab, then some sniffling. The plague had destroyed curiosity. I tried to think of something light to say, to ease their minds, but my mind had gone cold as a glacier. That glibness I'd been so proud of was now just a sour taste in my mouth.

5. MACKINAC ISLAND

Brianna and Charley didn't say anything for hours as we crossed Ohio and turned north into Michigan. When Brianna turned on the DVD, I remembered that our visitors in Niagara had mentioned a radio. I had her scan the AM band, finding nothing, but at 107 FM we found a weak signal.

The transmission was obviously on an automatic repeat. "This is Alpha Nation North. If you are picking up this transmission, be warned that the territory north of Gaylord, Michigan, including the Upper Peninsula east of Copper City, is quarantined. Anyone with Holt's disease attempting to enter this area will be shot on sight. This is the only warning you will receive."

As ominous as the words were, I felt a glimmer of the hope I'd not dared acknowledge in a long, long time.

"What do they mean by Holt's disease?" Brianna said.

"Zombie Plague," Charley said, who loved to show off his smarts. "The lead scientist on the project was named Holt. He was trying to find a drug that would put wounded soldiers into a stable coma until they could receive treatment. That's why people look like they're dead in the first phase of the disease. He also created the vaccine. Which worked for about one in twenty of us."

"Lucky us," Brianna said, her voice heavy with irony.

We ran into a checkpoint north of Gaylord. The approach to the barricade was lined on both sides of the road, for over a mile, with abandoned vehicles.

I didn't even have the chance to offer the bribe I'd prepared: a basket full of canned food, alcohol, and an almost-full bottle of my mom's Oxycontin. The figures in the hazmat suits took one look at me and indicated, by waving their rifle barrels, that I was to turn around and leave. When I popped my door open, three guns were shoved in my face.

I swung the Peterbilt around and drove east, looking for another way north. Before we hit the next checkpoint, on North Rt. 23, I put on a stocking cap and makeup.

It did no good. As soon as they spotted our truck approaching, the guards pulled a deuce-and-a-half across the road between two grenade launchers and waved for me to retreat.

We ended up parking in Alpena, on the shore of Lake Huron, that night. Little Charley, having slept late, was now wide wake, so we sat watching stars appear in the gathering darkness, like sugar thrown into a fire. I found myself wanting a cigarette, although I'd quit twenty years before. I also had a hankering for something to eat, but I couldn't quite figure out what.

"Why are we really here?" Charley asked.

Without C.B., I didn't have the heart to continue the charade.

"You and your sister don't belong in Storm Lake. In six months, there won't be anybody else left alive. You probably figured that out already, right?"

"Even you?" he said, staring at the ground.

"Even me, Charley."

"Then I'm going to die, too."

"You know better, kid. You and your sister are among the few that benefited from the vaccine. There are a few survivors of every disaster."

"Then where are all the dinosaurs?"

Sometimes I hated that he was so smart.

I woke early the next morning and walked the docks, finally coming back to an eighteen-foot fishing boat with an Evinrude outboard that had avoided extensive damage.

The battery was dead, but the engine was equipped with a backup rope-pull starter. I filled the tank from gas cans and changed the plugs. It fired right up.

The kids peppered me with questions about what we were doing as I loaded the boat.

"Trust us," Brianna said. "We're not kids any more."

I explained about Mackinac Island.

"And you think there are others like us there? Other kids? Adults?" Brianna said.

I nodded. "I don't know. But I hope. That checkpoint is the first sign of a civilization we've seen in a thousand miles or more."

Little Charley smiled for the first time in weeks.

"Sounds wonderful," Brianna said. "I can't take any more dead people."

I gathered up all the full gas cans I could find, a box of the canned food from the truck, our sleeping bags, C.B.'s portable GPS unit, his lighter, and the lucky bear charm he wore hunting. We shoved off at dusk.

We put a mile buffer between us and the coastline, out of sight of shore guards, before turning north. Charlie and Brianna fell asleep after a couple of hours. The slap of water against the bow brought back memories of fishing on Storm Lake with C.B. I'd lost my virginity on the deck of his father's bass boat while watching the Fourth of July fireworks from a quiet inlet.

Just before dawn, I turned back toward land and pulled us into the mouth of a shallow, sandy river south of Rogers City. The beach was swarming with black flies, but we found a vacant fishing cabin nearby.

The cabin smelled of fish and dirty socks, but the screens kept out the bugs. The kids found some board games and played them while I slept.

I woke up to the smell, the incredibly mouth-watering smell, of bacon frying.

"Canned bacon," Brianna said when she saw my eyes open. "Who'd of thought?"

We made poor progress that night, as the wind shifted into our face. Every time I checked the GPS, we'd been blown off course and had to recover. Around five a.m., as we worked our way around Nine Mile Point, Little Charley said he could hear another engine. I killed ours immediately and knelt in the bottom of the boat.

I could hear it too—low, throaty—an inboard motor between us and the shore. Luckily, fog and cloud cover diminished the moonlight.

A spotlight arced toward us from a spot high enough above the waterline to tell me the boat was the size of a Coast Guard cutter. To our relief, the light stopped short of our boat. In five minutes, it was barely visible, and the sound of the engine gone with the wind.

We floated silently for half an hour anyway, sharing a can of cold beets and some pudding, before we resumed our journey. By dawn, we had reached the southern tip of Bois Blanc Island, only a few hours south of Mackinac Island.

We landed at a sailing club that had burned to the ground. We found a tent in one of the half-sunken boats and pitched camp behind the old sail house.

After we woke, I made the kids promise not to peek while I crept down to the small beach, stripped naked, and walked out into the icy waters of the lake, hoping the cold would quench my new appetite. Through the crystal-clear water I could see my foot, now more green than pink. A large flap of skin floated free of it in the current, like the tailfin of a fish. The bruising on my side now extended unbroken from my hairline to my knee. I ached—God, I ached.

We waited until dark and set off again. I kept my hand on the engine housing. The heat felt good as the temperature dropped.

An hour later, we got our first glimpse of Mackinac. A fire burned on the hill at the center of the island. As we entered the Straits of Mackinac, more lights came into view, many obviously electric.

Little Charley and Brianna leaned forward, drinking in the first signs of normalcy they'd seen in months. I had just pulled life jackets from the bait locker when a spotlight hit us like a firecracker. A cutter had approached from downwind with lights off, and, with our eyes fixed on the island, had been able to creep so close I almost jumped out of the boat in surprise when the voice came over their loudspeaker.

"Ahoy the boat," it said. "Cut your engine."

I killed the motor and stood unsteadily in the boat, rocking in the wake of the cutter.

"You're trespassing." The speaker sounded like he'd said the same thing a million times.

I cupped my hands and shouted, "My children. They're clean. They had vaccine. They want to join you."

"They?" Brianna said, pulling on my sleeve. "You mean, we."

There was a pause as the cutter floated closer, until we were only thirty feet apart. The light was still full on us, blinding me.

"All of you strip," the voice said, "and turn around."

"What?" Brianna said.

I pulled Little Charley to his feet and began pulling off his clothes. "Strip," I told Brianna. "They want to see that you're clean."

She sat on the bow and reluctantly unbuttoned her jacket.

As soon as Charley was naked, holding his hands over his pecker and blushing bright red, I turned him toward the light. I pried his arms up so they could see the undersides, then turned him around like I was showing off a prize pig. His skin was fish-belly white and as unmarred as a baby's.

"And the girl, and you," the voice said.

Brianna stepped out of her pants. Chewing her bottom lip, refusing to make eye contact with me, she unhooked her bra and shrugged it off, and wriggled out of her panties. She faced the spotlight as though it was an execution squad.

With her back to me, I saw, in the small of her back, a dark bruise the size of a grapefruit that had never been there before. Jagged on the edges, as though reaching out for more skin.

The temperature dropped suddenly. I put my arm around her shoulder. "You have to take my children," I yelled to the light. "They're here to help you rebuild the world."

"Why do you keep saying they?" Brianna said.

"Turn her around. And you strip, too," the voice said to me.

"No need for me to strip," I said. "I've had it. I'm not going to try to fool you. It was these two got the vaccine."

"Doesn't matter. We don't need more people. And we won't separate kids and their parents under any circumstances."

"But they have no home," I said. "Nobody has a home anymore."

"Too bad," the voice said. "But we have no choice. The only way the plague is going to die is if the carriers die. Only survivors are welcome here."

Brianna grabbed my arm. "You're a survivor, Mom. Don't leave us here."

Little Charley stood trembling, seemingly unable to move. I picked up a life jacket and strapped it on him.

"Your children aren't welcome here," the voice said when he saw what I was doing. "Take your family home, lady. Love them."

Something snapped in my head.

"Love my family?" I screamed. "Why else do you think I'm here?" Flushed with adrenaline, I picked up Little Charley. Terror gave me strength I'd never felt before, and I heaved my son as easily as a sack of flour. Before he hit the cold water, I could see the anguish on his face.

I could hear people scrambling on the deck of the cutter. "He's your son, for Christ's sake," the voice said. "Pull him back in before he freezes." I could see the sailors dropping a skiff into the water.

Instead of following the voice's orders, I tugged the rope of the

Evinrude. It barked into life. I immediately twisted the throttle and we slowly pulled away.

"What are we doing, Mom?" Brianna said, tugging at the life jacket I was standing on. "What about me?"

"I'm doing what I have to do."

The skiff began moving in our direction. As soon as we were sufficiently clear of Charley, bobbing in the water, I let go of the throttle long enough to take C.B.'s knife and cut the anchor rope free from the boat.

Two sailors hauled Charley out of the water as I quickly wrapped the loose end of the anchor rope around my waist, then, hugging Brianna, took several turns around the both of us. My hand found the bruise in her back. The skin over it was loose.

The coast guard skiff started moving again, towards us.

"This is the only way I know of to show you how much I love the both of you," I whispered to Brianna. I felt her trembling in my arms.

As soon as the skiff came close enough that I could see my son's face, his teeth chattering, I blew a kiss to him and tossed the anchor into the water.

Brianna and I watched the rope uncoil until it pulled us over the side.

Mobly's Big Idear
Stephen C. Merritt and Alan M. Clark
with thanks to Cynthia Grissette Merrit

THE TWO COUSINS, MOBLY AND Harned, were destitute. For a month, battle between Union and Confederate forces had surged back and forth over the stony scrap of Tennessee hilltop that was the cousins' farm, destroying everything they owned.

"This," Mobly told Harned, "is the most excitin' thin' as ever happened to me an' you."

With nowhere else to go, they headed for the grand old city of Nashville, Tennessee, where, Mobly assured Harned, opportunities were boundless for a couple of enterprising young men like themselves.

The battle of Nashville was still raging. On the city's outskirts they saw mutilated bodies cooling in the winter wind.

Under cover of night, the cousins made it through the battle lines and into the city proper.

Although it had been long since Nashville was considered a frontier town, its residents were still used to the comings and goings of all manner of crude and rough men. Heads turned, however, when Mobly and Harned made their appearance.

They were rough-hewn, stooped of frame, obviously of poor stock. Being of the school that feared washing with water, they ran with greasy hair, the ratty shoulder-length brown and stringy variety. Their clothes exhaled little dust clouds and a medley of disagreeable odors. Their skin was mottled with sores. They kept ringworm, lice of two types, and passed impetigo back and forth like a jug of whiskey. Blackheads bred in their ears, ringed their bright eyes, and lay siege to their beaked noses. They considered themselves as above average men for their time and circumstances, and just a bit handsome to boot.

After three months in the city, however, they had yet to find their new lot in life. So far, they had tried and failed as ferrymen, dockworkers and night watchmen. They were presently in the grave digging trade.

Just two days ago, while talking with a colleague, the cousins learned that medical schools were "paying hunnerds fer corpses" because the religious Nashvillians were loathe to give up their dead for dissection.

Mobly had stopped digging, leaned on his shovel, and thought for a moment. Then turned to Harned. "Wit' the Rebels tryin' to take the city back from the Yanks, the countryside'll soon be littered with dead, an' we'll be in the thick o' it an' kin have our pick."

Harned's eyes brightened. The cousins dropped their tools at the same moment and walked away, leaving their colleague to finish the grave they'd been digging.

And so they found themselves, on the second day of their new enterprise, hunkered down in the trees edging a stump-filled clearing. Isolated sniper fire had drawn them to this ground, and they now hoped for a Union charge on the Confederate redoubt just up the hill. The temporary fortress had been hastily built, and wouldn't withstand a direct assault. At least that's what Harned and Mobly had been telling themselves. They'd been waiting since before dawn in the fog-laden cold.

Across the clearing Harned saw the day's first prospect, a gray-clad soldier who had dropped his pants and squatted to relieve himself in the slight protection of a clump of tiny saplings.

"That dumb ass is gonna git hisself shot. Ye want I should jus' kill 'im?" Harned asked.

"I *do* think they's holdin' up the fight fer 'im," Mobly said.

A shot rang out, and the soldier dropped dead, smack dab in his stool.

"Not anymore they ain't," Harned giggled.

As they crawled on their bellies across the clearing, Mobly whispered, "When we git to 'im, I wants ye to grab 'im by the right foot, I'll git t'other."

"But Mobly, tha's jes' gonna leave a shit-streak up his back."

"Jes' think o' all the scratch ye'll git an' shut your fool mouth 'fore we git ourse'ves shot."

They struggled to drag the soldier back to their buckboard, but had only made it ten feet before the screaming Yanks began their charge across the clearing. Harned let go of the soldier and bolted for the nearby trees. Mobly smeared some of the blood from the soldier's head wound onto his face and collapsed atop him, playing 'possum. Just in time too, for it wasn't long before the charging blue line surged around him on either side.

Soon the minié balls were whistling overhead, and shells from the redoubt were screaming down, bursting, spraying a rain of red-hot shrapnel that pattered about. A bone-jarring explosion shattered the air, and the breath was knocked from Mobly with a great *whoof*!

Harned saw the surprise on his cousin's face when Mobly opened his eyes and found, as if it had taken root atop his chest, a bearded head, its expression as startled as that of his own. With the deafening sounds of the battlefield, the only evidence of Mobly's scream was his overlarge Adam's apple bobbing on his long, scrawny neck. His frightful shudders rolled the head off his left shoulder, and it lay beside him, its lips firmly planted on his cheek in an endless kiss.

The sounds of battle were dying down as Harned made his way onto the field to rouse his cousin. "Mobly, c'mon, git up!" Harned shook him, shouted in his ear, but Mobly did not stir. "Deafened by the goddam 'splosions, are ye?" Leaning close, he shouted into his cousin's face. "I ain't one o' them soldiers, aimin' to shoot ye." Finally, he grabbed Mobly by the feet and dragged him to the wagon.

It was only when he was hefted up and tossed onto the already half-loaded buckboard that Mobly opened his slitty, little eyes. Surrounded by stiffening corpses, realization seemed to dawn as he looked up at his cousin. "Goddammit Harned," Mobly hollered, "ye cain't sell me to the medical school!"

"Naw, Mobly, I weren't!" Harned pleaded, backing away and holding his hands out defensively, "I's jes' lookin' out fer ye, I swear!"

Mobly was off the buckboard in an instant, launching himself at Harned's throat, when they heard the pud and plat of musket fire striking the wagon and corpses. Without a word, they leapt aboard just as the panicked horse yanked the buckboard free of the underbrush, and they bolted into the trees.

As the sun set through the smoke-filled twilight, the cousins sat swapping stories as they guarded their regiment of dead in an abandoned shack.

"…and that's how I almost got Mr. Spoonbread shot off, " Harned concluded his latest yarn, grabbing his crotch and smiling toothily, "but didn't."

"Aw shit," said Mobly, "ye jes' made that up, that ain't real, I saw ye out there—"

A great farting interrupted them. They turned toward the sound and gazed with troubled eyes down the corridor between stacks of dead soldiers. A slow and powerful stink filled the shack. The two men fanned their noses with disgust.

Mobly chuckled uncontrollably. "Did somethin' dead crawl outta you? That stinks plum awful."

"Twarn't me. It musta been one o' them."

Mobly thought for a moment. "The first sign…" he said, ominously.

They nodded their heads and quickly headed out to the cook fire they kept in the front yard. Mobly stirred up the banked coals and laid on some fresh wood while Harned started a pot of cold beans.

"Ye got any more o' them sheet-iron crackers we got offa them soldiers?" Harned asked. "I'll crumble 'em up in some corn whiskey if'n ye want."

"Yeah, tha'd be good."

Harned fetched the hardtack, and they warmed themselves as they went about their preparations.

Harned was the first to see the little blue ghosts rising from the fire. The rippling flames chased each other toward the windows and door, but were scattered by the breeze before reaching the shack.

"Another sign," Mobly said, nudging his cousin.

Harned grabbed at his mojo bag, and Mobly smiled his approval.

"Tha's right," Mobly said. "There ain't nothin' to be a'scared of. Ye got yer juju."

Harned opened the bag and examined its contents.

"What kinda juju ye got?"

"Aw," Harned said, emptying the contents of the bag into his hand, "various an' sundry, ye know. But since we was gonna be dealin' wit' ghosts, I thought to ask ol' Black Sally what was best an' she gimme this." He held up an oddly curved bone. "It's the dick bone from a three-legged, yaller dawg," he said, proudly.

"Mm, mm, mm, that sure is somethin'."

"What 'bout you?"

"Aw," Mobly said, shaking the contents of his own bag into his hand, "nothin' as good as that."

"Tha's awright." Harned patted Mobly's shoulder. "This here's got enough juju fer the both o' us."

* * *

The shack, being as it was so close to the fighting, afforded them a good base of operations during the following weeks spent gathering bodies. They needed to consider how to do business with the medical schools, but somehow they never quite got around to that detail.

"Damn it's hot!" Harned said, wiping the sweat from his brow with a well-stained rag.

"Truly, it is," said Mobly. He fanned himself with the top of his shirt, setting free a foul stench of body odor and an insect trapped since last fall. Hauling himself to his feet, he walked over to the front door and fanned it back and forth in a vain effort to dissipate some of the wretched air.

"Where's all this heat comin' from?" Harned asked. "It ain't nat'ral. The puddles out front're all frozen, but I'm sweatin' like a pig with the door wide open."

Mobly's face collapsed with the intensity of his thoughts. Then he beamed at his cousin. "It's them cannons. All that firin' builds a mighty heat that drifts aroun' like a cloud. It prob'ly come right down the chimney an' fired this place right up."

"Man alive, Mobly." Harned stared with wide and bulging eyes. "You smart just like a steel trap."

"Thank ye kindly, Harned. Now go open them winders in t'other room, an' I'll git these'n here."

Harned stepped into the back room and considered the window. It was separated from him by a waist-high stack of dead cavalry. When he leaned way over to get to it, a grinning sergeant let out a prolonged moan.

"Jes' yew shet yer mouth," Harned told the corpse, reaching for the sash, his balance precarious. "I know it's hot in here. I'm gittin' it."

As if in retort, the sergeant's claw-like hand shot out and caught Harned hard in the stomach.

"Oof! Dammit that hurts!"

"Unnnh," the corpse answered, as Harned lost his balance and fell forward.

Trying to break his fall, he extended an arm. It plunged deeply into the stack of dead bodies and sank up to the elbow in something warm, wet, and slimy. "Oh Jesus!" he shouted, his pants leaking as he leapt to his feet. A thick layer of slime coated his arm. From it came a reek so potent he could taste it.

"What is it?" Mobly called out, rushing into the room.

Harned shook his arm, bespattering Mobly and the room with stinking splats of goo. "I done figgered out why it's so warm in here."

That evening, they were startled by a hammering at the front door. Harned answered to find a stern, red-faced Union soldier. "Evenin', Cap'n," Harned offered, a little too cheerfully.

"Name's Corporal Rice. I've been sent by Major Buttes to look into reports of strange noises and foul odors emanating from this vicinity." The corporal coughed, and Harned pounded him on the back.

"It's jes' all these here dead soldiers we done collected," Mobly said.

The man took a step inside. His eyes went wide as he looked around. Then his face turned green, and he doubled over and vomited on the floor.

"Harned, why don' ye fetch the good corp'ral somethin' to drink?"

"What in God's name has been going on here?" Rice demanded, coughing and trying to regain his composure.

"Don' git all riled up," said Mobly. "We's only collectin' 'em fer the medical school!"

Rice stood up straight and wiped his mouth. "More like collecting a heap of trouble," he said.

"They wasn't doin' nobody no good rottin' out on the battlefield."

Harned set down the cup of cold coffee he had fetched, grabbed up a loose board, and slipped up behind the corporal.

When Rice was hogtied, and they had lifted him onto the nearest stack of bodies, the cousins paused to consider each other.

"Mobly, I cain't even see no more my eyes is burnin' so bad." He wiped at them, but it only seemed to make things worse. "Tomorrow, we gotta git these dead to the medical school, but fast."

"Hell, Harned, I don' even know where the medical school is, an' there ain't nobody gonna buy these bodies now, anyway. They's too ripe. Every time I try to move one, its limbs pull right out o' the sockets."

"Well what do ye 'spose we do, then?"

"I don't know about yew, but I'm leavin'."

"Mobly, ye reckon the corporal will be all right if we was to jes' leave 'im here?" Harned asked, a bit late, as they walked toward the road in the quickening dusk.

Before he could answer, a family of four, two goats, and a fully laden wagon came to a stop before them. A boy leveled a shotgun at the two as a

man spoke up angrily. "Stop where ye are, both o' ye!" The man aimed his lantern in their direction. "What're ye doin' on our property?"

Mobly squinted in the light. "Well...sir...," he said as slowly as possible to give himself time to think. "We...thought...we saw...some ...uh...rogues skulkin' round out here, an' thought we'd look inta it."

"That's mighty neighborly o' ye," said the woman.

"Lower yer musket, son," the man said to the boy. "Meaning no offense, but I'm sure yew kin appreciate our suspicious nature in times like these."

"These are trying times," Harned agreed.

"Jeb," the woman asked, "could ye offer these gentlemen a drink o' whiskey fer their trouble?"

"Naw, thank ye," Mobly said, as they sidled past the wagon. "We'd best be goin'."

They hurried down the road as the man, oil lantern held high, moved toward the house and opened the door.

Brilliant and deafening, the night slapped them off their feet, and the cousins found themselves face-down on the road, their ears ringing. Looking back, Harned saw only smoking fragments of the shack. There wasn't much left of the wagon, but the horse, now dead, still stood in its traces. There was no sign of the family. "Where'd they go?" he asked.

The powerful reek of the cabin assaulted his nostrils once again. Then he was pelted by odd gobbets falling from the sky. He looked to his cousin.

"I guess," Mobly said as the human downpour began in earnest, "that dick bone wasn't enough juju after all."

Harned pulled out the bone and tossed it away.

"But I tell ye what," Mobly said after a moment, "all this here flying flesh gives me another idear! Let's see if'n we cain't hurry an' scrounge us up a bucket or two 'fore it stops."

Mummies
J. D. Smith

Egypt's dead, put on display,
Still have the power to attract.
They're doing well for men of clay.

Curators stash some finds away
(e.g. the Grecian urns stay packed)
But Egypt's dead go on display.

The public will quite gladly pay
To see them glass-encased, intact.
They're doing well for men of clay.

Though their curse is null today:
They lie in state, right where they're stacked.
So Egypt's dead go on display.

Safer now than where they lay
At home, where scarabs' jaws attacked.
They're doing well for men of clay.

In these late days it's hard to say
What's human, what's an artifact.
Egypt's dead go on display.
They're doing well for men of clay.

The Mummy Lost Her Sarcophagus Where a Mother Found Her Soul
Martel Sardina

Y*OU CAN'T ALWAYS GET WHAT you want. But if you try—* Chelsea punched the preset button on her car stereo, flipping the channel. What the hell did Mick Jagger know about getting what you need? What Chelsea needed right now was a little relief from the two-year-old antichrist screaming his head off in the car seat behind her.

Chelsea pulled her cell phone out of her purse and speed-dialed her sister Karen.

"Is that Christopher?"

"Yeah."

"What's he crying about?"

"He wants me to turn on the *Sesame Street* tape."

"So, turn it on."

"If I have to listen to that tape again, you'll have to check me into the crazy house."

"I thought you liked *Sesame Street*."

"I did until I had to listen to it every time I got in the car."

"I'd rather listen to that than Christopher screaming."

"You wouldn't say that if you'd heard 'C is for Cookie' as many times as I have."

"If you didn't want to listen to kid-music, then maybe you should've thought twice about having a kid."

"That's easy for you to say, but seeing as how you don't have kids, I'd ask you not to judge."

Karen sighed.

"Look, I didn't call you to fight. I need you to do me a huge favor."

"What?"

"Can I drop Christopher off at your place, and can you pick up Julie from school today?"

"Why?"

Chelsea took a deep breath. "I'm just having a really bad day, and I need to get away from the kids for awhile." Chelsea felt guilty for misleading her sister, but it was only a little bit of a lie.

"Do you want to talk about it?"

"Not if you're going to play armchair quarterback."

"I was just kidding. What's wrong?"

"Your nephew is demon-spawn, for starters. He threw a tantrum in the bank because they didn't have any lollipops. He grabbed the deposit receipt out of my hand and ripped it in two. When I was strapping him back in his car seat, he knocked the keys out of my hand. I bent over to pick them up, and he kicked me in the head."

Karen laughed.

"It's not funny."

"It is kind of funny to think that a two-year-old can get the best of you. He really knows how to push your buttons. Maybe that's why I like the kid. We're kindred spirits."

"You like him so much? Maybe you can adopt him. At this moment, I'm not so sure I want to be his mother."

"You don't mean that."

"If Christopher would've been born first..."

"I know...you would've had your tubes tied, gotten Don a vasectomy, gone back on the pill, and used condoms faithfully." Karen laughed again.

"I'm not joking. I'm actually kicking myself for not having my tubes tied when I had the chance."

"I don't think you really mean that."

"Yes, I do. I can't take much more of him. After his tantrum at the bank, I actually wished he'd never been born."

Chelsea waited for Karen to say something, offer some sympathy. Static crackled in Chelsea's ear. Karen said nothing.

"It was the weirdest thing. I wished it after I saw every bad thing he's ever done flash before my eyes. The broken VCR, CDs, my new wood floor painted with sunscreen, my whole house covered in a dust cloud of baby powder."

"What about the good things? First tooth, first word, first step? That dimple he gets when he smiles?"

"That dimple is proof that he is demon-spawn. If he hadn't been in such a hurry to be born so he could get into this world and cause trouble, God would've had time to put one on the other cheek too."

"Got to admit it makes him a cutie."

"In a devilish way."

"He's only two. He wants to explore the world."

"That may be true. But he knows when he's doing something he's not supposed to. I'll tell him 'no,' he'll look right at me and do it anyway. It's infuriating."

"He'll grow out of it."

"Only if he lives that long. At the rate he's going, I can't make any promises."

"Don't you think you're overreacting?"

"Look, you don't have to do this 24/7. You see the kids on your terms, take them out, spoil them, bring them back to me loaded up on cookies and candy. You get to be the fun one. You don't have to discipline them. You don't have to clean up after them. It's just like with Don and me. He's the good cop. I'm the warden. It's not fun to be the warden. I don't want to be the warden. I can't do this again."

"Again? What are you talking about? You're not...?"

Christopher wailed. Chelsea clenched the steering wheel tighter. The knuckles on her left hand turned white with the increasing pressure.

"Can you watch the kids or not?"

"Sure, sure. No problem."

"Thanks. I'll be dropping Christopher off in a few minutes. Julie gets out of school at three-fifteen."

"Okay. See you soon."

Chelsea flipped the cell shut and put it back on the passenger seat.

Motherhood wasn't supposed to be a part of my destiny. She couldn't say it was an accident. Her first pregnancy had been planned: not because she had an overwhelming desire to be a mother. It had been a way to escape the pressure from her husband, family, and friends. They wanted her to have a baby. She knew she had no maternal instinct, but not wanting children made her less of a woman, somehow. At least, that's how they made it seem. They wore her down. In the end, she wound up discounting her own instincts, giving up what she knew was right for her, in order to please them.

The throbbing in Chelsea's head intensified. She thought about the phone call she'd gotten just before the trip to the bank. The nurse confirming what she already knew. Her stomach turned over, and then she noticed that she couldn't hear Christopher. She knew he was crying because she could see him in the rearview mirror, but it was as if the audio track had been removed. Maybe it was a defense mechanism; listening to the crying had so disturbed her that her body just shut it out.

After dropping Christopher off, she pulled around the corner and parked the van. She pulled her wallet out of her purse. *Was it in there?* She fumbled through the stack of cards until she found what she was looking for—the business card the nurse had given her earlier. She flipped the cell open and punched in the number.

"I'm calling to confirm my six o'clock appointment."

She flipped the cell shut and dropped it next to her wallet and the business cards that were now scattered across the passenger seat. She noticed her Museum of Science and Industry membership card. She had time to kill and needed a distraction. Maybe she'd go see that Body Worlds exhibit everyone raved about.

Traffic crept along the Eisenhower, and by the time she got on Lake Shore Drive, it was nearly rush hour. She exited at 57th Street, following it around to the entrance of the museum's underground parking garage.

Chelsea passed Christopher's favorite exhibit, The Jollyball, on her way to Body Worlds. The exhibit, an oversized pinball machine showing the sights of Switzerland, was constructed from recycled trash and scrap metal. The last time she'd brought Christopher, it was being repaired. Remembering his tantrum, Chelsea found she wanted to get as far away from The Jollyball as possible. She came here to forget; about him, the nurse, and what she was about to do.

"Enhance today's experience with our Body Worlds audio tour." While she normally would've passed on the museum's attempt to extort more money, Chelsea decided she deserved to treat herself today. She plunked four dollars down on the counter and walked away with a device similar to a television remote but equipped with a speaker. If she punched in the exhibit number, a recorded message described the item in detail.

Chelsea walked by a glass case containing preserved specimens of various components of the human ear. She glanced at the objects casually until she reached the first whole body plastinate. The skinless man, Exhibit 623, entitled "The Hand Shake," posed with an outstretched hand and welcomed Chelsea into his world. Viewing the body stirred up a mixture of emotions. The only corpses she'd seen outside of a funeral home were the Romero zombies that plagued her dreams. She hoped the plastinates wouldn't take on that role as well.

The next exhibit, "The Orthopedic Body," disturbed Chelsea. The man had been subjected to multiple surgical procedures, presumably to show the world that Humpty Dumpty could be put back together again. Surgical forceps held back muscles to show the metal plates where his humerus and tibia used to be. She wanted to tell him it was a good thing he was dead because there was no way he'd ever get through airport security after what they'd done to him. He looked like he wanted to say something; perhaps he agreed.

She noted his joint replacements, the pacemaker, all the broken bones with different methods of repair, and that's when she noticed that his genitals were intact. She tried not to stare. She knew the purpose of the exhibit was to promote an understanding of the human body, but was it really necessary to leave these "people" exposed? Chelsea was mortified on their behalf.

"All of the specimens were donated willingly to Dr. von Haegens, to his cause," the audio guide said. The statement reduced Chelsea's discomfort. She now felt it was okay to look at the naked figures; they had granted permission.

The combination of science and art, life and death, overwhelmed her senses. She half-expected to smell raw meat as she looked at the skinless figures.

She wandered farther in, looking at preserved cross sections of various body parts. The largest specimen in the case, a non-smoker's chest cavity, looked more liked a rib eye steak than Chelsea cared to admit.

Museum rules forbade touching the items on display. Chelsea knew that the figures would not feel the same as a living human being, but she couldn't quite imagine what they would feel like. She wanted to know. The morbid curiosity grew with each new figure she passed.

In the next corridor, she passed a display of the forearm: hand and fingers comprised of the veins, blood vessels, and arteries with the muscles, bones, and skin removed. She studied the intricate detail and doubted that the same systems were at work within her.

Chelsea saw the entrance to the final room of the exhibit. *I don't need to see that. How do I get out of here?* A mother with a toddler throwing a tantrum blocked the exit. *Crap.* She retreated to the curtained exhibit. *At least plastinated babies can't cry.*

The first display case in this room contained embryos from four to eight weeks' gestation. The skeptics around her commented on the preservation process, staring at the four-week-old embryo, disbelieving that they really saw the beginnings of arms and legs. By eight weeks, the limbs and other vital organs were easily discernable. Chelsea scanned each one to convince herself they looked more like blobs of tissue than anything else. She knew she was denying the truth.

She'd cried at the early ultrasound when the flash of a heartbeat appeared on the monitor. She'd been six weeks pregnant then; she was further along now.

She had to distance herself from what she had been brought up to believe: that life begins at conception. She needed to believe something other than abortion is murder; she settled for believing in self-preservation. The way things were going with the two kids she had, not terminating this pregnancy would likely result in...

Chelsea shuddered at the memory that had resurfaced. Something she hadn't told Karen. Something she couldn't tell anyone. She hadn't just wished Christopher hadn't been born. She saw herself squeezing her hands around his throat, saw herself smothering him with a pillow, and the images had calmed her.

Fetuses from nine weeks' gestation through full-term were displayed in cases that lined the outer walls of the room. In the center of the room, Chelsea saw the "Reclining Pregnant Woman," whose midsection had been cut open so that her internal organs and unborn son were exposed.

There was no avoiding the display. The exit was on the other side.

Chelsea had heard people talk about how pregnant women "glowed," but she never saw past the extra weight, stretch marks, and varicose veins until now. Something about the pose—the tilt of the woman's head, the parting of her lips, the way her body was draped across the platform—reminded Chelsea of a piece of Renaissance art. The once-grotesque pregnant form had now been rendered beautiful.

The vacillating emotions left Chelsea confused. What was she was supposed to feel? Awe that this stage of pregnancy was preserved for medical and educational observation? Sorrow for the loss of the life that had to occur in order to make the display possible? Outrage the baby hadn't had a choice? Her stomach twinged. She didn't want to look anymore, but she couldn't look away, either.

Chelsea didn't remember pushing the exhibit number on the remote as she heard a woman's voice begin to speak.

"I never gave much thought to what I'd do in the afterlife because I didn't think there would be one. I guess I was wrong about that."

Chelsea pulled the remote away from her ear and looked around. No one was talking to her. Other patrons mulled around this portion of the exhibit, but most of them stood at the far end, near the Reclining Woman's feet. Chelsea had been standing there, but now found herself on the other end looking into the Reclining Woman's eyes. She put the remote back to her ear.

"Don't be surprised," the woman continued. "The modern day mummy can talk, hear, and think."

Mummy? Chelsea wanted to say something. But there were so many people around. If she was going crazy, she didn't want to make a scene.

"Plastination, the process by which I was perfected in death, is the modern equivalent of mummification."

Chelsea supposed that made sense. What she didn't understand was how the woman knew what she was thinking.

"I can hear your thoughts. That's how I know whom to talk to. That's how we all know whom to talk to. Just because we're dead doesn't mean we don't still have jobs to do."

All of you talk? Chelsea raised an eyebrow.

"See that man over there?"

Chelsea peeked around the curtain that separated this room from the main exhibit hall. She saw a morbidly obese man wiping sweat from his brow with one hand and holding a remote up to his ear with the other.

"He is being told to go back on the diet he just quit. That the inside of his body looks worse than the specimen on the table."

Chelsea watched as the man leaned closer, examining the display with a look of grave concern. He paused, then looked around the room. She wondered if the man would go back on the diet.

"I don't know the answer to that question. We are only messengers. We never know for certain what impact our words have."

What's your message for me?

"To not take the gift you have been given for granted."

What's that supposed to mean?

"I wanted to be a mother since I was a little girl. I remember rocking my dolls to sleep in the wooden cradle that my father built. I'd sing them lullabies and rock them gently. When the ritual had been performed to my satisfaction, I crawled into bed and dreamt about the day when the dolls would be real.

"At first, I denied that what the doctors told me was true. Being pregnant, I could believe; but the other part, the part about not living to see that dream come to fruition, was the part that just didn't seem fair. Motherhood was part of my destiny.

"When the doctor asked if I'd like to donate my body to science when I passed on, I said, 'Why not? Whatever you're going to do to me can't be worse than what I'm going through now.'"

Chelsea sighed, wondering what the point of all this was.

"Do you want to know what being eight months pregnant while enduring a terminal illness is called? Try nightmare. Try Hell. I might have even called it my personal Golgotha, but that would imply that I still believed in God, which prior to my death, I did not. And now? Let's just say the two of us aren't exactly on the best terms."

Chelsea didn't feel her own relationship with God was on the best terms at the moment, either.

"That's part of the reason I'm supposed to talk to you. We're not that different. I was angry too. The anger I felt when I learned of my diagnosis surprised me. The anger I felt then was nothing compared to the anger I felt when the doctors told me I had two choices: have a late-term abortion and get chemotherapy so I could live, or have a Cesarean so my baby could live knowing that my *condition* gave me a slim chance to survive."

The woman laughed. "It's funny how people can hardly bring themselves to say the word 'cancer.'"

Chelsea wondered what the woman's family thought of her choice.

"The hospice staff helped me to determine that the best course of action for me, mentally, was to not terminate the pregnancy. I needed something to focus on other than my *condition*."

Chelsea looked at the baby again, still in the womb. *What went wrong?*

"Turns out there was nothing that the doctors could do for me or my unborn son. After all, they are only practicing medicine."

Get a grip. This doesn't change anything. What happened to the Reclining Woman was horrible, but...

"Don't pity me, and don't you dare pity yourself."

The disgust in the woman's voice surprised Chelsea.

"You should feel guilty. You have everything. You have a life that most people would envy. And what are you doing? Instead of enjoying it, you're looking for reasons to be unhappy."

Chelsea felt her neck got hot. Her nausea turned to anger. *You don't know what you're talking about. You don't know me.*

"Think what you want. All I know is I'd have given anything to hold my son in my arms just once. You have three children, and you don't deserve any of them."

The words hit Chelsea like a roundhouse right.

She dropped the remote.

Maybe I don't. Chelsea poked the woman in the shoulder, against the hardened, unyielding flesh. *But that makes me wonder...what did you do to deserve this?*

Chelsea ran her finger along the unborn child's thigh. No amount of sandpaper could give the boy's skin that silky, smooth feel.

Christopher's skin never felt this rough, not even in winter. Chelsea was forever bathing him, coating him in baby lotion. The baths were a result of his frequent mischief, coloring himself with markers or Chelsea's makeup, whatever he could find. How he'd laugh when she set him in the sudsy water. Chelsea would give in and laugh too, until Christopher splashed water out of the tub, soaking her jeans.

As she changed into dry clothes, she'd curse him for...for being two, Chelsea thought...*what did he do to deserve a mother like me?*

The voice that answered was not the Reclining Woman's.

"Ma'am, there's no touching the exhibits," the security guard said as he swatted Chelsea's hand away. "If you do it again, I'll have to ask you to—"

"Don't worry, I'm leaving." Chelsea picked the remote up and walked away from the woman, toward the exit. She stopped at the counter. The remote fell from her shaking hand.

"Something wrong, ma'am?" the attendant said.

She walked through the turnstile exiting the exhibit and made her way out of the museum. She stood on the sidewalk and saw Lake Michigan across Lake Shore Drive in the distance. The setting sun's reflection in the waves told Chelsea six o'clock had come.

Chelsea put the remote to her ear and approached the Reclining Woman in the Franklin Institute of Science's Mandell Center.

"Why are you in Philadelphia?" the woman said.

You said you were a messenger. That you never knew for sure what impact your words had.

"What of it?"

I thought about what you said. I've wasted a lot of time trying to find a life that I wanted, instead of wanting the life that I already have. Thank you for that.

The woman said nothing.

I'm sorry.

"For what?"

That your dream never came true. For thinking you didn't deserve it.

Don pushed the stroller next to Chelsea. The baby cooed as he turned his head toward the Reclining Woman.

Christopher tugged on Chelsea's pant leg. "Up please, Mommy."

Chelsea balanced the remote between her shoulder and her ear as she picked Christopher up.

The Reclining Woman said, "When you get frustrated, try to keep things in perspective. Remember me."

How could I forget?

Julie said, "Mommy, I think that lady just smiled at me."

Don laughed. "No, honey. That's impossible. She's almost entirely made of plastic."

Chelsea knew better. The dead can smile, especially to celebrate a job well done.

Hell's Deadline
Suzanne Church

EVERY DAY IN HELL SUCKS. I wake on the floor then roll over into a patch of my own vomit. Never fails.

The countdown clock on the wall advances. Today's day thirty of thirty.

The shower doesn't work, so I rinse myself with the water from the toilet.

I squirm back into my soggy clothes and head for the kitchen. The bread smells of mold, but it isn't blue. I shove two slices in the toaster. They pop up light and soggy. Doesn't matter how many times I toast the bread, it won't get any darker.

Hell's about the details.

The S-man left a note. I'm careful opening it, but I slice my finger on the envelope. The boss has a sense of humor that keeps on giving.

Dear Debs:
Good luck. I'm rooting for you.

I head for the door and grab the key from the hook on the wall. I've scribbled "Jamie" above it in black marker, but it's not my brother's key. Maybe it's the trigger—the deciding factor that buys me a ticket north.

Outside, the gravel of the path crunches under my feet. The air's humid and still, like the worst day of summer. Reeks of exhaust too, though I don't hear or see any cars. The trail leads to the same place no matter which direction I follow. Today, I head right.

The smells around me thicken; sap laced with rotting leaves. The birch and poplar trees close in until the light vanishes and I can't see past my hand, stumbling through the brush, hearing the growls and padding paws of the creatures who track me. My nerves ignite.

I stumble on until the woods brighten. I've reached the stand of towering pines growing toward the reddish sky, planted in endless rows.

I follow the fourth corridor to my left. Between the giants, the lower branches are broken or dead, protruding like sharpened talons. They scratch my face and arms, dig into my legs, tear my pants.

I duck past mammoth trunks, picking one aisle then another, searching for safe passage. No matter how many times I change direction, I reach the shed as the sun is setting.

Mom's screaming.

I don't want to use the key, but I do. Gotta fix things so I can get the fuck north.

Inside smells like smoke, sweat, and raw meat. My eight-year-old brother Jamie is cowering under the table in his usual hiding place, his hands pressed over his ears, tears smudging his cheeks.

Dad's gripping Mom by the hair with one hand and pounding her with the other. He's right handed, but he's switched to his left jab.

"Get your hands off her," I say.

"Mind your own fucking business," he says.

I step closer.

He drops her and faces me. Nose to nose. I can smell his breath. He's rotting from the inside out. I imagine killing him, cooking him, the taste of his flesh vile, like poison. Like victory.

"I never liked you," I say.

He grabs my breast. "You like this, though, don't you."

The knife appears in my hand. I don't know how, but it's always ready when his fingers pinch my nipple.

He closes his eyes.

"Debs?" Jamie's out from under the table.

"Get back and hide," I say.

Dad's hands are lower, in my pants.

"I don't want you to see this," I say.

Jamie shoves Dad from behind.

I don't know if this part's new. I can't remember what happens from when the knife appears until the deed's done. This performance is how I earned a ticket south. Stabbed my father with a kitchen knife over and over until he stopped twitching. The *why* doesn't change the verdict. Despite motive, I rode the down escalator.

Jamie grabs my wrist. "Don't." He yanks the knife handle.

I hold tight. "Hide!"

"Not this time."

We fight over the weapon. The old man stands frozen, uninvited to the party until we siblings agree.

Jamie shrieks, "It's my turn."

I look down. He's got the glint, the one I've seen burrowing in my own eyes. The one that says, "Fuck the consequences, I've waited my whole life for justice." That's why I wrote his name over the key.

I release the knife.

He holds it close to his chest, triumphant. Then he turns on the beast. For a split second, I want him to do it, to take the rap. He's young; maybe they won't ship him south.

No.

I obstruct his arms mid-lunge. He fights, but I seize the knife. Dad unfreezes. I kill him.

Blood splatters us.

Mom sobs, mumbling about how Dad didn't mean it.

Then I'm walking through the woods with the knife. The carnivores race towards the blood. A few wolves to my left, a bear beyond. An immense cat screams.

"Come and get me." I drop the knife, blade down. It sinks into the loam.

The wolves advance, baring their teeth. I welcome them.

"Nice work."

The S-man's beside me. He waves the carnivores away.

"You had your ticket north."

I shrug. "Jamie wouldn't survive here."

The S-man buttons his blazer. "Kids are resilient." He's smiling like he knows a secret.

"I'm never leaving here, am I?"

"Contracts are tricky," he says.

"I did the world a favor."

"You broke the rules."

I nod. "What now?"

He shakes his head. "No point spoiling the surprise."

I wake in a bed. A bug-infested, half-rotten, bare mattress, but a bed, nonetheless.

The shower works. Clean clothes hang over a chair. The toaster's still broken.

I bite into my soggy toast and use the butter knife to open the S-man's note. No paper cuts—I'm learning.

Dear Debs:

You've earned another thirty days to solve the riddle in the shed.

The countdown clock on the wall says day one of thirty. No time to lose.

Naked Lunchmeat
Brian Hodge

THE TRAINS DON'T RUN ON time anymore. It gives us a sense of gambling, we stand on the platform at the 14th Street Station and play the odds whether the train will come before any meatfolk catch wind of us on the stale ozone breeze in the tunnels of the underbelly, and come shambling out to investigate.

The train is late again, and here we are sharing the platform with the usual suspects, and we all look at each other like we don't really trust our eyes to tell between the living and the dead. Only the old Hasidic stands there with a sense of peace in his rheumy eyes. I figure it's because his faith forbids a belief in an afterlife and so he doesn't believe this shit is actually happening. Evidently we must be his idea of hallucinations. In black he already looks like an undertaker.

Today we lose, and people start to scatter with the practiced panic of retreats that leave their dignity intact after the first of them notices the meatboy lurching out of the mouth of the tunnel. When winos and bag ladies still slept down here, meatfolk bred like blue rats. He shows his saggy ashen face and the warmbloods run for the stairs and the streets, forgetting about their spent tokens. No thought to economic sacrifice. The solitary meatboy crawls from track level up onto the emptying platform, and I can hear his slobbering grunts and it still makes me wonder what all the fuss is about. The meatfolk all sound like asthmatics to me.

"Time for toasties," says Frazzle, and he takes the meatboy by one shoulder while I take the other and before he can snap at us we pitch him down below again. He lands on the third rail and starts to smoke and pop and flop like somebody's grey steak and a gas buildup blows out the back of the meatboy's pants and shoots him off the rail, between regular tracks. Everything's quiet and we're looking at each other through the charbroiled haze. The old Hasidic views it all without judgment, turns away.

Frazzle's got the works in his hand even before he jumps down off the platform. Clears the rails like a kid playing hopscotch, and I think I start to sweat when he kneels by the moaning meatboy who's sluggishly waving a pair of burnt matchstick arms in the air. Frazzle sinks the heavy bore needle into the meatboy's skull, better than a doctor. He hits the pituitary every time, like an old junkie finding final life in a bruised and flaccid vein. The syringe fills and he leaves the cripped-up meatboy for the next train, whenever it decides to show, and I can already hear the squeal of brakes and the shear of meat from bone and bone from socket.

"It's already cooked for us, even," says Frazzle.

"Fuck the tokens, we bail," then I turn to the old Hasidic's back. "Shalom."

We hide the works like couriers like spies like jesters of greed and take the stairs three at a time and the afternoon sun slams us bright in the face. We almost can't wait until we get back to the hotel room before tying off and nailing up. After transfer, we slide the smaller needle home, staring at that beautiful plumage of bloody backwash in the syringe, its second of blown-crystal perfection before it thins out, dilutes, drains back into the arm. Always the last aesthetic we appreciate.

Death's a bitch, and then you live.

The H dealers are out of business now, most of them, because dealers sell a product they don't make. Dealers are smart but not particularly creative, so they can't figure out how to make any profit off selling a fix that anyone can go out and find for free, or if not, and they have no moral objection to murder, manufacture for themselves. Meatfolk everywhere, for the taking or the making. Dealers have to shut down in an economy like this, but the way I see it, they just don't try hard enough to find the really stupid, lazy, rich junkies, if there are such things, the kind can be convinced of anything, *my* meatboy is better than *your* meatboy and it'll cost you, you know what I'm saying?

Some new kind of kick: Pituitary extract drawn from recently reanimated corpses, then treated with heat; cooled fluid medium bears attenuated form of virus known among scientific quarters as Quayle-Beta Syndrome, otherwise known informally as Pitchback Fever, the Resurrection Rag, Cancelled Ticket, Highway to Limbo, God's Little Joke, the Indiscretion of a Lifetime, Rotten Johnny, etc etc etc. Attenuation renders virus incapable of cannibalizing host cells. Intravenous injection results in purgatorial death trance, is metabolized out after six to ten hours.

"The times, they be a-changing," said the East Village's Twitching Kalvin Khrist before he shot himself through the eye with a nail gun. Here was a man who truly lived for his work. He was still sitting on a half-kilo of junk at the time. When we find him we have a shooting match and it just like the old days, all the old familiar addictions in all the old familiar veins.

The city's now filling with meatfolk and we suppose it really is possible to have too much of a good thing because they don't surrender their pituitaries without a fight, then there's their own habit to support. More of the slow groaning stinkers every day. In a sense I figure there's a karmic balance at work here, we two species each feeding off the other, the last cannibal couple each trying to sink the teeth while slow-dancing in the grey hungover morning.

So we hot-wire a Lexus, stock the trunk with fresh meatfolk heads, and start west.

We come out of the northeast looking for the last free town in Amerika, because it's the way we feel ourselves. For the first time in our memories uneaten by the fluid charcoal reclamation, we're not tethered to our connections. We score in cornfields as easy as Bleecker Street now. You know what it's like when God pukes manna, you don't ask questions, just stoop for the harvest.

Eight hundred miles and then Frazzle gets weird on me, tells me how every Christmas he took down his decorations and threw out the tree, and listened to Christmas records backwards and heard Satanic messages oozing from the speakers. These spells of his, never the same twice. Tomorrow he'll be singing the last stock reports to Gregorian chants or blinking Morse code haiku in a broken mirror. We get cold in the car as the Lexus' heater broke down in Indiana so we slice up the back seat and start to burn the pieces in the hubcaps set in the floorboards until the smoke forms a cataract over the windshield. I draw maps in the soot, Byzantine aortas from some other peeled body under the gloom, never mine.

The trunk of heads runs out west of Kansas City and it's desolate country, fields of nothing waiting to grow. Not even the meatfolk stayed around here. Sun goes down and we shiver. Sun comes up and we cry. Sun goes higher and jonesing we face hard facts, remember a time when they said junkies shared their last fix. A time we never lived through, never wanted to live through until now. A time we never even believed in.

"Cowards die many times before their deaths," Frazzle say. "But so does everyone else now. And we give it a shot, you and me Hallucinogenius One and Hallucinogenius Two."

"I regret I had but twelve veins to give for my sickness."

"Explorers are never so honest as to explain what they're really looking for, so history invents it for them."

"How will we go down, you think?"

"In flames, most likely." Frazzle dries day-old tears. "Make it quick, if you're going to."

So I stab him in throat with gnawed bone. Frazzle tries to hold in his life for a minute then gives up and watches it puddle in his lap, pool of old secrets where avatars lie submerged and suffocating. Ten minutes and he's back again, so I bust out his teeth with the Lexus' tire iron, Frazzle looking out at me with a toothless frown and handfuls of desiccated ivory, sad in his way. It's not fun when they're strangers, even less if you know them. I'm not as good with the heavy bore needle as Frazzle was, but it's a learning experience, and for a moment he almost seems to turn his head to give me a better shot at the pituitary, something of the old Frazzle remaining to help me along.

I cook him down and he goes into my arm, in burnt clouds of hellfire and a hundred discussions with whispering maggot voices. For a few hours I think maybe I know what it's like to be Frazzle and dead, dead for real. All the rest of them, they're no role models, stumbling around way they do, that's no death. This is something to hope for? They all stumble for oblivion, are too fucked up to find it.

But Frazzle knows now, he teaching me from the veins out.

It gets me down the road another day, still not afraid to die because now I remember again, but then there's always tomorrow, and you know me. I forget easy.

I left the highway in western Kansas, the time feeling right when I came upon a green exit sign with a plank boarded over the upcoming town's name. The old town dead, it had begun life anew. TARTARUS, someone had painted across the new wood, black block letters that wink subtle invitations when the sun hits them at precise angles. I find a town under martial law and underlying chaos.

A newcomer, I am assigned to the employ of Dr. Amway, of the Tartarus Clinic for Applied Research. My job being to report any activity within the perimeter of a postmodern death nature, or soon to be deceased. My judgment will be invaluable, they inform me, for my status as newcomer leaves me unencumbered by prior prejudices or allegiances.

Dr. Amway was a pathologist and medical examiner in one of the western metropoli, has since assumed a new mantle of command combining now-usurped control systems of medicine and law. He is a man of numerous facelifts, with four square inches of original face left, stretched tight over his skull.

"I am the man with his finger up the ass of the nation," he tells me. "How would you define deviance?"

"I wouldn't, but I know it when I see it."

"Splendid," and he clapping, then lead me to rows of cages filled with meatfolk. They eyeing us with confused dead glimmers and reaching with broken-nailed hands, but not as eager as average meatfolk beyond the perimeter. I remark that some progress appears to have been made here.

"I am the great white heterosexual overlord," says Dr. Amway. "And by that divine mandate I am eminently qualified to convert these poor blue heathen. I must admit, the task might be safer from the go if custom still insisted we sew the mouths shut immediately upon death, but I enjoy a challenge."

[Note: During Colonial and westward expansionist phases of American history, the lips of the newly dead were stitched closed, a custom brought over by European immigrants. Reportedly this practice still goes on in remote areas of Appalachia. Its function was spiritual in nature, to prevent evil entities from gaining access to the deceased and taking up residence. This measure would obviously be a failure in light of Quayle-Beta Syndrome, but I purport it might still be of use in thwarting their appetites.]

Dr. Amway waves one hand about. "You see the stubborn dead, but I see a roomful of potential. Actually, their chance at becoming productive citizens is greater now than it ever was. They're so much more pliant now, all they lack is the proper conditioning. Somatic and neural trigger experiences to remember that in their old lives, they were motivated not by hunger, but by sexual desire. They have forgotten that. They'll eat anybody now, without discrimination. It's a roomful of raging bisexuals, as far as I'm concerned, but I'm convinced they can be reconditioned to behave as God intended.

"I feed the males a steady diet of Rocky Mountain Oysters, keeps them virile. The females I don't feed at all. Keeps them slim and, I should hope, inordinately vain. The restorative potential of enforced anorexia cannot be exaggerated. Next week I shall introduce full-length mirrors into the females' quarters. They'll thank me then, just you wait and see."

Dr. Amway has a meatboy brought out and stripped, chained securely to the lab floor by knees and elbows, then he liberally applies K.Y. He dons a stovepipe top hat of stars and bars and fucks the meatboy in the ass. Ropes of saliva stream from dead jaws to puddle on the floor, and I thought the meatboy looked confused before.

"He'll learn, he'll remember," says Dr. Amway, now out of breath. "Only a matter of time. And if the ungrateful wretch still refuses, well, I can always sue the bastard."

Inhibitions fall as frequently as the night, the warmbloods of Tartarus making revel mockery of their old lives, or trying to resurrect them in bacchanalian ritual. Few dare talk with a newcomer, for fear of betraying themselves to a watchful agent of the ruling regime, and so I am invisible. I soon understand that their displays are considered unmistakable proof that they are alive.

On a typical night, swing-shifts of wailing penitents beat their breasts before the god of their choice, or possibly several, and pray for deliverance. Housewife strippers undulate wildly onstage while straying husbands stuff supermarket coupons into their garters. Two transvestite priests kneel before altars while genderflecting nuns dispense antacid hosts upon their tongues. Lonely schoolboys with tentacled acne meet for masturbatory excess over piles of burning magazines. A dominatrix professor in rubber lactates stale theorems into imbecile mouths that gape like baby birds. Shopkeepers in back rooms shit into relabeled jars and boxes, then sell them for spiraling prices. Suburban social pillars invade the homes of despised neighbors, lock them in cellars with hungry, transubstantiating rats. The Tartarus aristocracy preens along the streets, holding tight to leashes collared to surgically reconstructed meatchildren; their knees fold backwards as they obediently chatter like Rhesus monkeys, are rewarded with raw cubes of indeterminate origin.

"At last," the aristocracy cries, "we have reason to bury all the elder bipartisan hatreds. Even within Apocalypse can the wise find Shangri-La."

In certain hard-to-locate bars, frequented only at night, meatboys and meatgirls sit bolted immobile into wooden chairs, mouths clamped shut, while surgically implanted shunts drain off pituitary extract. The runoff collects in receptacles over gas flames, then is channeled into intravenous drips. Coded bathroom graffiti informs the careful reader that this technology is the work of Dr. Amway, as means of controlling the restless and ill-contented living. By 3:00 a.m., the only sound comes from dozens of groaning meatfolk, each bar filled with comatose warmbloods in their grave-spangled purgatorial trances, heavy inside with the cindery burnt comet empathic visions of those on the far side of the perimeter. It is their new lives we wonder and worry about, their eternities.

I am without choice on a biological level. Sit down next to grimacing meatboy hookah and plug in. Avoid the eyes and find the vein….before long I may be confusing the order in which things are done. But paradoxically, I will die, if it's the last thing I do. Hard to get that wrong….but then, look at the meatfolk, though I am not so sure they deserve quite all the blame.

SUBJECT 92

He occupied a suite of rooms on the top floor of the Tartarus Clinic for Applied Research. In the eyes of the staff, "Subject 92" replaced his given name of Leland Lovejoy, and behind him lay the terrible abattoir of misfortune which had led to his residency at the clinic, where he hobbled about with some assistance.

Subject 92 had lost various bodily parts in nine separate attacks by the walking dead. While drunk on a potent concoction of Sterno and Gatorade, the then-itinerant Leland Lovejoy was set upon by a trio of corpses who chewed his left leg off at the knee before he fought them away. While sedated in an emergency room, he then awoke to find a newly-deceased woman from an adjacent room drooling into his face, after which one eye was sucked from its socket like a cocktail onion. In later attacks over the coming months, several of which were alcohol-related, he lost an ear, a flap of scalp, three fingers, his surviving baby toe, most of his right bicep, half of one cheek, plus assorted divots of flesh estimated to total seven pounds.

"Well, I used to hate them," he frequently told his attending staff, speaking of the ambulatory corpses who had so bedeviled him, "but then I realized, no matter what, it's still nice to be wanted. And they've done a lot for me, in their way. Three squares a day and a roof over my head and a fistful of remote controls, you think I ever had it this good when I was on the streets?"

"But the price you paid to be here," said one of his nurses. "Some people would call what you lost an exorbitant fee."

Subject 92 dismissed all misgivings with a noxious cloud of cigar smoke and a wave of a four-fingered hand. "Lemme tell you something. They left my pecker and my nuts alone. They'd've taken those, yeah, I might be singing a different tune. But everything vital's still in place, and what's gone, I can't say I miss all that much. Hey, you know anyone needs a kidney? I got one to spare."

Subject 92's usefulness came as a result of his being the only known living human to sustain bites in one, let alone nine, attacks and then fail to succumb to infection by the Quayle-Beta virus. The Tartarus Clinic for Applied Research was an inevitable destination, as medical science had long known that if you want to learn how to defeat a disease, study who does not have it.

He was much beloved by Dr. Amway, who routinely had Subject 92 brought down to the labs, where they would freely, and with great exuberance, converse on topics as diverse as cheap alcohol substitutes, sightings of the Virgin Mary within foodstuffs and bathroom mildew stains, and post-amputation phantom pains.

"Excellent progress, we're making excellent progress with you. You really are quite the miracle man," Dr. Amway would tell him, and praise him effusively for his courage. "In fact, we're making such excellent progress that I am almost ashamed to inform you that we need a few more tissue samples for further analysis." He would then toy with a sterile, gleaming scalpel and surgical spatula.

And Subject 92 would look at him with an inaudible whimper, remember his home several floors above, with all its fine and expensive trinkets, sigh, and roll up the skin of his stump.

THE PARKING LOT

Thad in his suit, grey, Savile Row and tailored to a perfect 40-Regular frame. Always told, be a model, Thad smiling with mild indulgence but flushed with flattery. Bess in her Dior strapless, a diaphanous sweep to just below her perfect knee. Had turned down eleven proposals of marriage, but the night was young. Each were with friends at different richly cultured oases in the same plaza of trends, where rehabbers made killings and the dead were not allowed. This was where the beautiful could still come for a night devoid of worries, while they still could, here at civilization's last stand, at least any civilization that truly mattered.

A determined, intermittent blare muscled through the refined chime of crystal and china and harp, and Thad saw the world through a red mist of irritability as he left the table.

"Pardon me," to his companions. "My car, I believe. If someone's dinged it, I'll bring back a foreskin as a trophy."

The plaza oozed smug propriety beneath a sick orange sodium haze, cars in orderly rows like rounded steel hummocks, or burial mounds, their windshields gleaming with indifference. It was not a light to flatter human faces, but Thad found her lovely just the same. Bess stretching to delicate tiptoe, craning her neck after her rush down from her own dinner, own drinks. Thirty feet and four cars away from him, and he knew love all over again. From somewhere in the assembly of cars, a horn droned its repetitive pattern, three quick toots, then two longer ones, over and over, loud as gunfire.

"My mistake," Thad called over to her. "I thought it was my car!"

"And I mine." A vision, she was. "I guess we're both wrong."

Standing tall and tottering on stiffened legs, they scanned the lot again for the trumpeting car.

"There it is!" She pointed. "See the lights flashing?"

"Come along," and dazzled, he took her by the wrist as they hurried between cars like mischievous trust fund heirs, until they stood beside the empty, convulsing auto. One fender appeared stricken with a fresh wound. No one else was in sight.

"And it's only a Mazda," Bess said. "Some people, you wonder what goes through their minds...."

Thad held her surrendered hand, turned the diamond ring down, and directed her reach toward the windshield where, together, they etched in the glass: CLEAN THE WAX FROM YOUR EARS, YOU FUCKING CRETIN LOSER, after which they laughed and fell into each other's arms. Some nights it really was possible to love a lifetime's worth in five minutes.

But then the dead crawled from beneath a dozen cars, Beemers and Mercedes and Volvos, and surrounded them in a stinking ring of grey sodium putrefaction and maggot runoff. Even their clothes were as ragged as their skin. Who knew they were smart enough to set traps? Who knew they possessed the skills of pack hunters?

Thad and Bess were brought down in screams and threats of litigation, evoking the names of lawyers and aldermen, as business cards spewed like feathers in molt. Their buttocks were eaten away, until denuded pelvic bone showed through the tears in pants and dress, respectively, but the dead stopped when Bess groaned, newly revived, and they recognized in her a kindred lack of soul.

She waited at Thad's side until he, too, roused, and together they straggled their raw bony asses upright.

They returned to one restaurant, together still and forever, and they never even knew the difference.

Quick, now. Wake up to the sound of maggot jaws but I realize it's just another flashback. Got to rub the head before dreams sink seeds too deep and become the reality. Maggots eat their way back out. I assume it hurts, but might be a cure for narcolepsy.

Stumble out into the street in the grey deathly morning, a sky like moldy old cheese and winds full of sand to scour loose skin from brittle bones. "Bring out your dead," the meatwagon on morning rounds. The bonegrinder pulls her lever whenever they get one. Got to maintain warmblood order in Tartarus until Dr. Amway's proper conditioning reintegrates the meatfolk back into my world. Like I really want them? Just another new immigrant to hate, or hire, depending on your politics.

Bonegrinder grins. The mulch makes wonderful fertilizer, all that bone meal. Calcium is our friend.

Crying children sit filthy and naked around dead televisions with gutted insides, fires burning in the cavities, fed by random books. New billboard goes up, blue collar joes hoisting like the flag on Iwo Jima, says I AM NOT RESPONSIBLE, giant red letters. Another in the next block:

WHAT ARE *YOU* LOOKING AT?

Prostitutes linger exhausted around red-lit houses after a long night, bungee cord labia snapping in the dawn. "Disease-free," they call. "Checked every other Monday. Come on, you got something better to do? Our pussies moan like the Gyuto Monks."

Too fast now, at the perimeter wall before I know it. Up and on top, I balance between worlds. Stare over the desert, burnt brown like shoveled ashtrays. They move out there, they swim in it, they eat it because they can't get to us. They eat sand and shit glass. A million of them now, too stupid to climb the wall, but maybe not so stupid after all....patient, they know we'll come to them eventually. We still the ones winding all the clocks.

A thousand fathers sire a thousand offspring, a thousand mothers gagging on placental screams in the wretched morning. A thousand whipping boys cover their asses and weep with midnight despair, crying, "This is the life you gave me? This is what you wanted me for? You offer me nothing more than this?"

"We did the best we could."

"Ignorance is no defense in the eyes of the law of nature. 'tis better to create than merely to consume."

From my pocket I pull the works, syringe filled with extract of bootleg meatgirl five blocks back. Never paid money for one before. Why had I started now, of all days?

Slap the arm and rouse the vein, lazy worm that it is. I probe around with the needle, more than I need, long after the vein is found. Deeper

—deeper.

There is a corpse under my skin, just waiting to get out.

I'll find it.

Before it find me.

Death be not proud….just prompt, a definitive end. And you know me, I'm easily satisfied.

Charlie Harmer's Last Request
Brendan Detzner

MARK AND HARRY HAD THE radio turned up just loud enough to hear. Not the music, just the noise and some of the words. "This is Charlie Harmer on WBLI classic radio, joining you on a wonderful Monday night…"

Harry sat in the passenger seat watching the barrier fence bounding the edge of the interstate roll by.

It was dark; the streetlights loomed overhead like vultures, continuing at regular intervals ahead and behind them as far as they could see, leaving only a thin black space between each one. The fuel gauge had been hovering near empty for a few miles now, but there was no use pointing it out to Mark; he always let things ride to the last minute. It was just how he was.

A cop appeared in the rearview mirror. Mark took a quick glance at the back seat.

It was a mess, overflowing with junk, giant old books with leather covers, road maps, tapes, photo negatives. Most of the bad stuff was in the trunk. Pills, a candy tin full of weed, a fancy silver knife Mark saw in a head shop in San Francisco and insisted had "something" to it. There was also a gun in the back of the glove compartment. Supposedly it was for emergencies, but they really kept it just for the thrill of having it.

Nothing was out in the open.

The cop went past them and disappeared over the horizon.

"We really ought to find a hotel," Harry said.

Mark didn't answer at first.

Harry wondered how tired he was; it was impossible to tell through the sunglasses. For all Harry knew, he was already sleeping and just kept his hand steady on the wheel through force of habit.

Finally Mark said something. "Yeah. I'll get off at the next exit, and we'll look around."

Harry leaned back in his seat. "Great."

"I don't know why we keep coming back to Chicago," Mark said.

Harry closed his eyes. "We had some luck last time."

"We saw an old woman pushing a shopping cart."

"Her head was in the cart."

They'd seen better. They'd taken notes and snapped pictures, bragged about it on the Internet; they'd met like that, Mark and Harry and a few others. In Cleveland, they sat on a piano player's grave and heard music, and in Jacksonville they'd watched a tree bleed. They'd walked through the front door of an abandoned house in the middle of nowhere in Iowa and woken up two days later on the front porch, naked, with their hands around each other's throats.

At the beginning of the trip there'd been half a dozen people, but that had been months ago. Now there were only the two of them, and Harry was thinking about just pulling the plug on the whole thing and going home. It had been a long time since his parents had died. It wasn't that he felt any better, this just wasn't helping anymore.

They came to an exit. The Beach Boys were singing about summer. They ran out of lyrics, and the song faded out in perfect harmony.

They found a hotel and got a room. They went in; Harry fell down on the covers. A minute later he was sleeping soundly. Mark waited by the door until he was sure Harry wasn't moving.

He stepped back outside and got into the car. He reached into his hip pocket, found a black thread, and pulled. The thread had a small teardrop crystal hanging from it. He tied the crystal to his rearview mirror. It looked like something you'd buy from a hippie at a flea market.

He started the engine, pulled out of the parking lot, and got back on the interstate. The crystal began to spin gently, back and forth. The streetlights overhead shone through the glass, casting tiny slices of green and yellow light on the dashboard.

He turned up the radio. For a moment he wondered if he had the wrong station; he heard a piano playing what sounded like classical music. He reached tentatively for the dial, not sure where to go.

But then a girl started talking, slowly and just out of rhythm with the music, something about wanting to dance, her parents not liking her boyfriend's motorcycle, fifties greaser shit with a wall of sound behind it.

He pressed a button on the dash and set the trip odometer to zero.

The song ended, and the deejay started talking.

"Charlie Harmer here on WBLI classic radio, glad to have you here with me on a Tuesday morning. It's too early for the farmers, so I just want to say hi to all of you out there in radio-land on the tail end of a good time and thank you for spending it here with us. If you've got anything to say, all you have to do is speak up and say hello. In the meantime we've got another great set of music..."

Mark realized the deejay hadn't given a phone number.

"Hello?" he whispered hesitantly.

"Glad to hear from you son," the voice on the radio said. "What's your name?"

"Mark," Mark said and felt silly.

"Nice to meet you Mark, I'm Charlie. You sure seem surprised for somebody who went to so much trouble to get in touch with me."

"But..." Mark tried to think how to say it. "You're not dead."

"I sure am, for twenty-five years now. But still broadcasting. Did you get the crystal from Billy?"

Mark nodded.

"So you know what the rules are, right?"

Billy told Mark the rules when he gave him the crystal: Hang it from the rearview mirror, have your radio tuned to the right frequency. Travel for twenty miles, and don't drop below the speed limit.

"I know the rules," Mark said.

"That's good. Speed limit here's fifty-five. You're really going to want to be careful about that."

"Do I tell you who I want to talk to?"

"The way it works is that you only talk to me. But I can pass a message along to whoever you want and tell you what they have to say back to you."

Mark reached into the back seat with his right hand and pulled out a notebook and pen. There wasn't much light, but he managed to make out the first name on the list.

"A man named John Burris robbed a bank about twenty years ago. They caught him a few days later, but they never recovered the money. He died in prison. I want to know where he hid it."

"It'll take a little while to patch through."

"How long?"

"Not really sure. Wouldn't mind chatting a little bit in the meantime though. I don't get to talk to people much."

Mark didn't want to talk, but he didn't want to upset whatever it was that was talking to him.

"All right."

The odometer turned over; eight miles had gone past.

"Thanks, I don't get to talk to people that often. Last person who got in touch was Billy. How is Billy?"

Billy was an old man Mark met in a bar in St. Louis. He was fat and wore a plain red baseball cap and had trouble speaking in complete sentences. Mark had figured him for a drunk, but he went to the bar several times and never saw Billy drinking that much, definitely not enough to account for how fried he was. If he hadn't heard him muttering something about dead people, Mark never would have given him a second thought.

"He looked pretty messed up."

Charlie sighed. The sound was a low rush passing through the speakers.

"Yeah, well. Fifty-five, Mark, be careful. So tell me something else. Most people don't seek out ghosts, how did you get interested in doing something like that?"

"I saw some people die in a traffic accident."

The speakers were silent. Mark was offended; he felt like that deserved a reaction. "Are you still there?"

"You bet. Just took a second for John to come through. He buried the money in a forest preserve." Charlie gave him the directions. It wouldn't be too hard to find the spot.

He checked the next name.

"Al Capone. There's got to be something."

The trip odometer hit eleven.

There were more names on the list. Charlie wanted to know how some baseball teams were doing. Mark didn't know anything about baseball, but he was able to fake his way through it.

"I was kind of hoping I could ask you what it's like to be dead," Mark said.

"I'm not a poet." It was the first time Charlie sounded anything less than friendly. "Another one's coming. This one's complicated. Get ready."

Mark spent almost five minutes writing as fast as he could. He finished one sheet, turned to the next one, and filled about two-thirds of the page before he was done.

"All right," Mark said. "Thanks."

"No problem, but I think you're running out of road."

"Just one more. The name of the guy I've been traveling with is Harry Lund. His parents died a little over a year ago.

"It'd speed things up if I knew how they died."

"A traffic accident."

He waited for Charlie's answer, but the speakers were quiet. Slowly, music filled the car, the volume started low and gently crept up. A simple song with three chords.

"You make my heart sing..."

The car was moving at sixty miles an hour. Mark cut back on the gas very slightly. The dial on the speedometer dropped down and hovered between the white lines above the fifty-five mark. By the time the song was done, the odometer was halfway through its seventeenth mile. Charlie's voice came back over the radio.

"I'm sorry, but you're going to have to pass on this one. By the time they come around, you'll be out of time."

Mark slowed the car down to forty. For a moment, everything was quiet except for the sound of the wheels turning underneath them.

"You really shouldn't do that. It's not going to buy you enough time anyway..."

Mark pulled over to the side of the road and put the car in park.

"You're making a huge mistake."

"Just let me know when I can talk to Harry's parents."

A minute passed in silence.

"All right, they're here."

"Tell them that I apologize." Mark pulled back onto the road.

"I told them, they heard it."

Mark watched as the speedometer rose past thirty-five. He heard a siren. He looked in his rearview mirror and saw spinning lights behind him.

"Is that a cop?" Mark asked and immediately felt like an idiot, and anyway he got no answer. He pulled over. The police car pulled up behind him, and a large man got out and walked down the side of the road. He was hard to see. Even from only a few feet away, he was still only a black shape, a pair of shoulders floating in the air.

Mark rolled down the window. "Is there a problem?"

"The speed limit is fifty-five."

"I was going forty."

The man outside the window nodded. "That's too slow. There's a fine."

"How much?"

"It's not that kind of a fine. Step out of the car."

Mark pictured Billy, sitting at the bar dead sober but still muttering to himself, his eyes wandering aimlessly around the room.

He took a deep breath and forced himself to forget. Fear was a signal. Once you heard what it had to tell you, there was no point keeping it around.

"You're going to be needing my registration, right?"

The man outside raised his hand hesitantly, like he was about to say something. Mark reached into the glove compartment. He spun back around with his arms outstretched and the gun in his hand. He pulled the trigger three times.

The sound was like a hammer smacking against his eardrums; he didn't feel anything else until a moment after. His wrists were sore, and he could smell smoke in the air. He looked out the window and saw something on the ground a few yards away that looked like a pile of black felt.

The speakers came back to life with a hum of low static. "I've got to say, I've never seen anybody try that before. Won't kill him, though."

The pile began to stir. Mark saw hands pressing against the ground, shoulders rising into the air.

"He'll catch you."

The car gently lurched forward as Mark shifted gears.

"Wait," Charlie said.

Mark stomped on the brakes without thinking.

"Check his car."

Mark stayed frozen in place. He kept his feet pinned down, one on the clutch and the other on the brake. Each one felt like it had a jackrabbit inside of it trying to get out. He didn't know what to do.

Fuck it.

He shifted to reverse and pulled back alongside the cop car. He got out, ran over to it, and stuck his arm through the window. It was dark inside and cold like a meat locker. He reached toward the steering wheel and felt something metallic, and when he pulled his arm free of the window, there was a car key in his hand.

He looked up the road. The man he'd shot was on his feet, standing tall, lit up by the headlights. It was a cop; he was wearing a blue uniform. He had three fresh bullet holes in his chest and another much older one right between his eyes.

Mark ran around his car as fast as he could and climbed into the driver's seat.

He hit the gas pedal; the tires shrieked as the car cut across the lanes. A shot was fired, then another, behind him now. He straightened out the wheel and pressed down on the gas pedal.

He just went and went, and soon the man shooting at him was gone, a tiny black shape in the rearview mirror getting harder and harder to see.

It was just a key. It had no logo on it; it looked like a spare you'd have made at the hardware store.

"He won't get too far without that," Charlie said.

Mark didn't say anything. He looked at the odometer. Eighteen miles had gone past.

"On the other hand, he has no problem walking for a long time, and he doesn't like people stealing his things."

Mark shrugged. "I'll figure something out."

"That's the spirit, I guess. So tell me something…"

Mark reached for the volume.

"That's no way to treat somebody who just did you a favor. It's kind of funny, you killing somebody in a car accident and your travel buddy's parents dying in a car accident."

Mark put his hand back down on his knee and kept steering with the other one.

"I said there was an accident," he whispered. "I didn't say anything about killing anybody."

"I've heard both sides of the story now, Mark. Does your friend know?"

Mark didn't answer.

"All that time on the road and you never told him?"

Still nothing.

"All right, then."

The odometer turned over. Nineteen miles.

"Did they accept my apology?" He was still whispering.

"Sure. Dead people get to be pretty understanding about this kind of stuff. They just hope that you're a little more careful in the future. We've about reached the end of your ride, is there anybody else you want me to try and ring up real fast?"

Mark shook his head. "No." He looked down at the key again. "Are you going to be in some kind of trouble?"

Charlie laughed. "It's a little late to be worrying about that. Trip's almost done anyway. Let me play you a song."

Music filled the car, three men singing in harmony and snapping their fingers. The odometer hit twenty.

The next exit was a cloverleaf. Mark got off and went back the way he'd come. By the time he reached the place where he'd been pulled over, he could see sunlight in his rearview mirror.

He went back to the hotel, took the notebook with him to the room, and put it on the table by the window. He opened it, took a pen out of his pocket, and wrote in the margin.

HARRY—

HERE YOU GO. IT'S BEEN A GOOD TRIP.

Then, after thinking for a second:

I'M SORRY.

—MARK

He looked over the notes. If even half the tips were good, and Harry followed up on them, he'd be set for life. Mark threw the car keys down on top of the notebook and left.

There was a gas station next to the motel they were staying at, and on the far side of the station was a pay phone with a yellow pages on top. He flipped through it, found the number of a cab company, and gave them a call.

He found himself playing the accident over in his head while he waited. It was something he used to do all the time, but he hadn't done it for a while. He'd been a little drunk; when he made the turn, he saw the headlights coming, and he knew it was going to be close, but he'd been sure he'd just make it, just close enough to give the other guy a jolt without their cars ever touching. When he woke up in the hospital and heard what had happened, his first reaction was to get angry at how unfair it all was. A few inches difference and he'd have been fine.

The cab arrived. Mark climbed into the back seat. The radio was on.

"This is Julia on WBLI classic radio. Charlie Harmer isn't going to be with us for awhile, but I hope you'll stay tuned, we have a lot of great music coming your way…"

She played a song older than the ones he'd been hearing, a woman with a deep voice and an orchestra behind her.

"So where are you headed?" the driver asked him.

Exodus
Lawrence Schimel

JUST BEFORE DAWN, THE VAMPIRE stumbled towards home, drunk as a camel (since they don't have skunks in Egypt, and also because that was how he felt right then, he had drunk so much blood). The streets ran with blood, and he had drunk his fill and then past his fill, bloating himself to capacity, unable to stop drinking all that glorious fresh blood flooding around him, as the spring-flooding Nile—like all water—turned to blood. He grabbed his doorframe and leaned there, heavily, for a moment, while he fumbled for the keys to his house. His bloodied hands left a stain upon the lintel. He entered the welcoming darkness of his dwelling and, bloated as he was, fell promptly asleep.

He slept for days.

Frogs swarmed through the streets, but his windows were shuttered, and he didn't notice them. They slithered under the door on their pallid white underbellies, croaking their loud calls from atop his bed, even, but he did not hear them. He was fast asleep, dreaming about the floods of blood. He had an erection. Eventually, the frogs left.

In the frogs' wake swarmed all the vermin that had fled before the onslaught of those thousands of hungry, sticky tongues. Bed bugs snuggled into bed with him and bit him. Lice burrowed into his scalp. Fleas and ticks and chiggers and the entire panoply of minute parasites that sting and bite attacked him. But he did not notice. And, bloated as he was, he had blood to spare for them.

Wild beasts stampeded outside his dwelling, but their pounding hooves and neighs and coughs and trumpets did not wake him. He slept unperturbed. The vermin were intrigued by all the noise, however, and all that furry flesh to infest, and set off for wild and uncharted territories in search of excitement and blood that wasn't secondhand.

From the filth of the excrement left behind after the wild beasts had departed for greener pastures, came a pestilence which struck down all persons who moved about the streets. Fast asleep as he was, the vampire remained uninfected.

However, from the poisoned bites and stings and scratches of the vermin and the eggs laid under his skin, his body erupted in horrible swollen boils.

He looked as if the frogs' warts had been contagious, but took a few days to manifest. But the vampire did not scratch them. He did not even feel them. He slept as if drugged, so bloated that he could not feel his skin.

The temperature plummeted. Hail the size of grapefruits pounded the roof. The vampire hardly noticed at all, but in his sleep he pulled a sheepskin over his body to stave off the chill.

When the hail ended, a swarm of locusts descended upon the city, devouring every comestible in their path. In minutes they stripped away his roof of thatched reeds. The vampire murmured against the sudden bright sunlight and burrowed deeper under the sheepskin, but he did not wake. In moments, the world was submerged in a preternatural darkness, which quieted the vampire's somnolent discomfort.

The Angel of Death stopped outside his door, and the vampire again cried out in his sleep. The Angel of Death was curious and lifted his hand towards the doorknob; it had been a long time since he had taken one undead, one who had eluded him once. But he saw the blood upon the lintel and was sworn to pass by. This one, too, would come to him, in time, and receive his due punishment. Twice now, this one had eluded the Angel of Death, and the Angel of Death was not pleased.

A Jewish neighbor came to the vampire the next night and at last roused him from his torpor by banging on his door.

"What do you want?" the vampire growled as, sleepy-eyed, he opened the door. He was still quite full from his binging during the floods, but his anger at being awakened from such blissful dreams woke the tiny spark of hunger that had managed to dry itself off in his belly.

"Come, we must flee. It is time to go. We shall be free!"

"Leave? You've got to be kidding! What if this happened again, and I missed it?" The vampire shut the door on his neighbor and lay down again, his thoughts already turning toward the flood of blood he would dream about, until the Pharaoh's soldiers came.

Cold Comfort
Michael Penkas

"Do you believe in ghosts, Ms. Gramm?"

Candace shuddered. Not from the question, but because it was ten degrees, and she was dressed in a Catholic schoolgirl outfit. She could feel goose bumps rising on her ass, and there was no way that would look sexy. "What? Sure."

Father John unlocked the front entrance to the dormitory. It was three days before Christmas and, besides the two of them, it appeared the college campus was deserted. As with all her clients, the agency had run a check on the priest and said he was safe; but Candace still tended to trust her own instincts more than the agency.

They walked into a front lounge area, and she was surprised that it was nearly as cold indoors as out. "I guess they turn the heat off when the students leave."

The priest turned to look at her. He was somewhere in his late forties or early fifties, with grey hair, grey eyes, and a lean, weathered face. "Are you cold?" There was only curiosity in his voice, no concern.

She fluffed out her plaid skirt. "This isn't really winter clothing."

"I'm sorry about that, but I thought it would help."

"It's okay. I mean, you're the customer and if this is what you like…"

The priest shrugged and turned towards the stairway at the opposite side of the room. "I think it will be warmer upstairs."

She followed, again feeling uneasy about the client. The agency had told her that he had no criminal record, but he'd never done business with them before. Candace clutched her purse tightly as she began ascending the stairs, still feeling the cold. Inside her purse were condoms, her ID, a cell phone, cab fare, and a retracted six-inch switchblade. Three years earlier, she'd killed her pimp with that same switchblade in an act of self-defense.

She'd gotten off the streets and signed up with an agency after that happened, but she still kept the knife.

"Have you ever seen a ghost?"

"What?" What was it about the priest and ghosts? Were priests even supposed to believe in ghosts? "Um, no, I haven't. Why?"

Halfway up the stairs, Father John stopped and turned to face her. "This dormitory is haunted. Two months ago, a young man tripped on this stairway, fell, and broke his neck. His spirit hasn't left this place."

"Oh." There wasn't much that Candace could say in response to something like that. Why was he telling her? For conversation?

"Does it bother you?"

And suddenly she had the priest figured out. She tried making her face, her voice, as cold as the stairway. "No." He was the kind of man who liked scaring women. She'd worked with this sort of client before.

"I suppose you've seen a lot of strange things," he said.

"Yes."

They stared at one another for a short time, perhaps half a minute, before the priest finally looked away from her. "I'm sorry. I haven't been very forthcoming with why I hired you. I didn't know how to explain what I wanted over the phone. I thought, when I was with you, in person, maybe it would be easier." They reached the top of the stairs and began walking down a long hallway, with doors on either side of them.

"The agency didn't tell me much," Candace offered, trying to warm the mood between them. What the agency had told her about him was that he wanted a young woman in a schoolgirl outfit for some role-playing and possibly sex. It wasn't so unusual. The man had specifically requested a woman who wasn't easily freaked out. That also wasn't so unusual.

Halfway down the hallway, the priest unlocked one of the doors, and they entered a stripped down dorm room. There was a bunk bed without sheets, a desk with nothing piled on it, a dresser with the drawers all opened and emptied out, and several bottled waters sitting on top of the dresser.

The priest sat down on the lower bunk and Candace sat beside him, keeping a respectable two-foot distance between them. Looking at the floor, Father John continued. "After the students left for Christmas break, I was called in to deal with…the ghost. His name is Theodore Quisp. It's been five days and I think I have a solution."

"You were called in?"

"Yes."

"You handle a lot of ghosts?"

"When needed."

She tried to sound compassionate, tried not to laugh. "Father…John. Look. If…you're not really a priest? If this is just…a scene you like to play out? It's okay. You can tell me, and I'll play along. But you have to be honest with me."

Father John turned to look at her. The coldness was gone from his eyes. There was something naked and honest there, for the first time since she'd arrived. "I took my vows seventeen years ago, and in that time I have performed thirty-three exorcisms. Looking back, I believe eight of them were for people who just had mental problems. I have seen ghosts and demons. There is a ghost in this dormitory, and I believe you can help me to put him at peace."

All Candace could say in response was, "Um?"

"Sometimes, a spirit remains if his death was particularly horrible. Theodore's death was quick and almost painless. Sometimes, a spirit will not understand that it has passed on and will linger as if still alive. I believe he knows that he's dead. Sometimes, a spirit will stay if there is some business that it feels is unfinished. I believe this is what's happening here."

"Okay."

"Despite dying in a women's dormitory, I believe that, when Theodore Quisp died, he was still a virgin."

"Okay." The priest was silent, merely looking at her. "Wait." The priest said nothing, but nodded slowly. "You can't be serious?"

"I don't know if it's even possible, but I would be willing to pay you to try. I think the schoolgirl uniform will…enhance the illusion that you're a student rather than a…professional."

"Is this a joke?"

"It's not a joke."

"I don't even know how I would…what am I supposed to do?"

"Even though he died on the stairway, for some reason his presence seems to linger in this room. That's why it's been emptied out. The women staying here couldn't stand it any longer."

"They saw him?"

"They felt him. I'm hoping that, if we stay here for a short time, we'll feel his presence as well." A cold draft seemed to glide through the room. "Would you like some water?" He reached for one of the bottles.

"No, thank you. I wish there was something warm to drink."

"Coffee?"

"There's coffee?" She looked around the room again. There was no coffeemaker.

"Downstairs, in the lounge. I can go down and make some, give you a few minutes to consider things."

Candace nodded. "Yes. That would be nice. Thank you."

The priest got up to leave. "Theodore Quisp isn't cruel. He's just restless. And lonely. If you decide to…try it, I don't think you'll be in any danger." Then he left.

In five years of work, Candace could say quite honestly that she'd never cheated a client. Even when it would have been easy, even in cases like this where she could cheat the priest, just put on a show, and he'd never be any the wiser, she'd never done it.

She was still trying to figure a tactful way out of this situation when her arm began goose-bumping. Her flesh bunched up into bumps just below her shoulder, then down to her elbow, towards her wrist and then over the back of her hand. Almost immediately, her hand warmed up again, and then her knee went numb with cold. She reached out to touch the draft and her hand grew cold again.

The priest had closed the door to the dorm room when he'd left. But there was still a draft.

It seemed to creep back up her arm, under her blouse, and across her shoulder before reaching her neck. Her breath was freezing in her throat, stinging as if sharp icicles were forming inside. A quick breath blew out of her mouth like a cloud. As the chill ran up her neck and over her face, the room grew brighter, more colorful. It was as if the cold air brought with it a cold vision. As she felt her eyes freezing over, the room seemed to change.

There were clothes piled on the dresser and books piled on the desk and some boxes in the corner, landscape photograph posters on the wall. A girl, maybe eighteen, stood in the doorway. She was fully clothed, but her blouse was unbuttoned. She looked at the floor between Candace's feet, and Candace followed her gaze. A pair of blue jeans, white socks, worn tennis shoes, and stained white briefs were crumpled there.

Candace began to stand up, but something like a strong gust of wind blew against her, surprising her back down. The chill seemed to spread across her ears, making her clutch them for warmth. She could still hear what the girl across from her was saying. *"Well, Theo, it looks like you're ready. Are you ready?"* There was a pause, a silence so deep that it made her want to cry. *"Am I your first?"*

Still smiling, the girl reached for the doorknob to the room and, before Candace could figure out what was happening, she pulled it open and the room was filled with bright white light and laughter. She closed her eyes to the light, but the laughter grew louder.

When she opened her eyes again, there were five girls standing just outside the doorway, laughing, cameras in hand. Her shuddering was from more than the cold. Tears froze to her eyes. The doorway seemed to draw closer as the girls stepped aside, still laughing, from the hallway that she'd crossed minutes earlier. She heard the sound of ragged breathing and sobs. The doorway and the stairs seemed to loom forward as she passed through the door and descended the stairs. A quarter of the way down, the sound of girls' laughter still echoed behind her. Without warning, everything changed direction. The ceiling, walls, and stairs all mixed into a jumble as she spiralled down.

There was a crack like a tree branch snapping.

And then she was sitting in the empty room once again, the chill receding until it just filled her hand. She turned her hand over, palm up, and closed it when it grew colder. "Oh."

The room remained silent for another minute before she spoke again. "Theodore, that's…women can be assholes. Especially when we're young. I've met a lot of guys who've…who just can't deal with relationships because of that. I think that Father John was wrong about how you died. I think it was terrible. I think you just can't get past it. What they did." Her hand grew so cold that she almost cried out.

She slowly stretched on the bare mattress. "I don't love you," she whispered. "I don't know you, but I won't lie to you. I won't laugh at you." She began to unbutton her blouse, revealing a lacy white bra beneath. "It's okay with me."

It was like she was having sex outside in the ten degree weather, the cold running over her skin like a breeze. She looked down to see tendrils of frost creeping out from the edges of her bra. She unfastened it to expose her breasts. "Gently," she whispered.

The breeze focused on her breasts for a while. She was vaguely aware of a door opening and then closing again; but when she looked, the room was still empty. The breeze ran across her stomach, tickling and making her smile. Then the breeze edged beneath her skirt.

She remembered a client who liked playing with food. A lot of clients liked licking things off her body, but this one had been different. He'd given her popsicles and asked her to masturbate with them. After she'd finished, he'd eaten the popsicles and then paid her, leaving a nice tip.

It was like that. Like masturbating with popsicles, except the popsicles had grown slicker and softer and warmer as she'd used them.

There was no way of knowing how long it went on. Her panties were hanging off one ankle, but she didn't recall stripping them down. The sensation wasn't pleasurable, but it was tolerable. It wasn't exactly painful. The shuddering was from the cold and not pleasure or pain or revulsion. Everything from her thighs to her stomach felt like frozen meat.

Her ragged breathing was still visible, like a mist, as the warmth began to return to her skin. After a while, the door opened a second time and Father John stood in the doorway, two cups of coffee steaming in his hands. He looked at her questioningly.

She nodded. "You can come in. I think he's gone." She reached out for one of the coffee cups while the priest looked slightly sideways away from her. Looking down at herself, she could see that her blouse and bra were still undone, her panties were on the floor and her skirt raised up, exposing her red frozen skin. "Oh."

She sipped the coffee, not bothering to cover herself. The priest's discomfort satisfied her in a very unprofessional way.

He asked, "Are you all right?"

"Just cold. I think...I think he's going to be okay."

There wasn't much left to say after that. She'd gotten dressed. While the priest had already arranged payment through the agency, he nevertheless handed her something extra as they walked back downstairs. It wasn't the best tip she'd ever received, but it was far from the worst. She caught a taxicab just off-campus and decided that she would treat herself to a long, hot bath before checking her messages to find out where the agency would send her tomorrow.

Interlude: Blood, Snow, and Sparrows
Joshua Alan Doetsch

DESDEMONA USED TO TRACE THE stars with her finger, connecting the dots, naming her own constellations.
    I call upon her name.
Desdemona.
I call her name when I want to remember.
Desdemona—who gave me thirty-one birthdays when I had none. *Desdemona*—who laughed and made snow angels on rooftops because the snow there was cleanest, the closest to Heaven. *Desdemona*—who made an angel of snow and blood in the dirty street on the day I lost her.
    I remember this, now, as Zeek struggles in my arms, anger and fear evacuating his body in crimson spurts, and my smile dislocates my jaw. Zeek with the shroud-eye, one eye glaucoma clouded, said it was his evil eye, said he could hex a body with a stare, cast a pestilence. But, see, I knew better. I knew it was Zeek's dirty needles that killed the kids. And the night collapses with primate shrieks as Zeek tries to lift his bloody gun and...
Freeze.
Too far.
Backtrack.
Once upon a time, Desdemona Mercer giggled in frustration and joy and chucked her astronomy textbook off the roof we made love on. She connected the dots and named her own constellations, and when the winter wind came, we folded in on one another, seeing how close we could get in my sleeping bag. We spent hours seeing how close we could get.
    Now, I stare in the cracked mirror, and I connect the track marks on my body, form constellations with them. I name each one. But then the memories cut too deep, and I give up on the angry stars burning in a pale Milky Way of collapsed veins, and I plunge the needle behind my eye and inject.

I count the bullets: *one, two, three*…and wonder how many good deeds it'll take.

I love you, Dez.

I slam the clip home.

I miss you, Dez.

The little, vicious, mechanical conspiracy of a switchblade lurks in my pocket.

I'm coming home, Dez.

I drop the syringe, close my eyes in prayer, and wait for the drug to take hold. December wind slithers in through the cracks of boarded-up windows and thrills my pale, track-starred galaxy to goose bumps. In the winds of December it's easy to remember; there are ghosts in December wind.

Today is my birthday.

Yesterday was my birthday.

Tomorrow will be my birthday.

When I feel the golden flash-fire burn from synapse to synapse, I smile. Any fuckwit can shoot up heroin or PCP. But creation…see, that's art. Desdemona said that if I applied myself more, I'd make a great artist or chemist. Desdemona once told me that medieval alchemists tried to turn lead into gold, and I know that the dealers dancing the alley shadows would kill to know how I transmogrify the chemicals and narcotics, spin caustic shit into gold liquid-fire. But it's my recipe, my cocktail, *my* alchemy, and I'll never tell, though the dealers would murder their mothers to know.

I never knew my birth mother. I was born in a heroin apartment, spat out from a heroin womb, in my birth month of December. Weeks went by before my mother's head cleared enough to take me to the hospital. She couldn't remember what day I was born on. The other orphans teased me, the boy with no birthday, told me I had no soul.

And I grew and I developed under that assumption, strong and hollow, a predator in the jungle. I swam through an ocean of chemicals, blood, and screams before I found Desdemona.

"Happy birthday, Gabriel," she would say. Everyone had always called me Gabe, but she called me Gabriel. She said I was named after an archangel.

"You have a soul, Gabriel," she would say.

"How do you know?" I'd respond, tracing her tattoos with a forefinger. Here her smile spelled mischief, as she placed her eye on my bellybutton.

"I can see it through here!"

Too deep. I kick the mirror and millions of tiny me's rain down onto the filthy floor. I raise my gun, aim it at the luminous, broken angel, above. I yell at him, tell him his boss is a bastard for what He did. But I don't pull the trigger. The broken angel, busted and incomplete, is the last beautiful thing in here, the only remaining stained-glass window left, my only company, squatting in this burnt-out church.

Desdemona wouldn't break it.

Desdemona celebrated my birthday every day during December. She called it my birth month. She ignored the fake date that social services had given me as a consolation prize for being shat into the world. She gave me thirty-one birthdays when I had none. That was her alchemy. She could turn blackness into gold.

With my cocktail burning in my head, I leave the church. With the gift of my alchemy burning in my brainpan, I begin to time travel. Suddenly, I'm blocks away from the old church.

My vision bends in waves of dream alchemy as lines fade away and colors bleed into one another, chromatic orgies of a melting wax world. Desdemona liked to take me to museums. Once she showed me a row of expressionist paintings. My cocktail turns my surroundings into expressionist art, and it takes me a minute to recognize the street. This is where I pushed my first dope. The other kids played football, and I was earning. I don't remember my first customers; they were older than me.

I remember the cicadas screaming. I felt sorry for them. They spent decades getting ready, underground, earning their wings, whispering to each other, speculating what wonders they'd see above. But, see, when the time came and they ascended, it was just to fuck and die. They'd earned their wings just to fuck and die, and they were screaming in chainsaw decibels at the unfairness of it all.

My cocktail plays funhouse pranks on my ears, and I almost jump when I hear a dragon approach. But the 'L' train passes overhead, turns a corner, and the rickety sounds fade into a marching skeleton parade.

It starts snowing again.

Desdemona wore a black leather jacket, a man's jacket, many sizes too big. I used to watch, fascinated at how gracefully she swam in that jacket, pale skin contrasting dark leather, hair so blond it looked white. My snow angel.

I didn't deserve you, Dez.

Cicadas and ghosts make a haunted house of my head when Zeek shows up, across the street, standing under a flickering light, his evil eye casting hexes this way and that. He's waiting. A deal is going to go down. I know his satchel is full of contaminated needles. He's Santa Claus of the plague.

I wait in the alley shadows. I check the gun and the knife. But it's hard to be quiet when my alchemy circulates in my blood, when my brain screams cosmic secrets in my ear, and I'm suddenly afraid Zeek might hear my heart pounding.

"Gabriel, the archangel, whispered secrets to you, in the womb," she said to me.

"Secrets?"

"Yeah, it's Gabriel's job to watch over the unborn, and he whispers to them, tells them all the secrets of the universe."

"Then, how come I can't tell you those secrets now?"

"Because he put a finger to your lip," and she smiled and placed her finger against my lip, *"and he said, 'Shhhh.' And that's how you got that little dent under your nose."*

In the shadows, I clamp my mouth shut so hard something pops. See, when you're this high, you feel like you have access to universal secrets and they're playing in my head and it's all I can do not to start laughing. But laughing would alert Zeek. So I hunker down in the darkness and wait to do my good deed.

I never deserved Desdemona. I'm not a good man. These hands have pushed junk and a rainbow plethora of poisons. These hands are stained. These hands have killed. What had I done to deserve Desdemona? But, see, miracles are the undeserved gift. I never understood why she came to me, why she healed me, and she was taken away before I could figure it all out.

She challenged me in a race across the snowy street.

The truck.

The scream.

The driver lived. But, see, nothing is as graceful as a drunk. Nothing is as indestructible. I held Desdemona and her arms and legs jerked spastically, with none of her grace. Eyes open but unseeing, she kept calling my name, *"Gabriel...Gabriel...Gabriel?"* I answered but she didn't seem to hear, just called my name, over and over, and I sometimes pound my head into walls at night, wondering if she died thinking I wasn't there for her, that I didn't answer. She just called my name, and her arms and legs jerked around, and she made an angel of snow and blood.

The memories release me, and I look to Zeek and see I've almost missed my chance. Three kids, in gang colors, are already there and negotiations are underway. Three kids and they don't look like they're in high school yet. Three kids about to buy the plague from the man with the evil eye.

See, Zeek is smart enough not to sell bad needles to repeat costumers, but twisted enough to give them to others, just for the thrill. *"Better than sex!"* he once hissed to me, in a bar where the waitress had two black, panda-bear eyes. "Getting inside stranger after stranger, poisoning their blood and they don't even know it." People think monsters grown on chemicals and sent rampaging through the city are the stuff of science fiction, but, see, Zeek's as real as cancer.

The transaction underway, Zeek smiles like a slit throat, makes introductions, pleasantries, sets prices. The three kids open their mouths, and through my alchemy I can see the slang and obscenities crawl out, fanged moths flapping in the sodium light. Slang in the mouth is a dangerous thing in the jungle. Words evolve. Some fly into pop culture. Some burrow underground. Others grow hungry and cannibalize their brothers, grow extra limbs and claws and change, to survive in the jungle.

I remember Desdemona took a class in street slang. Some people were outraged that it was even offered, didn't consider it a serious subject. But, see, this is deadly serious shit. This is what proves your mastery in the jungle. If your growl has the right bite, other predators might not eat you. This is the shit that gets narc agents killed. How many undercover cops died to slang? How many of them knew their clothes and their mannerisms and their perps and their marks and their P's and their Q's only to come up short, impaled by a misplaced word, dangling and bleeding and dead.

Kids have the most dangerous mouths, the quickest evolving slang, more fluid, and now these kids are letting fang-mawed predators hatch out of their faces, and some of these monsters I don't recognize. I used to know them all. But I've been away from the jungle. I was a predator, but maybe it's my time to go to the elephant's graveyard.

But not *yet.*

I still have a good deed to do.

I lift my arm and take aim.

Gunshots are loud, but misfires are deafening. *Click,* says my gun, apologetically. The tiny sound stops the night. Zeek and the three boys look over and even the streetlight flickers, interrupted.

Click-click-click-click-click

Fuck.

I drop the gun. The best laid plans…

Zeek's slit-throat-smile turns upside down, and he looks at me through his good eye, curses me with his evil eye, then stares me down with his gun barrel.

"Gabe?"

He laughs. Strings of words follow but I can't follow them; my cocktail turns my brain into hummingbird heartbeats, a hurricane in a fucking teapot, and I can't decipher the words anymore.

I charge.

Zeek doesn't expect me to move this fast, to cover that much ground, but my alchemy is a beautiful thing.

Zeek's mouth barks four letters.

Zeek's gun barks a single syllable.

The shot goes wide. I barely feel the burning caress along my shoulder, as the grazing bullet kisses me and goes on its way, just like they always do in the movies. But bullets don't usually behave this way. Bullets aren't usually this polite.

I time travel though an impressionist stream punctuated by sounds—the crack of Zeek's wrist as I turn his gun on himself—the distant explosion of the bullet—the gurgle and suck of blood and air trying to move through the hole in Zeek's throat.

Both of us go down. The world comes into focus; bullets in the flesh can harsh any buzz. Zeek tries to lift his gun, but his arm won't obey him anymore. He sputters and gurgles, trying to form words—maybe to curse, maybe to beg redemption, I'll never know. I press my finger to his lips and say, "Shhhh," leaving a red line between his nose and lip.

Zeek's arms and legs flail in the whiteness, and I see the mark he leaves on the ground, and I wonder who this angel of blood and snow who haunts me is, and the flickering streetlight goes out. Blood is black by moonlight and the dark angel in the snow looks up at me…

Bad-time metaphors hover out of reach when I realize the kids are talking, mutant slang directed at me. I look close and realize these are not kids. They've seen too much, *done* too much. They grew up too fast, stunted. One of them has a gun out. Maybe he's already made his first kill. None of them are concerned about the dead man; they just ask me if I'm willing to sell them the shit. Bathed in Zeek's blood, blood now cooling, I realize why superheroes don't exist.

What do I say to these children-who-walk-as-men? They've heard every cherry-flavored anti-drug song. Christ, one of them is wearing a D.A.R.E. T-shirt. How do you do a good deed in this place?

I charge—

faster than sin—

my alchemy coursing in my arms.

I grab the D.A.R.E. kid by the throat, slam him into a wall, his head skips off the brick like a June bug, and I slide him upwards, feet dangling off the ground. My switchblade hisses out of hiding, and I press the point to his throat, forming a tiny indent in his Adam's apple.

"Listen, you little cunt. You ever take the shit again, I cut you. You ever buy the shit again, I cut you. You buy a suspicious amount of NyQuil at the Quick 'n Easy, I cut you. I'll know. I'll hear about it. The guy selling might be one of mine. And you don't tell about me, either. I don't exist. I'm a boogeyman. You break any of those rules, I will gut you with my knife. I know where you live. I'll come through your window. No one can stop me. I'll stick a needle through your chest and pump shit straight into your heart until it stops. And if I don't want to waste the money, I'll just cut your balls off, let you bleed out between the legs; it takes fifteen minutes. You look at the shit again, and I swear to the Devil, I will be there, and your mother will sweat blood when she's seen what I've done to you."

His face is slick with my saliva, and my eyes bulge open so wide I can hear, over Tommy-gun bursts of heartbeat, hear my skull-sockets groan.

I punctuate the words, press the knife a little harder; just enough to bring a trickle of blood, to make sure it sinks in—but it ain't easy—my alchemy is not good for fine manipulation—it's everything I can do not to shove the knife through the throat and three inches into the brick.

I hear urine flow in his pants, smell the sour scent.

It sank in.

And they're off like a light, heading for home.

And their faces aren't hard anymore. I cut down deep. They don't walk as men, they run as children. You can still reach the child in these lost-kids, if you cut deep enough. There are places, inside, still afraid of the dark.

And I time travel.

I leave the money Zeek had on him at the doorstep of Mrs. Stone. She's sick. She's saving up for an operation. She's so nice to me when I come to the diner.

And I time travel.

I'm back at the church. The busted, stained angel looks down at me, but doesn't tell me if it was enough. He never does. I climb up on the roof. It's covered in white. It's snowing and I'm bleeding. I know the blood's gone bad—too many needles. I know there will be repercussions for tonight. A bullet or a knife will find me, if I last that long. I don't have long. But it doesn't matter. I just need enough time to earn my wings.

I go cold, watching the snowflakes melt in my blood.

Desdemona.

I call upon her name. I scream like a cicada.

Desdemona. And the memories manifest, summoned by offerings of snow and blood. I can see her, swimming in her black jacket, an elf in an inkwell. I could never afford to give her diamonds. When I told her this, she just frowned, shook her head, and said, *"Diamonds are forever, and snowflakes are more precious because they melt."* And we held each other, on the rooftop, and I gave her snowflakes.

There's a dead sparrow on the roof of the church.

I pick it up.

"The Archangel Gabriel sends a sparrow to escort each soul," Desdemona once told me.

"Wake up," I tell the cold sparrow.

"Wake up," I say, rubbing the sparrow, and my voice breaks. I hug the still bird to my chest and cry big tears. I bleed and I cry, thinking of some lost soul, out in the dark, waiting for a sparrow.

"Wake up…"

I fall down, on my back in the snow on the rooftop, the cleanest snow, the closest to Heaven. Clutching the sparrow, I make a prayer to one of Desdemona's constellations. I flap my arms and legs, and I make an angel of snow and blood in the dark.

About Our Authors

Tom Barlow
Tom Barlow is a Central Ohio writer whose stories have appeared or will appear in *The Intergalactic Medicine Show*, *Steel City Review*, *Coyote Wild*, *Afterburn SF*, *The Hiss Quarterly*, *Apalachee Quarterly*, and other journals. He apologizes to anyone who may interpret his story as a slight against the corporeally-challenged, because he has nothing but the utmost respect for the dead. In fact, he plans to become one some day.

Edo van Belkom
Edo van Belkom is an award-winning author of more than 30 books and 200 short stories of horror, fantasy, mystery, and science fiction. He won the Silver Birch Award for his young adult novel, *Wolf Pack*; other novels in the series are *Lone Wolf* and *Cry Wolf*. As an editor, Edo has compiled several anthologies, including the collections for teens, *Be Afraid!* and *Be Very Afraid!* As a non-fiction writer, he has penned the how-to books *Writing Horror* and *Writing Erotica*. vanbelkom.com

Bill Breedlove
In addition to his short fiction collection, *Most Curious*, Bill Breedlove's work has appeared in publications such as *The Chicago Tribune*, *RedEye*, *InSider*, *The Fortune News*, *Restaurants & Institutions*, *Encyclopedia of Actuarial Science*, *Bluefood.cc* and *Playboy Online*. His stories can also be found in the books *Tales of Forbidden Passion*, *Strange Creatures*, *Tails from the Pet Shop*, *Cthulhu and the Coeds*, *Blood and Donuts*, and *Candy in the Dumpster*.

Eric M. Cherry
Eric Cherry writes, critiques, and edits in Chicago. He has been published in the Twilight Tales anthology *Spooks!* and at a handful of online publications, such as NewMysteryReader.com. Eric schedules and emcees the weekly Twilight Tales reading series. cherry_eric@sbcglobal.net

Suzanne Church
Suzanne Church lives in Ontario, Canada, with her two children. She is an outlier and a media junkie who, when cornered, becomes fiercely

Canadian. She is a 2005 graduate of the Clarion South Science Fiction Writers' Workshop. Her fiction has appeared in *Shadowed Realms, Neo-Opsis, Chimeraworld #2, Book of Shadows (Volume One)*, and will soon appear in *CICADA*. She is a contributing reviewer for *Tangent*. www.suzannechurch.com

Alan M. Clark & Stephen C. Merritt

Alan M. Clark illustrates fiction, non-fiction, textbooks, young-adult and children's books. His awards include the World Fantasy Award and four Chesley Awards. His short fiction appears in magazines and anthologies. *Siren Promised*, his Bram Stoker Award-nominated novel with Jeremy Robert Johnson, was released in 2005. His two-book series with Stephen Merritt and Lorelei Shannon, *The Blood of Father Time*, will be released by Five Star in 2007. www.alanmclark.com

C.S.E. Cooney

C.S.E. Cooney runs Kate the Great's Book Emporium on the north side of Chicago. By day she hawks literature; by night she and her colleagues collaborate with local theatre companies, art galleries, musicians, and writers to "ascend the brightest heaven of invention." With a B.A. in fiction and theatre from Columbia College Chicago, Ms. Cooney writes whatever she can whenever she can, then performs the results wherever she can.

Scott A. Cupp

Scott A. Cupp is a short story writer from San Antonio. His first published story appeared in 1989 and was nominated for the John W. Campbell Award for Best New Writer in 1991. Most recently, he edited *Cross Plains Universe: Texans celebrate Robert E. Howard* (FACT/Monkeybrain Books) with Joe R. Lansdale. He is a former part-owner of the fabulous bookstore, Adventures in Crime and Space.

Sukie de la Croix

Sukie de la Croix is, by day, a regular run-of-the-mill reporter for assorted Chicago news outlets, but after darkness falls he can sometimes be found—wearing nothing but a powder-blue bra and panties—dancing barefoot on the graves of his ancestors. His ambition is to raise the dead through the magic of art, music, poetry, puke, and lightning.

Stephen Dedman

Author of *The Art of Arrow Cutting*, *Shadows Bite*, *A Fistful of Data*, *Foreign Bodies*, and more than 100 short stories. He's won two Aurealis Awards and a Ditmar, and has been nominated for a Bram Stoker Award, a British Science Fiction Association Award, a Seiun Award, a Spectrum Award, a Sidewise Award, and a sainthood.

Brendan Detzner

Brendan Detzner's work has appeared in Gothic.net and Chiaroscaro. He lives in the Chicago area, appears regularly at the Twilight Tales open mic, and elsewhere around the city. You can keep track of what he's up to at www.myspace.com/brendandetzner and get in touch with the man himself at brendandetzner@yahoo.com.

Joshua Alan Doetsch

While you sleep, Joshua Alan Doetsch weaves words in the plasma cauldron of his computer screen under the twilight laughter of a black-light, advised by a rubber raven and his pet snake, Lenore. Joshua's first novel, *Strangeness in the Proportion*, will see print in the near future (by White Wolf Publishing)…and he is currently scrambling in the laborious enterprise of gathering enough body parts to sew together and animate into an unholy, lurching demographic to sell his books to.

Andrea Dubnick

Andrea Dubnick, president of Gallowglass Academy, Inc., is a fiction writer and performer who believes that not only historical, mystery and crime fiction need authentic details; scenes of fantasy combat ought to be believable, too.

Jo Fletcher

Jo Fletcher is a winner of the International Society of Poets' Critics' Choice Award, the British Fantasy Society's first-ever Karl Edward Wagner Award, and the World Fantasy Award. She has edited several anthologies, both alone and with multi-award-winner Stephen Jones; her first poetry collection, *Shadows of Light and Dark*, was shortlisted for the British Fantasy Award. She is currently editorial director of Victor Gollancz, one of Britain's largest genre fiction publishers, responsible for, amongst other things, the Fantasy Masterworks list.

Richard Gilliam
Richard Gilliam is the author/editor of nearly two dozen books, numerous short stories, and countless essays. His anthologies include *South from Midnight*, *Phantoms of the Night*, and *Joltin' Joe: The Best of Joe DiMaggio*. The first two tales in a series of stories set in his hometown of Greenbay, have both debuted in Twilight Tales chapbooks.

Sèphera Girón
Sèphera is the author of twelve published novels, and is a lifestyle journalist and astrologer for several magazines. *Hungarian Rhapsody*, an erotic vampire tale, will be out in 2007, as well as her Kama Sutra Seductions Deck. Sèphera is also a tarot counselor and reiki practitioner. She lives by the lake in Port Credit. www.sff.net/people/seph

Ken Goldman
Ken Goldman, former English and Film Studies teacher, shuttles between a new home on the Main Line in Pennsylvania and a beach condo at the Jersey Shore. (Yes, life is good!) His stories appear in over 445 publications in the U.S., Canada, UK, Ireland, and Australia. He received honorable mentions in *Year's Best Fantasy and Horror* 7th, 9th, 16th, and 17th Annual Editions.

Christopher Fulbright and Angeline Hawkes
Christopher Fulbright and Angeline Hawkes (2006 Bram Stoker Award nominee for *The Commandments*) write individually and collaborate as a husband and wife team. They have been published in the small press for several years with works appearing in magazines, anthologies, collections, and novels. Fulbright and Hawkes first joined forces with their novella, *Then Comes the Child*, published by Carnifex Press.

Brian Hodge
Brian Hodge is the author of ten novels and close to 100 short stories. His most recent works include *Hellboy: On Earth As It Is In Hell* (Pocket Books), *World of Hurt* (Earthling Publications), and the forthcoming crime novel, *Mad Dogs* (Cemetery Dance Publications). He lives in Colorado, where he also indulges interests in music and sound design, photography, and the bounty of local microbrews. www.brianhodge.net

Tina L. Jens

Tina L. Jens has worked as an author, editor, and publisher in horror and dark fantasy for fifteen years, and is a three-time Stoker Award nominee. She has nearly fifty short stories published in major anthologies. Tina's first novel, *The Blues Ain't Nothin'* (Design Image Group), won the National Federation of Press Women's Award for Best Novel and was a finalist for the Bram Stoker and Int. Horror Guild Awards.

Chris Kozlowski

Chris Kozlowski is an artist, poet, percussionist, and all around "Renaissance woman." She practices art therapy at a shelter for children, teaches art to children at the School of the Art Institute of Chicago, and fills in as an "on-call chaplain" at Northwestern Memorial Hospital. She is also the Volunteer Coordinator for Estrojam, a Chicago-based women's music/performance/art festival that gives women in the arts an opportunity to have their voices heard. She lives on Chicago's north side with her two dogs.

Randy Miller

Randy Miller lives in Tampa, where he is an associate professor of journalism at the University of South Florida. His short stories have appeared in the critically-praised anthologies *Excalibur, Phantoms of the Night, Joltin' Joe DiMaggio* and the Bram Stoker Award-winning *Horrors! 365 Scary Stories*. He served as associate editor for *The Tampa Tribune's Fiction Quarterly*.

Jude Walter Mire

Jude lives in the wilderness near Chicago, where he composes fiction and keeps an eye on the squirrels. 2007 marks his first fiction sales. He is an open mic regular, despite the trek from the suburban fringes. He can be reached at The Red Lion Pub on Monday nights.

Yvonne Navarro

Yvonne Navarro lives and works in the high desert of Southeastern Arizona, in a climate that's supposed to be warm. Alas, leftover cold from Chicago seems to have followed her there. A Bram Stoker Award winner, she's had twenty solo and media novels and over a hundred short stories published. She's accumulated two rescued Great Danes (Goblin and the

Ghost) and a husband (Weston Ochse), not necessarily in that order.
www.yvonnenavarro.com

Katherine Norem
Katherine Norem is spending the money she received for her contribution to this book on black eyeliner and a new studded collar from Hot Topic. She has also written poems about vampires and thus considers herself well-rounded. She lives in Chicago with one man, two cats, and innumerable tiny snails.

Craig D.B. Patton
Craig D.B. Patton is thrilled to be among the living who contributed the dead to *Book of Dead Things*. He has previously been published in *Strange New Worlds* (Pocket Books) and online at Dred Tales and Hellnotes. Additional stories are forthcoming in *Hell in the Heartland* (Annihilation Press) and *All Hallows*. He thanks his extended family and the BosMob for their ongoing support of his writing. He lives in Chicago with his wife and sons.

John Peel
John Peel was born in Nottingham, England, home of Robin Hood. He moved to New York to get married, and remains there with his wife and thirteen dogs. He has written tie-in novels for TV shows such as *Star Trek*, *The Outer Limits*, *The Avengers*, and *Doctor Who*. He is also well known for his teen fantasy adventure series *Diadem*, which is currently up to book ten.

Michael Penkas
Michael is a librarian. He lives in Chicago. In his spare time, he drinks coffee and writes stories. He began haunting The Red Lion Pub in late 2004. He also has a story in the upcoming *Tales from the Red Lion*, due out this summer from Twilight Tales.

Bruce Holland Rogers
Bruce Holland Rogers is a multiple award-winning author of short fiction. His stories have won a Pushcart Prize, two Nebula Awards, the Bram Stoker Award, the World Fantasy Award, and have been nominated for the Edgar Allan Poe Award and Spain's Premio Ignotus. He lives in Eugene, Oregon.

Martel Sardina

Martel Sardina blames her warped imagination on her addictions to Pepsi and chocolate, as well as a chronic case of insomnia. In addition to writing, she is co-editing *Hell in the Heartland*, a horror/dark fantasy anthology, due out in 2007 from Annihilation Press. www.martelsardina.com

Lawrence Schimel

Lawrence Schimel, author and anthologist, has published over 80 books, including *The Future is Queer* (with Richard Labonté), *The Drag Queen of Elfland*, and *Fairy Tales for Writers*. His *PoMoSexuals: Challenging Assumptions about Gender and Sexuality* (with Carol Queen) won a Lambda Literary Award. His poem "How to Make a Human" won a Rhysling Award. Writing in Spanish, his picture book *No Hay Nada Colo el Original* (illustrations by Sara Rojo Pérez) was selected by the Int. Youth Library for the White Ravens. His writings have been translated into more than twenty languages. He lives in Madrid, Spain.

Alan Smale

Alan Smale grew up in Yorkshire, England, but is now in the US to stay, His fiction has appeared in many venues, including *Realms of Fantasy*, *Paradox*, *Dark Regions*, *Writers of the Future #13*, *Low Port*, *A Wizard's Dozen*, and *A Nightmare's Dozen*. Alan labors for a well-known Government Agency in darkest DC, sings bass with high-energy vocal band, The Chromatics, and performs occasionally in community theater. www.alansmale.com

J.D. Smith

J.D. Smith's works include *Settling for Beauty*, *The Hypothetical Landscape*, and *Northern Music: Poems About and Inspired by Glenn Gould*. His children's book, *The Best Mariachi in the World*, is forthcoming from Raven Tree Press in 2008. His poems have received three Pushcart nominations, and his essays and reviews have appeared in *American Book Review*, *Grist*, and *Pleiades*. His literary and crime fiction has been in *Orchid* and *Thug Lit*, among others. His work currently appears in the anthologies *In a Fine Frenzy: Poets Respond to Shakespeare*, *Poetic Voices without Borders*, and *Illuminations: Expressions of the Personal Spiritual Experience*.

Thomas J. Strauch

Thomas J. Strauch owns the Design Image Group, which in addition to its normal humdrum commercial activities, maintained a well-received horror fiction micro-publishing side business. Tom was obviously raised a Catholic, based on his creepy nun fixation. www.designimagegroup.com

Karen E. Taylor

Karen E. Taylor is the author of *The Vampire Legacy* series of novels, published by Kensington Books. To date, the series stands at seven titles and has earned a cult following. Her short stories have appeared in numerous anthologies, including *Love Bites*, *100 Vicious Little Vampires*, *100 Wicked Little Witches*, *A Horror Story A Day*, and *Seductive Spectres*. In 2001, she was nominated for the Bram Stoker Award for best short story for "Mexican Moon."

Dan Waters

Dan Waters lives and writes somewhere in the Northeast. His first writing sale was to *Cemetery Dance Weekly*, where his horror music column "Dead Beats" ran for a few months. He still has enough fingers on one hand to name off all of his short fiction sales, but is pleased to report that "Perfect Rings" was tallied with his pinkie. His novel, *Generation Dead*, is scheduled to be released in the Spring of '08 from Hyperion.

John Weagly

John Weagly has had over 25 plays produced by theaters across the country and over 50 short stories and poems published in a variety of media. *The Undertow of Small Town Dreams*, a collection of his Currie Valley stories, is available from Twilight Tales Publications. www.johnweagly.com

Robert Weinberg

Bob Weinberg is the author of sixteen novels, two short story collections and more than a dozen non-fiction books. He's also scripted comic books for Marvel, DC, and Moonstone comics. As an editor, he's compiled more than 150 anthologies and short story collections in the horror, fantasy, and mystery fields. Bob's work has been published in fourteen languages. He's a two-time winner of the World Fantasy Award and also a double winner of the Horror Writers Association's Bram Stoker Award. And he's perhaps the only horror writer ever to serve as Grand Marshall of a rodeo parade.